SUNBREAKS

BY GREG MESSEL

Order this book online at www.trafford.com
or email orders@trafford.com

Most Trafford titles are also available at major online book retailers.

Note for Librarians: A cataloguing record for this book is available from Library
and Archives Canada at www.collectionscanada.ca/amicus/index-e.html

Printed in Victoria, BC, Canada.

ISBN: 978-1-4269-1509-3 (sc)
ISBN: 978-1-4269-1510-9(dj)

Library of Congress Control Number: 2009932985

*Our mission is to efficiently provide the world's finest, most comprehensive book publishing
service, enabling every author to experience success. To find out how to publish your book, your
way, and have it available worldwide, visit us online at www.trafford.com*

Trafford rev. 9/9/2009

www.trafford.com

North America & international
toll-free: 1 888 232 4444 (USA & Canada)
phone: 250 383 6864 ♦ fax: 812 355 4082

To My Beautiful Carol
Who Has Taught Me Much
About Love

INTRODUCTION

I AM A middle-aged man who had my fifty-third birthday last fall. I am beginning to show some of the onset of middle age but I try to keep the clock from advancing too fast by staying active and fit. I am about six feet tall and have thick blond hair, which is quickly becoming more gray than blond.

I have lived most of my life in Portland, Oregon. The office building where I work is called the Public Service Building. The name traces back to the days when it was the headquarters for the power company, which has since moved to the Lloyd District. Back in the day, it would have had neon signs featuring Ready Kilowatt, the cartoon character who represented the electric generation business for decades.

I loved my building, with its red tile roof capping its fifteen floors. My favorite part about it was its Art Deco design, which had been beautifully maintained since the 1930s and made it something special.

It now housed various companies including the insurance company where I worked. Working for my company wasn't exactly like saving the rainforests or providing drinking water to African villages but it was decently interesting work. It provided a means to an end to make my life possible. When I was a small child, I don't ever remember saying, "I want to work in insurance when I grow up."

Directly across the street from my office building is a large hotel of equal height to the PSB. It is interesting that people somehow think they are invisible when they are in hotel rooms. I have a clear window looking directly into the uncovered windows of their rooms. Why do they think I can't see them? Some people seem to believe that they can't be seen doing bizarre things when they are in their cars.

Over the years as I gazed out my office window towards the hotel, I saw darn near everything. There were stories in my office, amongst the guys, of seeing beautiful women doing erotic things through the hotel windows. I must have missed those. It seemed I just saw middle-aged traveling salesmen getting out of the shower.

On the downtown Portland grid, the street running parallel to Sixth Avenue is Broadway, which was the source of some of my favorite activities. There were new gleaming office towers, which had multiscreen movie theatres on the ground floor, which I frequented. I loved those theatres but missed the old vintage ones they replaced.

I used to go to movies at the old Broadway Theatre, a holdover from the 1920s, which showed movies from the golden age of Hollywood. Down the street was the Music Box Theatre. The last time I went to a movie at that theatre was shortly before it was demolished. I saw a restored print of *Lawrence of Arabia* there. It was a wonderful experience but the old theatre was breathing its last. There were buckets to catch drips of rainwater from the roof where the front two rows of seats used to be. The theatre was so hot and stuffy that I felt like I was in Arabia.

One old movie palace that was saved is the jewel of Portland called the Schnitzer Concert Hall. It is a treasure of Italian architecture that was built in 1928 and was restored in the 1980s. It now houses the symphony, other cultural events, and concerts.

A block off of Broadway are the "Park Blocks." It is a series of twelve blocks stretching through the heart of downtown Portland. Each Park Block features artwork, consisting of various statues and fountains. The blocks form a cathedral of tall trees with a thick carpet of green grass underneath, leading to the Portland State campus at the end of the expanse of carpet. It is a wonderful place to spend some moments away from the concrete of the city.

Sitting adjacent to the Park Blocks is the Portland Art Museum. If I were a wild animal, these few blocks would be my natural habitat. It has everything I like and need.

Portland has its flaws but it is like a lover; I am willing to overlook its faults because of my love for it. In a word association game anywhere in the nation, if you mentioned Portland, the first response would be—rain.

Portland's rain is usually more like mist than the gully-washer rains some parts of the country get. It may take Portland days and days to accumulate two to three inches of rain. That much rain can fall in an hour or so in places like Houston, New York City, or Miami.

There are four months of the year—the summer months—when an average of only five inches of rain falls. During this time are the majority of the sunny days we will see for the year. The temperature is usually mild with low humidity and no swarms of bugs. You can usually count on the five inches of summer rain coming when you are camping, having an outdoor wedding, or planning your biggest barbecue of the summer.

The other eight months are going to be rainy but most of all gray. The grayness and heavy overcast drive some people crazy who move to Portland. They wonder if the sun will ever shine again. It can be disheartening. But to me the city is always bathed in a soft, muted light, which adds to its beauty and magic.

During the eight months of gloomy weather, Portlanders are anxious to hear the word "sunbreaks." Portland weathermen and -women find an amazing array of phrases that simply mean "It is going to be cloudy and rainy." It is a little like the challenge of meteorologists in San Diego. There are only so many ways to say "75 degrees and sunny."

In Portland, when the weatherperson says, "Today we may have sunbreaks," it means that sometime during the overcast day, the clouds will part and the sun will brightly shine. The sun may shine briefly or for several hours, but it will provide a welcome change from the grayness and gloom.

My life had been gray and gloomy for almost two years. I didn't know how to overcome my demons and chase the clouds away. Then one day the clouds parted and there was a glorious sunbreak.

Chapter 1

LOVE AND COFFEE

THE FIRST time I remember seeing her was on a rainy, dark morning in January of 2004.

When my son from San Francisco visits me, he always says that Portland smells like coffee and everyone wears black and gray. It was on one of those black and gray mornings that Erika made her first appearance. It was raining steadily when she entered the coffee shop, wearing a tan raincoat. The hood was pulled over her head, obscuring most of her face as she entered. She got in line to get her coffee and tried to shake off her umbrella while holding onto her large purse. I took note of her entrance but became very interested in watching her when she pulled back her hood, revealing her beautiful face.

She gave everyone she encountered a kind smile and seemed to be a very warm presence. I wondered if this was the first time she had stopped by this coffee shop in the morning. I would have surely noticed her, even in my semi-alert state early in the morning, as I ingested my first caffeine jolt.

Erika was a tall, slender woman with large light-blue eyes. Her face was surrounded by long, thick black hair, which hangs below her shoulders. Her hair formed a perfect frame for her face. I guessed she was about five foot nine or ten, and I pegged her age at somewhere in her thirties.

She was a beautiful woman, but what made her extra attractive was the way her face lit up when she talked. As she talked, her face was very animated and her eyes twinkled. It was a stunning combination. I found that I could not take my eyes off her from the first time I saw her.

It wasn't just that she was a beautiful woman … there was something else drawing me to her that I couldn't quantify.

I was sitting by the window in the Starbucks across the street from the office building where I worked. I was half-reading my morning paper and half-watching the scene outside the window as people rushed to get out of the rain and make it to work on time.

It is a habit I had developed each morning recently. I couldn't stand to spend the rainy, dark winter mornings alone in my house as I prepared to go to work. I headed into downtown Portland, where I worked on Sixth Avenue, each morning about 6:15 AM, sometimes earlier. Since my wife's sudden death a couple of years ago at the hands of a drunk driver, I couldn't sleep very well anymore. I no longer enjoyed being in my house alone. Whenever I got up, I generally took my morning shower and headed out regardless of the time.

I found the coffee shop on the corner of the block by my office was ideal. It was an all-glass cube with windows from the roof line to the sidewalk. There were tables and chairs and even overstuffed chairs positioned near the large windows. I found comfort in sitting there, drinking my morning coffee and easing into the day. It was entertaining to have a front-row seat to the morning street scene as I watched humanity pass by the windows. I always felt happy when I was downtown. Unfortunately, I lived in the suburbs.

After getting her coffee and a muffin, she sat across the room from me on the opposite wall. I felt a little guilty as I continued to watch her. I couldn't stop looking at her. I noticed what long, graceful fingers she had as she delicately tore off small pieces of her muffin. I tried not to stare, but she was by far the most interesting thing in this coffee shop.

A few minutes later this beautiful, tall woman began to gather her belongings and head out the door. I got caught looking and she flashed a brief smile at me as she exited the coffee shop and walked back into the rain. I would think that she was used to being noticed. My office was a left turn out of the coffee shop door. She turned right and headed down Sixth Avenue.

I took note of her entry each time she came into Starbucks. Some mornings she came, and sometimes she didn't come in while I was there. I thought she was a pretty woman, one of many attractive women who can be observed downtown each day. But I found myself being disappointed on mornings when she didn't make an appearance.

There are many, many people you see in your work environment each day. They are familiar faces but you never know their names. You see them on the elevator and recognize them as someone who works in your building. You see them on the bus riding to work. You see them at the lunch-spots downtown or at coffee shops. This woman was becoming one of those familiar faces, and I would likely never know her name or her story.

This morning ritual continued for the first few weeks of January, with little variation to the seemingly scripted series of events that occurred in the confines of the coffee shop. Then an unusual set of circumstances broke this routine. They seemed to be random events that would normally never happen. A few minutes difference either way, then the chain of events would have had a different outcome. The timing had to be perfect, or Erika and I would never have interacted. It was good luck for me. It was a turn of events that would alter my outlook on life after all that had gone on in the last two years for me. Was it just random? Some would say, fate was taking a hand in our destinies. I don't know what it was, but it was extremely coincidental.

One morning late in January, I was finally making a long-delayed trip to the dentist for a cleaning and check-up. I scheduled it for the first thing in the morning. My dentist's office was near my house. I would go there first and then drive into the city. It was a very rainy, blustery morning, and we were in the midst of an unusually strong storm. The day was the kind of windy, rainy day where you have to battle with your umbrella as the gusts tried to turn it inside out.

It did not occur to me that by getting to downtown around 9:30, all of the usual parking spaces and lots would be full. I had never encountered this problem because I always came so early. All of the lots around my office building had "Lot Full" signs blocking the driveways. I was beginning to get frustrated and wondered where I would end up parking. I finally found a parking lot a couple of blocks off Broadway. It was not an enclosed lot but wide open to the pounding rain. I was in for a wet walk of about five blocks to my office.

As I pulled into the lot, I noticed a woman struggling to get a large box out of the back of her car. She was completely covered by her raincoat and hood. The woman was also struggling to hold her umbrella over her head. I was certain it was a woman since there was a beautiful, slim pair of legs and red high heels below the raincoat. She looked like she needed help.

As I exited my car I couldn't quite get there fast enough to help her. Before I could help, she dropped her large purse, spilling its contents out onto the rainy pavement. I now ran quickly to assist her. I extended my umbrella over her head and said, "Let me help."

She lifted her head and when I could see inside the hood of the raincoat, my eyes met two large blue eyes and the beautiful face of the woman from the coffee shop. My face must have registered surprise.

"What a nightmare morning," she said.

I suggested that I take the box and that she concentrate on recovering the contents of her purse and holding the umbrella.

"Thank you so much," she said. "You are going to get wet."

"I think it is probably too late for that. Let me help you get this hauled to your destination."

"Oh, no ...," she started to say.

I interrupted and said, "I work over on Sixth Avenue, where are you going? Let's just get out of this rain."

She said, "I work on Sixth Avenue also, just a few blocks over at the investment firm, on the third floor."

I said, "You take your purse and the umbrella, I will get the box while you lead the way."

"Thanks so much," she said.

We were walking silently, trying to manage our bundles without getting even wetter than we were already. I finally asked a question, and of course I already knew the answer: "I think I see you in the coffee shop on some mornings. Do you go to the Starbucks on Sixth Avenue?"

I was hoping she wouldn't say, "Oh, yeah, you are that kind of creepy guy who is always staring at me."

Instead she said, "Oh, yes, that is where I have seen you. I thought you looked familiar."

"How did you get caught in all of this?"

"I usually come before 7 and never have any trouble finding parking, but today was a total nightmare," she said. "I had to go pick this stuff up at the copying center for a presentation later today. I ended up parking in that lot a few blocks away and then discovered I couldn't get it all hauled to my building. I guess I pictured pulling into the covered lot by my building and then getting a hand-truck or something to haul it to my office. That plan didn't work."

"I am never here this late either and got caught with the parking problem too. I went to the dentist this morning before I came," I said.

"Wow, the dentist and now this," the woman said. "Your day is off to a great start."

Then she added, "Turn here," as she pointed to the walkway of her building. "You don't have to do this ..."

"We are almost there ... I assume," I said.

"Yes, we are. Let me grab the elevator."

I entered the office behind her. It was a nondescript series of cubicles like most of the other offices downtown. She had a window seat facing my office building. I realized my hair was dripping on to the box.

"Just set it here. Perfect. You are so kind. You poor man, let me get some paper towels to dry you off." She scurried off towards the women's bathroom and quickly returned with a fist full of paper towels. "I am so sorry, and it was so, so nice of you to rescue me. It was a dumb thing I was trying to do."

I noticed her nameplate on the cubicle, which read "Erika Stevens."

"Really, it was no big deal, glad I could help. You must be Erika," I said, pointing to her nameplate.

"Yes, and I owe you a coffee, at least, when I see you some morning," Erika said.

"I am Tom Walker, and it is very nice to meet you, Erika. It was my pleasure to help."

"Where do you work?" she asked.

"Right there," I said, pointing out her window. "The thirteenth floor."

"I love that building," Erika said. "Wow, the thirteenth floor; does it bring you bad luck?"

"There is only so much I can blame on my location in the building. The rest of my problems are probably self-inflicted," I said, attempting to make a joke.

She laughed and thanked me again.

I said, "I guess I better get going. Good luck on the presentation today."

"Thanks again," she said. "I definitely owe you a favor."

With that, I walked out of the building, trying to readjust my wet coat and hair. I thought I must have looked pretty bad. She certainly didn't. Erika. Nice name. She was even more stunning up close and personal. As I walked down Sixth Avenue with the rain pounding on my umbrella, I mused about the strange turn of events. I was amazed to find the "coffee shop woman" under the raincoat hood in our chance encounter.

I was now curious as to what would happen the next morning in the coffee shop. It was kind of a silly thing. I wanted to arrive early to the coffee shop. I didn't know what I expected to happen or what coming early would do. Maybe it was the chance to have some interaction with someone new and interesting. That had not happened for a really long time. I am not sure I even wanted it to happen. I might get to talk with Erika and see how the rest of her day went. Then, it would probably be the end of "our moment."

I sat on the usual side of the coffee shop the next morning but moved one table closer to the door. Around 7 AM, Erika came through the door. She smiled when we made eye contact.

"Hi," she said. "Have you had your coffee yet?"

"I will have one of whatever you are having," I said as a way of short-circuiting the extensive list of options. I had already been there for half an hour and had enough caffeine to keep me bouncing off the walls all day. She placed the order and then came to the table.

"Please join me," I said gesturing towards a chair. "How did the rest of yesterday go, Erika?"

"Pretty well ... Tom, right?" I nodded. Then she added, "Thanks to you."

"You are very kind," I said, "but I think helping you with a big box in the rainstorm is the least I could do."

"Well, you saved my day and I really appreciate it. Did you get dried out okay?"

"Oh, yeah, I have lived in Oregon long enough that I will not rust," I said. "Go ahead and sit down and I will pick up our order. Did your presentation go well?"

"Yes, it did. I did it with two other people but I was the one who was compiling it. I was getting it put together over the weekend. I decided to do the materials at the copying place in the condo building so I could run back and forth with changes. That was a convenient plan until I had to haul the stuff to the office in the rain yesterday."

"Oh, so that is what happened," I said as I brought our coffee to the table, with a muffin for Erika. "Where is your building?"

"I have a condo over in the Pearl District, and there is a Kinko's on the ground floor."

"Now I am really impressed that you have a condo there," I said. "I have always wanted to live over there. I love that neighborhood. I run at lunchtime and I always run through that area just because I like it so much."

"Really? You probably run by my building. It is the one on Eleventh Street by the Jameson Square Plaza fountain. Do you know it?"

"Oh, yeah, I know the area. I love the plaza, and there are so many great galleries and restaurants."

Erika said, "So you run each day?"

"Yeah, I have a group of buddies that I run with to try to stay in shape and prevent further deterioration," I said.

She laughed and said, "Good for you. I need to do something and quit being such a slacker."

Right, I thought, you really need to do something about your slovenly appearance. "It is a nice break in the day," I said, "and it gets you outside and reduces stress too."

"I presume you don't live downtown," Erika said.

"No, I live in Beaverton but would like to be downtown. I am a downtown kind of person."

"So you're a commuter," Erika said. "Are you married and have kids in the suburbs?"

"No, I am not married. My wife died a couple of years ago and my two children are both adults living other places."

"I am sorry about your wife. I guess I was being snoopy."

"No problem. Thank you. What about you?" I asked.

"No, I am single," Erika simply said.

"How is that possible?"

"I was divorced a couple of years ago, and I have spent the last two years working on my MBA," she said. "It seemed like a good time in my life to take the plunge and get it done."

"Sorry, that was a stupid question. It was none of my business. My social skills are a little rusty, I think," I said.

"Not at all. How did you lose your wife?" Erika asked, with a concerned look on her face.

"In a car accident; she was hit by a drunk driver. She was a real estate agent and on the way to an appointment when this guy ran a red light and hit her."

"Oh, my gosh, Tom, I am so, so sorry. That is terrible."

"Yeah, it was quite a shock. So I have been getting used to a new life as a single person. That is something I never anticipated."

"I can relate to that," she said. "It was very disappointing that my marriage didn't work out, and I wasn't expecting to be single either. I guess I thought I would live happily ever after or something ..."

It was mesmerizing to talk to her at close range. When she turned her beautiful blue eyes on me, it was impossible to not be fascinated by her every word.

"Life does take some unexpected turns for sure. I am sorry things didn't work out for you, Erika."

She looked at her watch and said, "Yikes, I better go."

"Thanks for the coffee and the conversation. It was a pleasure to meet you," I said.

"Thanks again for being my hero and rescuing me. I will see you again, I am sure."

"Join me for morning coffee and conversation any time. I enjoyed talking with you."

"Have a good day," Erika said, and she was out the door.

Erika definitely brightened a room when she entered, and she certainly brightened my day.

The next morning, I was at my station in the coffee shop at my usual time, but there was no Erika that day. I thought it was odd that I was suddenly so enamored with her and looked forward to seeing her. I don't know what I expected would happen. I tried to put her out of my mind and thought my close encounter with Erika was probably over.

However, the following morning, she came into the coffee shop earlier than I had seen her before. I nodded to her and smiled when she entered. I decided to not take the initiative and not seem overly aggressive towards her. These strange rituals are hard to understand or interpret.

Erika smiled, said hello, and got in line to order her coffee. She waited to pick up her order, and then, to my surprise, she approached my table.

"Do you mind some company?" she said. "I don't want to bug you if you need some solitude."

"No, no, I would love to have you join me." I continued, "If there is one thing I have, it is a lot of solitude. It is nice to have some conversation with a nice person."

"I try to be a nice person, and I am not a stalker," Erika said.

"Good. That is a load off my mind. That is something I have to be cautious about. I come in the coffee shop each morning, and there are always hordes of young women staring at me and stalking me."

She laughed. Then I added, "I assure you that I am not on some watch list, nor do I do weird things on the Internet or stalk beautiful young women in coffee shops or parking lots."

"I know you didn't sabotage me in the parking lot so we could meet," she said. "I seem to not need any help sabotaging my own life."

"It is a jungle out there, isn't it? Being single presents all kinds of craziness that used to not be an issue. Have you had trouble adjusting to all of that, or have you liked the freedom?" I said.

"I have had trouble with that, and I have not wanted to get back into the dating games. I have really not enjoyed being alone," Erika said.

"You never know; sometimes with a divorce, it can be a good thing to get away and be alone again," I said.

"True, but my ex is an okay guy, it just wasn't working out," Erika said. "What about you? I bet it has been tough to suddenly find yourself single. Where are your kids?"

"It is something I never expected to happen to me, for sure. My son lives in the San Francisco Bay area and is a lawyer. My daughter is married with two children and lives in Denver with her husband, who works for the federal government."

"So you really are alone then? But you have grandchildren?"

"Yeah, two girls."

"Show me pictures," Erika said.

"I don't really have any with me," I said.

"What kind of grandparent doesn't carry pictures of their grand-kids?" she teased.

"One who doesn't like to sit on a big lump of a wallet all day," I said.

"You need to bring pictures to show me," Erika said.

So it began. There was an amazing connection between us immediately. It seemed like we already knew one another. We fell into the routine of regularly talking each morning. Erika rode the cross-town streetcar from near her condo to the downtown core, a trip of just a couple of miles. She would occasionally miss a morning because she got a late start or missed the early streetcar.

We discovered that we both had a love of the restaurant scene in Portland, which had all kinds of affordable, cool little places to eat. We also discovered that we both loved movies. She said she had not gone to the cinema much lately because she didn't like to go to movies alone, and she had been busy with school. I told her I went alone all of the time because there wasn't much of an option. I told her of some of my favorite movies of the last couple of years and also my favorite places to go to movies in Portland.

We also talked about music. One morning we exchanged iPods and looked over one another's music collection. "You have some great stuff on here," she said. "You like so many of the same bands that I do."

"What did you expect, Frank Sinatra and Ricky Nelson?" I said.

"Who is Ricky Nelson?" she asked.

"Never mind," I said.

Then one morning, I decided to take a chance and propose going to lunch sometime. I had noticed one of her little quirks over the course of these morning rendezvous. I loved the way she ate a muffin. I had never seen anyone do it quite the way she did. Erika ate it a small pinch at a time. She would delicately unwrap the paper from the muffin. Then, with her long fingers, she would take small pinches of the muffin and put it in her mouth until it was gone. It would take me hours to eat a muffin that way.

As she began this ritual, I started smiling.

"What?" she said.

"Nothing, I just like the way you eat muffins," I said.

"Are you making fun of me?"

"No, not at all. I think it is charming and adorable."

"Now you are embarrassing me; what am I doing wrong?"

"Nothing, please don't change, I think it is great."

Then I changed the subject. "Would you be interested in meeting for lunch sometime and trying out some of these places we have been talking about? There are some places I would like to show you."

"I thought you ran at lunchtime," Erika said.

"Well, I will skip a day," I said.

"I don't want to be a bad influence on you," she said. "But sure, that would be fun. Usually midweek is okay for me but we can check with each other in the morning to see if there are any schedule problems."

So, about the first part of February, Erika and I began to meet once a week for lunch and saw each other most mornings in the coffee shop. One morning, a coffee shop employee began tacking up pink and red hearts and "Happy Valentine's Day" signs.

As I noticed this, I said to Erika, "Oh, no; it's Valentine's Day again."

She said, "Oh, yeah, I almost forgot. Don't you like Valentine's Day?"

"I guess I used to like it. I have not enjoyed the last couple of years. Being single and not connected on Valentine's Day is not fun."

"I agree," Erika said, "it seems manipulative. Just because the greeting card company or someone decided this was the designated day to show that you love someone, suddenly you have all of this pressure on you."

"What have you done the last few Valentine's Days?" I asked.

"Well, all of my girlfriends were out with their boyfriends, husbands, or whatever. They said I should get out with someone. Somebody has a friend who would be just right for me, blah, blah, blah …. Just because it is February fourteenth, I have to get someone …quickly. So I have been home doing homework mostly. What about you?"

"Last year, I went wandering into one of my favorite restaurants by myself to get dinner, and I had trouble getting a table. I thought, what is going on here? Then I noticed all of these couples and realized it was Valentine's Day. How pathetic is that?"

Erika smiled and said, "I feel your pain."

"Then two years ago," I continued, "it was a few weeks after my wife's funeral, so that was not a really great time. I went to my beach house and noticed the beach was covered with couples walking, holding hands or with their arms around each other. That really helped a bunch. Just what I needed, being reminded how much I missed my wife."

"Aw, that is so sad," Erika said. Then she brightened. "Wait a minute; did you say that you have a beach house?"

"Yeah."

"Shut up!" she said. "Now I am the one who is jealous of where you live."

"I don't live there but I have thought about it. If you are going to become a recluse, why don't you just do it right? Live on the beach, stop shaving and bathing … just drop out."

"I don't think you could become a recluse. You would break quickly. You couldn't go forty-eight hours without going to a restaurant or a movie," she said.

"I guess you have me figured out, huh?" I said.

"So where is your beach house?"

"Lincoln City," I said.

"That is so awesome, do you go there often?"

"Not as often as I would like, but chicks dig the beach house."

"Oh," Erika said, "do you take all of your girlfriends to the beach house?"

"Well, just a few obstacles there. I haven't had a girlfriend for about thirty years, and I married into the beach house. It was my wife's. She inherited it from her parents when they died."

Erika laughed. "That is very cool to have a beach house. Is it right on the beach?"

"Yeah, it's an awesome location."

"I am very impressed. I have a proposal for you," Erika said suddenly. Then she backed off. "No, never mind, it would be dumb."

"Whoa, you can't do that to me. This exciting young woman says she has a proposal for me and then says 'never mind.' It's too late; you are not going to get away with that one. I am listening ..."

"Alright, but if you don't want to do this I will understand."

"Erika, the odds are greatly in your favor that I will want to do anything you suggest."

"Well, since you and I are both depressed by Valentine's Day and are tired of being alone ... how about if we meet somewhere for dinner on the fourteenth? We can just be two friends going to dinner together in a non-Valentine's date. Would you like to do that?"

"I would love to do that. Gee, let me think; I could go home by myself or go out to dinner with you. Hmm ... that is a tough one. I accept your proposal."

She laughed and extended her hand for me to shake. "It's a deal. We will go on a non-Valentine's Day, non-date together. That will be fun."

"Should we just meet on top of the Empire State Building on Valentine's Day if we still feel the same way we do now?"

"What?" she said.

"Never mind, it is a movie thing," I said. "It is on. It would be my pleasure. Are you sure you are comfortable going with me at night? So far you have only seen me in public places in the daylight."

"Actually, I have done some checking into your background, Mr. Walker. There are some disturbing things," Erika said with a wry smile on her face.

"You did a background check on me? Oh no; I am really planning to pay that Visa down as soon as possible."

She laughed.

"What do you mean, you are checking on me?"

"Well, I ran into someone I knew from college who works with you. I hadn't seen her for a while and when I asked where she worked, she said she works in your building, on your floor."

"Yikes, I hope it is one of the people I am nice to," I said.

"She had some interesting things to say about you and was very complimentary."

"Who?"

"It is no one who works directly for you."

"That figures," I said.

"No, it is Rachel Sizemore. Do you know her?"

"Oh, yeah, I do. You went to college with her?"

"I did," Erika said. "She said you are a real sweetheart and everyone loves you. She told me about when your wife died and how nice you are."

"Wow, really? I need to be nicer to Rachel."

"Apparently, she thinks you were pretty nice to her already," Erika said.

"Was anything else revealed in your investigation?" I asked.

"No, all of the credit reports, FBI checks, terrorist watch lists, sexual predator lists came back clean, so I guess we can go to dinner."

"Wow, dating in the twenty-first century—this is going to be tough."

"No, silly man," Erika said. "I just ran into Rachel and she gave me a very glowing report. She only confirmed my suspicions."

"Nice. How do I know I am safe with you?"

"I guess you will just have to take a walk on the wild side and throw caution to the wind."

Chapter 2

THE PEARL

THE PEARL District is an area located just north of downtown Portland. It is an area that formerly consisted of warehouses, light industrial facilities, and railroad yards. It is now noted for its art galleries, upscale businesses, and residences. The area has been undergoing significant urban renewal since the late 1990s and now is one of the hottest, hippest neighborhoods in Portland.

It now consists of mostly high-rise condominiums and warehouse-to-loft conversions. An old brewery building was converted to a great venue for live theatre, and the neighborhood is the home to one of Portland's most famous icons—Powell's City of Books. Powell's is a massive, multistoried bookstore that covers a whole block in the Pearl District.

The story goes that a local gallery owner coined the name "Pearl District," suggesting that its industrial buildings were like crusty oysters, and that the galleries and artists' lofts contained within were like pearls. It became the Pearl District, according to local folklore.

Now chic galleries and restaurants abound. Erika's condo building faces the Jameson Square and fountain, which simulates a tidal pool that is periodically filled by artificial waterfalls and then drained into grating. It is a popular spot on beautiful summer days when the fountain is full of waders, both large and small. But those days were months away on Valentine's Day.

It had rained earlier in the day but it was dry for our Valentine's outing. The restaurant where Erika wanted to meet was actually on the ground floor of her condo tower. As I walked down Eleventh Street, I could see the window gleaming in the soft darkness that was descending on the city. The wet streets and sidewalks were shiny from the rain. Then I saw her.

Illuminated in the restaurant window sat Erika. All of the surroundings were shades of gray but she sat in the window and shone like a pearl inside the oyster. Tonight, she looked very different. She wore a bright pink sweater, black skirt, and black boots. The bright color was very flattering. Erika seemed to have a slightly anxious look on her face as she waited for me. What a change a year or two have made, I thought to myself. Now this gorgeous, fun woman was waiting for me and we would spend the evening together. When her eyes met mine, she broke into a warm smile.

"Sorry, I am late," I said.

"You are not late. I had a little shorter trip than you had. I just got on the elevator and pushed '1,'" Erika said.

"By the way, this is for you," I said as I handed her a single red rose.

"Aw, you are so, so sweet. You didn't have to …," Erika said.

I came to know that her beautiful eyes softened and got moist when something really touched or pleased her. I was having that effect on her now, as she smiled at me.

"It's Valentine's Day and this red rose seemed like it needed to go to someone like you," I said. "I couldn't resist."

"This was our non-date, so you didn't need to do this," Erika said.

"I know. This is a non-flower; does that make you feel better?" I said.

"You have already made me feel very nice, thank you so much."

"You look very nice, Erika," I said.

"Aren't you the charmer tonight?" she said.

"I can be quite devastating when I have been awake for several hours. You always see me when I have been awake for about forty-five minutes. Sorry, I didn't mean to overdo it …"

"Don't misunderstand, you have nothing to apologize for, you are off to a very good start. I would give you a perfect ten for your first five minutes. I haven't been treated this nice for a long time," Erika said.

"I will see what I can do to correct past errors in judgment by others who didn't know how to act," I said.

"Wow, where have you been hiding?" Erika said.

"I was thinking, as I was walking up the street, how my fortunes have suddenly taken a nice turn," I said. "I have gone from lonely, depressed, and sad to looking forward to spending a nice evening out with my new friend."

"Let's try to help one another get happy again. You make me smile, and it is nice to be having fun again," Erika said.

"I couldn't agree more on all counts. Suddenly, I am feeling better about Valentine's Day again," I said.

We were interrupted by the waiter. It was time to order at this charming little Asian restaurant.

"I will defer to you, this is your restaurant. That is very cool, to have your own restaurant," I said.

Erika was up to the job and ordered a few dishes we could share and an appetizer she especially liked. "Is that okay?" she asked.

"You go, girl, I am with you," I said.

There were a few moments of silence after the waiter retreated, and then Erika touched my right hand, which was lying on the table. "Is that your wedding ring?"

Surprised by the question, I said, "Yeah, it is. I contemplated not wearing it any longer, but I didn't want to do that. I decided to move it to the other hand. I guess that is kind of dumb, it really doesn't make any difference which hand it is on. Nobody really noticed that I don't have a ring on my left hand anymore."

"I am so touched that you did that," Erika said. "It touches me deeply that you are that loyal and loving. Someone did notice."

"Thanks. I guess it wasn't my choice to not have her any longer."

Erika lightly touched her eyes with her napkin and said, "You are going to make me cry."

"I am sorry ...," I started to say.

She cut me off and said, "Stop being sorry, just talk with me about anything you want. Geez, how did I find the sweetest man in the world? You know I continued wearing my wedding ring for a while after my divorce. That is kind of weird, but I just wanted to be left alone. I didn't want anyone to know I was single again. I wasn't ready for that. I even had one guy in my MBA class say, 'I can see you are married, but are you happy?' Can you imagine that? That is the kind of stuff I didn't want to deal with."

"First of all, you should know that you understandably caused a bigger stir by becoming single again than I did. I can understand how a guy would notice something like that. Rings are kind of losing their significance now, in many ways," I theorized. "I don't know if you don't have a ring on because you are single, or you are living with your boyfriend, or you are gay, or whatever. All I know is that when I removed the wedding ring from my left hand, it was met with a huge collective yawn by the female population of the planet."

"I doubt that," Erika said. "There would be lots of women who would love to have you."

"If you could supply names and phone numbers, it would be helpful," I said.

"How about 503-555-2784?"

"What?" I said.

"That is the cell phone of a woman named Erika Stevens."

"Whoa, that is the greatest pick-up line of all time," I said.

Erika blushed and said, "That wasn't intended to be a pick-up line ..."

"No, don't spoil it. I am savoring the moment when a hot young woman used a pick-up line on me. What did you mean?"

"What I said. You said to give you the name and phone number of a woman who would be interested in you, and I gave you one."

I was still trying to regain my footing when she added, "Tom, what if you and I become very good friends? What if you and I starting having nothing but fun together? What if you and I were companions to one another to go out and start enjoying the things we both love? We are both tired of being lonely. We could have fun and not have to worry about all of the dating games. Is that something you would be interested in doing with me?"

"You are proposing a platonic relationship, kind of, where we will be just good friends and go do things together, but as friends, right?"

"Yeah; if you don't want to, I would understand ...," Erika said.

"Of course, I would like to be with you, Erika. It makes me very happy to be with you, and I look forward to seeing you each day," I said. "It would be wonderful to have you as my friend and companion."

"That would be awesome," Erika said.

"Are you sure you want to do this? I don't want to make a pest of myself, but I will likely want to be with you a lot."

Erika said, "We both will always have the right of refusal, if we are busy with family or other friends or just don't feel like hanging out with one another some time."

The waiter then brought our food. I raised my wine glass and said, "Here is to Tom and Erika and all of the good times that are ahead for us."

Erika smiled and touched her glass to mine. "To us," she said.

As we settled in to distribute the dishes we were sharing, we began to notice a crowd gathering on the sidewalk in front of the building across the street. We both took note of it but were busy sharing our food with one another.

The conversation settled into an exchange of information to fill in the holes in our biographical puzzles. Erika's mother lived in the area and had been divorced when Erika and her brother were fairly young. Erika remained close with her mother and her brother. Her brother and his family lived in the Sacramento area. Erika was born in Medford in southern Oregon and moved with her mother and brother to Portland after the divorce. She had lived in Portland ever since. Erika's mother, with her two children in tow, was apparently brought to Portland and placed under the protective wing of their grandparents. When Erika's grandparents died, there was apparently a fair amount of money left to her mother and to Erika as well. This provided a security blanket for Erika and her mother, especially as divorced women.

I told Erika that my father had passed away and that my mother still lived in the Metro area. I confided that I was frustrated with my mother since my father's death. My mother had seemed to become very scattered and was always meddling in the details of my life, not an easy thing to deal with, considering what had been going on in my life for the last two years. I don't know if my father had been able keep her focused and was able to deal with her strange behavior, or maybe she became that way since my father's death. But either way, she was a handful to deal with right now. I told Erika of my only sibling—a brother who lived near Cleveland, Ohio, with his wife and three teenage-children.

Meanwhile, the crowd was getting bigger in front of the building across the street.

I gestured towards the street and said, "What do you think that is all about?"

"It is like a Valentine's party that has spilled onto the street or something."

"New Year's Eve parties can spill onto the street, but usually Valentine's Day parties are not that raucous," I said. "Besides, this is the Pearl, not East LA or something."

Either way, Erika and I had a front-row perch by the window, which was directly facing the gathering mob. Suddenly, Erika said, "Oh, my God, no way."

Her eyes widened as she looked down the street, directly over my shoulder. I turned to see a young man wearing a suit of armor approaching on a large white horse. I turned and looked at Erika. We both thought we must be hallucinating.

The knight in shining armor on the white horse stopped in front of the crowd across the street. They began cheering wildly and then became very quiet. The knight got off of his horse and knelt on one knee in front of a blushing young woman at the front of the crowd. He produced a small box, which apparently contained an engagement ring, and was talking to the embarrassed maiden. We could not hear any of the exchange, but apparently she said yes. The group observing them began to cheer wildly. All of this drama had attracted the attention of everyone in our restaurant. Our fellow diners broke into applause after the knight was apparently successful.

"Aw, that is so awesome. How romantic ...," Erika said.

"I will have to remember this one, except I don't think I could get off a horse in a suit of armor. Actually, I don't think I could get on a horse in a suit of armor either," I said.

Erika was laughing and still watching the unfolding scene out our window.

"Boy, that guy really laid himself on the line, what if she had said no?" I wondered.

"What about her? What if a guy you didn't want to marry rode up on a white horse with a crowd of people watching?" Erika countered.

"Ah, Valentine's Day in Portland. There is nothing like our quirky little city to produce the bizarre. Have you ever seen the people at the Blazer games in the Rose Garden who propose while being shown on the Jumbotron screen?"

Erika said, "I have never been to a Blazer game."

"What?!" I said. "That is one thing we will have to fix. Anyway, I saw one guy propose to a girl as it was being shown on the big screen in front of 20,000 people during a timeout. She said no. The whole crowd starting booing and she had to leave the Rose Garden. "

"Gutsy chick," Erika said.

"I think she should have said yes, watched the rest of the game, and dumped him later in a more private ceremony," I said.

Erika began to laugh. "And by all means finish watching the game, right?"

"Exactly. Then there is one of the most romantic gestures our unique city offers—being married in the Church of Elvis."

"What?" Erika said.

"No way, you really have lived a sheltered life," I said. "You can be married in the twenty-four-hour Church of Elvis over on Couch in Old Town. For real."

Erika was laughing hysterically.

"I can check into the details of it if you are interested. The last time I checked, I think you could get married for $25 or do a two-fer for $20."

"The last time you checked?" Erika said. "You are the only person I know who has checked the price list at the Church of Elvis."

"I had suggested to my wife one time that we do a renewal of vows there. For $5 you can get a non-legal wedding with a trip around the block, a 'Just Married' sign, and cans. I think it costs more to get 'Elvis' to sing."

"I am sure it does," Erika said. "What did Liz think of this wonderful idea?"

"She never wanted to do it," I said sarcastically. "Maybe next year on Valentine's Day we could do the non-legal; non-binding wedding and we could pool our money and have Elvis sing."

"Wow, tempting," Erika said, tongue-in-cheek, as she continued to snicker. "I will think it over and get back to you," she said, winking at me. "I can truly say that you are the first man who has invited me to go to the Church of Elvis with him."

"See, I am taking a chance to make a *romantic* proposal to you like that. You know, Erika, a man really exposes himself to pain and vulnerability when he steps out there in pursuit of the woman he loves," I said.

"Oh, really? Apparently, I am about to be enlightened in the mysteries of the male psyche," she continued to laugh.

"A man is like a banana ...," I began.

"I have always thought so," Erika said.

"No, I don't mean that ...," I said.

She interrupted, speaking to herself, "Some are actually more like pickles, but all of them think they are bananas ..."

"That is not what I am talking about. Behave. I am trying to give you a metaphor ..."

Erika said, "I really hate to think about where this is going."

"No, I heard this metaphor in a movie once and ..."

"Oh, this is a serious metaphor, it must be true then ..."

"As I was saying before I was interrupted," I said as Erika giggled with her hand over her mouth. "A man is like a banana, he has a tough outer protective skin …"

Erika was laughing uncontrollably now. "Sorry," she said mockingly, "I know this is a serious matter."

"A man has a tough outer protective skin like a banana. But for the woman he loves, he will peel away that protective skin to expose his soft, squishy insides because he is willing to take that risk for her."

"Aw, how sweet," she said mockingly, "that is mostly a crock … but I know there must be a point in there somewhere. Are you telling me you are willing to make yourself vulnerable as we begin our new friendship and relationship?"

"Yes."

"The way you got around to that simple sentence was much more entertaining, and I am not sure what piece of fruit I am, and I hate to think how I somehow interact with the banana … but thank you, I guess. I trust you too and am happy to expose my … what was it? 'soft, squishy insides' to you." Then she started laughing again. "Did I get it?" Erika asked.

"It sounds kind of dumb when you recap it."

"Were you under the impression it sounded good when you explained it?" Erika said amid her giggles.

"Okay, maybe it didn't come out right," I said.

"You are so cute and so funny. Don't stop being you," Erika said.

"Was that a compliment?" I said.

"Sure. You are a hoot on a date."

"Not bad for a guy who hasn't been on a date for … thirty years or so," I said.

"Thirty years?" Erika said. "It has been thirty years since you were on a date?"

"Well, yeah. I got married and most wives take a dim view of their husbands continuing to date after the wedding."

"Wow, that is like the seventies."

"Thanks for that. I meant to ask you if anything changed while I was away," I said.

"How would I know? I didn't know what it was like in the seventies, since I might not have even been born yet."

"Oh," I groaned and grabbed my chest. "You have wounded me to the heart. Nice thing to say."

She said, "So how old are you, Tom?"

"Uh, well, I am fifty-three," I said.

"I just turned thirty," Erika said.

I was somewhat surprised by that answer. "Wow, I guess I thought we were a little closer in age than that," I said. "I don't know why but I guess I thought you were a little older .... I mean that in a good way ..."

"Does our age difference bother you?" Erika asked.

"Well, no, but does it bother you?" I responded.

"We have just been talking about how much we are enjoying being with one another. Then we reveal our ages. Should that mean that we now can't enjoy being together after all?" Erika asked.

"No," I said. "I enjoy being with you more than any other person for a long, long time. I still feel the same way. However, it would be more fun to be the younger one than the older one. Are you okay with that and don't feel like you are hanging out with some old guy?"

"You don't seem that way to me at all," Erika said. "What you perceive yourself to be is not how I see you through my eyes, okay? I want to be with you and I want to be happy again. Being with you makes me happy."

"Erika, it is remarkable the way you and I have such a connection," I said. "I want to be your friend and your companion. I am tired of being sad. I have felt like I have been lost in the gloom and couldn't find my way out. You seem to be the light shining through all the clouds."

This same conversation would be repeated in various forms over the coming year. The assurances and the anxieties would be the same each time. All other issues aside, the important thing was that Erika wanted to be with me, and I couldn't remember the last time I felt this happy.

Erika concluded by saying, "I don't want you to be sad any more. I don't want you to be alone."

"Thank you, Erika. I am excited about the possibilities of all the things we can do together. There are a lot of things I want to show you and do with you."

"I can't wait," Erika said. "Perhaps I should start by showing you my condo. Would you be interested?"

"You know I was not being patronizing when I said I had always dreamed of living in a Pearl District condo," I said. "I actually went on kind of a home tour here with my wife and some other Realtors. I loved it. I could never get Liz to go for it. But it has always been my fantasy."

"Let's go," she said.

Erika gave me a short primer on how to enter her building. I would go to the keypad and hit the buttons "9-1-2," and it would buzz a phone in her condo. She could either talk and buzz me in, or just buzz me in. Erika showed me that she had a security card she could swipe to activate the elevator, which would take her to the ninth floor.

"What happens if you forget your card?" I asked.

"I think you are screwed," she said. "I don't want to know what happens so I always, always have it with me." We got on the elevator and ascended to the ninth floor. I entered condo 912 for the first time. There would be many times to come, and it would be ground zero for my life for the next year. It was impossible, in these early moments of our relationship, to imagine what lay ahead for both of us.

I had not been this excited about anything for a very long time. We opened the door to a beautifully decorated, compactly designed condo.

"This is awesome. You know what? This looks like Erika's condo."

"What do you mean?" she said.

"It is beautifully done, with a real eye for detail. It is you, and that is a compliment, by the way. I love it, Erika."

Erika seemed so pleased with my reaction, which was genuine. She had decorated the living room with earth-tone-colored walls. Her furniture and accents were chocolate brown and turquoise, which had a great impact. The small kitchen was separated from the living room by only a bar with stools. Then there was the balcony. It was small but just big enough for a couple of chairs and a table.

The view was breath-taking. There was the city, the lights twinkling in the moist air on this February evening. "Oh, Erika, this is incredible. You have chosen well, and you are an awesome decorator. Well done."

"Thank you so much. I love it and have really put a lot into it."

"It shows."

She took me into the bedroom, which had the earth tones again, with red accents scattered around the room and a red comforter on her bed. It was great. There was a small master bath off of the bedroom. Down the hall was a small guest room, which was just big enough for a double bed. It would become an important room to me.

After the tour was completed, I said, "You have blown me away. Very, very nice. I am so jealous but you are very deserving."

"Thank you," she said. As we made our way to the door, Erika turned and hugged me for the first time. It was unexpected and wonderful.

"Erika, this is one of my best Valentine's Days, or any day, for that matter," I said.

"I feel the same way," Erika said. "Thanks for being my friend. I look forward to many more wonderful times that lay ahead for us."

"Me too. Thanks for being my friend. You are something very special."

She hugged me again and said, "See you tomorrow."

I left apartment 912 floating on air. It was a feeling I would have often during the next year.

Chapter 3

TWO YEARS EARLIER

Today, January 12, 2002, I buried my lovely Elizabeth. She was the love of my life, the mother of my two children. Liz was my partner, my lover, and my companion for nearly thirty years. I am still too numb to even begin to sort out how things will ever be the same or how I will continue with my life from this point.

Last Tuesday afternoon, January 8, I was sitting in a meeting at work that was supposed to end at 4 PM. It was dragging on as someone was making a point that I thought had already been made several times. My cell phone, which was on the silent mode, started vibrating. I looked at the display screen and saw "Liz" flashing on the illuminated portion of my phone.

Liz was a Realtor and was running around all over the Metro area, showing houses and meeting clients. Liz was starting to really enjoy the success of her hard work. She was just coming off of her most successful and lucrative year as 2001 ended. Liz was really excited about her possibilities in 2002 in the hot Portland housing market.

Liz and I routinely checked in with one another via cell phones throughout the day. Her schedule could suddenly change, and she kept me posted on her plans. I didn't take particular note that she was calling me in the late afternoon. Normally, I would have returned her call which came in just before 4 pm.

I could call Liz after the meeting, but in all likelihood, Liz would just leave a message, telling me about her latest schedule change. As I sat in the meeting, I watched the screen stop flashing, indicating she would be leaving a voice mail. I didn't know that my last chance to ever talk with Liz had just passed me by. I would never hear her voice again, except in the recorded message she was leaving. Much of life's routine events take on a greater significance when there is a sudden death.

We spend each day under the false impression that we are in control. We plan our day; we have schedules; we monitor our schedules on electronic devices; and we keep detailed "to-do" lists. We are managing our time and our day. Then something startling can happen that proves that control is only an illusion. Our life is very fragile. Life can be snuffed out in seconds. Fate does not consult our Outlook schedules or our "to-do" lists.

The nation had been hit between the eyes with a stark reminder of the fragile nature of life exactly four months before Liz's death. Terrorist attacks on New York City and Washington, D.C., had suddenly ended thousands of lives on September 11, 2001. It had a chilling impact on all of us that fall.

A week after the attacks, Liz and I attended a memorial concert in the Park Blocks in downtown Portland. We went with our best friends, Brian and Christina Mayer and our neighbors and best friends, Jerry and Shelly Long. We had known the four of them for twenty-some years. The memorial requiem was being played by the Oregon Symphony inside the Schnitzer Concert Hall. Behind the concert hall, speakers had been placed throughout the Park Blocks to broadcast the symphony to the crowds that had gathered outside. Lighted candles were everywhere in the Park Blocks. It was a poignant and sad scene I will never forget.

The six of us, who had experienced so much of our adult life together, sat arm-in-arm soaking up the special moment, listening to the sad music, and remembering those who were lost. During those weeks, it seemed you cherished those you loved just a little more. Everyone seemed a little kinder and more understanding of one another. The events of September 11 reminded me how much I cherished Liz and my four best friends.

It made me think of my children and grandchildren. Our newest grandchild had just entered the world. Liz flew to Denver in the late summer to help our daughter, Michelle, as she brought this new family member into the world.

There were people who worked for the same insurance company that employed me who barely survived the collapse of the World Trade Center. Some people from our office were in New York City on that beautiful autumn morning. After the first plane hit the World Trade

Center, the small group from our Portland office was being evacuated. We had heard stories in our office that the Portland group, for some reason, ran to the right as they exited the building. It was moments after their dash to the right side of the lobby that the first tower collapsed. Apparently, if our employees had run to the left, they would have been crushed under the mountain of debris.

The randomness of the fatalities on September 11 was stunning to me. There were those who were out retrieving coffee for their co-workers, getting haircuts, picking up children at school, and going to the doctor that day and coincidentally were out of the office towers when the tragedy struck. There were stories of people who missed boarding the hijacked planes for a variety of seemingly random reasons. There seemed to be so many who had "good luck" that day and avoided the catastrophe. Then there were thousands, and their extended families, who suffered cruel twists of fate that day.

As I marveled and was saddened by those stories from the September 11 tragedies, it was impossible for me to know that I would soon suffer my own cruel twist of fate. A random act, which could easily have happened many different ways, would soon take Liz from me. My mood had been generally somber that fall, even before the events in New York and Washington. My father, who was my best friend and my constant companion in many ways, had died in April. It was sudden and unexpected.

I had the great fortune of being raised by a wonderful father. He and I had spent so much time together in the last several years. We watched sports, went to Blazer games, helped one another with home projects, and played lots of golf together. As the nation mourned, I was still reeling from losing him in my life. I didn't think things could get worse. They could.

Amidst the gloomy events we had been dealing with as the holiday season approached at the end of 2001, we did have a joyous Christmas and New Year's celebration. Liz and I flew to Denver for Christmas and spent time with Michelle, her husband, Rob, and our two granddaughters, including our newest family member, Emily. Much of the nation was still very skittish about flying, but security was tight that holiday season. Everyone harbored mostly unspoken fears of another terrorist attack during the holidays.

When we returned to Portland, we went to our beach house in Lincoln City on the Oregon coast, with the Longs and Mayers to ring in the New Year. It was a joyous occasion to let go and have some fun after a grim year. Our four best friends came down and spent four days with us at the beach house. We had unseasonably good weather and spent a lot of time on the beach.

On New Year's Eve, which fell on a Monday that year, we cooked crab over our beach fire. Over the next two years, I would remember this moment as the last time I could remember being happy. We had a great time and toasted the New Year. Eight days later, Liz would disappear forever.

On the last day of Liz's life, Tuesday, she called me while I was in the meeting and left a message. Her message said, "Hey Tom, I just wanted to let you know that I will be a little later than I thought. I just found out about a property in Tigard that I need to take a look at. I am headed there now. We will catch up later. Love you."

Tuesday, January 8, began in a very ordinary way. There seemed to be nothing special about it. Liz had worked late on Monday night showing a property. Consequently, she decided to sleep in on Tuesday morning and start her day a little later. She didn't have any appointments until late morning.

I tried to be extra quiet as I arose and prepared for my day. I turned on just one light in the bathroom and showered by indirect light so I wouldn't disturb her sleep. I quietly dressed, and then, in the dim light, I walked to the edge of the bed. I looked at my beautiful golden-haired wife lying peacefully, snuggling under the comforter of our bed. I couldn't resist a final touch before I left. I touched her face and then put my hands under the cover to feel her soft skin.

"Don't," she said, making a face, "your hands are cold."

"Sorry," I said, withdrawing my hand from under the covers. Then I said, "Good-bye Liz," and kissed her on the cheek. Liz didn't react and continued to sleep peacefully. I would never look upon her face again.

I headed out into the steady, cold drizzle that was falling on this January morning. I gave little thought of Liz that day during the routine chores of a busy, rainy Tuesday. After her message, which I received just short of 4 PM, I assumed I would just go home and wait for her. We would probably catch a late dinner at a nearby restaurant.

As darkness fell, I waited in our house. It was not particularly unusual for Liz to be running late due to the unpredictability of her schedule. Then the phone rang. There had been an accident and I was supposed to come to the hospital. There was no indication of the seriousness of the accident, other than that Liz had been injured and I should come quickly. I was very concerned. I wondered about the condition of the car. I somehow pictured that, upon my arrival at the hospital, I would see Liz in the emergency room with a bandage on her head or her arm in a sling.

Upon my arrival at the hospital, I was told that my wife had suffered severe trauma in the accident and had "expired." This apparently had just occurred while I was on my way to the hospital. I kept wondering if there had been a mix-up and they were talking to the wrong person. Liz was dead.

I didn't know what to do next. Someone suggested I call some family or friends to come and help me. Alan had just started his new job in San Francisco. Michelle and her family were in Denver. I thought of Jerry and Shelly, my neighbors and friends.

The rest of the events I hardly remember. Jerry and Shelly were wonderful. They took over and helped me through the steps needed. The part of that evening I will never forget was my phone calls to Rob and Michelle. I cannot get out of my mind the shock and pain I heard from them.

Michelle cheerfully answered and said, "Hello Daddy," as she saw my name pop up on her caller ID screen. It would be some time before I would hear that happy voice again. I would talk to her many times in the aftermath of Liz's death, but her voice was devoid of the happy, cheerful lilt. Michelle probably imagined that Liz and I were calling to check in and ask how the granddaughters were doing.

I will be forever grateful that Jerry and Shelly came and slept at our house on that Tuesday night. They slept in the nearby guest bedroom and were there to protect and comfort me. The Longs spent much of that night on the phone, notifying people of Liz's death and making arrangements. They even offered to call Michelle and Alan for me, but I insisted on doing that myself. I gladly let them do the rest, including contacting the people in my office.

On Wednesday morning when I awoke, I experienced, for the first time, the wrenching moment that would be repeated many times over the next couple of years. In my earliest moments of consciousness, I wondered if the events of Tuesday were just a bad dream. I instinctively looked next to me in the bed. I was hoping to find Liz lying there, and that would confirm that it had indeed been a horrible dream. Liz wasn't there.

Michelle and Alan caught early planes on Wednesday to rush to Portland. Rob's parents were on their way to Denver to stay with the girls. Then Rob would fly to Portland. The funeral would be on Saturday.

I started having all kinds of discussions that seemed surreal to me, and I had trouble focusing on what people were asking me. The man at the funeral home told me Liz suffered "considerable trauma" in the accident but said I could make the decision about a viewing. I immediately said, "No, and I don't want to see her either." I didn't want my last image of Liz to be whatever she looked like now. I didn't know what "considerable trauma" meant but I didn't want to know.

It rained the night Liz was killed, typical of Portland January weather. I don't remember a single moment, from her death on Tuesday to the final moment at the cemetery on Saturday, when it wasn't raining. It added to the grimness of the week.

I was never one for organized religion. I wasn't sure what I believed, but I generally had issues with organized religion and many churches. I was in the "undecided" column, I guess. I believed in God. I never believed that life had no purpose and when you die, that is it. That made no sense to me. However, I didn't understand what God was like. I didn't understand why things happened the way they do in life. I suppose I believed that life had a purpose. But I didn't know what that purpose was. I believed that you continued to exist in some form after you die.

Heaven and hell ... I guess so. Little devils with pitchforks are a bunch of nonsense. So are angels floating on clouds playing harps. Can you be a good person without going to church? I am certain of it. My father was the best man I ever knew. He didn't need to be validated by some church.

However, Liz grew up in the Catholic church. It was very important to her. I conceded, and our children were raised in the Catholic church. I had trouble understanding the philosophy, but I thought the church was wonderful. It provided a moral structure for my children. There most definitely are things that are right and things that are wrong. I supported Liz. I had many friends in the Catholic church, and I participated in many charitable efforts by the church over the years.

I became friends with Father Raymond Matheson, who was a good and kind man. He was important to my family. He was our priest, and he conducted Liz's funeral in the Catholic church where my family had always attended. Father Ray was wonderful to me in those days before and after the funeral, even though I never took the plunge myself.

The program handed out at Liz's funeral contained the phrase, "Busy

Hands Now Rest." I know the last thing Liz wanted was rest. Especially "eternal rest." She was in the prime of life. She had everything going her way. Her business was thriving, she had a new grandchild, and we had recently become empty-nesters when our son graduated from law school. Everything seemed possible now for Liz and me after all of the years of hard work and raising children.

I never imagined that I would ever attend Liz's funeral. I was a couple of years older than her, and I never considered the possibility that I wouldn't die first. Liz is the last person who deserved this fate. She was always so careful about her health. Liz was devoted to a regular exercise program. She was in great shape. At her annual physical, she was always a textbook specimen of a healthy woman. Liz was very careful about what she ate and often chided me for my slothful eating habits, even though I ran almost every day.

She was always extremely disciplined and focused on doing the right things. Now some irresponsible idiot, who was drunk in the middle of the afternoon on a Tuesday, slams into her car and kills her. The story was pieced together in subsequent days after her death. A man in a large pickup truck, who was legally drunk, ran a red light and slammed into the side of Liz's car as she proceeded through the intersection. He was charged with manslaughter.

On a gray, rainy Saturday in January, Alan, Rob, Michelle, and I stood at Liz's graveside, beneath black umbrellas, to say good-bye. I remember the whole day being shades of black and gray. It turned out this really wouldn't be our good-bye. It would take us a long time to come to grips with these events. We were all devastated. We were also touched by how many people were so kind to us and expressed their love for Liz. I intimately knew my wife, but I had no idea she had touched so many lives.

Michelle and Alan stayed a few days with me after the funeral. Then everyone left. It was then that the enormity of what had happened started to settle in on me.

I made the mistake of going to the wrecking yard to see Liz's SUV. I was supposed to recover some of her real estate stuff, which filled the car. The vehicle's driver's side door was smashed well into the interior of the car. The hit had been directly on the door. Liz never had a chance. No one could have survived the direct hit. I so wished I had never seen her vehicle.

I went to the intersection one day to survey the layout and try to reconstruct the accident. I don't know why I felt I needed to do that.

Maybe I was wrestling with the idea of how this could happen. I needed to think it through.

I stood on the corner under an umbrella as a steady drizzle fell. I positioned myself at the intersection of the roads where the accident occurred. I was standing inches away from the traffic light the drunk driver had ignored seconds before killing Liz.

The main street was four lanes, two going each way, divided by a small island between the traffic lanes. The street ran north and south. Liz would have been northbound. A small two-lane road ran up the hill to my left. The drunk driver would have come down the hill at a high rate of speed, presumably. He ran the red light and proceeded into the intersection at the very second that Liz was passing by in the northbound lane.

I marveled at the logistics of this accident after I saw the intersection. The traffic on the four-lane road was heavy, with lots of cars traveling quickly through the intersection. How could the drunk have gotten to Liz to hit her? It would have to have been at the precise moment that there were no cars in the southbound lanes. Otherwise, the drunk driver would have struck one of the southbound cars. Even at that, there was heavy traffic northbound.

The accident could have happened a million different ways. In the majority of the scenarios, Liz would have survived. There could have been a car stopped at the light, on the two-lane road, which would have blocked the drunk's access to the four-lane road. There could have been any number of cars in the southbound lanes, which would have taken the hit before the drunk got further into the intersection.

If you tried to re-create this accident, it would be almost impossible. It would take split-second timing. If you started two cars at different points of departure and tried to get them to rendezvous so the pickup hit the SUV's driver's side door precisely, you probably couldn't do it. I would think ninety-nine out of a hundred tries would result in the accident not happening the way it did.

Liz had been randomly struck down by a completely freak accident. It shouldn't have happened. That is not even taking into account the hundreds of things that could have happened differently that would make Liz late or early to the point of impact. If Liz had even been hit in the back panel of the SUV, she would have survived.

As I left the intersection and walked back to my car, I felt total despair. I put my hands on the steering wheel of my BMW and stared straight ahead. I buried my face in my hands and started to hysterically sob. This should have never happened. It so easily could not have happened. Why did it have to happen to her? We had both been the victim of the worst possible twist of fate. Where was God that day? Why couldn't I have caught a break? Just this one time, and I would never ask for anything ever again. All I needed was a few seconds to change the outcome.

Of all of the verbiage that rolls out of the churches in the world constantly, how come no one can tell me where my wife is now? Why can't anyone explain this basic question? There is so much useless information and total nonsense. How come no one can answer the most important question of all? Why did she have to die? How come all of these horrible people get to live, but my beautiful Liz had to die?

It is all blackness and confusion. I now must figure out how to walk alone. I was fifty years old when Liz was killed. There should be many more years. There should have been many more for Elizabeth.

Chapter 4

RETREAT INTO DARKNESS

IN THE aftermath of Liz's death, I began a slow but steady withdrawal from all the parts of my past life. In nine months, I had lost my father and now Liz. Everything I enjoyed doing and the two most important people in my life were suddenly and shockingly gone. The withdrawal began slowly, and I had no predetermined plan. I was just trying to cope with overwhelming grief and being so alone.

I had taken time off work, bereavement time, which was available. In the week after the funeral, I wasn't sure when I would go back to the office. Everyone wanted to talk to me about Liz's death, and I wasn't ready to do that. I know people were trying to be kind but I did not want to have conversations about it.

On the positive side, it restores your faith in the state of humanity when a crisis like this arises. There seemed to be so many people being kind and caring to me and my family in the wake of Liz's death.

The first couple of weeks, there were lots of people around helping. I felt like I was still numb. It was after that, when everyone went away and the numbness wore off, that I began having great difficulty. I also began having dreams. Sometimes, I would be just doing routine things in my dream, except Liz was with me. She was still alive. I felt happy and then I would wake up.

One night, I had a dream that Liz and I were making love in our bed. It seemed so real. In the dream, I kept asking her, "What are you doing back?" She wouldn't answer, but just smiled at me. I touched her in my dream; she was alive, soft, and wonderful. I was holding her in my arms. Then when I awoke, it was dark in the house and no one was next to me.

Everywhere there were artifacts left behind of her unfinished, interrupted life. The book she was reading was on her nightstand, with her reading glasses neatly folded on top of it. There was a bookmark about three quarters of the way through the book. She would never know how the book ended.

I attempted to wash some clothes. In the hamper were the clothes that Liz wore on the last few days of her life. The clothes and her pillow still smelled like Liz, her body, and her perfume. Her real estate paraphernalia was all over the garage. There were stacks of signs with her picture and name on them. I was still getting phones calls from people asking, "Is Liz there?" After a few of those, I stopped answering the house phone. The message on our voice mail was still Liz, cheerfully asking you to "leave a message and we will get back to you." I didn't want to answer the phone any more. Those closest to me would call my cell phone.

I started having people tell me that my house phone mailbox was full and not accepting messages. I told them I would take care of it, but I didn't plan to do that. I had listened to Liz's final message left on my cell phone several times, just so I could hear her voice. I couldn't bring myself to delete it. I truly understood one of the saddest things I saw after September 11.

Alarmed family members wandered the streets of Manhattan with pictures of their missing loved ones. They were asking people if they had seen this person or had any information regarding their whereabouts. It was so sad to watch this spectacle unfold on cable news. Everyone knew the person in the picture was likely dead in the debris of the collapsed World Trade Center. However, if the loved ones could hold onto hope a little longer ... "missing" was not "dead." That meant your loved one was still in the world.

I found myself reacting that way. Signs of her existence were everywhere. If I got rid of those things, then that meant she was gone. It even carried over into a concert I attended at the end of February with the Longs and Mayers.

Liz had been the alpha dog in our pack of friends. She was the one who was always proposing things to do and making plans. It was Liz who proposed going to the coast together for the weekend, she watched the concert calendars, and she seemed to be in the know about new restaurants or plays. Without her guidance, the five of us seemed a little out of synch.

Liz had always been a huge Bruce Springsteen fan. We got six tickets for his appearance at the Rose Garden at the end of February. We were all excited about seeing "the Boss" and had extensive discussions about the upcoming concert on our New Year's weekend at the beach. Springsteen had recently reunited with his E Street Band, and it was going to be a once-in-a-lifetime opportunity.

As the concert date approached, my neighbor and friend, Shelly, gingerly asked, "Tom, what would you like to do about the Springsteen ticket for Liz? Will it bother you to have an empty seat? Do you want me to take care of that?" Shelly was so sweet and sensitive to my needs. The ticket to the concert could have been sold in a heartbeat. It was a super hot ticket. I had what I thought to be an odd reaction. I wanted there to be an empty seat. I knew how much Liz had looked forward to the concert. I wasn't going to give her ticket away.

There must be a moment in your cosmic consciousness when you realize that you are now dead. I pictured Liz approaching the "pearly gates," or whatever the entry to the hereafter is, and throwing her hands in the air, protesting, "Hey, I had Springsteen tickets!"

At the concert, there was an empty seat and we remembered Liz again. It was a bittersweet occasion. The concert was the best ever. I was seated between Shelly and Liz's empty seat. Several times during the concert, Shelly held my hand or put her arm around me.

I returned to work at the end of January. Everyone was very kind and I just tried to regain my bearings. I tried to do the minimum, take it slow and easy, and get back into the flow of life again. It had an unreal feeling to it. It was actually good to try to think about something else ... anything else. The difficulty came when I went home after my first day back at work. The house was pitch dark. I would have to do something about that. I can't handle the dark house each night.

It was then that I purchased some timers so there would be several lamps on when I entered the house. It was funny. It was not like I was afraid of the dark, but I guess, in reality—I was. It really unnerved me to come into the dark house. Everything was just as I had left it.

I found that when I was home, I would turn on the television and just let it run. I wasn't watching it necessarily, but I needed some sound in the house. If I left for a short time, I would leave the television or music on so there would be noise when I returned. It was a very strange sensation.

I had certainly been alone at home in the past. When Liz was gone or out of town, I would be home alone. I actually relished such opportunities to have some personal time. But this was something different, something I had never experienced.

Another poignant reminder of Liz's absence was when I hit the garage door remote button. As the door lifted, the garage was empty. Even my garage reminded me that she was gone. Where there had been two cars, there was now only one. Everywhere, there were signs that she was missing. She was missing when I went to bed. She was missing when I sat at the kitchen table. Unfortunately, Liz was missing when I was with Jerry and Shelly and Brian and Christine.

As the two years dragged on, I found myself avoiding being with my four best friends. I still loved them, but the dynamic was broken. I felt out of place with them. I think they felt odd too. It was a relationship of couples. Now there were an odd number of people. This was perhaps my most critical mistake of all, to push my friends away. They could have provided great support and comfort to me, but I started withdrawing from them.

It seemed that I was pretty strong early on after Liz's death. I thought maybe it would get easier. To my surprise, I seemed to be sinking with each day that passed since I lost her. I couldn't shake my feelings of sadness. It was getting worse. Sometimes, in the middle of the night I would wake up and think about standing in the intersection where the accident occurred. I would get so angry that I could feel my heart pounding. It shouldn't have happened. It was such amazingly bad luck. Liz should be with me now, except for a total fluke.

Valentine's Day came about a month after Liz's death. In my current state, I didn't think I could handle being in the city alone on that day. I decided to take a few days off and go to the beach house. It was the first time I had been there since New Year's Eve. We had printed some pictures of our festivities on the beach on New Year's weekend. The six of us had shared our photos. There were some left over and laying on the kitchen table at the beach house.

When I entered the beach house, I sat down to look at them. There we were on that happy night. In the pictures, we were gathered around the fire on the beach. In one picture, I was seated on a log by the fire. Liz was next to me, and I had my arm around her. She was smiling and laughing. Liz looked so happy. The fire gave her face a golden glow, and her blonde hair was tussled and in disarray. But Liz was still my golden girl.

There was another picture of Liz seated between Jerry and Brian, with her arms around them. She had undoubtedly been teasing them and exchanging barbs with her friends. Both men were laughing in the picture, and Liz had her mouth open, apparently saying something.

There were a few other pictures with various combinations of the six of us. Everyone was so happy. When I looked at all of the faces catching the glow of the beach fire, it made me realize this was my last happy moment. Hopefully, there would be others some day, but for now, this was the last happy moment.

Little did any of these happy, laughing people know that a devastating blow was waiting for all of us. The most unlikely person to be suddenly taken from the six of us was Liz. She was the youngest; she was the most fit and the healthiest.

Valentine's Day came, and I planned to spend it in solitude at the beach house. I didn't want to be reminded that I was alone. It was a cool, clear day. There was sunshine, but a cool, clear day at the Oregon coast in February means it will be cold.

I bundled up and grabbed a cup of coffee to go sit on my deck and watch the sunset. I had not processed the fact that the Oregon coast is one of the top destinations for people in Portland to celebrate Valentine's Day. Many couples go to beach houses or rent cabins and rooms to be there for a romantic getaway. As I sat sipping my coffee at sunset, the beach was dotted with the silhouettes of people standing together, two-by-two, watching the sunset. I had done that so many times with Liz. Sunset at her beach house was one of her favorite moments.

You could tell that many of the couples had their arms around one another or were holding hands. This beautiful moment reminded me of another reason to be sad. I couldn't get away from it.

As the spring and summer of 2002 came and went, I seemed to not be making any progress. Many expressed their concern. I felt I was barely functioning and easily distracted. I started to lose weight. I was shocked when I got on the scales one morning. I was still running regularly but not particularly doing anything to control my intake. My weight was dropping. It would have been a happy result most times, but it was alarming under the circumstances. I felt I was falling apart.

During this time, I seemed to have more nightmares. I even had a recurring dream of being in a car with Liz and bracing for the impact of a crash. In the dream, I was frantically trying to do something to protect Liz. I would always wake up before the impact. I didn't know the results of the crash. It was deeply disturbing. I would startle awake and be in great despair.

I started to frighten myself. One beautiful summer weekend, I awoke early on Saturday morning. I thought there was no point to getting out of bed. If I wanted to lie there all weekend, who was going to stop me? I remained in bed most of the weekend.

Something had to change. I began a long and steady withdrawal from all that I had known before. My safe haven appeared to be going to movies. I had always loved movies but always liked to share them with friends and discuss the movies I saw. Now going to the movies seemed the perfect retreat. I could go there alone, in the dark, and no one could contact me. I was completely anonymous. There was nothing there to remind me that Liz was missing.

Besides, part of the joy of going to the movies is that you could vicariously live someone else's life for two hours. That was perfect. I felt safe and secure when I was going to movies alone. No one expected anything of me. No one asked me how I was coping. I began a serious and prolonged binge of movie watching. It was like being an alcoholic on an extended bender, but I thought I was not harming anyone.

I would often stay downtown on evenings and go catch something to eat at a restaurant and then go to a movie. Sometimes, I would skip the restaurant and do two movies—a 7 o'clock show and another at 9. It was perfect. I was enjoying my movie binge, and it made the evenings go away. I did this for most of the next two years. I would go home to sleep and get the mail.

In the morning, I would wake up and get out of the house as quickly as possible. On the weekends, I would mow my lawn or do whatever needed to be done to keep my house minimally maintained, and then I would head downtown.

I had always loved my house. It was my favorite place I had ever lived. My children grew up there. I had twenty of my prime years with Liz there. Now I hated my house. It was like a tomb. When my father died, I hated going to the viewing. His lifeless, wax-like body was lying in the casket. I hated seeing him like that. Whatever was the essence or spirit of my father—the twinkle in his eye; his sense of humor; his voice—were all gone. He was gone to wherever it is we go, and there was only this shell left. My house was now like that. It was a lifeless shell. All of what I had loved about my house was gone.

Out of obligation, I would try to check in with my mother a couple of times a week. I probably talked with Alan and Michelle once a week.

Other than that—I had checked out. I spurned my friends and only did what I had to do at work.

During the two years after Liz's death, I probably saw Alan three times. I flew down one summer weekend and went to a Giants baseball game with him in San Francisco. We spent the weekend together in the city. Alan flew home to Portland and spent that first Christmas with me.

I did fly to Denver for the first Thanksgiving without Liz. I enjoyed catching up with Michelle and Rob and seeing the girls. Michelle and I spoke little of Liz. We were both still in pain as the one-year anniversary of her death approached. She asked me what was going on in my life now.

I said, "Nothing." I was not exaggerating or oversimplifying. "Nothing" was the truthful and correct answer.

I should have gotten counseling. I should have turned to my friends for solace. I should have drawn closer to my children and comforted them. I did the opposite in all cases.

One Saturday, late in the summer, my doorbell rang, and it was Jerry and Shelly.

"Hi, guys," I said as I greeted them at the door.

"Where have you been?" Shelly said. "You are the invisible man. Sometimes, I get worried about you not coming home."

"I know, I have just been staying in the city a lot lately. Catching up on work, going to a movie, catching dinner at a restaurant," I said. "I just try to stay busy and not just sit around in my house by myself."

"That is good to get out," Jerry offered. "We just miss you and wondered if you were okay."

"Brian and Chris are coming over tomorrow for a cookout. Please come and see us," Shelly pleaded.

I had been regularly putting off people who invited me over and even those who wanted to go to lunch with me. I was always giving some lame excuse for not going with them. I don't know why, I just didn't want to be with anyone.

This one I couldn't pass up. I felt I shouldn't, but additionally I knew the four of them well enough that I would be harassed and hounded if I didn't go. It would be good to see them all.

Sunday came and I went over early to hang out with Jerry and Shelly. It felt good to be with them. Brian and Christine came, and we warmly greeted one another. They treated me normally, which was wonderful. So many others, I felt, reacted like, "Aw, look, it is poor Tom." Then the women would tear up and hug me, and the men would pat me on the back. I was tired of being "poor Tom."

Much of our conversation, particularly between me, Brian, and Jerry, had always been bantering back and forth and teasing one another. I guess I wasn't being my usual self, so there was none of that. Jerry or Brian would occasionally fire off a one-liner, but I found I just laughed. I didn't engage in combat with them like I usually did. I had definitely changed. I am sure they noticed.

They asked me what I was doing these days.

I said, "I am just kind of going through the motions. I wake up, go to work, try to function as best I can, and then do it again the next day."

"What a thing to go through," Brian said. "It is unimaginable what you have had to cope with, buddy."

"Thanks, it has been bad. In a way, I am still kind of numb," I said. "It is like you have gone to the dentist and your mouth is still numb. At some point, it is going to hurt like hell and you will need some pain pills, but now you are just kind of in the fog."

Shelly said, "Chris and I miss Liz so much. It doesn't seem possible."

"No, it still seems unreal," I said. "I don't think I ever told you guys about the day I went out to the accident site."

"No, you didn't," Brian said. Then you could hear a pin drop on the patio as all eyes focused on me.

"When did you do that?" Christine asked.

"About a week after the funeral," I began. "I went out and stood there and tried to understand how it could have happened. Are you familiar with that intersection?"

Everyone shook their head, and finally Jerry said, "No."

"I went out there and looked. There are four lanes of heavy traffic. Two northbound, two southbound, and Liz would have been in one of the far northbound lanes from where the drunken guy entered the intersection. I stood there for fifteen minutes or so. The traffic was heavy in both directions. If a dog tried to run across that street, he wouldn't get three feet before being ran over by multiple cars."

All eyes were glued on me, and no one said a word. I continued, "The guy in the pickup would have come down the two-lane road, running downhill towards the intersection. He would have had to come at the precise moment when there was no traffic in the two nearby southbound lanes. He would have to have had a clear shot at Liz's car as it entered the intersection. How those circumstances lined up between four and five o'clock in the afternoon on a weekday in Tigard is beyond my comprehension. How could this have happened that way?"

They all looked at me with pained expressions on their faces, but said nothing.

"It pisses me off. I can't seem to shake this part of it. It is so random, so freaky, how the hell could that have happened? I know everyone thinks death of a loved one is not fair but this ...," I concluded.

Thankfully, I was able to express my feelings to them. No one rushed forward to hug me and start crying. I was glad for that. They just sat there with concerned looks on their faces, trying to process what I had told them. Chris put both of her hands over her mouth and closed her eyes. Then Shelly hit the nail on the head.

"We all got screwed, Tom. We all got robbed of our beautiful Liz. It shouldn't have happened, and it damn sure shouldn't have happened to her."

I just nodded in agreement. "Exactly," I said.

The barbecue occurred about eight months after the accident. I had to make some changes. I was not certain as to what I should do. I was grasping at straws to try to stop my downward descent.

"Can I ask a favor of Christine and Shelly?" I said.

"Anything," Christine said. Shelly nodded in agreement.

"I need to get Liz's things taken away or packed away or whatever. It is getting too difficult to see them every day. The house is virtually like it was the day Liz died. I have to find a way to start climbing out of this. Could you two deal with that for me?"

"We would be glad to," Shelly said.

"I know Michelle will want some things. I was going to set aside most of Liz's jewelry for Michelle. You two would be good judges of what Michelle might want. Both of you can take whatever you would like for yourself. I could just go away and give you the key to deal with it, if that isn't asking too much."

"We would be happy to do that," Christine said, "for you and for Liz."

A couple of weekends later, I decided to go to the beach house for a final summer weekend. I had always loved the beach house, but it was taking on greater significance for me since Liz's death. It was a place away from the city and a place of solitude. That weekend, I found myself sitting on the deck a lot and just staring into space. My mind was going a hundred different directions. What I was doing was not good. I knew it. I had to find a way out of this.

Sunday I returned home. When I entered the house, everything that belonged to Liz was gone. The house was cleansed of any of her personal items. It had the opposite impact on me than I anticipated. I started to cry uncontrollably. It was like she had never existed. Liz was really gone now. I didn't want her to be gone.

As the months went by, I couldn't stand to be alone. I liked to be out in public. I liked to be with people but, strangely, not with anyone I knew. I liked being anonymous and just observing others. Spending my free time downtown, going to movies and restaurants, was perfect. It was always lively and interesting but I was a fly on the wall. No one would be talking to me about things I didn't want to talk about. No one would be giving me advice I didn't want to hear.

This was my new routine. It isolated me from all of my friends. I still continued to do runs with my buddies, but I actually preferred to just listen to music and run alone.

I had limited contact with the Mayers and Longs. I still knew they were there but I only got with them when they cornered me and left me no choice.

Sometimes, I could see the four of them taking off on the weekend for an outing. It was the kind of thing Liz and I always did with them. I did not fault them for not taking me. Five wasn't the right number. They were trying to move on also and just wanted to go have fun. I wasn't exactly a barrel of laughs these days. If I were them, I would want to leave my morose, manically depressed friend home this weekend.

I continued to disconnect and sneak away from the rest of those around me. I rarely answered my phone, especially on weekends.

Another year passed, and little changed. I wasn't getting better. I wasn't moving on. But I had settled into my new solitary routine. I was comfortable with it. It made me happy when I was alone. I was only uncomfortable when I was forced to interact with others. This carried over into my second holiday season without Liz. On Christmas, I dodged everyone and lied to some, so I could just be alone.

But as the last day of 2003 approached, I was starting to feel an urgent need to change my life. I didn't like who I had become. If I continued on my present course, I thought I would be a really unhealthy person. I couldn't go through 2004 this way. Something serious needed to happen. I needed to chase away the blues. I was sure I was suffering from depression, maybe worse. There had to be a way to get out of this.

I would always miss Liz. However, I seemed to be over the crushing grief that I had felt earlier. Something inside of me was sending me warning signals. I was entering a danger zone unless I took some corrective action. I promised myself that there would be some changes made.

But what? Should I sell my house, which I had come to feel was a prison keeping me mired in the past? Should I start dating again? I wouldn't even know how to begin. I didn't know what to do.

All of these things were rolling over in my mind as the end of 2003 arrived. I wanted to change my life. I spent New Year's Eve home alone. The last year had been a miserable, lonely year. I decided to go to bed about 10 PM. If I went to sleep, it would make 2003 end sooner.

I was waiting for a sunny day to end the gloomy existence I had. If I couldn't have an entire sunny day, I at least needed a sunbreak.

Chapter 5

FALLING SLOWLY

"E RIKA, DO you believe that a person has a soulmate?" I asked one night over dinner.

"There are so many definitions kicking around for that word," Erika said. "What is your definition?"

"To me," I offered, "a soulmate is someone that you have an unusually strong connection with from the beginning of your relationship. I think there are a variety of people you could pair up with and be happy. But I think it is even rarer to find my definition of soulmate."

Erika looked pensive and said, "I think I agree with your definition."

"So, do you think you have ever found your soulmate?" I said, pressing forward.

"Do I need to consult with my attorney before answering that question from you?" Erika said.

"No, no, I meant no harm and your answer is nonbinding. I was just curious, since there is so much talk about finding your soulmate. I have thought about it a few times," I said.

"Finding your soulmate does not necessarily equate to living happily ever after," Erika said after some thought. "It takes a lot of effort to make it work, even if you have a real connection to your partner."

"I agree with that," I said. "I can see that even someone as wonderful as me could at times be irritating."

"I agree with that also," Erika slyly said.

"That I am wonderful or that I can be irritating?"

"Both."

"Thanks, I will take that as a compliment," I said. Erika just smiled.

"There are people that you really like," Erika surmised, "but that is very different from falling in love with them. But then there is love. I actually think I believe in love at first sight. I think that happens. True love is definitely achievable. That is what keeps life interesting." Erika continued to hold her cards very close to her lovely chest.

"Then there is lust," I offered.

"I am sure you are an expert in that category," Erika teased.

"Now, now,I meant there can be lust at first sight also," I said. "I think some people get off on the wrong roads as they try to find the right person, when physical appearance overrides everything else."

"Oh, for sure," Erika said, "there are gorgeous people that I would not want to spend five minutes with."

"That is comforting when you look like me," I said.

"You are not hard to look at," Erika said. "Do you know what my first impression was of you?"

"Oh, oh … I am not sure about wanting to know this. I generally have not wanted to know what women really think about me," I said. "I would prefer to live in a fantasy world …"

"Do you want to know?"

"Okay, but be gentle, please … I am very fragile," I said, wincing. "Did you think I was the creepy guy who always stared at you in the coffee shop?"

"That is amazing," Erika teased. "How did you know that? No, no silly man … I thought, now there is a very kind, gentle, together-look-ing person. He is handsome and looks very pleasant."

"Really?"

"Of course," she said. "It is very attractive to see someone who has it together, is kind, is funny, and … you know … you just get a feeling about a person … if they are a good person or not. I don't know if it is an aura, or a spirit, or whatever. So, what was your first impression of me?" Erika asked as her blue eyes got much bigger and she smiled coyly.

"Well," I began, "first impression …"

"Yes."

"I thought … there has got to be an incredible body under that rain-coat …," I said.

"Oooooh, you are so awful. No, really."

"No, no, I was just kidding … let me do this right," I teased.

"Truthfully, that was my second thought about you ... but my first impression ... I was stunned by your beautiful face and your eyes."

Erika started to speak but I said, "No, let me finish ... but the most impressive part was when I saw you talk to other people. It was the wonderful, warm smile that you gave everyone; it was a warmth or a sweetness that came from inside of you. You are a beautiful woman, no doubt about it. But there was something intangible that was beautiful, coming from the inside."

Erika was quiet for a minute and then tears welled up in her eyes. "That is the nicest thing anyone has ever said about me," she said after a few moments.

"When it comes to first impressions, you must go around blowing people's doors off all the time and don't even know it," I said. "You are something else, Erika."

Erika was carefully dabbing her moist eyes with a napkin. "You see my first impression of you was correct. You are kind." She touched my hand and smiled at me.

"But as for computer dating," I said, "I would never be lucky enough to get someone as dazzling as you. I would get several women from Sun City, Arizona, or a woman who's first three husbands all disappeared under suspicious circumstances."

Erika started laughing and said, "No, you wouldn't. But that is why I would prefer to do my own match making. I had pretty good luck one morning in the rain."

"So did I," I replied.

This conversation came after some light-hearted speculation about computer dating. We wondered what type of people we would get matched up with if we had a profile and were involved in some of the on-line services. I suggested that it was highly unlikely that Erika would be on my list of matches coming back.

I had ulterior motives in pursuing this line of conversation. I usually did when I started philosophical discussions with Erika. I had started to notice changes in myself over the last few weeks. I was kind of giddy and could not stop thinking or talking about Erika. I am sure my friends thought I was annoying. I could steer any topic of conversation back to something about Erika.

It reminded me of the Groucho Marx line, "Enough about me, let's talk about you. What do you think about me?"

When I was alone, I seemed to not think of anything but Erika. I couldn't get enough of being with her. I came to the realization one day that I was very smitten. I had not felt this way for a really long time. I had loved Liz for many, many years. Our relationship matured like fine wine. I never stopped loving Liz, but it became an advanced relationship. This is why it took me a while to recognize what was happening to me—I had fallen in love with Erika.

I totally bought into the concept we developed over dinner on Valentine's Day. I loved to just have her as my platonic, good friend and companion. I thought it sounded wonderful to be able to enjoy the things I loved and share them with this incredible young woman. But I now recognized that I had completely and totally fallen in love with this woman.

Confirmation came in a silly way from a most unlikely source. I was bored sitting in the waiting room at my dentist's office. My eyes scanned the pile of six-month-old magazines on a table in front of me. One article in some women's magazine that I have never read caught my eye: "How to Tell if You Have Fallen in Love." I picked it up and started to scan the article. It listed six ways to tell. I had not just symptoms of the malady, but I had a raging case of being in love on all six counts. Using this criterion, I had gone over the cliff some time ago and did not realize it.

I really didn't want to fall in love necessarily, but it made me so happy. I didn't know what the implications of this would be, but several friends and associates had remarked recently that I "looked different." They used words like "happy," "relaxed," and "excited" to describe how I appeared to them.

I am not sure what this will ultimately do to Erika and me. But I seemed powerless to resist it.

One day, as I was heading for my weekly lunch rendezvous with Erika, I noticed that the schedule was out for the Portland International Film Festival. That is one of my favorite activities of the year. It is about twenty days of foreign films that you rarely get to see outside of the film festival venue. I would sometimes drag Liz through the festival, but she was more tolerant than enthusiastic. Often I would stay in the city and catch some of it after work while Liz did something else.

I wondered if Erika would like to go. I pitched the idea as soon as I saw her.

"That sounds really cool," she said. "I have never done anything like this, and I will have you as my experienced guide."

"My suggestion," I proposed, "is to go to two films Friday night, which is the opening of the festival. They sometimes have the stars of the movie or the director there on opening night. Then, on Saturday, we could catch a couple more in the afternoon."

"Geez, that is like four or five movies in twenty-four hours," she said.

"Yeah, I get a little revved up about this," I said. "If it is too much, you could just go to opening night with me or anything else you prefer."

"No, no, it sounds interesting," Erika said. "I have never known anyone who has done this."

"Probably because you don't hang out with geeks or nerds," I said.

"You are hardly either one," Erika said. "Let's do it."

"I am excited because I have a friend who might be interested in doing these things with me," I said.

"Did you go to the film festival alone the last couple of years?" Erika asked.

"Well, yeah," I said, "I have pretty much stayed to myself."

"Aaaaaw, I am so sorry; I would love to be your partner. We will go to anything you want, and it will be a new experience for me," Erika said.

I just smiled and before I could reply, the waiter came for our order.

"I just had a thought," Erika said after we ordered our food. "If we are going to be out late Friday night and then go to movies during the day on Saturday, why don't you stay at my place instead of driving back to your house? You could pack some clothes and stay in my guest room, and I will make you some breakfast on Saturday morning. Would you be all right with that?"

"That sounds like a good plan if that works for you," I said. Privately, I was stunned. I not only got to go to the film festival but I was spending the night at Erika's condo. I told her I would get the tickets today and that the screening theatres were just a couple of blocks from both of our offices. As lunch broke up, we both walked back down Sixth Avenue towards our offices.

When we got to her office building, she hugged me and said, "See you soon."

I was so excited about our plans. It was then that I noticed two women from my office, who nodded and waved to me. They had apparently witnessed the hug. I would undoubtedly hear about this, or maybe they thought I was taking my daughter to lunch.

My thoughts returned to Erika, as they always did when I wasn't with her. Now, though, I was trying to take in the plan for our "sleepover," and I was thinking about what it meant. It probably meant just what she proposed, but it also was an indicator that she was feeling pretty comfortable around me. Erika was so free and didn't seem to worry about what others would think. That was remarkably refreshing, but I was scrambling to catch up in that department. Was I supposed to be reading between the lines here, or was I being delusional and it was only what it appeared—a convenience saving me a drive to the suburbs?

On Friday, I awoke excited, not just about the film festival, but today I would see her for a significant period of time and even stay at her condo. The world seemed like a brighter and happier place on any day when I was going to be with her. I marveled at the remarkable transition that seemed to be going on with me. I knew this was a dangerous place to be but I couldn't seem to help it. I didn't want to help it.

As I reflect on our relationship, I wonder at what point I actually fell in love with Erika and she stopped being just a friend to me. I really have trouble pinpointing the exact time. What was the event, or series of events, that made me conclude I really loved this woman deeply? I honestly don't know, but when I reflect on 2004, I can never remember not loving her.

After putting in a couple of hours at work, I went downstairs to the bistro on the ground floor to get a drink. A little caffeine would be needed to get me across the finish line.

I heard the voice of one of my running buddies, "Well, look who is still around."

I turned to see my friend Dave with a couple of co-workers at a table in the bistro.

"Come and join us, we have some catching up to do," Dave said. "So are you still doing the Shamrock Run with us next week? Can you work us into your schedule?"

"Of course I am in the Shamrock Run with you, why wouldn't I be?" I said.

The Shamrock Run was an annual St. Patrick's Day tradition, which we used as our spring fitness goal. We had done the 15K race together for about ten years.

"You seem a little preoccupied these days," Ryan chimed in. "You never seem to be available for early morning runs anymore, and you are hard to catch on your cell phone. Could it have anything to do with the luscious young chick I have seen with you lately?"

I was caught off guard and said, "What are you talking about?"

"What am I talking about?" Ryan responded. "Are you hanging with so many hot young chicks now that I need to be more specific?" This brought a chorus of chuckles from my wise-guy friends.

"No, that is Erika, she is just a friend I have started doing some things with," I offered.

"Just Erika? Damn man, we way underestimated you, good for you," said Dave.

"When have you guys seen her?" I asked.

John, the other member of the trio, chimed in, "You are busted, dude. We have seen you at the coffee shop and walking around downtown, all starry-eyed, at lunchtime."

"We don't blame you for not noticing us noticing you. If I was with her, I wouldn't be looking any direction other than at her either," Ryan said.

"You guys are so funny," I said sarcastically.

"No, seriously, I think it is great news," Dave said, "good for you."

"Yeah, don't get defensive, we just haven't had a chance to talk with you for a while," Ryan said, "and it is apparent you are undergoing some changes in your life. She is beautiful. More power to you, my friend."

John said, "If you don't mind me asking, how old is she and why is she with you?"

"And if I did mind?" I asked.

"Gotta love John, he always cuts through the crap and gets to the point," Dave said.

"Do I have to love him?" I said. I continued, "Erika is in her thirties and I guess animal magnetism is the answer to your second question." This brought loud laughter and hands extended in offers of high-fives.

"How far into her thirties?" John pressed.

I shook my head amid the chuckles. "I am not sure of her exact age, but we are just beginning to be casual friends."

"Whatever," Ryan said.

"I would love to have a casual friend who looked like that," Dave said.

"Speaking of the Shamrock Run," I said, "I will be there and will be ready."

"We are doing a tune-up run this Saturday morning to make sure we are ready; you up for that?" Ryan said. "We will meet downtown and run the exact Shamrock course as a warmup."

"Saturday morning will not work for me," I said as my mind went back to the planned overnighter at Erika's.

Ryan said, "Saturday morning doesn't work? Saturday morning works for everyone. That is why we do these things on Saturday morning."

"No, sorry guys, I can't, but I promise I will ready," I said.

Ryan said, "Well, don't let your casual friend wear you out too much. It must be hard for an old guy like you to keep up with a smokin' young woman, but we will see you on race day."

"By the way," I said, "I haven't had the chance lately to tell you guys what jackasses I think you are."

They all laughed. "We are not attacking you, man. You seem a little sensitive on this subject," John said.

"We think you are awesome but we especially think she is smokin'," Dave said.

"Have fun," Ryan said. "We are jealous. I am glad you are getting out again."

"It isn't like you think," I said. "She is really nice."

"Of that I have no doubts," said Ryan.

Now that the day of reckoning with my friends was over, I could concentrate on my excitement at having an extended period of time with Erika. As I sat in a meeting, which was holding no interest for me on this Friday afternoon, my Blackberry vibrated about 3:30 PM. I glanced at my Blackberry under the table.

There was an e-mail from Erika: "Can't wait to get this week over and spend some time with you. See you soon." Now I really lost interest in the meeting.

A crowd was gathering on Broadway in front of the theatre, and it was an extra hectic Friday evening downtown. There was the rush of everyone getting away as the work week ended and the bustle of Friday night downtown. Crowds poured into the core of the city to go to the theatre, movies, restaurants, and a variety of entertainments. Darn, I started to feel raindrops. I thought it wasn't supposed to rain tonight.

I saw Erika working her way through the crowd with a stressed look on her face. I waved to her. When she spotted me, her face lit up into a beautiful smile. I love that moment when she sees me and the lights go on.

As we stood in line, she talked in her animated way about her work week and her day at work. I listened but I was more interested in just watching her explain her life to me. It was a great evening, and I loved sharing the film festival with her.

As we waited in line for the second and last screening of the night, the lobby was full of classic movie posters. Erika quizzed me about how many of these movies I had seen. There was a poster of the Woody Allen movie *Manhattan*.

"What is that one?" she asked.

"What is that one?" I asked incredulously. "That is my favorite Woody Allen movie."

"Isn't Woody Allen that little weird guy who has a thing for younger women?" Erika asked.

"Whoa," I said. "First of all, I love Woody, so you can't start bagging on him. Second of all, do you think all older men who like younger women are weird?"

"I totally hope not but you will have to answer that one," Erika said.

"Funny girl," I said. "Seriously, tell me you have seen Woody Allen movies—" I began to list them: *"Annie Hall, Manhattan Murder Mystery, Everyone Says I Love You, Bullets Over Broadway, Crimes and Misdemeanors* ..."* She continued shaking her head.

"Young lady," I said, "there is a gaping hole in your life and your education. I have DVDs of nearly all of his movies, and I need to introduce you to great cinema."

"You seem to be my guide and my Sherpa through movie land, so I am at your disposal," she said.

I was still stunned and asked how she could have missed these movies. It was a big occasion when I was in college and as a young adult, when a new Woody Allen movie came out. He has put out one new movie a year since forever. She pointed out that she was probably being potty trained or learning to walk when most of those movies came out.

"Nice," I said, "you certainly know how to burst my bubble."

"I am just teasing, you are so fun to tease," Erika said. On reflection, maybe I would skip showing her one of Woody's best movies, *Manhattan*, which is about a thirty-something-year-old man dating a seventeen-year-old. Perhaps the theme is a little too close to home for now.

As the second film concluded, we walked to my BMW, which contained my overnight bag. We drove to her condo. As we went up the elevator, we chatted about how much fun the night had been and how she really liked the foreign movies.

We went to her small balcony and looked out on the city lights.

"This is stunning," I said. "You have an awesome view of the city."

"I would love to have some outdoor space," she said.

"You can have my outdoor space. Let's swap house keys and call it even, and I will even throw in my lawn mower."

She laughed and said, "You need to show me your house." I said I would.

I went into her guest room to call it a night. I was ecstatically happy to be under the same roof with Erika and breathing the same air she was breathing.

When I emerged in the morning, I wore a t-shirt and some sweat-pants. I wanted to get out there and not sleep in once she was awake. She was not out of her bedroom yet but I could hear activity inside. Erika emerged in a white terry cloth robe, looking radiant.

"I tried not to look so gross in the morning with you here, but I am not there yet," she said. "So cut me some slack until I get my makeup on."

"Yeah, it is shocking to see you in the morning, Erika."

"I am really letting you into my inner circle by letting you see me in the morning," she said.

"I bet you say that to all the guys who do sleepovers with you."

"Just to the only guy who has ever had a sleepover with me. How did you sleep? Is that bed okay?"

"It was wonderful," I said. "This condo is so nice. There are some re-ally clever design features to maximize space."

To this she replied, "You have cute feet."

Startled, I said, "Cute feet? No woman has ever said that to me. Great butt, amazing torso ... I hear those things all the time, but never cute feet."

She laughed. "No, seriously, a lot of people have ugly feet, but you don't."

"Well thanks, I guess. By the way, I haven't mentioned to you about the Shamrock Run yet," I said.

Erika said, "I hope you are not suggesting I run in a race."

"No, no," I said, "but I am committed next Sunday morning to run with some guys from work in the race as part of a St. Patty's tradition. We have done it together for several years."

"Cool," she said, "how far is it?"

"It is 15K around downtown. There is a 5K version, and an 8K, but we always do the 15K."

"I have a question," she said. "How and why do you do that?"

"You know how when they build a coal-fired power plant they have to plant trees somewhere as a carbon offset to keep the world in balance?" I offered.

Erika said, "What?"

"Because of my love for restaurants, I have to run far enough to offset the damage I do to my waistline."

Erika put down her utensils and bent over laughing.

"It is fun and is a good way to stay in shape, or try to," I further explained. "It is too bad you don't run, you have the perfect runner's body with your thin torso and long legs. If you showed up in a t-shirt and running shorts, other runners would be afraid."

"The only thing that might scare them about me in running shorts is seeing the cellulite on my legs," Erika said.

"Yeah, whatever, Erika."

"Yeah, totally," she said. As she prepared our breakfast, she turned and pulled up the hem of her robe, showing me the back of her legs. Her legs were long, tan, and perfect. Maybe the most beautiful legs I had ever seen.

I threw up my hands in mock horror and said, "Don't ever do that again; I see what you mean."

"Seriously," she said.

"Knock it off, Erika," I said. "I have not found any part of your outside or inside which is not beautiful. You are so silly."

"That is why I keep you around; you are so good for my ego. I will come to the race and support you," Erika said.

"No, no, you don't have to do that. It will be early on Sunday morning and just a lot of standing around for you," I said.

She said, "I know I don't have to, but I will. I think it is awesome that you can do this. I have never done anything like that. You continue to expand my horizons. I will take you out for breakfast after the race …"

I think she was about to say more but my cell phone rang, interrupting our conversation. I picked it up off the coffee table; the display screen showed "Michelle."

"Hello," I said, "how are you?

Erika kept fixing breakfast but cocked an ear towards me.

"Not much. Actually, I am out running errands right now and I am going to the film festival later today. I will call you later when we can talk more, okay? Are things going alright Michelle? Good, we will talk later, I promise."

"Is that one of your other girlfriends checking up on your whereabouts?" Erika asked.

"Right, I have so much trouble keeping them all happy," I said. "That was actually my daughter, Michelle, who lives in Denver."

"So you just totally lied to your daughter?"

"That would be one way to put it. I could have said, 'I am kind of busy, I just rolled out of bed at an attractive young woman's condo …'; would that have been better?"

She laughed. "I see your point, but I don't want us to have to lie to people about what we are doing because we are not doing anything wrong."

"I agree," I said as we sat down to breakfast. "But my daughter is probably ticked off at me that I put her off with the excuse I gave her. So I am pretty sure she could not handle the truth. My daughter is a pretty feisty little chick."

"Nothing wrong with that."

"Why did I have a feeling you would say that? I love feisty, assertive women, I wanted Michelle to be like that, but adult children seem to have a problem with their parents having a life," I said.

"These darn twenty- and thirty-year-olds are so self-centered and are not like us, right?"

"That wasn't nice. Touché. I mean that children in general, even adult, mature children with their own children, seem to have certain expectations about their parents."

I continued, "No kid thinks their parents were ever in love, made out in a parked car, or had sex, or continue to have sex, for that matter. After Liz's death, I am having a little trouble dealing with my kids' expectations. Was I sad? Of course. Was I devastated? Yes. Do I want to maintain my house as a shrine to my dead wife? No, I can finally answer. That is probably where I have been for the last couple of years. I would now like to move on, and you, Erika, are really helping me do that."

"That is very sweet of you to say so," Erika said. "You deserve happiness after all of the sadness you have endured. It makes me happy to see you being happy. It is hard for me to imagine this bright, alive, cheery person that is you, being sad and alone for a couple of years."

"You would be amazed to know how I have begun to turn around," I said. "Has anyone noticed you being with me and asked about it?"

"A few friends have. The Goddesses."

"The Goddesses?"

"Yeah, that is what my girlfriends and I call our group. The Goddesses have nights on the town, go to dance classes and Pilates together, and of course do a crazy amount of shopping. I will have to introduce you to them," Erika said. "They would totally love you."

"Do you really think they would or would they wonder why Erika is wasting her time hanging out with some middle-aged guy?"

"They would not think that because they are my friends. I have told them about you. You don't have to be apologetic for our friendship," Erika said.

"I would never apologize for knowing you," I said. "I just wonder what others think or what they assume our relationship to be."

"Let's get a couple of things straight," Erika said.

I feared I had crossed a line. I was scrambling mentally to try to recall what I had just said.

Erika said, "Our parents conceived us at different times, roughly twenty years apart. Society assigns a number to us called 'age.' The numbers do not mean anything unless we let them. As far as our friendship, that is a private matter between you and me. What it is or isn't, is nothing anyone else needs to worry about. If I want you to spend the night with me at my condo, it is no one's business. I like to be with you because you make me happy, you make me laugh, and you are one of the most alive people I have ever met. Even though you are fifty-three and I am thirty, you act younger than many of the other men my age or younger. If people have a problem with us, then they don't have to be our friends. Are you okay with that?"

"Yes, I am. You make me happy too. Thanks for the pep talk."

"Have some of your friends given you a bad time about me?" Erika asked.

"I faced a bit of an inquisition yesterday from my running buddies at work that I haven't seen for a while," I said. "I haven't talked with anyone about us. I guess I was a little oversensitive about it, and they were kidding me but happy that I was getting out again."

"Did you tell them that you were staying at my condo this weekend?"

"Hell, no," I said. "I stopped telling my friends about my dates when I was in high school. Looking back, it was just good-natured kidding from some guys I have known for a long time. They are happy that I am re-emerging back into the world. I was probably being a little touchy."

"Good. Just remember we do not have to explain anything, and our private life is private. Don't let people label you or me."

"Agreed. You seem so in control of the impact of others compared to me. You have never said much about your ex-husband, what would he think if he knocked on your door right now?"

"It is no longer his concern what is occurring in this condo. That is why he is an ex-husband. We married when we were young, and as we matured, we seemed to go different directions. It seems that one day we both mutually decided that we wanted to move on," Erika said. "We just sort of fell out of love."

I said, "I have always wondered about that phrase and how people 'fall out of love,' like it was something that could not be avoided."

"I will fill you in sometime, but let's go have some fun. I need what you can give me. Make me happy and make me laugh, okay? Do you want to take a shower?"

I must have looked startled at that sudden request. "I meant, do YOU want to take a shower? Not us."

"Yeah, I knew that," I said.

She just smiled a wry smile and said, "Feel free to use my bathroom."

When we emerged from our bedrooms, we were both wearing jeans and black turtlenecks. We both laughed.

Erika said, "We both look very film festivally today."

"All we need are black berets to be totally bohemian," I said.

"Should I change? Do I look stupid?" Erika said.

"No, don't change a thing. You most definitely don't look stupid."

"Let's go enjoy our day and forget everyone else and their problems," she said.

Following the afternoon films, Erika and I returned to the Pearl District near her condo. We went to what would become "our restaurant." It was the Asian restaurant on the ground floor of her condo tower.

It was the restaurant where we met for Valentine's Day. I still remember the table where she was sitting when I first spotted her on our Valentine's rendezvous dinner. Throughout the year, we would often go there when we were together. It was easy. We enjoyed cutting a huge swath through Portland's good restaurant scene, but this was our default eating place—an extension of Erika's kitchen.

As the year progressed, the waiters and waitresses always called us by name and greeted us when we returned. They usually would sit us at our "Valentine's Day" table. I would always fondly remember this restaurant and those magical evenings, watching the world go by the rain-streaked windows and talking about my life and my hopes with Erika.

Chapter 6

TOM'S GHOSTS

DURING THE following week, as the Shamrock Run race approached for me, I did not mention it or remind Erika of the event, which was to occur early on Sunday morning. I decided to let it drop and not impose on her. I could go run the race, spend some time with my buddies, and then go home. Maybe I would call her later in the day.

Sunday morning was overcast and cool. It was going to start out as a cold run, but hopefully I would get warmed up and my muscles would loosen up. That is always a concern when you do a lot of standing around on a cold day before the race.

The race would be a 15K, just over nine miles, around downtown Portland. I would not be the fastest of my friends. I never was. Some of them were track stars in high school and even college. I was just a baseball player who took up running when my arm gave out. My goal was to finish sometime around the seventy-minute mark, which would mean I would be running eight-minute miles. Any faster than seventy minutes would be a major accomplishment.

I started out running slowly and methodically, until I got warmed up. I was running reasonably well as we headed into the second mile and I was starting to warm up and break a sweat. My running had been a little spotty recently with the wonderful distraction of spending time with Erika. As I neared the halfway point, I was running a good pace to hit my goal. I was starting to really enjoy my run. There is a moment during races like the Shamrock Run where you wonder why you rolled out of bed early and paid someone to let you run on a cold morning.

As I neared the final turn, I could see the banner labeled "Finish" up ahead. That is always a welcome sight. I was going to try to run as fast as I could to finish strong. There wasn't much gas left in the tank, but I would try. As I neared the finish line, I saw one of my friends toweling off after finishing, and then I heard a cheer go up: "Go Tom, woohoo!" It was Erika. She was moving forward to stand near the finish line as I crossed.

"Hey, you," I said, while trying to catch my breath.

"You are my hero, you are awesome," Erika said.

"You are so nice to come; you didn't need to but I am glad you are here."

"I wouldn't have missed it, I wanted to see you run," Erika said.

"I hope you weren't expecting too much," I said.

"You were awesome, I would drop dead a hundred feet down the street if I tried this," she said.

By then Dave, John, and Ryan were gathering around. We were congratulating one another for another successful race but all eyes were on Erika standing nearby.

"Hey guys, I want you to meet Erika," I said.

Erika turned on the charm and said, "I have heard a lot about this group and I am very impressed by your running."

John said, "Tom told you about us? That is surprising."

Amid chuckles, they all talked briefly with Erika as I pulled on my sweatpants. It was a cool day, and standing there in a wet shirt and shorts quickly became uncomfortable.

Dave asked, "So do you two have plans today?"

Erika fended him off by saying, "Oh, yeah, I am sure we do." Then she flashed her twinkly smile and told them how much she enjoyed meeting them. Nicely done, I thought. As Erika and I began to walk away, Dave called after me and said, "Tom, let's go to lunch next week. It has been awhile."

"Okay," I said, "let's do Tuesday." He agreed.

I couldn't resist looking over my shoulder once as we walked away. My three buddies were standing together, and they watched our every move. I smiled to myself. I was fairly certain they were not watching me.

"Did you drive over or walk?" I asked Erika.

"I walked over, since the start and finish lines are not far from my neighborhood. I just came down the waterfront park," she said.

"My car's over here," I said, pointing to a parking lot a few blocks ahead. I wiped off the sweat, which continued to pour from the top of my head and drip off my chin. "Do you want to go to my house with me, I could shower and then we could do something if you want?"

"Perfect. I am open today; I am all yours if you want."

She had no idea how good that sounded to me but I said, "Sounds like a good day, I have wanted to show you my house anyway."

We headed to the suburbs for the first time together.

As we drove towards my house, Erika said, "How far did you run today?"

"About nine miles."

"What is the farthest you have ever run?" she asked.

"Actually, last summer I ran a half marathon, which is about thirteen miles."

"Oh, my God, why did you do that?"

"A reasonable question, to be sure. One I asked myself several times as I was running. My thought was that one time, before I die, I would like to run a full marathon. All of my friends have, so I did this to help prepare."

"How did it go? Are you going to do a marathon?"

"I went from saying I need to do this before I die, to I would rather die than do this."

Erika laughed.

"I really admire people who do a marathon but it was unimaginable to me that, as I crawled across the finish line after thirteen miles, I would only be half-done with a marathon. There were several milestones that psyched me out. One was when my running-watch passed the two-hour mark and I was still running. Another was when my iPod was playing the 278th song and I was still running."

Erika was laughing loudly now as we pulled up to my house, which was in Beaverton, a nice suburb of Portland. My house was probably twenty years old. Liz and I bought it when it was brand new and we were among the first residents of the new subdivision. Our next-door neighbors became our best friends. It had been a wonderful place to live until the last couple of years. Even before that, as we became empty-nesters, I had tried to convince Liz how much fun it would be to live downtown, but to no avail.

The house was a cheery, pastel yellow with white trim. It was a two-story with three bedrooms and three-car garage. It had a nice large patio out the back door, which was a great place to spend beautiful Portland summer afternoons and evenings. It was by no means a mega-house but was a comfortable 2,000 or so square feet, just right for a couple with adult children. However, it was too big for a widower living alone.

As we pulled into the driveway, Erika said, "This is it? Wow, this is nice."

As I pushed the remote garage door opener, I said, "I am trying to remember how piggy I left the house this morning."

"Don't worry," she said.

"Liz always had a rule that we don't bring guests in through the garage. We use the front door, but of course, we are under new management that is not that classy," I said as Erika laughed. "So pardon the dust or whatever."

As we entered the house, Erika continued to compliment what she saw. "This is an awesome house," she said. "I am impressed."

"Well, let me take a shower and get decent," I said, still sweating from the race. "Just make yourself at home, Erika, look at pictures, open drawers, and look in medicine cabinets, whatever. It will confirm what a boring person I am. Pardon my dusty tables, I try to maintain certain standards but I fall a little short in the dusting department."

"Okay," Erika said as I headed up the stairs to shower.

When I returned downstairs, Erika was in the living room studying various family pictures, which filled a large table behind the couch.

"How are you feeling?" Erika said.

"Fine; at this point, any race you can walk away from is a good one."

"Get a duster thing and I will help you dust. Then you can tell me about the pictures, is that okay?" Erika asked. "You have a beautiful house, by the way."

"I don't deserve most of that credit. You don't have to dust, I was just kidding, but I will be glad to tell you about the pictures."

"I would be glad to help," she said. "These are great pictures."

I walked with Erika into the laundry room and opened the cupboard, looking for a duster. "I don't spend a lot of time in here," I confessed.

"Here it is," Erika said as she grabbed a feather duster.

"Oh, is that for dusting? I thought it was the worst toilet brush I had ever seen."

That stopped Erika in her tracks, as she stared at me. Finally, I had to say, "Just kidding."

"Good. But you are in the top percentile of single men if you realize you even need a toilet brush, however," Erika said.

As we started to go through the framed pictures on the table, Erika said, "There are some cute pictures of you from your past."

"Yeah, I used to be cute," I said.

"That isn't what I meant," she said. "Is this Liz?"

It was a picture taken on the beach about ten years ago. It was a close-up shot from about the waist up. Liz had her arms around my neck and we were both smiling. Liz's blonde hair was still long then and she looked radiant. It was one of my favorite pictures of her.

"Yes," I said, "we were at the beach house about ten years ago."

"She is so pretty," Erika said. "You both look so happy."

"Liz is very pretty," I said, "and it was a happy time. Liz always had long hair but went to a shorter style in the last five years or so."

"She looks like a very nice lady," Erika said.

"That she was. I feel certain that you and Liz would have really liked one another," I said.

Erika didn't respond but continued to look at the picture. Then she said, "What about this one, are these your grandchildren?"

Erika was holding a picture of my daughter, Michelle, and my two granddaughters. I will have to admit that I didn't like to be thought of as a "grandfather" by Erika. I am embarrassed that I felt that way. I am proud to be a grandparent, and I have two wonderful granddaughters, but the label "grandpa" seems to be one of those labels that conjure up certain images and certain limitations in our society.

"Yes," I responded, pointing to Michelle, "this is my daughter Michelle and this is Brooke and the little one is Emily."

"They are so, so darling," Erika said. "Michelle looks like Liz."

"Definitely. Michelle has long blonde hair like Liz. I have always thought she looks like actress Reese Witherspoon," I said.

"She does," Erika agreed.

"And when she smiles, I can see her mother," I said. "The bad news is that Michelle hasn't seemed to smile at me a lot lately. She seems very concerned about some of my decisions."

"Really?" Erika quizzed. "Like what?"

"I have talked about downsizing from this house, and I have tried to find ways to move on to some kind of life without Liz. My amateur psychological assessment is that Michelle is really angry about losing her mother. She seems to be kind of channeling her anger at me for some reason. I think Michelle doesn't want me to move on without

Liz. I have to find a way. It is not disrespecting Liz; I just can't stay in mourning for the rest of my life. Michelle is my little sweetheart but she seems to be having issues with me trying to make changes."

Erika looked thoughtfully at the picture and then at me and said, "It must be so difficult for both of you. How old are Brooke and Emily?"

"Brooke is just starting school and is five. Emily is almost three. Emily had just been born when Liz died. It makes me really sad to think that those little girls will not know Liz and that Liz was robbed of all of the years she would have had with her daughter and two granddaughters."

"But they have the world's nicest grandfather," Erika said, trying to put a positive spin on the conversation.

"I need to make sure that is the case," I simply said.

"Is this your son?" Erika said, picking up another picture.

"Yeah, that is Alan when he graduated from law school at Lewis and Clark."

"Is he younger than Michelle?" Erika asked.

"Yes, by two years or so," I said. "Michelle was born in '75 and Alan in '77."

"Oh, okay," Erika said, "they are basically my age since I was born in 1974."

"You were born in '74?" I asked. "I kind of forget that sometimes. It is very disturbing to me."

"Don't let it be," Erika said and we moved on.

Next, Erika picked up a picture of Liz and me with our four best friends.

"What about this one?" she asked.

I smiled and said, "Well now, that's a story." Pointing to the first two people in the picture, I said, "This is Jerry and Shelly Long, who live right there," gesturing out the window. "They have been our neighbors for twenty years, and we have been best friends all of that time. These two are Brian and Christina Mayer. We met them through the Longs. Brian and Christina are basically old hippies from Eugene."

Erika started to giggle. "Are you at some kind of party?" she said.

"Basically," I said. "It is a Jimmy Buffett concert, which is in reality just a big party."

"Really?" Erika said.

"Oh, yeah. Brian and Christina were old 'Deadheads' in college and spent their early years chasing the Grateful Dead, in their VW bus, all up and down the West Coast, going to concerts. In their later years, they have become 'Parrotheads.'"

"Parrotheads?" Erika asked.

"Yeah, the devoted fans of Jimmy Buffet, who follow him around going to his concerts."

Erika laughed and said, "They don't look like hippies now."

"No, they are undercover and have assumed legitimate roles in society. Christina is in real estate and was the one who got Liz started. Brian is in banking, of all things. He really 'sold out to the man,' to use the sixties jargon. From potheads to Deadheads to Parrotheads. Liz and I always speculated that the Mayers were probably still potheads."

"You have colorful friends," Erika said.

"Oh, yeah, and it gets better. They have all bought Harleys and are into that now. They always wanted Liz and me to get motorcycles but we were too chicken, I guess. We would take weekend trips with them, the four of them on their Harleys and us following in the car. Ironically, Liz was always afraid of having an accident. The four of them are a real kick, however."

Then Erika picked up a picture of me and my father, taken at a golf tournament several years ago. I always cherished that picture because it reminded me of being with Dad.

"What about this? You look way cute in this picture; who is the man?"

"That is my dad," I said.

"Oh," Erika said reverently. "I haven't heard you talk about him. Is he still alive?"

"No," I said. "It is probably time I told you that story."

"Oh, I am sorry, Tom, I didn't know," Erika said.

"You have nothing to be sorry about. Let me tell you about my father. I had the great fortune to be raised by a wonderful father. Everyone loved my dad, and he was nice to everyone."

"Sounds like you," Erika said.

"That is a wonderful compliment, and I can only aspire to be like him," I said. "My dad became my best friend really, especially in the last several years of his life. He and I helped one another on weekend projects. We talked almost every day. We watched sports together and went to Blazer basketball games and golfed. All of the guy things I did with my dad."

I lowered my head and said, "I really, really miss him."

"Tom, how long has he been gone?" Erika asked.

"He died about nine months before Liz was killed," I said.

Erika's beautiful eyes began to fill with tears and she said, "Oh, Tom, I am so, so sorry. I had no idea you were dealing with that pain as well." Erika reached out and grabbed both of my hands. "You dear sweet man, you have really suffered such tragedy. I had no idea."

"I lost the two most important people in my life in a nine-month stretch. I feel like I have been reeling ever since and can't regain my balance. I haven't even played golf since Dad died. I didn't want to, without him. There was a huge hole in my life. Then Liz. Everywhere I looked reminded me that she was missing. I couldn't sit at the kitchen table without realizing that she should be sitting right there across from me. She was missing from my bed. I had to stop thinking of 'my side' and 'her side.' When I was with the Longs and Mayers, it reminded me that Liz was missing. I can't even go into my damn garage without being reminded."

This last statement seemed to puzzle Erika. I explained, "There used to be two cars there, now there is only one since the other was destroyed with Liz."

Erika pulled me near her and hugged me as we sat on the couch. "Oh, Tom," she said. "How have you coped with all of this?"

"Not well. I am sure I did all of the wrong things and should be seeing a shrink or something. I withdrew from everything that reminded me of Liz being gone. I stopped hanging out with my friends; I became aloof to everyone including my children. I am sure it was the wrong way to handle it but I couldn't make it work otherwise. One day I was even wishing I was dead and wondered if anyone would care. That deeply disturbed me and I thought I had to make changes."

Erika continued to hold my hands and look at me with a pained expression.

"I just withdrew from everything possible. I couldn't make the pain stop. One day, I called my friends, Shelly and Christina, and asked them to come and take everything out of the house that was Liz's personal items. I just couldn't do it anymore, and I couldn't remove them myself. I went to the beach house for the weekend and asked them to take care of it while I was gone. I asked them to take anything they wanted and to save anything for Michelle that they thought she would like. I set aside Liz's jewelry box and was going to give it to Michelle. I so appreciated both of them doing that for me. When I came home, it was like magic, everything was gone. I thought it would bring relief but I just cried because now I really was alone."

"I am so sorry to bring all of this up," Erika said. "I didn't mean to make you sad, I was just interested in your family."

"Do you know that you are the only person I have ever talked to about this? It has made me feel better to talk to someone. And you, Erika, are not just someone. Do you realize what you have done for me?"

Before she could speak, I said, "You are helping me emerge from this dark place. It is a cold, lonely place where I had gone to hide from life. When I met you and we started doing things together, that was the first time I had re-emerged. That felt so good, and I am so grateful to you for making me look forward to getting up in the morning again."

"I think you are giving me too much credit ...," she said.

I interrupted and said, "No, Erika, no I am not giving you too much credit."

"I don't want you to be sad any more, Tom. I don't want you to be lonely. I want to be your friend, and I want us to have fun together. Okay?"

"I don't want to be this damaged person who is so needy," I said.

"You are not. I look forward to being with you each day," Erika said.

She hugged me and said, "You are not alone any more ... I am here."

Chapter 7

A NOTE OF CAUTION

M<small>Y GUESS</small> would be that most of the people walking down the crowded sidewalks of Broadway each day in downtown Portland do not realize that they are walking "over" the best hamburger joint in the city.

There is a simple unmarked stairway that leads down below the street level. It almost looks like a stairway leading to the New York subway. Most of the people on the sidewalk just walk by the stairway that leads to the subterranean regions and probably take little notice of it.

It is as if when you descend the stairs, a smell of greasy food begins to permeate your skin pores. There is simple black door with a window stating the name of the restaurant—Blue Note Burgers. It is the kind of place where there is no need for a fancy menu. The only question is—do you want cheese and onions on your burger? Other than that choice, just sit down and shut up—your burger will be there soon.

They serve hamburgers and then they serve cheeseburgers. You will get fries regardless. This isn't the kind of place where you order a salad with the dressing on the side. If you really cared about your health, you wouldn't eat here to start with. So there is no reason to pretend otherwise.

To drink, you can have a Coke, Diet Coke, or Sprite, but you can also have a milkshake—the old-fashioned way. They bring you a tall glass and then give you the metal container off of the milkshake maker so you can refill your glass as it starts getting empty. It is amazing that when you enter this "secret" place to eat lunch, you find that it is packed. To eat lunch here is to be a part of a secret society that cannot be spoken of above ground among the rest of the population.

I have wondered if it used to be a speakeasy. Or maybe it was a hold-over from Portland's rowdy days when there were "Shanghai tunnels" below some of the bars. The Shanghai tunnel legend tells the story of loggers who would be drugged as they consumed liquor at the bar. The drugged loggers would then be dropped through a trap door, or some other device, down to a lower level. They would then be trans-ported out through a tunnel to a waiting ship on the Willamette River. When the sleeping logger awoke, he would be out to sea—literally, as he found himself an involuntary crewman on a ship. It was part of the "Portland Underground," and supposedly "white slavers" used these tunnels to steal women too.

I don't know if the Blue Note had that exciting of a history, but it was certainly off the beaten path. My friends, who were avid runners, were also avid Blue Note Burger guys. I tried to convince them that a couple of lunches there probably negated all of the good that comes from run-ning miles and miles each week. But it was to no avail. Most people (who were predominately male) who ate there would be willing to give five years off of their life span to enjoy these tasty burgers.

Blue Note was the site of my promised lunch with my friend, Dave, following the Shamrock Run.

We hadn't gone out together for a while, and I was looking for-ward to spending some time with him. He was already waiting for me there and had already ordered for both of us. We exchanged chitchat and talked about the race. Then the topic turned to more provocative topics.

"I just want to say, despite our teasing and harassing, how good it is to see you more like your old self these days," Dave began. "You have had a long, sad time after Liz died, and it is so good to see you coming back."

"Thanks for noticing ...," I began.

He interrupted and said, "Oh, I think everyone notices. You seem like a completely different person than you have been for the last cou-ple of years. I just want to sincerely say how nice that is to see."

"Thanks, it feels really good to me also," I said. "I am tired of being sad and depressed. Now I have found a way to get re-involved and be-gin a new phase of my life."

"Too bad it will be cut short by eating lunch here ...," Dave joked.

"Yeah, well ... I can hear my arteries clogging before I get to the bottom of the stairs when I come here," I said.

Dave laughed and said, "So what has been going on with you? I know Erika is a big part of that but tell me how all of this has happened."

"Well, I would like to tell you that I had an epiphany or I reached down into my inner core and summoned my strength and decided to be a better person," I said, "but that isn't what happened. I was tired of being so depressed and alone, but I didn't know how to break out of it. Just as one day Liz was taken from me ... one day Erika walked in the door."

"Of all the gin joints in all the towns in all the world, she had to walk into mine," Dave said in a bad Humphrey Bogart impersonation of a famous line from *Casablanca*.

"Nicely done," I said, and then added, "but it was a coffee joint and am I ever glad." I then told him the story of Erika coming into the coffee shop and my rescue in the rain. I told him of our Valentine's Day dinner and our "agreement."

"Wow, that is quite a development. So you are not doing Erika?" Dave asked.

"It is so nice to be back with people who can handle sensitive and delicate matters with such discretion," I said sarcastically. "I would like for you and the guys to think so, it would improve my image, but no, we are just friends."

"But I have seen you kissing and hugging, and the way you two look at one another doesn't make me think 'platonic relationship,'" Dave said. "Don't you want Erika?"

"No, I really don't think of her that way, the poor little ugly mutt," I teased. "I guess some men would find her attractive ..."

"I really hope you are kidding, or you need some serious professional help, man," Dave said.

"No, of course, I think Erika is one of the sexiest women on the planet," I said. "She gets better looking every time I see her ... and I see her a lot."

Just then there was a shout-out from behind the counter: "Dave!" This means you have about thirty seconds to come and get your stuff or they will give it to somebody else. That was the Blue Note way of saying, "We hope you gentlemen enjoy your lunch."

"So now take me through this relationship again," Dave said.

"We are just having a good time for now. We go out a lot and have great conversations and a lot of fun."

"And that's it? Are you are okay with this?"

"Having this type of relationship beats the hell out of being alone … just for starters. I tell you, it is incredible to look into her beautiful face, to watch heads turn as you enter a restaurant with her, and besides, she is so much fun to be with."

"Are you satisfied with that?" Dave asked.

"For now, but I think there is a good chance for our relationship to become more … much more," I said.

"Really, what makes you think that?"

I continued, "For one thing, I have come to the realization that I have fallen hard, head-over-heels in love with Erika. I can't wait to see her every day. I can't think of anything else. This hasn't happened for a long, long time but it has most definitely happened now. I am really excited and happy."

"Does she feel the same way, do you think?" Dave queried.

"Not yet, but I think she will come around," I said. "There is really something special between us."

"Have you told her that you love her?" Dave asked.

"No, I am just kind of waiting for her to catch up. I will be patient until she feels that way too," I told Chris.

"So how is it that someone who looks like Erika is still on the market?"

"She divorced her husband a couple of years ago," I explained.

"A fabulous babe, a real bona fide beautiful, hot woman like Erika, has been on the bench for two years? She doesn't impress me as a member of a lonely hearts club. I would think someone like Erika would need an administrative assistant just to manage the volume of offers and scheduling she would need in the singles market."

"Erika has been working on her MBA the last couple of years. She said she didn't want to get involved in the dating game yet."

"Since her divorce?"

"Yeah," I said, "she said she wasn't ready to start playing all of the dating games. That is what appealed to her about our relationship. Erika could be shielded from all of the singles rituals, but we could still have fun together."

"This is the woman you are now crazy in love with?" Dave asked with a troubled look on his face. I nodded in the affirmative and smiled.

"Be careful, man," Dave warned. I was taken aback by this reaction. It was not at all what I expected.

"Why do you say that?"

"Something doesn't seem right," Dave said with concern etched on his face. "Maybe she isn't ready for a serious relationship yet like you are."

"I realize that," I said defensively, "but I can wait. She is worth it."

This didn't seem to satisfy Dave's concern. "I mean, you struggled … struggled mightily to cope with Liz's death. But the day came, though, when you had put it behind you enough to be open to a new relationship. Even though Erika sort of dropped into your lap, you were ready to have a relationship with a woman."

"Right," I said, but he had more on his mind.

"But Erika seems to have not moved on and doesn't seem ready for a new relationship. She is just kind of stalling for time," Dave surmised. "Do you think she still has a thing for her husband? Is she hoping that he will come back? Does she still love him?"

"From my conversations with her," I said, "she broke it off with him. She was the one who pulled the plug, and I don't get any feelings of fondness there."

"I hope you know I am saying this with love in my heart for my friend Tom. No one deserves happiness more than my friend Tom. And if it is with some incredible woman like Erika … God bless," Dave offered, "but maybe hold back a little of yourself. Hold back a little for your own preservation. It scares me to think of you re-emerging from two years of hell only to get slam-dunked by a beautiful woman who you have fallen in love with. I just don't want that to happen."

"I appreciate your concern so much, Dave, I really do," I countered, "but I think it will be okay. I will try to go slow."

"It is just when someone gets ready for a new relationship, they have already taken the necessary steps to move past the old relationship," Dave warned. "If a person is still mired in the old relationship, then they may be keeping their options open … you know what I am saying?"

"I do, Dave, I really do," I responded. "Thanks for your concern. It is something I will need to be careful about. You have given me a good reality check."

"I am sorry, this is total unsolicited advice and is none of my business," Dave said.

"But that has never stopped you before," I said.

"Good, just so we understand one another," Dave responded.

"Seriously, I am just concerned that you will be okay. There is a big age difference."

"I know, but you know, just because we have this number assigned to us ...," I began, parroting the Erika dissertation, "doesn't mean we can't be together."

Dave just listened silently, perhaps because he felt he had said too much or perhaps because he wasn't buying my story.

I continued, "There are lots of phony rules made by society to define what is acceptable. Who is permitted to be in love and who is permitted to be together? We both remember a time when two people could fall in love but society deemed they could not be together because one had black skin and the other white skin. Who makes these rules? It is not the Capulets and the Montagues. Who says Erika and I can't be together?"

"No one," Dave said, as he seemed to be pulling back before saying too much. "I am sorry if I rained on your parade. I just want you to be careful. Keep your options open and try to protect yourself a little until all of this shakes out."

"I will, and thanks for your concern," I said. "You know, being fifty and single really sucks. I don't mean to sound fatalistic but you really don't know how many chances you have left for finding someone ... or finding happiness."

"I can only imagine. It could happen to any of us, and that possibility should scare the hell out of everyone," Dave said. "I know it is not easy to deal with all of these problems that were thrust upon you over two years ago."

"There are some really nice desirable people out there, but there are also a lot of people who are seriously damaged," I said. "So to even get an opportunity to be with someone like Erika is extremely rare. Sometimes, when I am with her, I just look at her and think, 'Wow, she is with me.'"

"Oh, yeah," Dave agreed, "I can see how she would be very intoxicating."

"That is the word for it, too," I replied. "When I am with her, she really casts a spell on me. I can't get enough of her. It is not just how she looks either."

"Hang in there," Dave said. "I sincerely hope it all works out. Erika is incredible and no one deserves this wonderful stroke of luck more than you."

"It is amazing that people can even get together. Just think of all the happenstance that has such a major impact on our lives," I mused. "You could be walking right by someone downtown, and they might be 'the one.' But unless some weird thing happens, like Erika and I meeting in a rain-soaked parking lot ... then you will never find that person."

"That is why there are the singles Internet things," Dave said, "to bring people together."

"You know, my mother keeps calling me every time she sees some show on cable news about a dating scam," I said. "She calls me and says I should be careful because she has seen a story about women who are taking advantage of men, or vice versa, on some Internet dating scam. It always turns out to lead into sexual depravity or someone gets their bank account cleaned out," I continued.

Dave laughed and said, "I would love to hear those phone calls. Your mother is a piece of work."

"I keep telling her that if a woman wants to sexually exploit me at this point in my life, I am actually okay with that," I offered.

Dave chuckled and said, "It is a fairly low risk."

We were quiet for a moment as we pondered my last point. Then, I said, "Speaking of a sudden turn of events, guess who has been dropping by a lot lately?"

"Who?"

"Theresa. She has recently been showing up to chat with me. I will just turn around and see her sitting in my cubicle."

"Theresa!" Dave exclaimed, suddenly coming back to life. "That would get my attention. Now there is somebody who is back in circulation also. I hear that she and her husband got divorced a while ago. She is single again."

"Really?"

"Now, Theresa could keep you warm on a rainy night," Dave offered. "She is amazing. Am I just an old horny guy or is her body getting better with each passing day?"

"Both things are true," I said. "I am not sure if her improving body is an 'all natural' process but who cares?"

Theresa was a beautiful, middle-aged woman with stunning red hair and a great body. She worked in our office. Dave has worked with her for several years.

"Meaning no disrespect to Erika," Dave began, "but if I had Theresa sniffing around my office, and I was single, I would be all over her. Even if I wasn't single."

"How would your wife feel about that?"

"Yeah, well … you know what I mean," Dave said.

"For the record, I have asked Theresa to quit sniffing. But a more serious point is that I am not sure Theresa crosses you off the list just because you are married. I think she may only view marital status as a minor inconvenience," I said.

"What?"

"Never mind. I will tell you a story sometime," I said. "Theresa can be pretty aggressive."

"Beautiful, sexy, and aggressive …," Dave summarized. "I am trying to see a down side here."

"Stay tuned …"

"So, let's say it did work out with Erika," Dave said, changing topics. "Where do you see this going? Are you going to have children with her? In your mid-fifties, are you going to start with diapers and bottles and elementary school programs and all of that again?"

"A sobering thought, to be sure," I agreed, "but love sort of leads you into lots of paths you might not take otherwise. If Erika wanted to marry me someday, if Erika wanted to have children, then I guess that is what would happen."

"You would really want to start over again?"

"Not really, but I can't not have Erika. If that is what it would take, then to me, it would be worth it," I said. "I guess it is hard to be logical and analytical when you are in love."

"Just be careful. I am just afraid that at some point, the age difference is going to bite you, and Erika will move on," Dave warned.

"It is a legitimate fear," I responded. "I am aware of the risks. I guess I am just ready to take the risk."

I thanked Dave for his concern and good advice. I ascended the stairs back into the world above the Blue Note. As I reached the top of the stairs, my cell phone suddenly went crazy, beeping and vibrating. My first thought was that there must be some type of crisis at work. My cell phone display screen showed "Erika—5 Missed Calls."

The Banfield Freeway enters downtown Portland from the east side of the city. It is one of the main arteries into the city. It funnels traffic from the entire east side, plus a significant amount of commuter traffic from Vancouver, Washington. It is really the tail end of Interstate 84, which snakes its way across the western United States. Everyone in Portland calls the section that runs from near the Washington State border into downtown Portland "the Banfield." I am not sure why, other than "Banfield" was Thomas Harry Banfield, who was the chairman of the Oregon Transportation Commission in the 1940s.

Everyone in Portland just refers to it as "the Banfield." It has very few exits once you enter it. It has three lanes with large cement walls on the sides and very narrow shoulders. There is an exit to the Hollywood District of the city and one more at the Lloyd Center area, before you take a downtown exit and cross the Willamette River into the downtown core, where Erika and I work. It seems to always have heavy traffic.

If there is an accident or a stalled car in one of the three lanes, traffic will quickly stack up to the Columbia River, which is the Washington-Oregon border. I think all Portland drivers should have a glass case in their car containing a cyanide capsule. If your car stalls on the Banfield, the best thing to do would be to break the glass and take the capsule.

It has always been a nightmare scenario for me. It always makes the morning and evening traffic reports when some poor soul breaks down, especially in the middle lane. There is no way you could get out of your car without being immediately cut down by oncoming traffic. The only option you would have is to sit in your car and hope someone has mercy on you. If that happens on a rainy day, it doubles the fun.

Apparently, while I was in the subregions of the Blue Note, I had no cell service. Upon reaching the top of the stairs, my bars came back and so did several rapidly placed phones calls from Erika. I was immediately concerned that Erika had been frantically trying to reach me.

I instantly speed-dialed her.

"Tom, where have you been ... please help me!"

"Erika, what is wrong?"

There were all kinds of noises and she was practically shrieking, "My car is broken down on the Banfield! I can't get out of my car ... I am so freaked out ...!"

"Okay, okay, have you called anyone yet ...?"

"I have been trying and trying to reach you!" she screamed.

"I know. I am sorry. I meant a tow truck ... or something?"

"No, I don't have any phone numbers ... I am such an idiot," she said.

"Calm down, I am on my way. Where are you?"

"On the Banfield!" she shrieked.

"I know, but where? Please try to be calm, sweetie; I will come and get you. Where?"

"I am just short of the Lloyd Center exit, and I am in the middle lane!"

"I am on my way, I just got back to my car, I am on my way. Do not, whatever you do, try to get out of your car, okay? Wait until you see me."

"Okay, please hurry," she said, and then she hung up.

I immediately drove as fast as possible over the Burnside Bridge to the other side of the river. My thought was that I would get on the Banfield and pull up behind Erika to help her. It was way too late for that, I would discover. I was also anxious to let the Oregon Department of Transportation (ODOT) emergency response people know that Erika was stranded.

I was also way late for that. EVERYBODY now knew Erika was stranded, or at least they knew some poor woman in a blue Volkswagen was. All four local news stations have lunchtime broadcasts, and their news helicopters patrol the Metro area like hungry wolves looking for a kill. I am sure they flashed their "Breaking News" crawler across the screen as they got the feed from their live helicopter shots. I am certain Erika was on all four stations—live and real time.

As if things were not complicated enough, it was starting to rain, and the closer I got to the Lloyd Center District, the harder it was raining. My new strategy was to call ODOT and the tow service to get help on the way. I pulled the numbers off of my Blackberry and dialed while I raced through the streets. Near the Lloyd Center exit from the Banfield, there is an overpass over the freeway. I parked my BMW and ran out on the overpass to look over the Banfield. I could see Erika's car with the emergency flashers going and cars stacked up behind her as far as the eye could see.

My first instinct was to start running down the off-ramp and try to get to Erika. Then a little voice inside of me said, "Don't even think about it." Running on the shoulder of the Banfield, in the rain, against the flow of traffic, with an open umbrella, was probably an almost certain way to die violently.

On the overpass, I had a panoramic view of the entire problem. I could see the ODOT emergency response truck making its way on the narrow shoulder to try to get to Erika. Once there, they would turn on the lighted arrows that would divert traffic away from her car and make her safer. For now, I could only pray that some idiot didn't come up behind her and hit the back of her stalled car. Then in the distance, I could see the tow truck making its way down the narrow shoulder in the bumper-to-bumper traffic. Its progress was impeded by people's reluctance or inability to move over in the lane to allow the large tow truck to pass.

I called Erika.

"Tom?"

"Erika, help is on the way. The tow truck should be there in a few minutes. DO NOT get out of your car! They will just load your car onto the flatbed of the tow truck and bring you to where I am. Do you see me? I am on the overpass waving my open umbrella."

"I can't see you. It is raining too hard."

"Turn your key on and turn on your wipers."

I could see that she was doing that. "Now can you see me?"

"Yes, I can."

"Erika, I am here waiting for you. The tow truck will bring you here. You can ride with me, and we will follow the tow truck to the Volkswagen dealer. They know your car is coming. I am having them take your car to the dealer back down the Banfield the other way—out by Gateway, okay?"

"Alright," she said.

"Hang in there a few more minutes. I can see the tow truck coming, and the ODOT truck is right behind you."

The tow truck finally fought its way through the congested traffic and was positioning itself to attach the winch to the front of Erika's car. The loading was now under way. I had talked with the tow truck dispatcher earlier, and they knew to meet me at the top of the Lloyd Center exit.

He pulled over in a safe stopping area right by my BMW. I went to the back of the truck and motioned for Erika to get out of her car. She walked tentatively on the flatbed truck bed, which was several feet above the ground. I took Erika's hand and I told her to jump and I would catch her. She did. I caught her and lowered her to the ground.

Erika would not let go of me and immediately buried her face in my shoulder and continued to hug me. She was getting wet and trembling but she continued to hold me tightly. "You are safe now, sweetie, everything is going to be okay," I kept saying. She still held onto me. I told the tow truck driver, "Go ahead, we will meet you at the VW dealer."

He said he would and got back in the cab of his truck.

This brought Erika out of her trauma, and she said meekly, "My stuff ..."

"We will get it out of the car at the dealer," I said as I walked her around to the passenger side door and opened it for her.

"Are you okay, Erika?"

"I am really cold and wet."

I removed my black leather coat and put it over her and turned up the heat. As we headed back down the Banfield following the tow truck, I explained the arrangements I had made to get the problem solved.

She seemed to ignore that and said, "Why didn't you answer your phone? I was in such a panic and I am so, so sorry."

"Erika, it is alright; you have just gone through one of my most feared experiences, right up there with family death and my house burning down. Panic is understandable."

Then I explained, "I guess I wasn't getting cell coverage down underground where I was eating. When I came to the top of the stairs, my coverage kicked back in and I noticed that I had five or so missed calls from you."

"You ate lunch underground?" she asked.

Before I could answer, she said again, "I am so sorry how I acted. I was just running errands at lunchtime and my car just cut out, then stopped, and all of the lights on the dash went on. I was stranded." Erika was wiping tears from her eyes as she told me what happened.

We then pulled into the dealer, and I told Erika to wait in the car and I would take care of everything. I got out and talked to the tow truck guy and signed some papers and gave him my Visa card. I then went into the service department and told them what happened to Erika's car. I gave them my cell phone number and Erika's number as well. I asked them to call when they discovered the problem.

It was now almost 3 PM. As I re-entered the car, Erika was still very upset and wiping away tears.

"I presume we are not going back to work this afternoon," I offered. Erika's hair was wet from the rain and now hung limply. Her eyes were red from crying and being traumatized.

"Yeah, is it okay with you to not go back to work?" she asked.

"I called in and told them I had an emergency and to call my cell phone if there were any problems or people who need to talk with me."

"Tom, you are my hero. You came and rescued me." Before I could respond, she came to a realization and said, "Wait, you are so not going to pay for my tow and car repairs."

"I just gave them my Visa to get the ball rolling. We can square up later. VW is going to call later when they find out what went wrong with your car," I said.

I looked at Erika's beautiful face, her wet hair, and her reddened eyes, and she looked shattered. Before I drove out of the lot, I extended my arms and said, "Come here." She put her head on my shoulder and began to sob while I hugged her. "It is okay, sweetie," I said, "just let it all out."

After a few moments, she said, "You are so good to me, and I am such a witch to you. I will never be able to tell you how sorry I am." I was puzzled. What in the world was she talking about? I just let her meltdown continue.

At last I said, "Should we go back to your condo so you can get some dry clothes? In a little while, we can get you some food. I assume you had no lunch?"

As we headed back into the city, she said little but tried to regain her composure. She kept repeating how sorry she was and that she didn't know why I put up with her. I tried to just pass off her comments, but remained confused by her apologizing for her car breaking down.

As we neared her condo, she asked, "Did I totally ruin your lunch?"

"No, we had our lunch, and it wasn't until I got to the top of the stairs from the underground that my cell phone coverage returned and I realized you were trying to call me. I wasn't ignoring your calls, believe me," I said.

"I know you weren't, Tom, I don't know why I freaked out so bad, and my behavior was inexcusable."

"I know why you freaked out," I said, "breaking down in the middle lane of the Banfield on a rainy day is about as bad as it gets."

As we entered her condo, she said she would take a quick shower and change clothes. I said I would catch up on some phone calls. I noticed that I had gotten a couple from the office while we were driving back to the Pearl District."

"Tom, you don't have to stay. If you don't want to, it would be perfectly understandable. I have ruined your day," Erika said.

"No, you haven't. I am staying with you; go shower," I said.

Erika returned shortly in her white terry cloth robe. Her long black hair was still wet from the shower. I wasn't sure what else she had on but she suddenly looked fabulous to me as I chatted on my cell phone to someone at work.

"Is everything okay?" Erika asked when I concluded my phone call.

"Yeah, everything is good. I just asked someone to cover a meeting for me this afternoon; things are fine," I said.

Erika walked towards me where I sat on the couch. She knelt down on her knees in front of me. Erika then leaned forward with her hands on my knees. I would have really gotten excited but Erika's face looked completely distraught.

She began, "Tom, I owe you such an apology. I don't think I have ever acted so badly. I have never used that language before, and I want you to know that I do not use foul language like that. I also am so, so sorry about the things I said about you on the phone. I was freaked, and I temporarily went insane or something. Please give me another chance, but if you don't want to be with me anymore, it would be perfectly understandable."

I looked into her lovely, vivid eyes that reflected the extreme pain she appeared to be in. I was so confused. I took her face in my hands and said, "Sweetie, you have nothing to apologize for. What in the world are you talking about?"

"Why would you call me that?" Erika said.

"What ... sweetie ... I will stop if you don't want me to use that term. It is just a term of extreme affection, and I feel so bad for you."

"I am anything but sweet. I am such a witch."

"Erika, what are you talking about?"

"The messages," she said.

"What messages? I said.

Now she looked confused. "The ones I left on your phone when I kept trying to call you."

"Huh?" I said. "You left messages? I haven't listened to them, I guess; I haven't had time. As soon as I saw that you had called five times in a very short period of time, I was immediately alarmed and just called you. I didn't take the time to listen to your messages. I didn't think they mattered anymore."

"You haven't listened to my messages?" Erika asked with great intensity.

"No, what's the big deal?"

Erika buried her face in the couch and seemed to practically collapse with relief.

"Do you want me to listen to them? I am confused," I said.

"No!" she practically screamed. Then she resumed her position kneeling in front of me and looked very intently into my eyes. I was getting the full impact of her eyes burning into mine now. "I must ask you one more huge favor. Please promise me you will never listen to those messages. Can I have your cell phone now so I can delete them?" Without waiting for a response, she repeated, "Can I now have your cell phone?"

"Sure," I said as I handed her my cell phone. "What is the big deal?" I asked.

She quickly grabbed my phone and then said, "I freaked out and I said a lot of things I didn't mean about you—I freaked because I couldn't reach you. I used some terrible language, which got worse with every call I made. I am so, so sorry. I didn't want you to hate me or think I was a psycho or something. I am so ashamed how I behaved, and I assure you I have never, never in my life done that before. I promise I will not ever do it again. I was afraid you would just drop me off at the curb when you brought me home. I wouldn't have blamed you if you decided I just wasn't worth it."

Finally, I was catching up with her. I started laughing. "Now I really want to hear those messages," I said.

"No, Tom! Please, I am begging you," Erika said urgently.

I continued to laugh. "Erika, you are so worth it, and I was in real pain as I watched my sweet, kind Erika in peril as I stood on the overpass," I said. "I was so worried about you, sweetie ... and I call you that because you are a sweetie and that is how I feel about you."

"Oh, Tom," she said, keeping a death's grip on my cell phone, "I so don't deserve you. You are my hero. You rescued me."

"Please calm down, everything is okay now," I said.

She hugged me and thanked me again. "I guess you want me to get some clothes on," Erika said.

"Did I say that? I would never say that to you," I said. "Are you hungry?"

"Yes, my stomach is starting to settle down enough to eat," she said. "Can I delete those messages now?"

"Yes, by all means, Erika," I said, "delete them ... it never happened—so just calm down."

She smiled and immediately started deleting her phone messages to me. Erika gave me a warm, affectionate look; kissed me on the cheek; and said, "I will go get dressed."

When she returned, she appeared to be decompressing and becoming herself again.

"So are we good now?" I asked.

"Yes," she said. "I will never act like that again ..."

"It didn't happen, so I don't know what you are talking about," I said.

She smiled and asked if I was ready to eat. Erika had never gotten to eat lunch, for obvious reasons, and it was now nearly 5 PM.

I said, "Well, after eating at the Blue Note, I feel like a python that has swallowed a small mammal and needs several days to digest it. But I can get something light. We will go anywhere you want. You pick."

"What is up with this place where you ate?" she said. "I have never heard of it."

"That is because you are part of the population who thinks it is wrong for someone to eat a pound of hamburger for lunch." I then told her about the Blue Note. She began laughing and smiling again. It appeared she was back. I smiled to myself over the rest of the day, as I was extremely curious about what Erika had said in the messages. I wondered what she said about me that made her so ashamed. Ain't love grand?

As we left for a restaurant, the phone rang and the service department told us that the fuel pump on Erika's car had failed. It would be ready tomorrow.

I had little time since lunch to ponder Dave's words to me. I intellectually understood his warning. I felt it was valid. I had no way to know how to "hold back part of myself" emotionally from this wonderful woman. I continued to give myself over to her completely and wouldn't miss a minute of the ride, regardless of the consequences.

Chapter 8

SICK DAY

ERIKA USUALLY projects a very calm demeanor. Her slender body and always neat appearance tells you this woman has got her act together. Nothing is left to chance.

Erika's hair and makeup are always beautifully done. She also has a very polished and calm manner when dealing with people. Erika's sleek appearance and ultra-cool persona took a dent during the famous breakdown of both her car and her calm exterior. Now just ten days later, that carefully put-together image was about to take another hit.

It had been an ugly week of relentless rain. Generally, the rain and gloomy weather in the Northwest doesn't bother me; in fact, I like it most of the time. But it seems like there comes a time about April or May when you start waving the white flag and wondering if you will ever see the sun again. Such was the week that would end in a much unexpected way.

It had also been a week of frustration at work. Everything seemed to be going wrong. Erika seemed to be having a similar week and had to cancel our weekly lunch because of the crush of meetings extending into her lunch hour. I saw her only briefly a few mornings at the coffee shop. She promised we would do better and make up for it this weekend. The last time I saw her was Thursday morning, and the plan was that I would come by her condo Friday night and we would do a quiet dinner at a quiet restaurant and catch up. I was anxious to see her Friday, but she never showed up Friday morning at the coffee shop.

I sent a couple of e-mail messages to her during the day but they were not answered. That was very unusual for her. I called her cell phone and left a message. I thought she must be into something intense, and I didn't want to bug her or be a pest.

I would just try to chill out and not be my usual overanxious self. I would meet her at her condo after work to begin our Friday night. I walked to the main entrance and buzzed her unit number. There was no answer. I wondered if she had to work late. She would have definitely called if that were the case. Maybe it was an ugly day since she was not communicating and now not answering. I buzzed one more time.

I heard something that sounded like Erika; she called my name, and I confirmed that I had arrived. She said, "Oh no, I am so sorry," and then there was nothing else, but she did buzz me in. As I took the elevator up, I wondered what the heck was going on up there. Was she okay?

She opened the door just a crack, which caused me to catch myself so I wouldn't crash into her and the door. "I am so sorry, I have been sick all day and I can't go anywhere. I don't want you to come in and get sick with whatever I have."

"What is wrong with you?" I asked.

"I don't know, a horrible cold or something, I came home from work this morning and have been sleeping ever since. Sorry."

"Come on, let me in, I will take care of you."

"No," she said, "really. I am not going to be any fun tonight, and I don't want you to get sick. We can reschedule. Sorry I didn't let you know."

"It is okay, just please let me in for a minute," I pleaded. "I just want to help you and then if you want me to leave, I will."

Without saying anything, she just released the door, walked away, and collapsed on her couch, pulling an afghan over her.

"I was getting a little worried about you, since you were not answering your phone or e-mails." Both Erika and I had Blackberrys and used these handhelds as our primary communication device when we were not together.

"I know," she said, talking with her eyes closed. "I turned everything off and just came home because I couldn't function anymore." She remained on the couch with her eyes closed. I am sure I was irritating because I just kept peppering her with questions.

"Do you have any medicine, have you eaten anything, and what can I do?"

She just shook her head, and I am sure she wished I would just go away. There was a Bi-Rite Drug in one of the buildings across the street and a good take-out Thai place a block up the street.

"Let me go get you some stuff, and then you can buzz me back in."

"No, you don't have to do that."

"Someone needs to take care of you."

I think she realized I wasn't going to yield and would just keep yapping away. I am sure her honest answer to "what can I do for you" would be—"Go away!"

Erika said, "Just get my key out of my purse and use the card to swipe at the security thing."

I spotted her purse on the kitchen table. She always had a big purse in a variety of colors and styles to provide an accent color to her clothes. I think she was a big-purse kind of gal. I have never had any luck finding things in women's purses. It always frustrated Liz when she would tell me to get something out of her purse, and I could never find it and finally had to surrender.

Geez, Erika's purse was enormous. It was like a portable 7-11 in there. Does this woman really need all of this crap to function? No wonder she has great muscle tone in her arms. The pressure was on. I had to find the keys because I think if I had asked her one more question she would have thrown me out. I finally found them.

I said, "I will be right back." She didn't respond or move a muscle and had her eyes closed.

I scurried around the neighborhood and got some nighttime and daytime cold medicine and threw in a box of tissues for good measure. There were bunches of tulips and daffodils for $5 near the door and I snagged one of those also. Then I went down the street and got some take-out of Tom Yum soup from the Thai place, enough for her and maybe me, if I didn't get tossed out when I got back to the condo.

As I approached the main entrance, I was hoping that I could do the right things to regain admission. Having to buzz Erica again would be bad. It worked like a charm and I heard the door click. When I re-entered, she had obviously not moved. I went into the kitchen and got a bowl for some soup and got a bottle of water out of her refrigerator. I unwrapped the nighttime cold medicine. I put the tulips in the sink for now. I moved my supplies onto her coffee table. Now I had to convince Erika to submit to my attempts at nursing without annoying her.

I knelt down by her and touched her face and said, "Would you like a little soup?" I rubbed her cheek until she opened her eyes. She raised her head and nodded. As she tried to open and focus her eyes, she said, "What is all of this?"

"I just got some things that might help you feel better."

Erika weakly smiled and said, "Nice date. I don't want you to see me looking like this. This must be what you really wanted to do tonight."

Actually, I was enjoying helping her. I was hoping she would let me. She took a chug of water and sipped some soup. "I don't deserve you," she said.

"What happened to you, girl?"

"I don't know," she said. "I just feel better resting with my eyes closed. My head really hurts and feels like it is totally clogged up." She took one more sip of soup. "That was good but I think I am done. Thank you," she said, as she touched my face.

"Would it help with the congestion to take some of this nighttime stuff?"

She nodded and grabbed the bottle. Before I could get the measuring cup in position, she chugged a lot of the contents of the bottle. "Whoa, Erika, slow down, you will not wake up until next Wednesday," I said.

"I usually need a lot of this crap to make it work," Erika said.

She then slumped over again on the couch. I cleared the coffee table and had some soup myself while standing at the kitchen counter, watching her. When my limited domestic chores were done, I returned to the living room.

Erika was wearing sweats and baggy white socks and had her hair pulled back in a ponytail. The afghan was loosely covering her. Most women, especially the Erikas of the world, who always care very much about what they look like, would be humiliated to be seen like this. I thought she looked great. I felt like maybe I was being a pervert or voyeur watching her sleep. But the feelings inside were complete adulation.

There she was, my wonderful friend, the woman I was falling deeply in love with, but I could not tell her. She wanted me to be her friend, to not put labels on our relationship and just go with the flow. I was doing that but I was pretending. I did not want to be that vulnerable. Maybe I was psychologically damaged from the events of the past couple of years, and now I was obsessing about Erika. But I was going with the flow. I had come to the realization that I loved Erika and hoped someday she would feel that way about me. I didn't know if that was possible or if she ever would. But if all she wanted me to be was her friend,

I would do that for now until she agreed to be something different. I would take whatever she would give me.

As the nighttime shadows started to fill the condo, I got up from the chair and watched the sun setting behind the west hills through her view window by the balcony. Today, we were supposed to have "sun breaks." That usually meant you might actually glimpse the big ball in the sky through the dense overcast for a couple of minutes, if today were your lucky day. I always wondered, "Why do the sun breaks come only as the sun goes down?" That is kind of a rip-off.

There was an orange glow, which constituted the sun's brief peek at Portland today. The city lights were coming on and this beautiful city was switching into the Friday night mode as the lights shined through the mist as far as the eye could see.

I turned on a lamp on a table far enough away so it would not disturb Erika. Then I couldn't resist. I went to the couch and lifted her limp head, slid into a sitting position, and put her head on my lap. She briefly stirred, smiled, and squeezed my hand. Then she continued to doze. I was careful to not disturb her, but I wanted to hold her. Fortunately, this woman had taken enough nighttime cold medicine to put down an elephant.

I studied her face as she lay sleeping on my lap. I had never really looked at her this way before. I was used to seeing her beautiful, big blue eyes and her thick, long black hair dominating her face. Now the blues eyes were powered down for the night, and her hair was pulled away from her face. Her skin was absolutely flawless. There were no wrinkles or creases anywhere. There was little or no makeup on her face, yet it was so beautiful. I touched her full lips with my fingertip, and she was so soft.

"Oh, Erika, what am I going to do about you? I want you so badly," I whispered. "Who are you, how have you so smitten me that I can't think of anything else?" Yet I did not feel frustration. I wanted more from our "friendship," but all I had to do was to think back about a year ago, or even a few months ago, when there was no Erika in my life. The world was a cold, lonely place.

She was so warm and soft against me. Why couldn't I have her? Other men my age marry younger women. I went on a cruise one time and there appeared to be all kinds of men my age with women her age. Surely, if I give her time, it could work out, couldn't it? Let's see, when I am seventy-five, she would be forty? No, that can't be right. Oh, yeah, I blew the math. When I am seventy-five, she would be roughly fifty, probably, the age I am now. That would be okay, wouldn't it? Other people do it. Why couldn't I be with Erika? Plus, when I got to that point, I would have had twenty some years loving this wonderful creature and being loved by her.

My mind was going funny directions. So, I am twenty-three years older than Erika. That means when I was graduating from college, someone could have walked up to me with a newborn baby girl and said, "Meet the love of your life." No, that is not a good way to think about it; that is too weird. But it is like Erika tells me, "Age is just a number that is only significant if we think it is significant." Forget the age difference. I am gazing at the beautiful face of a woman I love with all of my heart. That is all that matters. How rare is that in today's world?

I want to love and nurture her and make sure she has a happy life. I want to make her happy. That is all I want. I couldn't resist a few more tender touches of her beautiful face before this moment would end. I loved to hold her and just look at her without any restraints. This night certainly took a different turn than I expected. In the future, I would recall this night and wish I could have it back. It was a moment in time when all was well with me and Erika, and I was caring for her on a rainy, cool night when she was sick. It was a profound moment for me, and one I would recall with great tenderness and yearning.

I gently lifted her head and said, "Come on, sweetheart, let's get you to bed." I put my arm around her waist and guided her into her bedroom. She was very groggy and said nothing. I pulled the covers back with one hand and gently lowered her to the bed. I swung her legs around onto the bed and pulled the covers up to her chin. I couldn't resist just one more thing. I put my face next to her face and kissed her and said, "Good night, my love."

I left her door ajar and decided to sleep on the couch. I removed my shoes and pullover sweater and crawled under the afghan, which was still on the couch. The couch was still warm from Erika's body, and I could smell her on the pillow. Eventually, I drifted off to sleep.

I slept really soundly, apparently. My first indication that I survived the night was Erika sitting on the edge of the couch and touching my face and saying, "Are you okay, you sweet man?"

I said, "Oh, hi, are you okay?"

"I am better," she said. "What happened here last night? It is all a blur to me. How did you end up spending the night? I can only remember a few things from last night. Oh no, how could I let this happen, oh, my God, I must have been a great sight last night. Swollen eyes, puffy skin, and snotty nose. Oh, no ... did I snore, did I snort? I was so congested. I must have been disgusting. I am so, so embarrassed. I have never been so humiliated."

I was struggling to catch up with her. "Wait, don't you remember letting me in?"

"Yes, and I told you to not come since I couldn't go out with you."

"Well, yeah, but I wanted to help you, you were in a bad way. I got you some soup and medicine and some water ..."

"I remember the soup and sleeping on the couch. How did I get into my bed?"

I said, "Well, I wanted to make sure you got a good night's sleep, so I moved you in there."

"You moved me in there? Why don't I remember that? Did you do something weird to me?"

I decided this was too good to pass up. "Well, that all depends on what you mean by weird."

"What?" she said.

"Well, I took you in there and undressed you but I couldn't find the right nightgown for you to wear, so I decided I had better put your sweats back on."

"Oh, no, I am so, so embarrassed."

I interrupted the neurotic meltdown by saying sternly, "Erika, chill. Seriously, I didn't do anything to you, and I only wanted to help you. I was extremely respectful of you and protected your modesty and dignity."

"I know," she said. "I know you are always a gentleman and would never do anything to me."

"You are putting words in my mouth. I never said I didn't want to do anything to you. I said, I didn't do anything to you."

"You are a naughty boy, and maybe you are a perv."

"Let's back-track," I said. "I was awakened by you gently calling me a sweet man and five minutes later you called me a pervert."

"No, I don't think you are a pervert. I am just humiliated that I was so gross and disgusting in front of you."

"Erika, you slept like an angel and looked like one."

"Why do I always treat you so badly, when you are so sweet to me? I was so hideous when my car broke down and totally lost it. Now this. I so don't deserve you."

"I agree," I said.

"So how did this all happen? I am still pushing back the cobwebs," Erika said.

"Erika, before we retrace the timeline in our magical night together, let me say one thing."

She suddenly looked very serious and waited for my words.

"Chick, did you ever wonder why they put those measuring cups on the nighttime cold medicine? You can't guzzle that like an ice-cold beer on a summer's day. I had to check a few times to see if you were still breathing."

"Okay, Daddy, I was a bad girl. Eeeew, I am so embarrassed. I must have looked horrible," she kept saying, while covering her face with her hands.

"Hey," I said, "I am the one who slept in my clothes. I feel really disgusting myself."

"Oh, I know, you are the kindest, gentlest person I have ever met," Erika said. "I don't know of any other man who would do this."

"Thank you. By the way, Erika, how are you feeling?"

"I am better. My head still feels stuffed up but way better than yesterday," she said. "I don't know what happened yesterday.

I said, "I tell you what, are you up for some coffee and a bagel?"

"Wow, that actually sounds good," she said.

"Okay, I will run down the street and get us some."

"I will take a really quick shower and try to not be such a pig when you get back," she said.

With that, I staggered out the door to retrieve breakfast. When I returned, she was wearing a bright blue, long-sleeved t-shirt and some tight, dark denim pants. She sure didn't resemble a pig. I noticed the tulips were in a vase on the kitchen counter. I had actually forgotten about them.

Erika asked, "Did you get these for me?"

"Ah, yeah ...," I said. "Where did you think they came from?"

"You brought me flowers when I was sick. Do you know no one has ever done that for me? You are the first and the best," she said.

I had no retort for that and just smiled. That was definitely worth the $5.

"Let's retrace our steps from yesterday," I said. "I couldn't get you all day. I didn't see you at the coffee shop. No big news flash, I was just checking in with you. I thought it was odd that you didn't respond but I thought maybe you were really slammed at work or in a meeting or something."

Erika said, "I started feeling really crappy Thursday and just really tired and draggy. I got up Friday morning and really didn't feel well but went to work anyway. About two hours into it, I just wanted to put my head down and close my eyes. My head felt terrible."

"You should have called me," I said. "I could have helped you get home."

Erika said, "You are sweet but I just came home about mid-morning and shut off my Blackberry and phone and just wanted to totally sleep. I thought I would sleep for a few hours. The next thing I knew it was 6 and you were buzzing down below."

"Wow, that is very unlike you. So you do remember letting me in?"

"Of course, I remember you feeding me soup and drinking some water. I remember you being tender and sweet to me and then it gets really fuzzy after that."

Uh, oh, I thought. I wondered how much she heard. I thought she was out of it. "When was I tender and sweet to you?"

"Probably all night but when you held me on the couch after the soup," she said. "That is about the last thing I remember until I woke up this morning."

"I wonder what kind of bug you got?" I said. "I am so glad you are better."

"By the way, you poor man, you look like hell."

"Don't sugarcoat it; just give it to me straight," I replied. "I tell you how beautiful you look even when you are sick, and this is what I get?"

"You deserve a big, wet kiss to show you how much I appreciate your many kindnesses, but I don't want to give you my germs."

"Yeah, the story of my life; my timing is always off," I said.

"I am going to make this up to you," Erika said. "You are going to get something special."

"I can't wait," I said.

"Well, we certainly broke through lots of barriers last night, I have no more façade. You have seen the woman behind the mask now," Erika said.

"Right, princess, who knew that you were so hideous underneath your makeup," I said. She laughed and before she could reply, I asked, "So are you careful about your security, I mean, you can tell who is buzzing your buzzer downstairs, right?"

"Of course, are you afraid I am going to let some guy in who will drug me with cold medicine and do twisted things to me?"

"There are people like that out there, you know," I said. "But seriously, you are careful, aren't you?"

"I am very careful, and I love living in a secured building. If you knew me before, you would realize how remarkable it is that I am so comfortable and feel so safe with you," Erika said.

"Good, I know you are a big girl, but I want you to be careful," I said.

"Go get some sleep," Erika said. "We will get in touch later."

"Just lay low this weekend and get better, okay?" I said.

As she walked me to the door, she hugged me and said, "You are the nicest person I have ever met, and you are such a good friend. Go take care of yourself."

As I descended in the elevator, I thought, "I am her good and nice friend." That is good. I suddenly felt like I had an itch that couldn't be scratched. Last night, I think I made it harder to continue to limit myself to that role.

Chapter 9

UNDERSTANDING ERIKA

THE DAY had finally arrived when I was going to meet Erika's friends—the Goddesses. I had heard her talk about them and the things they did together. Erika had mentioned their names but at this point, I could not distinguish one goddess from another.

Erika told me that her friend, Tamara, and her husband had just bought a new house and were having a house-warming party, and I was invited. I was open to the new experience but was a little nervous. I felt some pressure to make a good impression. Then I found out Erika's mother was also going to be there, and this would be my first chance to meet her.

Now I was starting to feel the heat.

When I expressed some trepidation to Erika earlier in the day, she said, "Relax, be yourself, everyone is anxious to meet you." The phrase "anxious to meet you" can cover a wide variety of situations to the insecure and neurotic. There could be "anxious to meet you" because I have got to see this to believe it. Is Erika really going out with a guy her mother's age? Or there could be "anxious to meet you" because I have heard so many remarkable things about you.

I had done some rough math. Erika just turned thirty in 2004. I had discovered Erika was the older of two children. She was born in 1974. It is likely her mother was twenty-something when Erika arrived, so we're going to be close in age.

Erika's mother had basically been dumped by her father after Erika and her brother were born. Her mother had spent a lot of years as a single mother. As nearly as I could tell, Erika and her mother had a good relationship. Her mother lived in the Metro area. Erika's brother lived in Sacramento. Apparently, the father was out of the picture and lived somewhere far away. I was not sure of the details involving him but it appeared he was basically not part of the family or Erika's life.

Erika picked me up in her car, since I didn't know where we were going. It was a new housing area in Camas, Washington, just across the Columbia River from Portland. It was a new development, where it is likely that the main demographic was new couples or young families in their thirties.

As we pulled into the driveway, I took a deep breath. I really don't like new social situations, and I am actually a little rusty in the social skills department after my "hiatus" of sorts from the outside world over the last couple of years.

Erika seemed to sense this and said, "Just be your lovable self."

"Oh, I thought you wanted me to be my unlovable self."

"Behave," she said.

There was quite a stir as we entered. It seemed everyone was there already. There were lots of hugs for Erika and people saying things like "So this is the famous Tom we have heard so much about." I have never known the correct social response to "So you are the one we have heard so much about?" Do you say, "Yeah, that is me."? Do you say, "That depends on what you heard."? Do you say, "Yeah, and it is all true."?

Besides Tamara, the other Goddesses were Jenna and Kristen. Tamara was married, Jenna was living with her boyfriend, and Kristen had a boyfriend but wasn't living with him, as nearly as I could tell. They were all very attractive and seemed to fit Erika's personality perfectly.

Then Erika's mother emerged from the back of the house. She was a very pretty, impressive-looking woman about my age. She was shorter than Erika but had the same sleek body. She had light brown hair, which was just beginning to show signs of graying ... much like my own. Erika's mother had her hair cut in a bob, which barely touched her shoulders. Erika's vivid blue eyes obviously came from her mother. The immediate impression of her mother was of a woman who had her act together and seemed very self-assured.

Erika rushed forward and said, "Tom, this is my mother, Tricia."

"It is so good to finally meet you," she said, moving forward with an outstretched hand.

"It is wonderful to meet you. I have been looking forward to meeting the key people in Erika's life—the Goddesses and you," I said. I quickly added, "I didn't mean to exclude you as a Goddess."

Everyone laughed.

"Oh," Tricia said, "we have heard about you," and she patted my arm. Tricia continued, "Sorry I wasn't here when you arrived, I was getting the tour."

"No problem," I said.

"Would you like something to drink, Tom?" Tricia asked. "Let me show you where the drinks are and what we have." I really did want a drink of something, and quickly.

I walked into the beautiful new kitchen with Tricia just as Tamara was exiting it.

"Beautiful place, Tamara," I said.

"Thank you so much, and thanks for coming," she replied. "I am borrowing Erika for a bit, okay?"

"Yeah, tell Erika I gave my permission, she would like that." Both women giggled as Tamara went bustling out of the kitchen to meet Erika.

"Want to grab a drink and go sit in the family room for a bit until Erika comes back from whatever they are doing?" Tricia asked.

"Sounds very good to me."

When we had positioned ourselves in two soft chairs, Tricia cut to the chase and said, "Thank you for bringing some happiness into my daughter's life."

I was a bit taken aback by the comment. I said, "I hope I do, but she is the one who I feel has really rescued me and given me a new outlook."

"Yes, Erika told me about your loss, and I am so sorry. Was that a couple of years ago?"

"It is about that," I said. "I am actually kind of astonished to hear all of you say you have heard a lot about me. I am not sure what you have heard, and I guess I was being kind of secretive about Erika and me."

"First of all," she said, "Erika talks about you all of the time. We know about your wife, we know how you met, we know you love to take her places, we know about how you rescued her on the Banfield, and we know about the night she was so sick."

"Uh, you know about that?" I said in reference to the famous sick night.

"Oh, yes."

"Well, that wasn't exactly our finest hour. It turned out a bit weird and I ended up sleeping on her couch, but I assure you …"

"Oh, you don't have to explain yourself to me," Tricia said.

"You sound a bit like your daughter when you say that, Tricia."

She laughed and then said, "You didn't consider that your finest hour? That surprises me, because Erika thinks it was nothing short of heroic."

"Really?"

Tricia explained, "Erika told me what a gentleman you were and how tender and kind you were to her."

"Oh, well, that is good to hear."

"Didn't she tell you that herself?" Tricia said. "That surprises me, considering what rave reviews you got from my daughter when she was telling me the story."

"She did express her thanks, and Erika is very sweet to me. I guess I am going through an adjustment period. I am a little unsure of myself in the social setting with a beautiful young woman like her."

"I can appreciate that …," she began but we were cut off by Erika as she burst into the room with her friends.

"What are you two talking about, over here in the corner?" Erika asked.

"Your mother is telling me the funniest stories about when you were in high school," I said.

"Mother!" Erika said.

"I am not, Erika, Tom is just teasing you."

"Erika, we are good. We are just getting to know one another," I said.

Erika was being rushed out of the room by her friends, who were onto the next room. She shot me a backward glance and flashed her blue eyes at me.

"Tom, you mentioned that you were being 'secretive' about you and Erika. Why is that? It seems like a pretty good stroke of luck for both of you," Tricia said.

"Secretive was probably a bad choice of words. Private is more like it. It is certainly not because I have any reservations about Erika. It is just that I have lots of prying eyes watching me now, it seems. After I lost my wife, I basically spent a couple of years to myself readjusting to suddenly being alone in my life. Some of the best friends my wife and I had happen to also be our next-door neighbors. They are good at noticing when someone is home and not. People at work, my mother, and other friends all seem to have great interest in seeing me with a woman again, especially a young, beautiful one like Erika."

"Oh, I know something about the advice that is freely given to people who become single," Tricia said. "After my divorce, I got that from a lot of friends and family."

"Yeah," I said, "you need to get out there; you need to quit hanging around the house; and my favorite, you need some closure."

"How do people react to your age difference? Are they giving you trouble about that?" Tricia asked.

"If you would permit an indiscreet question, Tricia, I assume you and I are about the same age, is that true? I am fifty-three."

"Yes, we are very close in age," she said.

"Wow, I can't believe I asked your age, I am sorry," I said.

Tricia smiled and assured me she wasn't offended.

"I embarrass myself with that question for this reason," I said. "It seems difficult for some people to not react to a middle-aged man with a young woman."

"You would do better than I," Tricia said. "Try a middle-aged woman with a young man."

"Point well taken, and that isn't right either," I said. "I actually did not know Erika's age when we started becoming friends. It really didn't matter to me. I was a little shocked when I did find out her age. I thought she was a little older. However, it didn't change how I felt about her. I still wanted to be her friend, and I have immensely enjoyed your daughter's company. As Erika reminds me, age is just an assigned number and doesn't change us as people," I said.

"Spoken like a thirty-year-old. Sometimes, in the morning, that number seems to have significance to me," Tricia said. "But she is right. Age is very much an attitude, as you and I well know."

"I agree. The other point is, Erika and I are friends. Everyone assumes all kinds of other things are going on. We are just friends, and I am not sure what kind of relationship Erika even wants with me."

"That, Tom, is one of the things my daughter so appreciates about you," Tricia said. "You are being patient and tender with her and not rushing into anything. You are letting things develop."

"That is nice to hear," I said. "She is just what I needed to bring me back into enjoying life and having fun again. I didn't realize how much I had retreated until I started spending time with Erika. I love her sense of fun and freedom."

"You have been just what she needed also," Tricia said. "Erika has had her own dark period."

"She did?" I said. "I knew about the divorce but Erika seems so in control and self-assured."

"That is what you have seen," Tricia said, "and that is the Erika we all know and love, but that is not how she has been since her divorce. Erika's dad and I split up when she was in junior high, and it was hard on her and her brother. I think from that experience, Erika never wanted to be a divorced woman. When her marriage ended, she was twenty-seven, and she felt like she had failed one of life's major tests.

"Erika's ex-husband is a nice kid but he was pretty immature and self-centered for my tastes," Tricia continued. "Maybe I am speaking like a mother-in-law but I guess I always wanted him to treat my Erika better. After her divorce, I tried to tell Erika that her whole life was ahead of her, but she really became depressed and had trouble dealing with failed expectations."

"I don't know where things will lead with us, but I love having Erika as a friend and a companion to just go have some fun with," I said.

"Keep up the good work, Tom. It is nice to see her so happy again."

Just then Erika re-entered the room. Those blue eyes were even larger when she noticed I was still talking to her mother. "Okay, you need to share him, Mother; leave the poor man alone," she said.

"Thank you, Erika, this woman has really been working me over," I said.

Tricia laughed, and Erika shot a glance at both of us.

Then I saw a golden opportunity.

"By the way, Tricia, I want to tell you something about your daughter," I said, taking Erika's hand. Erika looked warily at me. "You have taught Erika well. Your daughter has this incredible ability to stay cool under pressure. Like when she broke down on the Banfield ..."

Erika rolled her eyes at me as her mouth tightened into pursed lips. I saw a smirk developing on Tricia's face.

"Here she was," I continued, "the primary cause of traffic backing up into Vancouver and being televised live on all the noon news shows, but did our Erika panic ... no! She calmly gave me her milepost number, her exact situation, gave me emergency numbers to call ..."

With that, Tricia began laughing out loud. "It is too late, Tom— she already told me what really happened," and we both burst out laughing.

"I thought it was hilarious," Tricia said.

"So did I," I said.

With that, Erika slugged me in the arm and said, "You two are so not funny."

"Erika, you be nice to Tom," Tricia said. "He is so adorable."

"Tricia, I so enjoyed talking with you, and I am sure we will see each other again," I said.

"Any time, Tom; I enjoyed meeting you."

Erika took my arm and pulled me towards the crowd. "What were you two talking about for so long?" she said.

"Nothing really," I said.

"Whatever!" Erika replied. "You and I are having a long talk on the way home. Was she really grilling you?"

"Your mother was wonderful. She is a very impressive woman, very sophisticated, charming, and kind. You didn't tell me she was a hottie."

"Eeeew! You have been hitting on my mother? I am going to have to not leave you unattended," Erika said.

"I wasn't hitting on her; I just said she was pretty. What would you expect with a daughter that looks like you," I said.

"Nice comeback," Erika said. "I want you to talk with some other people. But we are so going to talk on the way home."

We spent some more time admiring the house and being congenial. My fears eased, as everyone was very nice to me, and it was fun to watch Erika interact with her friends. Finally, we said our good-byes and headed out the door. There was quite a bit of our Saturday evening left, and I wondered if Erika wanted to do something in addition to pumping me mercilessly about my conversation with her mother.

As we got into her car, I said, "So what do you feel like doing now? Want to do something else?"

"Yes," she said, "but I ate just enough snacky stuff there so I am not hungry, but I want to do something."

"I agree," I said. "How about a movie?"

"No, I want to talk," Erika said.

"So I gathered," I said. "Okay, we could go down to the waterfront and sit on a bench to watch the boats, we could go sit by that cool fountain in your neighborhood, and we could go to that cool little dessert place on Hawthorne, or we could ..."

She interrupted and said, "This is so awesome, having my own Portland tour guide."

"Sorry," I said. "I guess there are so many places I like to go with you."

Erika said, "Let's go somewhere quiet. I have to take you home eventually anyway. What if we just go hang at your place for a while?"

"Well, that is certainly a quiet place; most cathedrals are noisier than my house, but sure."

As we pulled into the driveway, I noticed my neighbors and friends, Shelly and Jerry, in the driveway doing something with their cars. Great. While Erika chattered to me, I gave a quick wave and headed for the front door, trying to avoid eye contact. I didn't want to have a conversation with my neighbors right now. I saw both of them checking things out and their eyes following us all the way into the house.

"It has kind of cooled off, don't you think?" Erika said.

"Yes," I said. "How about if I build us a fire in the fireplace and you get us some drinks out of the refrigerator?"

"Okay, sounds fair," she said. I reached up and flicked the switch to ignite the gas log.

"I did my part," I said.

"You are so mean; why did I trust you?" she said as she headed into the kitchen.

I decided to get all of the pillows off of the couch and position them on the floor in front of the fireplace.

"You don't need to do that, we can just sit on the floor," Erika said.

I said, "Call me in twenty years, sweetie. Trust me, I need to do that if we are sitting on the floor in front of the fire. By the way, Erika, you have a flair for home décor. What is it with women and pillows?"

"This is totally a guy's refrigerator. Two bottles of wine, about twenty cartons of yogurt, and the bottom shelf is totally packed with Diet Coke and beer. Have you ever heard of fruits and vegetables, mister?"

"That is why God invented restaurants," I replied. While she got out the wine glasses and looked things over in the kitchen, I said, "So, what is it with women and pillows? There have got to be fifty pillows in this house. Anytime I want to sit on the couch, I have to move the pillows. When I go to bed, I have to spend five minutes unloading the pillows before I can pull back the covers. Every night I was irritated by the pillows. I lived alone for a year and took the pillows off faithfully each night before it occurred to me, 'Why am I doing this?' and I threw them all in the closet."

"Liz trained you well. Pillows look nice. Now tell me about your conversation with my mom?"

"Yeah, speaking of your mother ...," I said. "How is it that a woman like your mother can still be single? Someone is really missing the boat."

"So, do you want me to set you two up?" Erika said.

"Now, don't get excited and go all Freudian on me. I was just wondering."

Erika said, "She has had boyfriends and 'partners,' I think, from time to time, but she has never really found someone she wanted to make the commitment to."

"That is too bad, she seems like a nice lady," I said.

"So, what did my mother say?" Erika pressed.

"What are you so fired up about? She told me how much she appreciated me taking care of her daughter, how her daughter seems to like me, maybe even a lot, she knew about the night when you got the flu or whatever, and she told me a little about your life," I said. I decided to not reveal her analysis of Erika's divorce. I didn't want to get in the middle of a shootout between mother and daughter until I understood the dynamics of their relationship a little more.

As she approached me with the wine and sat next to me, she said, "Great, let's just spill our guts about everything the minute someone asks, 'How are you?' What do you mean, she told you about my life?"

"Don't worry, it was very benign stuff, about how her daughter has always been a very happy and fun person and she is proud of you. I mean, what are you so paranoid about, are you a criminal on the run or something? Your mother was very positive and sweet. You want to see spilling your guts, wait until you meet my mother. My mother has lost the filter between her brain and her mouth."

Erika started laughing.

"No, seriously, every time she has entered this house since Liz died, she invariably says, 'Liz always kept this house so beautiful before she died.' Like there are rats running around the kitchen and rotting garbage sitting in sacks on the carpet and tumbleweeds blowing across the yard."

"Wow, are we being a little oversensitive here?" Erika asked.

"Wait until you meet her and see if you think I am being paranoid. Besides, you are the paranoid one about revealing family secrets. It is not like you are a coven of witches or something," I said.

"How do you know?" Erika said.

"That would explain a lot, actually," I said. "I am sort of under a spell when I am with you. I do anything you want now, how could you have more control over me?"

"You don't appear to be suffering. By the way, this is sooo nice sitting in front of this fireplace, hanging out with you and a little wine. We made a good choice for spending the rest of our day," she said.

"You know, I think I need to get rid of this place and move downtown," I said.

"You are kidding, this is awesome."

"Well, you saw what it was like when I came home. Welcome to my life. I walk in every night and it is cold, and dark and silent. It is very lonely, actually," I said. "I need about half of this house—tops. Something like your condo would be ideal for me, and downtown is where I want to be."

"I long for green grass and trees and flowers in the concrete jungle, and you have all of this," Erika said.

"How come everyone always wants whatever it is that they don't have?" I said. "When I am downtown with you, I love it and everything is so vibrant and alive. Then I come here, and it is dark and cold and lonely."

"I do like it downtown," she said.

"There is another possibility," I said. "Maybe it is not about the house or the condo. Maybe when I am in your condo and downtown, I like it so much because I am with you. I don't like my house anymore because when I am here, I am not with you."

"That is so sweet," she said, touching my face.

"I am just being honest," I said.

"I know you are, that is why it is so sweet," Erika said.

"This house is becoming my past. All of the pictures, the furnishings, the lifestyle I no longer have—lots of memories. Maybe too many memories," I said.

"I can understand," she said.

Chapter 10

ERIKA'S THANK YOU

ERIKA HAD been planning something throughout the week as her thank you for my "nursing" efforts on the night she was sick. She sprung the plan on me about midweek.

"You have a gas barbecue or grill or something, right?" she asked.

"Yes."

"It looks like Saturday's weather should be good, right?"

"I would say, 100 percent on the BBQ, 70 percent chance on the good weather Saturday."

"That is close enough for me," she said. "I want to make you my special barbecued salmon as my thank you. Remember, I told you I would pay you back."

"I remember, but sometimes it scares me when you say that," I said.

"Does that sound good—a barbecue, chilling out on the patio, and spending the day together?" she asked.

"Oh, yeah, definitely," I said. "What do you need me to do?"

"Be my friend and talk to me while I prepare this for you," Erika said.

"You know, it wasn't really so great what I did that night. I sort of blundered in after you asked me to leave and I …"

"Are you trying to talk me out of this? You don't know when to stop talking, do you?"

"Point taken," I said.

Erika arrived about midday Saturday and started unpacking her goodies. I started cleaning my gas grill before Erika saw it.

"What are you doing?" she said. "Sit, don't do anything, talk to me."

"I was trying to remember if I have cleaned the grill this century, so I didn't want to gross you out. I haven't done a lot of entertaining in the backyard recently."

Erika made herself at home and opened cupboards until she found what she needed. I sat on a stool at the kitchen bar and chatted with her. There was something surreal about seeing Erika in the kitchen where I had seen Liz for so many years. It seemed very comfortable to have her there.

"If you need me to get something down for you, just say so."

"No, I can get everything, no problem."

"I guess I am accustomed to shorter women, like Liz and my daughter."

Erika said, "No, you are with 'gargantuan woman,' no petiteness here. I can reach everything."

"That is nice," I said. "It is desirable to have long arms and be slender and tall."

"I never thought so," Erika said. "I got tall when I was still young and was always the giant girl in the pictures at school with all of the little, cute girls."

"And all of the little, cute girls wanted to have long, beautiful legs like Erika. What is it with women?"

"I would rather have had a different body," she said.

"Is that why all of the models on the Paris runways have bodies like yours, because it is such a hideous trait?"

"You are so kind," Erika retorted.

"I bet you were a real heartbreaker in high school, Erika."

"Oh, no, I was in high school in the big-hair era, you should see my prom pictures!"

"That is a great idea," I said. "Next time I am at your condo, it will be high school yearbook night."

"Not even, no, no, no," Erika said, "besides, all of that crap is at my mother's house, I think."

"Even better," I said. "Tricia is more cooperative with me than you are."

"I really need to watch the two of you …"

"What kinds of things did you do in high school?"

"Well, not too much, but I was a cheerleader," she said.

"Shocker," I said.

Erika smiled and responded as she mixed some ingredients in a bowl, "Are you making fun of me?"

"No, no, I assumed you were not the president of the chess club. Do you still have your uniform? Maybe you could wear it for me sometime."

"Like, I would fit in it now. You are such a naughty boy. What about you in high school?"

Just then I heard a commotion in the driveway. I got up from the bar stool and walked into the living room. The next sound Erika heard was a string of expletives coming from my mouth.

"What is wrong?" she said.

"My mother and her friend, Gladys, are coming up the front walk. Dammit. Go ahead and keep cooking."

The doorbell rang. As I opened the door, my mother said, "Oh, you are home. I noticed a strange car in the driveway and wasn't sure."

"Hi Mom, hi Gladys," I said as I hugged my mother. "What are you ladies doing today?"

My mother said, "We decided to run out to the sales at the outlet malls in your direction. I haven't seen much of you lately, so I thought I had better stop by since it appeared you weren't coming to my house anytime soon."

I looked at my watch and said, "Well, that only took about two minutes to drop your first guilt-bomb on me."

"Oh, Gladys, don't listen to him, he is always fooling around and being silly," Mom said. "Are you cooking, dear? I smell something good."

"No, I have a friend here."

The two ladies moved towards the kitchen, and my mother said, "Oh, a woman friend."

Thanks for noticing, I thought.

"Yes, Mom, this is my friend Erika. Erika, this is my mother and her friend Gladys."

"It is very nice to meet you, Erika," Mom said. "It is good to see he is getting a home-cooked meal. I try to get him to come over so I can cook for him, but he always has some reason he can't come. I guess I have kind of lost my touch."

Erika turned on the charm and saw a chance to jerk my chain. "I know what you mean," Erika said. "He does need some looking after. He can be very uncooperative."

"You are so right, dear, I just wish he would come to see me more often," my mother said.

"Well, he is kind of a busy guy, but I will encourage him to give a little more attention to his mother," Erika said.

"That would be much appreciated," Mom said. "It smells good, Erika, what are you cooking?"

"We are getting ready to have some barbecued salmon and some other goodies," she said.

"Well, we won't interrupt your private party," Mom said. "I just wanted to show Gladys your backyard." As she opened the back door, she said, "Is that okay?" No response was necessary, of course.

As my mother and Gladys stepped onto the patio, Mom said, "My late daughter-in-law always kept this house and yard so beautifully ..." I looked at Erika and rolled my eyes. Erika covered her mouth with her hand and turned away to stifle a laugh.

As the backyard tour concluded, Mom said, "You have things looking pretty good, Tom."

"Don't act so amazed, Mom," I said.

"You are so funny," Mom said. "We must be going. Erika, it is so nice to meet you, and it is nice to see Tom having friends over again."

"It was very nice to meet you both," Erika said. "Have fun shopping."

As Mom and Gladys made their way to the front door, Mom said, in a not-so-quiet voice, "Call me later, we need to talk, and you can fill me in on everything. Apparently, you have had a lot going on that I wasn't aware of."

"Sure, Mom," I said. "I will call you later."

"Well, alright dear," she said as she kissed me on the cheek and went out the door.

Erika started laughing. "She is a real hoot," she said. "She is not so bad."

"Really? You can have her if you want."

"Oh, she is cute, and I think it is funny how she still treats you like her little boy," Erika said.

"Yeah, it is darling," I said.

"Don't be so hard on her; she is pretty harmless and sweet. It *does* sound like she will want a full report on the strange woman in your kitchen."

"Oh, yeah," I said. "I will be counting the moments until that conversation."

Erika continued, "She did say the backyard looked nice."

"But it was the astonishment in her voice that made it a non-compliment."

"I take it you and your mother have issues," Erika said.

"It just kind of bugs me the way she is always fussing and mothering me," I said.

"You don't seem to mind when I do it."

"Go figure," I said.

"Chill, go back to your happy place," Erika teased. "It is almost time to put the fish on."

We were getting a great day to sit outside and have a little private cookout together. The sun was shining through the clouds. I raised the umbrella on the patio table to keep the "searing" Portland sun out of our eyes. It is an interesting thing in Portland. There are long periods when you don't see the sun, but when you do, everyone scrambles for the sunglasses.

I don't know if it is true or not, but I once read that Portland and Seattle had more sunglasses per capita than anywhere in the United States. That seems pretty crazy. It seems like there would be more in Miami or Phoenix or somewhere else. But there are a lot of sunglasses in Portland, maybe because we are pretty sensitive to sunlight.

Erika and I were now basking in the sun as she put the salmon on the grill. I hauled dishes out to the patio table while Erika manned the grill and the salmon.

"Now this is the way to do a weekend," I said. "I will have to continue to be nice to you if I get thank yous of this quality."

She smiled a warm smile at me and said, "I know you will always be nice to me."

We sat under the warm sun of late spring, and I basked not only in that warmth but also in the warmth of being with Erika. All seemed right with the world at this moment. I had brought the weekend entertainment section from the newspaper out to the patio for future reference. Maybe we could spot something we would like to do later.

"Oh, wow!" I said as I opened the entertainment section. "I know what we are doing tonight."

"I am always anxious to hear what follows you making a statement like that," Erika laughed.

"*Dial M for Murder* in 3-D," I said.

"What?" she said and began to laugh louder.

"So, the Alfred Hitchcock movie, *Dial M for Murder*—you have heard of it or seen it, right?"

"I have heard of it but I don't remember seeing it; maybe I have," Erika said.

"You poor child, I have so much work to do with you to turn you into a well-rounded person."

"I feel well-rounded after eating this much food. But you are referring to kind of like a *My Fair Lady* thing with me, huh?" Erika said. "Have I become your project?"

"Yeah, right. Now listen up, this is the original Hitchcock movie, except in 3-D."

"Oooooh," she said.

"Now you are making fun of me," I said.

"What was your first clue?" Erika said as she continued laughing and pushed her sunglasses up to wipe tears from her eyes.

"You are such a brat. Have you ever been to a movie when you wear the 3-D glasses?"

"You know, Tom, I can honestly say I haven't," Erika said as she continued to mock me and laugh louder with each statement I made. "You have undoubtedly seen *Dial M for Murder* many times and have seen a 3-D movie with funny glasses—but never *Dial M for Murder* in 3-D," Erika surmised.

"Exactly. How did you know?"

"Lucky guess." She bent over laughing and said, "You are so hilarious."

"If you don't want to go, we can do something else. If you think that sounds dumb ..."

She interrupted and said, "Are you kidding? I wouldn't want it on my conscience that I was the one who stood between you and the 3-D thing. Give me the pitch, what is this about?"

"We have seen several movies that were made before you were born, but I think this one was made before I was born."

"Wow, like a really old movie then," Erika said.

"I am going to ignore that ... okay, there is Ray Milland and Grace Kelly. It is a mystery and this guy wants to kill his wife, probably because she is always making fun of him like you are doing to me. It is plot with a lot of twists. 'Dial M' refers to how there used to be phones that you actually dialed, and a dial that had letters on it, not that you would know any of this."

"So, this is something you guys did in, like, the 1950s or something?" Erika said.

"No, not that 'you guys' did … I was once a small child too, you know, I wasn't born old."

Erika was now laughing hysterically. "This movie can't be more entertaining than you, telling me about it."

Referring to the ad, I said, "It says that this movie has not been seen in 3-D for many years, and it was the way Hitchcock intended it to be shown."

"Well, I sure wouldn't want to disappoint Alfred Hitchcock then," Erika said. "I am in."

"Seriously, do you want to go? If you don't, it is okay."

"Oh, yeah, saying I don't want to do this would be like taking Easter candy away from a small child. I'm in."

"Seriously, does that sound like fun?" I said.

As she rose to start clearing the table, she walked behind my chair, put her arm around my neck, and hugged me from behind. She put her face next to mine and said, "Everything with you sounds fun; you are just so much fun to tease and are so adorable."

"I will take that answer. We don't need to rush off, though, the movie isn't until later; there is one at 5 and one at 7:30. I am enjoying what we are doing."

"Me too," Erika said.

After we cleared away the dishes, we were both struck by what a great sunny day we suddenly had on our hands.

"Hey, I have an idea," I said as I pulled the two chaise lounges into the sunniest place on the patio.

"Very nice," Erika said. "Let's soak up some sun before it goes away."

Erika usually wore tailored jackets and slacks when I would see her during the week. This attire was always very flattering to her tall, slim body. However, today she was in her weekend-let's-have-a-barbecue attire. I thought she was being a little optimistic about the weather in what she wore, but the optimism was being rewarded with a spectacular, sunny afternoon. Erika had a long, white, loosely fitting skirt, sandals, and a pullover long-sleeved t-shirt.

There is a thing women do that puzzles me. There is that kind of twisty thing they do with their wrist as they grab their long hair in the back. When they are done twisting their hair, it is magically piled on top of their head and off of their neck. Erika did that maneuver as she sat on the patio and prepared to soak up the sun. How do women do that?

"I think I am going to catch some rays, if you don't mind," Erika said.

"Erika can do anything she wants," I replied.

She smiled, slipped off her shoes, pulled her skirt up to mid-thigh to expose her legs, and lay back in the lounge, relaxing with her sunglasses on.

"You look very happy," I said. "I think I will join you. Want something to drink?"

"Oh, yeah," she said.

I went inside to retrieve some drinks, but had trouble not stealing glances at her beautiful, long legs. It was really the first time I saw her in a dress, or with bare legs, and I was having trouble not being distracted.

When I returned with the drinks, she said, "You are the best, and it is wonderful to be spoiled."

Amid this tranquil scene, I saw my friend and neighbor glancing over the fence to see what was going on in my backyard. The curiosity factor about Erika remained high, it seemed. I wished everyone would just leave me alone. I felt like all of my friends and co-workers were gathering around and saying, "Hey, look, Tom is interacting with another human being. And it's a woman."

Maybe I had become a bit too much of a loner over the last two years. Maybe I had become accustomed to being ignored and anonymous. There is one side of me that loves being anonymous. I can go about my business as if I was invisible and no one is offering their opinions about what I am doing. Being with Erika makes it impossible to be invisible any more. When she walks into a room or I walk in with her, our arrival is immediately noted.

The powers of invisibility that I possessed before Erika were proven without any doubt one day during a noontime jog. I was jogging along the Willamette River, which runs through the middle of downtown along a bike and walking path called the Esplanade.

It is a wonderful feature of downtown, which allows bikers, rollerbladers, walkers, and runners to go along the banks of the Willamette and view the spectacular skyline of the city on the opposite side of the river. It can be especially beautiful during early morning runs, when the sun comes up over Mount Hood on the east and begins to light the downtown buildings in a soft rosy glow.

That was one of my favorite activities in the early morning before I met Erika in the coffee shop.

One day, as I took a noontime run, there was a beautiful young woman with long blonde hair running a few yards in front of me. She looked back as she ran ahead of me and smiled broadly. That got my attention, and then she looked back a second time and smiled flirtatiously again. She motioned with her arm and said, "Come and join me."

I was about to say something like, "Are you talking to me?" when a very rugged, muscular, handsome-looking guy in a tight t-shirt labeled "Portland Fire Department" ran past me and joined the beautiful woman. The beautiful young women apparently did not even know I was there. On her radar screen, I was not even a blip. It was then I realized that I had powers of invisibility, especially to beautiful women. I was just a potted plant next to the ruggedly handsome fireman. Actually, I was less than a potted plant. I was invisible.

So now, I was adjusting from being someone no one ever took note of, to being seen, apparently by more people than I knew, with an alluring young woman. I am sure Erika has never known what it is like to be invisible.

Just as I was settling onto the lounge next to Erika, I heard my neighbor Jerry say, "Hey, Tom, how are you doing?"

Great. Jerry is one of my best friends, but I didn't want to go shoot the bull with him right now. I didn't want to go hang over the fence, talking golf or discussing how much moss is in the lawn, while Erika was sunning herself in my backyard.

I said to Erika, "Go ahead and stay here." She assured me she had no intention of moving.

"Hey, Jerry, what's up?" I said as I walked towards our common fence.

As I got closer, he said in a lowered voice, "I could ask you the same thing. We never see you anymore. The house is always dark at night like no one is there. The only two times I have seen you lately, you are with your new lady friend."

"Gee, thanks for noticing. It is nice to know that I am being watched over," I said sarcastically. "That is Erika, and we were just having a relaxing afternoon together."

"Very nice," Jerry said. "This is a new exciting development, huh?"

"Yes, it is," I said. "We are just good friends and having some fun now. But thanks for asking."

"Shelly and I were talking about you the other day, and we are glad you are re-emerging after all you went through."

"Thanks, man; tell Shelly hi. Erika is a very sweet lady and has been really good for me."

"So, is she the reason no one is ever at your house anymore?"

"Partly," I said. "The other reason is I have nosy neighbors."

"So, I get it. I don't need to be hit over the head with a brick. Nice to see your biting sarcasm return to form," Jerry said. "Come and see us sometime if you get a break. You crazy kids have fun."

I just smiled at him and walked back to Erika's location on the sunny patio.

Just as I settled back onto the lounge by Erika, Jerry fired up his damn lawn mower. We had been listening to the birds singing, the gentle splash of the water in the fountain on the patio, and the squirrels rustling in the trees. Now it was Black-and-Decker time.

Is Jerry completely clueless? I know Saturday is a big lawn-mowing day, but did he have to fire up that friggin' thing now?!

Erika turned towards me and asked, "Are there more inquiring minds that want to know the truth about Erika and Tom?"

"Oh, yeah," I said, "you are actually good for my reputation. People think I am much more exciting and interesting than I really am since I have been seen with you."

I then told her the story of the fireman and the beautiful blonde girl.

She laughed and said, "Aaaw, but I noticed you."

"For that I am very grateful," I said.

The cinema where *Dial M* was playing is in one of my favorite older, hip neighborhoods in Portland. It is on Twenty-First Street near downtown. If cinema is your religion, this movie house is one of the temples. Here you can see old Fellini movies, or classic movies, as well as the latest edgy art-house releases. I once saw *Citizen Kane* here on the big screen, and that experience has made me love this theatre ever since.

Erika had never been there but loved the funky neighborhood and the theatre, which was a throwback to an era that preceded Erika's entry into the world. It had an old-style lobby with thick red curtains covering the entrance-way into the theatre. The screen was covered by a large curtain, which was raised as the movie began. It had a balcony where, by now, generations of people had made out and done other forbidden things in the dark corners. Erika laughed when we put on our 3-D glasses and looked at one another.

However, she was amazed when the movie started and we saw our first 3-D images on the screen. "This is awesome," she said to me, moving her glasses up and down to check the contrast between 3-D and non-3-D. As we left, she started reviewing the plot twists with me. "So now, walk me through the switching of the keys thing again."

It is one of the principle plot points in the movie and proves the husband was the murderer. It still confused me after about my sixth viewing but I pretended to get it all.

"To me, the most baffling part of this mystery," I began, "is, if I were married to Grace Kelly, why would I want to kill her?"

Erika laughed and said, "I would expect a comment like that from you."

We walked through the cool evening air back to where we had parked our cars and talked about our day. I followed her back to her condo and helped her get all of her stuff used in her "thank you" meal unloaded.. She gave me her customary hug at the door and thanked me for a great day. It was another perfect day with Erika.

By the way, today was the day I fell in love with Erika's laugh.

Chapter 11

TEMPORARY INSANITY

I RELUCTANTLY MADE good on my promise to call my mother to explain the "strange goings-on" at my house and in my life.

"Hello."

"Hi, Mom."

"Well, hello dear, I was wondering if you were going to call me."

"Well, I did."

"I wondered if I would hear from you yesterday but I guess you were very busy and distracted. How was your lunch with Erika?"

"Very nice. It was beautiful weather and it was nice to be outside. We went to a movie last night, so I didn't get home until late."

"So who is this Erika, and where did she come from?"

"She is someone I recently met and we have started doing things socially together."

"So she is your girlfriend?"

"I guess you could say that. She is my friend and she is a girl."

"You know that isn't the way I meant it. I mean, you are romantically involved?"

"We are just good friends. We like each other very much, but we are just taking things kind of slowly."

"I think that is a good idea, dear. She seems very young."

"No, she doesn't," I protested. "Erika is a very serious and accomplished woman. She works at an investment firm; she just got her MBA and is a very intelligent, impressive lady."

"I am sure she is, she just seems very young."

"I don't know what you mean by that. It sounds like she is popping her bubble gum and having me drop her off at the mall so she can hang out with her friends from school. Just because she is younger than me doesn't mean she is a child."

"I am just concerned that you don't waste too much time. You are not getting any younger. You need to date someone who you would seriously consider as a wife. She seems very nice but she is so much younger than you."

"Yeah, Mom, I noticed. She is younger than me but that doesn't really matter. We are just two people who are enjoying being together and like each other very much. This is how people find mates. I could take the fast track. I could go to some bar and get a woman liquored up and take her to Reno. That would be the fast way to find a wife."

Ignoring my sudden outburst, Mom pressed on, "So do you think this will develop into something and you are going to get married?"

"It is way early to say something like that. Our relationship is just as I have described and nothing more."

"How long have you known this woman?"

"We met in January, downtown in a coffee shop."

"In January and I am just finding out about her in May?"

"Well, I meet lots of people. I don't call you every time I meet someone."

"Yes, but it sounds like she is not just *someone*. Has she been married before? How old is she?"

"She has been married before but she is divorced. She is in her thirties."

"Thirties, that is a lot younger than you. It makes you wonder what happened in her first marriage, doesn't it?"

"Not really. There are some very nice people who get divorced."

"You can't be too careful these days. I saw this thing on Fox News about this woman who goes around picking up men and draining their bank accounts. You know ..."

I interrupted and said, "Mom, I keep telling you to turn off the cable news. You can't watch that crap for ten hours a day. It gives you a very warped view of the world. You met Erika, she doesn't seem like a serial killer, does she?"

"No dear, she seems very nice, but I am just saying these things happen."

"Thanks, Mom. You know if some woman picks me up at Starbucks and then wants to sexually exploit me, I am okay with that at this point."

"Oh, you are so silly and so naughty. I am just looking out for my boy."

"I know, Mom."

"Do the kids know you are dating again?"

I considered my next answer carefully but could see no way out of it. "No, they don't," I said. I knew my mother was like a shark detecting blood in the water now. She would be speed-dialing Michelle in Denver seconds after this call concluded. "There is no reason to involve them in everything. I can tell them, at the right time, when it comes up in conversation." That was a futile plea for mercy, which I knew would go unheeded. "Are you doing okay, Mom?"

"Oh, yeah. You know I have good days and bad days, but I am getting along alone somehow."

For the uninitiated, that was one of my mother's passive-aggressive shots across my bow.

"Good," I said. "You have anything big planned?"

"Oh, not me. Gladys and I are getting together later today. We like to go out running around on Sunday afternoons. It looks like it will be a nice day."

"Well, those are big plans. Have fun and I will see you later in the week. Let me know if you need something."

"Okay. Tell Erika hello. I am sure you two are getting together, right?"

"Have a good day, Mom. Love you, good-bye."

"Good-bye, dear, love you too."

After I hung up the phone, I let out a weary groan. I wondered if I called her phone right now, would it be busy? Enough of this, I thought, I did my duty.

The next morning, I gave Erika a homogenized version of my "chat with Mom." She laughed and told me I needed to lighten up on her. If I had been talking to a normal mother, she would have said, "I am so glad you are getting out again and finding happiness. Erika seems wonderful and is very pretty and very nice." Things like that would have been nice to hear. Boy, did I ring the wrong number if I wanted feedback like that.

I was slogging through my Monday when I decided I needed to go downstairs to the cafeteria and get a Diet Coke. My warm caffeine was wearing off, and it was time for some cold caffeine. My intent was to pick up my drink and return to my desk. I did have quite a bit going on this morning. There had been lots of phone calls.

Sitting at a table near the window, sipping a soda, was my buddy Josh. Josh was my "car buddy." No one knew more about cars than Josh. Cars were a religion to Josh, with *Car and Driver* and *Road and Track* magazines as his scriptures. Josh was probably around thirty years old and had recently been married. I met Josh when he and I used to work on the same floor in my office building. He had since taken another job within the company and had moved to a different floor.

I noticed Josh one day when I saw all the pictures of cars and models of cars that littered his cubicle. I stopped by and made a comment about some of his car pictures. That is all it takes to get Josh going. It comes pouring out of him. After that, I would often drop by Josh's cubicle and talk cars. I went to a car show with him one time. I loved cars and am interested. I am nothing compared to Josh. Since that time, Josh always kept me posted on the latest. There is a turbo version of this car coming out. Or "Have you seen the new redesigned" whatever?

Josh sent me e-mails directing me to Web sites about some car he wanted me to see. In the fall before Liz died, I bought my BMW 5 Series sedan with the gray metallic finish. It was a great car. I had always loved BMWs. It was probably my favorite car I have ever owned. That fall, I told Josh I was in the market for a new car. It was like throwing red meat to the dogs. He quickly prepared several alternatives for me with price ranges, horsepower, and the whole enchilada. He was amazing. I wondered what Josh did at work all day other than look at car Web sites. But he was awesome.

I rewarded his enthusiasm and diligence by inviting him to go car shopping with Liz and me. It was an orgasmic experience for him. He was like having a car robot with me. Josh corrected several things the salesmen told me. He was always right.

Today, Josh was not his usual super-wired self.

"What's up, Josh?" I said in greeting.

"Big changes, man. I need to sell my Porsche."

"No way, that is your baby, Josh." Josh owned a Porsche Boxster, which was about three years old. It was yellow with black leather interior and was magnificent. Of course, it was in mint condition because Josh cleaned it within an inch of its life and nurtured it like a child.

"Have to, man. Cheryl says we need a different car."

"That's okay with you? I thought you would just get a different woman if Cheryl ever said something like that. There are lots of women, but this is your Porsche."

"Thing is, Tom, she is right."

"Wow, you must really love this woman."

"We found out we are going to have a kid."

"Congratulations, Josh. That is awesome, buddy. Good for you."

"I am really excited," he said, "but I am headed for minivan-land, dude."

"Not my Josh. You are never going to be driving a minivan full of kids to soccer or Cub Scouts," I said.

"I need a different car. My Porsche days are over now, man. The time has come."

"You could put the kid up for adoption," I said. "There are lots of nice people who want to adopt a child."

"Not funny, man," Josh said. "I am way stressed out trying to figure out which way to go. I am checking Blue Books and doing some research."

"You are the man. If you were someone else with this problem, I would say, 'Hey, I need to hook you up with my friend Josh.'"

"I don't want to go to a full SUV, I am thinking some kind of crossover vehicle. But I am addicted to the German engineering. I don't know if I could drive anything and be happy after having the Porsche. You know what I am talking about with your Beemer," Josh said as he started to do a data dump on me of his thoughts.

"How much could you get for the Porsche?" I asked.

"I am checking it out. I am looking at what kind of comparable vehicles I could go with that would fill the bill," Josh said.

"Yeah, I am trying to remember what I paid for my BMW a couple of years ago," I said.

"Oh, I remember exactly," Josh said.

"Sorry, I forgot my head there for a minute and forgot who I was talking to," I responded.

"You got the cool extras on your Beemer 5 series, the nice deluxe package."

"Yeah, I am trying to remember who talked me into all of that stuff," I mused.

"Hey, you know who needs my Boxster?" Josh said, as his face brightened.

I knew what was coming. Josh was always trying to talk me into buying cars. When I would tell him I just bought one, he would say, "Yeah, but you have that big garage." Josh thought it was practically immoral to have a three-car garage without three cars. Now that I had just one, Josh thought there was no reason to not buy two more cars. Cheryl was in for an interesting life.

"Dude," Josh continued, "you are a single guy now. I am the married one with a kid. We should swap cars."

"Oh, yeah, right. I will get a Porsche."

"Why not?" Josh continued.

Once these doors are opened by Josh, they can be difficult to close.

Josh said, "If I were you I would. I was you and I did. When I was a single guy, I went for it. They are the most awesome cars ever, man."

"I have no doubt, Josh, but it would be dumb for me to do that. I love my Beemer," I said.

"BMWs are awesome, dude; you know how I feel about them. We are talking my Porsche Boxster here. Have you ever driven a Porsche, Tom?" Josh asked.

"Well, no, but I have admired them, and yours, from afar for years."

"Drive my car and it will be game over," Josh said.

"Josh, Josh, Josh …," I said.

"Seriously, dude, what are you doing for lunch? Let's go driving and you can buy me a burger."

"I can, huh? Well, I was planning to go for a run and … Josh you are crazy, man," I said.

"Come on. 11:45 in the lobby. We will go to the parking garage, and I am about to change your life, dude."

"That is what I am afraid of," I said.

At 11:45, I went to the lobby. Josh looked like a child about to meet Santa Claus.

"All right, Tom! I kept worrying that you would call me and dog me," Josh said.

I just shook my head and said, "No agreement yet, okay? We are just talking."

"No problem," Josh said, "but I talked with Cheryl and she is totally cool with the deal if you agree."

I just laughed. Then I said, "Cheryl knows it is futile to interfere with crazy-car-man once you get cranked up, right?"

"No, no, it is all good," Josh said.

When we got to the parking lot, he tossed me the keys and said, "You drive."

As we got in, I noticed the interior was immaculate. There wasn't one speck of dust. It had all been freshly detailed, and the dark carpet didn't even have a piece of fuzz or one pebble on it.

I started it up and heard the roar of the Porsche engine.

"Sweet, huh?" Josh said.

"Is this better than sex?" I said mockingly to Josh.

"It will be, once we get on the freeway," Josh said.

I pulled it out of the parking lot onto Fifth Avenue. "Hit it, Tom," Josh urged.

"This is Fifth Avenue, Josh, chill for a second."

We headed for the on-ramp and decided to get on Highway 26.

As soon as I merged onto 26, Josh said, "Punch it, dude. I have done this on-ramp at 80 before."

I started laughing. I did punch it. It was awesome. I was amazed at how it accelerated. It was unlike anything I have ever driven. This was incredible.

"What do you think, Tom? Did you feel that total kick in the ass as you floored it?"

"I wish someone would kick me in the ass right now. How could you not like this?" I said.

"No doubt. I told you it would change your life, man."

We pulled into a Burgerville for lunch. "Is it alright to eat a hamburger in this car?" I asked.

"It's your car, Tom, you tell me."

"Not so fast, slick," I said. "Seriously, are we eating in the car?"

"Oh, yeah, then I could show you a bunch of stuff."

As I munched my burger, Josh poured it on. "Notice, this thing will do freakin' 180 miles an hour, 0 to 60 in five seconds. It is air-cooled, light-weight, it will fly." Then Josh went through a complete demo of switches, gauges, cup holders, etc.

"I may not be smart enough to drive this car, Josh. The dash looks like the Millennium Falcon or something," I said.

"Trust me, you are going to wonder how you did without this stuff in a few weeks," Josh said.

"Josh, you are the best," I said as we put our burger wrappers into a paper bag for disposal. Josh quickly reached behind the seat and produced a canister of wipes to remove any fingerprints or residue of our meal. I smiled to myself. Josh put the used wipe into the paper bag and said, "Remind me to get rid of it when we stop."

The test drive continued as we re-entered the downtown core near my office.

"What do you think, Tom? This is your big chance. You will never get another chance to own a car like this. Especially not a car that has been treated like this one."

"That is not in question," I said. "Are you sure on the Blue Book and all of that? It seems like I ought to throw in some cash if we are to make a deal."

"So we are making a deal?"

"I am just thinking, okay?"

"Tom, think of it this way. You are a single guy. There is no reason to not do this if you would like to do it. There is no one to tell you no. You are the decision-maker. Do you want to take this one chance and have an awesome car? It will be more fun than you have ever had before. You will look forward to driving every day. You have always done the safe thing and the sensible thing … do something crazy and fun. You will be living the dream, dude."

"For the record, it is not always a bad thing to have a wife to tell you no. Sometimes, it prevents you from jumping off of the cliff. The fact that there is no one to tell me no, kind of freaks me out a little. Let me think this afternoon, and I will let you know."

We walked back into the lobby. "Are you sure this is okay with Cheryl? I don't want you to do something crazy that will cause a problem."

"Cheryl is totally fine with everything I am doing. She knows I won't do anything crazy."

Poor Cheryl, I thought. Then I said, "I will call you."

I had got to get back to work. I had a lot to do. Josh is a crazy man. As I tried to re-engage, I started thinking seriously about the car. Josh's words, "You have always done the safe thing and the sensible thing," rang in my ears. The more I thought about it, the more I thought the idea could be fun. It was an awesome car. Why not do something out of the norm? Why not do something that people wouldn't expect me to do? I should probably ask someone to slap me really hard across the face, and maybe I would snap out of it. It could work. Why not? I was trying to forge a new me. What would Erika think?

I called Josh to deliver my decision about 4 PM. He was ecstatic. "You will so not regret this," he said. "You are doing the right thing for both of us."

"I hope so. So we can exchange pink slips, I guess …"

"Yeah, I will get it all fixed up. Just bring your pink slip for the BMW tomorrow. I am psyched about the Beemer. I wanted the Porsche to go to a good home where it would be appreciated. This is awesome."

"Josh, check the Blue Book again and make sure I don't owe you some cash, because I will make it right."

"I will, don't worry. Let's meet in the parking lot and exchange keys."

"Tonight?" I said.

"Oh yeah, we can make it legal tomorrow. We can enjoy our new cars tonight."

I met Josh in the parking garage and asked, "Should we meet to get the crap out of our cars?"

"I don't have any crap in my car," Josh said, somewhat offended.

"Sorry, I forgot who I was talking to. I am sorry the BMW is not as clean as your car."

"No worry, I will detail it tonight," Josh said. He handed me the keys and said, "You now own one of the finest cars on the planet."

"Thanks, Josh. Always a pleasure. If there is buyer's remorse or Cheryl throws you out of the house or whatever, we can undo it tomorrow, okay?"

"It is all good. Enjoy your new car," Josh said.

"I have got to show this to my lady friend."

"Oh," Josh said, springing into action. "We have got to take the top down for your chick to see it for the first time."

"Isn't it a little cool outside?"

"Loosen up, Tom. Your lady needs you to pull up with the top down."

After showing me how it all worked, Josh put down the top of my new car. Then, Josh took off in the BMW, smiling and waving.

I was alone with my Porsche for the first time. What *have* I done? I had to call Erika. I dialed her cell.

"Hey, handsome, to what do I owe this sudden call?" she said.

"Where are you? Have you left the office yet?"

"No," she said, "but I was getting ready to leave."

"Are you free tonight?"

"Sure," she said.

"Meet me in front of your office building in five minutes. I will pull into the turn-out place."

"You are picking me up at work?"

"Yes, just do it, okay?"

"Is something wrong?" Erika asked.

"No," I said. "Just do it, okay?"

"Okay, see you in five," she said.

I circled the block and pulled in front of Erika's office. Erika was standing there, holding her purse and her briefcase, looking blankly down the street. She did not realize it was me—I guess she was looking for the BMW.

"Erika," I called.

Erika normally has a very expressive face but she went off the charts when she saw me.

"What is this?" she said.

"It is my new car," I said.

"No way," she said.

"No, seriously, it is," I said.

"Shut up!" Erika said.

"Get in quick," I said. She did and we pulled away from the curb. "What do you think? Do you know what this is?"

"Well, yeah, it is an awesome Porsche ... and a convertible," but she continued looking bewildered.

"It has been a very interesting day," I said.

"What happened to the Beemer?" Erika asked.

"I traded it for this," I said. "This is your basic high-profile car."

"No way. Yeah, we are getting lots of looks," Erika said. She waved to some people from her office that stopped and stared.

"Yeah, they are probably wondering what this moron is doing with the top down on his convertible in early May in Portland," I said.

"How did this happen?" Erika asked and kept repeating, "This is so awesome."

"It is a long story I need to tell you," I said.

"Aren't you the impetuous one these days?" Erika said. "Let's swing by my place so I can change clothes and then we can go do something decadent."

"I have already done something off-the-charts decadent. I should go home and open a can of soup for dinner."

Erika said, "We need to go to some high-profile place and show off your new hot car. Let's go down to the river and get some seafood. I will buy, since you are feeling poor now. You know this car is sooo you."

"This car is so not me," I retorted.

"This car is the new you, it matches what you are becoming," Erika said.

I looked at her and smiled. "So you like it?"

"Ah, yeah," Erika said.

"Good. I told the guy I bought it from that I wanted to show it to 'my lady friend' and that I hoped she would like it. He told me if my chick didn't like this car, I should get a new chick. So I am really glad I don't have to dump you tonight," I said.

"So now, in your office building, I am known as your 'chick'? I am sooo relieved that you don't have to dump me. Who is this jerk?"

"Just for the record, I have never referred to you as 'my chick,'" I said. "This guy is such a car fanatic. When I tell you the story, you will understand the comment," I said.

"Tell him your hot chick got all turned on when you pulled up in your hot car."

"He would consider that the ultimate compliment, believe me," I said.

"There is an interesting story ahead. Who else has seen this car?"

"No one but you. I bought it about fifteen minutes before I called you. You are the first, of course. Erika, do you think I am crazy? Maybe you need to hit me really hard in the face or on the side of my head so I will stop being stupid," I said.

"You *are* crazy, but I would never hit you. But, my friend, your car rocks. This is going to be awesome. I am proud of you for stepping out there. Look at you. I am so impressed," she said.

"So you think it is exciting when I am irresponsible and act like an insane guy in a mid-life crisis," I said.

"Yeah, you know us 'chicks' dig the bad boys," Erika said, laughing. "Tom always does the right and responsible thing. It is fun to see Tom cutting loose and having some fun. I think it is awesome."

"Thanks, that is the second time I have heard something like that today. See, I was feeling pressure to get a car up to the standards of the woman I hang out with. So I had to get the coolest car on the planet," I said.

She smiled and said, "Now that is a good answer. We so need to show this to someone tonight ... oh, you know who would love this? My mother."

"That sounds like a great idea," I said.

"Let me see if she is around." She dialed her mom's number. "Hi, Mom, are you going to be around tonight? Yeah, Tom and I want to come and see you. We have a surprise ... okay ... see you in an hour or so. Yeah. Okay, bye."

"Was that the best way to put that?" I said. "She probably thinks we are getting married or you are pregnant or something."

"Why would she think that? My mom loves surprises."

"I guess I am still adjusting to the idea that you are in a normal family. My mother and I probably consider all surprises bad and think the worst."

We pulled in front of her condo and decided we better put up the top. "You do like it, right? You don't think I am stupid or something? You see, I always have this buyer's remorse thing. I will wake up screaming tonight in the middle of the night. I will be in a cold sweat."

Erika put her arm around me. "You are so funny. It is amazing and so are you. This is incredible. I am dying to hear this story. It is so fun to see you having fun."

"You know, if someone had shown me the future a year ago," I said, "if they had shown me riding in this car with you, and said, 'This is what you will be doing a year from now' ... I would have thought it was impossible."

Erika hugged me and said, "You have way more going for you than you think."

I smiled and we headed up to Apartment 912.

Over dinner, I gave Erika the history of Josh. She thought it was a riot. Erika said she thought my involvement with Josh was another funny, quirky thing that she loved about me.

"So basically, you went down to buy a Diet Coke about 10:30 this morning and ended up buying a Porsche."

"Boiled down to its basic components, you have just described my day."

Erika was laughing loudly as she said, "That is some kind of world record for impulse buying. You are the most fun person ever."

As Josh would put it, "my chick digs my car."

After dinner, we went to the parking lot and I said, "It's your turn. You drive to your mom's house."

"Oh, no, I am afraid to ..."

"No, no, I want you to drive. You need to have this experience. Josh said driving this car is better than sex."

She looked at me warily. "If that is true, I can't wait to drive it. Okay ... I don't want to hurt it. It is so beautiful. I love the yellow color."

"I want it to still be yellow when you get done driving it, but come on, girl, you can do it. Where is the wild-child Erika that I know and love?"

She took the keys and fired it up. She eased it out of the parking space and moved out of the parking structure. When we pulled out onto the four-lane road, I said, "Punch it, Erika." I was turning into Josh. Erika floored it right on cue and was quickly going 60 miles an hour and climbing. She let out a whoop and said, "Oh my gosh—I would get so many tickets in this car." Meanwhile, I was checking out the sound system.

"Probably, so will I. It is important you know how to drive it so we can still use it when my license get suspended."

Erika laughed and said, "This rocks! Wooohooo!" she yelled as she floored it again.

Erika wheeled the Porsche over the Hawthorne Bridge towards the Laurelhurst neighborhood, one of the charming older areas of the city. When she pulled into the driveway, I asked her to stay in the car, and I would go get her mother. I knocked on the door and was greeted by Tricia. She gave me a big hug, which was very nice. "Come outside," I said.

Tricia followed me and saw Erika in the Porsche.

"Whoa, what is this?" Tricia said.

"I sort of had a mental breakdown today and bought this," I said. "Erika likes it."

"Yeah, I bet she does," Tricia said. "Oh, Tom, this is beautiful. It is incredible. I am blown away."

"Me too," I said. "Erika has spent the evening reassuring me. Get in. Take her for a ride, Erika. I will wait here."

Erika and Tricia took off. Erika was definitely getting into it.

When they returned, they were both laughing as they got out of the car and headed inside.

"Tom, you are incredible. That is the coolest car I have ever seen. Wow," Tricia said. "Come in for a little bit."

"Okay," Erika said.

"I love this neighborhood, Tricia," I said. "I always have. You and your daughter have excellent taste in places to live."

"Thank you, sort of like your taste in cars," Tricia said.

"Oh, Tricia, what have I done?" I said with my head buried in my hands.

"I have a suggestion," Tricia said. "Let it go, Tom. Have fun and don't look back with any regrets."

Erika told Tricia the story of my day. They both laughed hysterically. I loved watching Erika tell her mother the story. It was another wonderful encounter with Tricia. She and I really clicked, much like Erika and I have.

As I pulled in front of Erika's condo, I said, "I have an idea about what we can do with this car."

Erika reacted with her blue eyes widening and just listened for what was next.

"I say we drive it to my beach house and spend the weekend there. Does that interest you?"

"I am so there," Erika said.

"How about in a week or so?"

"Oh, yeah," Erika said. "Tom, my dear friend, you have topped yourself again. This has been so fun tonight. Now chill out, don't wake up screaming. Picture all of the good times you and I are about to have using your cool car. If you focus on that, you shouldn't wake up screaming … I hope."

She hugged me and flashed her beautiful smile. "Tell Josh hi for me and tell him I dig you and your car."

I should have bought a Porsche years ago.

Chapter 12

THERESA

I CONTINUED TO adjust to my new car and my new "image." I really hadn't bought into my new image but I was intrigued by what Erika had said the night I got the car. It was "sooo me," not the person I had been, but the person I was becoming.

The last thing on my mind when I swapped cars was to fancy myself as some kind of "swinging singles" guy. My mind continued to go back to the concept that I was in some type of metamorphosis into a new person. That seemed to be true, but had not occurred to me until Erika verbalized it.

All of the details got worked out with Josh. I did give him some cash to accompany the BMW. I thought it was the fair thing to do. I wasn't rich, but I had the money. I wanted to err on the side of being extra nice to Josh—a great young guy struggling to find his place and now adjusting to the idea that he was about to become someone's father.

On Thursday of that same week, I saw Josh early in the morning as I stood in the lobby, waiting for the elevator. He moved towards me. I teased him, saying, "Hey, man, I have been looking for you. That car you sold me is a piece of junk, I got ripped off."

Josh looked stricken, so I called off the joke early and said, "No, I am just kidding. It is awesome."

Josh said, "Whoa, dude, don't even kid about things like that."

"I am so sorry. I shouldn't do that. Your car is a work of art. I want you to know, I go into the garage, kiss the Porsche good night, and cover it with a blanket before I go to bed."

"I knew you would appreciate my baby. That is why I was stressin' about just running an ad to sell it," Josh said.

"You are the man, Josh. You have visitation rights. Come and play with the car any time you want. By the way, my lady friend thinks you rock and loves the car."

"You are the best, Tom." The elevator opened and he moved to exit onto his floor. He added as he left, "I told you, man, you are living the dream now." I just smiled to myself. I didn't believe cars were people with souls like Josh did, but he did have a point. Things were going pretty well now. Due to my neurotic nature and upbringing, I tend to get nervous when faced with what seems to be unbridled happiness. I was trying to take the advice I had received from Erika and Tricia—to move on and be happy.

Friday morning dawned bright and clear. The sun was rising over Mount Hood and bathing the city in a rosy glow as I drove downtown for my morning coffee rendezvous with Erika. The gorgeous blossoms of spring were everywhere. The dogwoods, azaleas, and rhododendrons were at their peak, coloring the landscape with a gaudy display of bright pinks, various shades of red, and purple hues. It was a good day to be alive. I was glad to see the good weather since today was our annual "employee appreciation" event at work.

I always thought it was a lot of fun. We worked in the morning and then, about noon, we headed to PGE Park, Portland's baseball stadium, which was the home to the Class AAA Portland Beavers. The appreciation day was always scheduled based on the limited number of afternoon games played by the Beavers. Today was one of only three day games on the schedule. Our company traditionally picked one for the afternoon away from the office. There was an area along the first base line where there were several tables and chairs. A barbecue was set up, and all of the company employees sat at the tables and enjoyed the cookout.

It was always a fun day at the ballpark and a very low-stress way to close the week. Today's weather looked perfect for this event. I have been at some of the May baseball games where you wanted a parka and hot chocolate, but today was going to be a good day for a cookout.

When I saw Erika at the coffee shop in the morning, she seemed to be excited about something. "I have a plan for tonight," she said. "I was looking in the newspaper's entertainment section this morning to see what movies were opening tonight. I didn't think there was anything good. But I did notice that there is a showing on the big screen of

Casablanca starting tonight over on Twenty-First Street. I would love to see *Casablanca* on the big screen, so I thought we should do that."

"Whoa, you have turned into me," I said. Erika started laughing. I almost obsessive-compulsively checked the Friday entertainment section to see what new movies were opening. Movies always changed on Friday, and this ritual was the highlight of my week for the past couple of years when my social life consisted of just going to the movies alone.

"What have I done to you?" I asked. "That sounds awesome. I don't think I have ever found you more attractive than right now. I am feeling kind of flushed and hot when I see you talking about movies like this."

Erika slapped my arm and said, "Knock it off. Do you like my plan?"

"You *know* that is my favorite movie of all time, and I would crawl on my hands and knees to see it on the big screen," I said. "You have the perfect plan. I am so proud of you."

"Perfect," she said. "But can we take the Porsche instead of crawling on our hands and knees?"

"Awesome," I said. "I will meet you right after work. I may get away a little early today since today is the baseball game thing."

"Oh, yeah, poor baby," Erika retorted. "You will be sitting in the sun, drinking beer, and watching baseball while I am in my cubicle looking at the sunshine out the window."

"Well, it is the appreciation thing, because I work so hard the rest of the year," I said.

"Whatever," Erika teased.

"Want me to give you a call on my cell about the fifth inning and let you know how it is going?" I asked.

"No, because you will just mess with me and tell me how good the beer tastes and how warm the sunshine feels on your skin, etc."

"I will call you later this afternoon and we can make our plan to hook up, okay?" I asked.

"Perfect," Erika said. "Did I do good on our plan for tonight?"

"You are the best, Erika. Your plans aren't bad either," I said. "Next weekend, we leave for the beach house, right?"

"Absolutely," she said. With that, we parted to begin our day.

The office was in a festive mood. It always helps to know that you will only work for three hours, instead of eight, on a sunny Friday. It seemed there were always enough workaholics, people who didn't like baseball, and people who didn't like fun or other people so that we could keep a skeleton staff to answer the phone. Everyone else was ready to party.

One of my favorite things was the annual statement from Human Resources, just before the appreciation event. Some HR person put out the memo that said, "In compliance with the corporate alcohol and drug policy, any employee partaking of beer at the annual employee appreciation event should not return to duty in the office later in the afternoon. If you intend to return to work in the office after the event, you should not partake of alcohol."

It became a big joke. The first thing most people did at the ballpark was to grab a beer and drink it and say, "Damn, now I can't go back to work."

As I was answering e-mails and attending to any matters that I absolutely had to deal with on this Friday morning, my friend, Theresa, slid into the extra chair in my cubicle for a visit.

I was facing my monitor and didn't notice her entry until I heard her say, "Well, look at you, with your furrowed brow, being all serious today."

"Hey, there. I promise I am about to get very not-serious. I was just looking serious to set a good example for my staff."

Theresa laughed and pointed to my staff as they stood in the hall, talking and laughing. "It looks like you have made quite an impact on them."

"Yeah, where would they be without my leadership? You are looking very summery," I said to Theresa. "I like your dress."

"Well, thank you. I was being very optimistic about what kind of day we would get." Theresa was about five foot four or five and had a long tangle of beautiful red hair. Her hair was kind of her trademark. Theresa had a great body. As a casual observer of Theresa's body over the years, she seemed to be bustier now than she had been in the past. I wondered if there had been some enhancements along the way, but either way she was a knockout.

I had known her for years. She was always a shameless flirt with me. I had flirted back with her over the years, thinking it was just a game. Then one day, a few years ago, she told me that if I ever got tired of Liz, she was interested in me. It was a serious proposal that had scared me off talking with her for a while.

After Liz's death, she had kept a respectful distance, it seemed, and would stop by occasionally to see how I was doing. But recently, it seemed our paths were crossing a lot more frequently.

Today, she was wearing a green sundress with thin straps and sandals. Theresa also wore a cardigan sweater over her dress as an insurance policy against disappointing weather at the baseball game. Theresa said, "Let's eat lunch together and catch up. It has been a while since you and I have had a chance to talk."

"Sounds good," I said. "We haven't talked for a while."

"See you then," Theresa said.

Around noon, the party was on along the first base line. The Beavers threw the first pitch to the Salt Lake batter, but the main concern was "Pass the mustard" and "Do you want cheese on that?" Everyone was milling around, greeting one another and separating into groups that would inhabit the tables. I spotted Theresa, who was making her way towards my table where a few others were chatting with me. I waved and motioned her to join us.

As we talked, Dave and John stopped by to say hello. I had shown Dave the new ride yesterday and word was spreading quickly. We exchanged "high-fives" and then John said, "What is this I hear about you?"

"Well," I said, "there seems to be so much conversation about me these days, I need to know which rumor or innuendo you are referring to."

All of this was happening while Theresa sat beside me, taking it all in.

"Well, you have a Porsche, apparently?"

"True, it is awesome. I am having lots of fun with it. I am still adjusting," I said, "but it is a new experience."

"Yeah," John said, "new experiences seem to be your specialty these days. So am I going to get a test drive at some point or even be officially told about it? Maybe you have just moved on and left your old friend John behind?"

"All right," I said, "you were next on the list …"

"Yeah, whatever," John said. "I bet I know who the first person to find out was."

"You are right," I said, "I went straight to my mother's house."

They both laughed raucously and John said, "You are so full of crap. So what does Erika think of it?"

"She likes it," I said.

"Oh, shocker to hear your hot young girlfriend likes your hot car," John said.

Dave asked, "How is Erika?"

"Doing well," I responded.

"She looked like she was doing pretty damn well the last time we saw her, "John retorted.

"It was so nice of you to drop by; too bad you have to be rushing off," I said sarcastically. "Seriously, John, I want to show you the car and go for a ride."

"Hey, I am always available. I don't quite have the demanding social schedule you do. If you get a few moments, call your old friends ...," John said.

"Seriously, John, I will call you," I said.

"You are amazing, dude; your legend continues to grow each day. You are full of surprises," John said as he and Dave walked away chuckling.

There was an uncomfortable silence and then the question hanging in the air between Theresa and me was finally verbalized. "Who is Erika?" she asked.

"She is someone I met and have been seeing some," I said, hoping that would suffice. It didn't.

"Sounds like there is a little more going on than that," Theresa said. "Is she that pretty young woman I saw you with at lunch one day?"

"Yeah, that was her," I said. I was being tight-lipped because I had a feeling where this cross-examination was going.

"Wow, she is very pretty. Very young and pretty. I think I saw you hugging her on the sidewalk in front of her office," Theresa said. "That didn't exactly look like a platonic relationship."

When did Theresa see that, I wondered? Sometimes I found Theresa really attractive and then sometimes she seemed kind of *Fatal Attraction* to me. There were times when I wondered if I would look out of my window at night and see her on the sidewalk in front of my house. She was pretty fiery and possessive sometimes—or at least I got hints of that side of her. In a few words ... her aggressiveness kind of creeped me out sometimes.

"Actually, that is kind of what our relationship is, we just do things together and have a good time," I said.

"Oh really, then she is not really your girlfriend?" Theresa pressed.

"I suppose she sort of is, but we are just getting started in our relationship, and things are still evolving," I said, hoping this would end the battery of questions.

"Oh, I see," she said simply and then was quiet for a moment. She mercifully changed the subject and asked what the car talk was about. I was very happy to tell her the story about my purchasing the Porsche.

"So is this your classic mid-life crisis thing?" Theresa asked.

"You know, it has occurred to me that I am going to be accused of that," I said, "but I always think it is unfair. Guys start a love affair with cars when they are little boys. Then, when they get to be middle-aged, they may, if lucky, begin to have enough money to fulfill some of their dreams. I have wanted a Porsche from the first time I saw one. Now I finally got my chance. It isn't because I am having a crisis. Things are pretty good, actually."

"Good for you, Tom," Theresa said. "I am so glad that you are finally having some fun. I have been waiting for Tom to break out some day. Now it looks like you have. It is understandable after all you have gone through; I think it is great, Tom. Are you going to show me your car?"

"Sure," I said.

"Hey, you and I live out the same direction. I used to see you on MAX [Portland's light rail train] a lot, but not so much anymore. Would you mind giving me a lift home and showing me your new car?"

I hesitated. I had planned to go home and change before meeting Erika. I assumed after sitting in the sun all afternoon sweating, it might be nice to freshen up before our evening out.

Then I replied, "I would be glad to. You will have to tell me where you live. I haven't ridden MAX for a while since I have been spending a lot of time downtown after work." Theresa gave me a sly look, which signaled that she suspected why that was the case.

"Good," Theresa said, "that will be fun. It is so good to see you again, Tom. We really didn't see one another for a while."

"Nice to see you too," I said as she decided it was time to shed her sweater.

"It is getting warm," Theresa said. "What a nice day."

"It is ideal weather for doing this. Ooooh," I said, as I reacted to a pitch that caused the Beaver batter to hit the dirt to avoid taking a fastball in the chin.

"You were a big stud athlete in college weren't you?" Theresa asked.

"No, I was more like a wimpy little guy who stopped playing because he got hurt," I said.

"You are being modest, I am sure," Theresa said.

"No, really. I played baseball in high school and for a couple of years in college before I hurt my arm and never quite got my pitching karma back."

"You have always stayed in great shape, Tom. You look great," she said. "Still running?"

"Yeah, still after it," I said.

"This redhead better do something about the sun. Would you mind putting some sunscreen on my shoulders and back?" Theresa asked.

"Sure," I said as she lifted her red hair to expose her shoulders and neck. I rubbed it on her soft skin and she responded, "You have very nice hands."

I wasn't sure what to say then, and I had a feeling this was about more than sunscreen.

"How about you?" Theresa said. "You have the blonde complexion, you need it too. Here, let me do your face."

I removed my cap, which I wore to protect my head from sunburn, and then took off my sunglasses. Theresa stood in front of my chair and bent over. She applied the sunscreen to my face. Her position allowed me to see everything contained in the top half of her sundress. Her large breasts were almost completely exposed in a display kept private for me by her red hair tumbling to obscure the view from anywhere except my location. She was gorgeous. It was extremely difficult to believe this was an accident. I knew she knew—we were not making eye contact during her application of the sunscreen.

"Thank you," I said as she smiled at me and returned to her seat at my side.

Our conversation settled into small talk about work, people at work, and remodeling houses. Theresa had just finished remodeling her kitchen. She was divorced a few years ago. I didn't know the story and was not sure what her private life was like.

The game dragged on and the Beavers were getting thrashed. A series of pitchers tried to slow down the Salt Lake bats but to no avail. "I am starting to lose interest," I said.

"Yeah, want to retreat up to the stands and get out of the sun?" Theresa asked.

"I think I have had enough sun too," I said, and we made our way up from the barbecue area to some empty seats in the shade of the grandstand. At last the slaughter was over and it was time to go home.

"Follow me," I said to Theresa, and we made our way to the nearby parking garage.

Theresa raved about the car once she spotted it in the parking garage. "Can we put the top down?" she asked. I couldn't help but think Theresa had already put her top down—now it was my turn.

"Sure, this is the day for it," I said as I maneuvered the top down. We headed for Beaverton, where I discovered she lived just a couple of miles from my house. As I accelerated on Highway 26 towards Beaverton, she squealed and then purred, "I love this," as her red hair seemed to fly all directions in the breeze.

I pulled into her driveway, as per her instructions, and then she asked, "Do you have a minute so I can show you how my remodeling turned out? You have never been in my house."

I glanced at my watch and then said, "I have a minute, but I have someplace where I need to be in a bit." I didn't want to go into her house, but it seemed inescapable without being rude.

"Do you have a date tonight?" Theresa asked.

"Well, yes, but some other things too," I said as I stretched the truth a little.

We went inside her nice house. She gave me the tour and then showed me the kitchen. I complimented her on her choices and said how nice her house looked.

"Want something to drink?" she asked.

Surprisingly, I was very dry-mouthed right then, and I was not sure all of it had to do with the heat of the day. I was, frankly, a little nervous.

"What's your pleasure?" Theresa said.

"You know, just a Diet Coke or bottle of water would be great right now," I said. Trying to keep it light, I said, "It looks like you and I got some sun today," referring to our pink cheeks and her shoulders.

"Go have a seat on the couch and I will bring it to you," she said.

Theresa brought a bottle of water and then put it on the end table by the couch as she sat on my lap. This got my full attention. "Can I ask a question?" she said. "When am I going to get my turn with you? I have been patient. I haven't pushed you, but when are you going to give me a chance with you?"

I didn't respond verbally, but looked into her green eyes as she leaned forward. I grabbed a handful of red hair and started kissing her. It was the signal she was waiting for and she went into full attack mode. She leaned into me and brought her legs up onto the couch. After several passionate, deep kisses, she said, "Give me a try, I think you will really like what you find. I think we would be great together."

She then took my hand and cupped it on her breast and said, "I am here for you, waiting patiently. You can have me any time you want to."

We kissed again and I rubbed her all over her body before pulling back and saying, "Sorry, I am a little mixed up right now."

"Don't be sorry, Tom," Theresa said. "I know you have to leave now, but just come back soon. Finish what you started here this afternoon."

I helped her off of my lap and she stood just inches in front of me as I arose from the couch. She put her arms around my neck and kissed me softly again. "When you get done playing with the girls and are ready for a woman, come back," she said.

Theresa followed me to the door. "Please think about me and about what I said," she said coyly as she looked at me through her open doorway.

"I will, Theresa," I said. "Thanks for a nice afternoon."

"It was my pleasure," she said as I started down her walkway towards the car.

"Hey, you," she called. When I turned around, she said, "I love your car."

I smiled and got into the car and drove away as she looked longingly out the door.

My mind was reeling as I made my way out of her neighborhood and drove to my house to quickly change. I was in shock. Wow, what came over me? After all of our dancing around for years, Theresa and I had finally laid our cards on the table. At least she had. I felt like I was unable to think. It is like, during the last hour or so, my systems had kicked into an involuntary shutdown and I was still in the "rebooting" process to restore my functionality. What just happened here?

As I pulled into my driveway and hurried into the house, I was sweating profusely. I never did get that drink. We got distracted—to say the very least. I was now trying to reset and get ready to be with Erika. I had some real thinking to do about where I was headed. There were definitely choices to be made.

I would really need to decide. Many men would try to have both, I suppose. I was wired towards being a "one-woman man." I never considered not being faithful to Liz. Now peculiarly, I was being wracked with guilt as I changed clothes. I felt like I was cheating on Erika. My mind was a muddle when I left the house and drove downtown.

One stray thought popped into my mind. "Is it the car?" Maybe it is. Maybe this is why I wasn't cut out to be a Porsche owner. I might lack the stamina. Is it really an aphrodisiac? Maybe that is why they cost so much.

What I thought would be a peaceful, stress-free afternoon had suddenly caused my life to go a little topsy-turvy. While I was still in this state, I noticed that it was after five o'clock and I was jumping into the heavy traffic, which stood between me and meeting Erika. Just then my cell phone rang. It was Erika.

"Hey, I am running a little late," I said. "I got kind of hung up."

Erika said, "What's the plan?"

I said I was heading back into the city and could be in front of her office in ten to fifteen minutes. I continued to battle my way through the traffic.

When I saw Erika, she said, "I thought you were just going to the game, I didn't know you were going home."

"I guess I didn't either, but I got pretty hot and sweaty at the game and decided to go change."

"You had a great day for sure," she said. "Should we head over towards Twenty-Third Street, get a parking spot, and then catch a restaurant there? Parking is always a nightmare there. Then we could just walk to the theatre on Twenty-First Street."

"Good idea," I said as I was trying to get re-engaged and clear my head.

"Is something wrong?" Erika said. "You seem a little stressed or quiet or something."

"I guess it was just sitting out in the sun and then battling the traffic back to Beaverton or something."

"Well, just chill, you are with me now and I will take good care of you, I promise. Are you excited about this tonight?"

"I am," I said. "I can't wait." I could tell, and I think Erika could tell, that I wasn't myself. I suddenly had a lot on my mind. I looked at Erika and smiled. It helped reorient me when I looked into the face I loved and was the recipient of her warm smile.

"I am so glad to be with you," I said. "I have missed you."

"That is very nice. I just saw you about eight hours ago, but I am glad you missed me," she said.

My affirmation of affection for Erika seemed to start getting me resettled after the afternoon encounter. How could I ever leave Erika? If I had never met Erika and had that moment of passion at Theresa's house this afternoon, we would be starting a torrid love affair, which would end who knows where. I really don't think Theresa is a slut or anything. I find her very attractive and sexy. I appreciate now what it is like to be fifty years old and single. I certainly know what it is like to be lonely. You need to go after the opportunities that are before you. I believe that was all she was doing this afternoon.

She is a very desirable woman and probably an incredible lover. These thoughts were racing through my mind as I looked blankly into Erika's lovely face as she told me about her day over dinner. I felt oddly disconnected and was trying to re-establish contact. I was gulping the ice water but I could still taste Theresa in my mouth.

After the waiter brought the food and interrupted Erika's chatter, she said, "Is anything wrong? You don't seem to be your usual self. Are you okay?"

"I am," I said. "I'm sorry. I need to just kind of clear my head and start enjoying my favorite thing—being with you. I will try to kick in here and be someone you want to be with."

"You always are," Erika said.

"So how incredible is it to see *Casablanca* on the big screen tonight?" I asked in a feeble attempt to refocus. I clearly had some thinking to do. However, I was going to try to put that all away and focus on my evening with Erika for now.

Another pleasant topic popped into my head. "Just think, Erika," I said, "next Friday night, we will be on our way to the beach house. I sure hope it is a day like today."

"Me too," she said. "I can't wait."

On Saturday, Erika had big plans with the Goddesses for a "girls day out." I basically had a weekend ahead by myself. This came at an interesting time, as my mind was still in a muddle about the events of Friday. I had some catching up to do with several people. I did go see John and took him for the promised Porsche ride and bought him lunch.

I called Alan in San Francisco and told him about my new purchase. He was really excited and wanted me to e-mail pictures immediately. Alan and I used to go to the car show every fall at the Coliseum together. It was one of our favorite father-son activities, especially when he was a teenager. I suggested he come up for the weekend in the fall and we could drive the Porsche to the car show. He thought that was an awesome idea and was going to try to work it out. Alan was dealing with the fallout from beginning a career at a large law firm, where the new lawyers were largely slave-labor working long hours.

I dropped by my mom's house to check on her. Her reaction to my new Porsche was predictable. She said, "It is a cute little car but seems very impractical." No kidding. Then she seemed to be under the impression that she was pointing out something I had not yet noticed: "You know, dear, this car doesn't even have a backseat. How will you haul things?" I asked her if she wanted to take a ride and she said, "There will be time for that later, I know you are probably busy today." Try to contain your enthusiasm. Saturday's check list—go see Mom—check, mission accomplished.

One thing I was looking forward to on this sunny Saturday was cleaning my Porsche in my driveway in a conspicuous way, so that my neighbors and friends, Jerry and Shelly, would notice. I didn't think they knew about the new car yet. Each Saturday, Jerry went through a weekly ritual, regardless of the weather, of cleaning and practically sterilizing his cars and Harleys in the driveway. I took great pleasure when I returned from my errands and saw Jerry look up, standing transfixed, with a sponge in one hand and water running from a hose in the other, when he saw my car.

I called Michelle. We probably had a lot to talk about. After exchanging small talk and asking about Rob and the girls, Michelle got down to business. "Grandma tells me you are dating again. She said it was some really young girl."

"Good ol' Grandma," I said. "Did she tell you the 'girl' was over eighteen?"

"What?" Michelle asked.

"Never mind, I knew she would give a distorted picture. She has a flair for dramatic presentation, you know," I offered.

"Well, she is getting old and is concerned about you," she said.

I can't imagine the spin Michelle gets in these conversations with Mom. "Well, here is what is really going on. I have met a woman. We are just having some fun together—going to movies, out to dinner, and things like that. She is younger than me, but we are just having fun. It is really great to be having some fun again, and I am tired of being lonely, Michelle."

"I know, Dad," she said. "I am glad to hear you are getting out. I know you have been through a lot. Grandma says this woman is younger than me. Is that true?"

"No, that is not true. She is in her thirties, but the relationship isn't any more than I just said. We haven't even known each other that long."

It was quiet for a moment and I decided on a diversionary tactic.

"Guess what I did?" I said.

"What?"

"I got a new car."

"You got rid of your car or got a second car?"

"I traded my car for a used Porsche Boxster that this guy I work with was selling," I said.

"You got a Porsche?"

"Yeah, it is so much fun."

Michelle pulled the receiver away from her mouth and yelled to Rob, "Dad bought a Porsche."

Michelle came back on and said, "Rob says you are awesome."

"Tell Rob thanks and to keep telling his wife how awesome I am," I said.

Michelle summarized, "So you have a girlfriend and a Porsche."

"Well, yeah," I said. "Is it disturbing to you to find out that I am an actual functioning person?"

"No, Dad, you know that is not what I meant," she said.

"I am having some fun again, and I did something out of the norm for me, and it feels kind of good," I said.

"Good for you, Dad. So when are we going to see you again?"

"Well, it kind of looks like I might have a business trip to Denver in the late summer or early fall. I am thinking I could extend it and spend some time with your family. Then are you guys still coming for Thanksgiving this year?" I asked.

"Yeah, we are planning on it. Sounds like you are pretty busy," Michelle replied.

"Well, I promise I will try to do better staying in touch. I have just been doing a lot of adjusting to my new life. I still really miss your mother."

"I know, Dad. Oh, Rob says e-mail pictures of the car."

Saturday night came, and I found myself missing Erika after only twenty-four hours. It seems silly but I really felt a need to see her. My thoughts were never far away from Theresa either. I wondered what I should do. Ignoring the situation and not taking some definitive action was not an option.

I have to admit that I also thought of Theresa physically. It preyed on my mind knowing that two miles away, there was a smoldering redhead, who had literally told me "come and get it." I could knock on her door and immediately rip her clothes off and have "rock-star, Hollywood fantasy sex" with a very attractive woman. It had been a long time. That was hard to resist. I did not want a one-night stand with Theresa. I cared about her and myself more than that. I also sensed that Theresa would not take well to being treated in that manner. If you tried to make Theresa a one-night stand, I am not sure what the results would be. I was certain it would not be pretty nor would she go quietly away.

Then there was Erika, the woman I deeply love. She is the woman who is the total object of my desire and hopes, the woman who makes me come alive with a simple smile or a gentle touch. Would she ever become my lover? Would she ever want me? I didn't know what my odds were. However, I couldn't imagine not having her in my life.

The house phone rang while I was deep in thought on these matters. I hoped it was Erika, asking me to meet her for dinner. As I ran to the phone, it occurred to me that Erika always called me on my cell phone.

"Hello," I said.

"Hi, Tom—it's Theresa."

"Hey, Theresa, how are you?"

"Okay, I guess. I have been fighting the urge all day. I can't stop thinking about yesterday. I wanted to hear your voice again, so I finally gave in."

"It was very nice yesterday, Theresa, and believe me, I have been thinking a lot about it too."

"You have? I am very glad to hear that."

"Yes, I want you to know that I take the things you have said very seriously, Theresa. I do care about you. I just need to work through a lot of things right now before I can talk to you about it."

"It can be so good, Tom. You know where I live and my door is always open to you. I am here for you, without restraints or reservations."

"I know. Just give me a little more time to work this out, okay?"

"Okay, but don't wait too long. We have already missed a lot of good times together. I can make you very happy, Tom. All I ask is that you give me a chance to show you how good it can be."

Just then, my cell phone rang. The screen was flashing "Erika."

"I will talk to you soon, Theresa, I promise."

"Okay, good-bye, have a good weekend, and think of me," she concluded.

I rushed to pick up my cell phone.

Erika said, "I almost gave up on you."

"I was on the other line trying to end the conversation before I lost you."

"Checking on Mom or the kids, were you?" she said.

"Yeah, I have had all kinds of calls today," I said.

"I was wondering … have you had dinner and would you like some company?"

"I haven't eaten and I could use an 'Erika fix,'" I said.

Chapter 13

BEACH WEEKEND

FINALLY, FRIDAY arrived and Erika and I were going to have our getaway. The beach house, which I had inherited, had been in Liz's family for three generations. Liz was an only child and it became her beach house after the death of her parents. It had always been an important part of our family and part of our children's legacy. It took on special significance to Alan and Michelle after the death of their mother. Michelle always referred to it as "my mother's beach house." I tried to not take offense at that but it made me feel like an illegitimate heir.

I had used the beach house several times on weekends since Liz's death. I had gone alone on weekends when I needed to get away from the loneliness of my house. I had also taken some days off during the week occasionally and went to the beach house to not only recharge my batteries but to try to find peace in some of my darkest hours. It was a place of solace and tranquility to me.

As the spring weather gave way to some beautiful early summer days, I wanted to share the beach house with Erika. I always tried to read the signals she sent me about our relationship. I seemed to sense its fragile nature. I did not want to push too far too early and make Erika uncomfortable.

Erika was excited about going to the beach house, and I wanted to go for a whole weekend, not just for the day. The purchase of the Porsche had only increased her enthusiasm … and mine too.

We had some memorable days together, and she seemed comfortable with the concept of "sleepovers," which allowed us to spend more time together but retire to separate bedrooms each night. I didn't want Michelle to find out I had taken another woman to "her mother's beach house."

After our Valentine's Day dinner, we seemed to set the outline for our relationship to begin. We began by seeing each other regularly at Starbucks to begin the day. Usually, we tried to meet for lunch some time midweek. Then we started to meet one weekend day or night for an outing together. Usually it was dinner and a movie. However, things had progressed to the point that we both wanted more time together.

I gave Erika some background about the beach house. It was located about two hours from Portland in the beautiful coastal town of Lincoln City. The beach was beautiful there and my house was on a slight rise, right on the beach. There was a deck off of the back, wonderful for sitting outside or having a meal. A short three steps down off of the deck, and you were standing on the beach.

It had one large bedroom, which Liz and I had traditionally used as "our" bedroom and two smaller guest bedrooms. The back half of the house was all windows, with a terrific view of the beach. In the past, we had even seen migrating whales passing by from the living room windows.

I picked up Erika at her condo Friday after work, she threw her small suitcase into the trunk of the Porsche, and we were off for a weekend at the beach house. I was thrilled that I would have the chance to share this with her.

"Are you psyched to drive your new car to the beach?"

"Oh, yeah," I said. "New cars are a major turn-on for guys. Did I tell you the theory about women's perfume I heard?"

"No, but I can't wait," Erika said.

"Well, I saw a comedian on TV who said women always have perfumes that smell like things women like. Like flowers."

"Yeah," she said with a skeptical look.

"What they should do if they really want to turn guys on is to have smells men like ... such as the new car smell or a Philly cheesesteak sandwich or something."

She laughed and said, "Philly cheesesteak? Good input, Tom. I will see what Sachs or Nordstrom's has in that department," Erika offered sarcastically, as she shook her head.

As we neared the coast, the sun was beginning to set. I pulled over at a lookout point near Depoe Bay. We were just a few miles from the beach house now but I didn't want to miss this great sunset. We leaned against the hood of the car, taking in the incredible beauty of the Oregon Coast at sunset on sunny days. We just smiled at one another without speaking. Finally, Erika broke the silence by saying, "I think this weekend is going to work."

As we drove into Lincoln City, we stopped at one of my favorite restaurants, then the grocery store for a few supplies. It was late when we pulled into the beach house. Erika said, "Oh, Tom, this is incredible."

"I can't wait to show you this in the daylight," I responded. We got things opened and set up for our weekend. After talking for a while, it was time to go to bed.

Erika put her arms around me and gave me a warm hug. "Thanks for this and thanks for being my friend."

"I find I can't wait to share everything I love with you, Erika," I responded.

She gave me one more squeeze and then said, "Good night," softly.

As I went to bed, my thoughts were completely of Erika. All of the events with Theresa seemed far away and unreal. At this moment, Erika seemed to be worth about ten Theresas. I could try to be objective about Erika, and my chances with her, when I wasn't with her. When I was with Erika, looking into her blue eyes, I was completely mesmerized. She had a narcotic effect on me. She was like a drug that I couldn't quite get out of my system before I took the next injection. All I wanted was Erika. Theresa was probably a much better choice for many reasons, but I couldn't apply logic or reason to my feelings for Erika.

When I first became conscious in the morning, I was immediately excited, knowing I was in the beach house with Erika. I quickly got dressed and opened my bedroom door. I could hear Erika stirring behind her bedroom door. She soon joined me, looking out the window to see the sun was breaking through the early morning overcast.

I looked towards the driveway, and before I could speak, Erika said, "Is it still there?"

"Yeah," I said.

"I was wondering if you were going to drive it into the other bedroom for the night …," she said.

Before responding, I opened the door onto the beach so Erika got her first look at the beach in the daylight.

"Wow, this is going to be so awesome," she said.

"Let's go."

As we walked along, we were struck by the beautiful colors of gray and blues that dotted the landscape before us. The sun was peeking through some clouds, and it made the wet sand and water luminescent.

It was a moment of incredible solitude and serenity for both of us. It was as if we were the only two people in the world. There were a few people on the beach, but any noise was obscured by the waves—the ultimate white noise. The only sounds I could hear were my own voice or Erika's. There is something extraordinary about walking on a beach with someone you care about and neither of you are talking. There seems to be communication on a different level other than verbal when that happens.

I broke the silence and said, "It doesn't get better than this. Thank you so much for coming with me, it really means a lot to me."

"Let's just savor this," she said, "I want to remember this moment."

"Me too, but I am open to repeats on this weekend, any time you want," I said. I don't remember the last time I felt this happy, to be at my favorite place with someone I was starting to feel I could not be without.

We walked silently, side by side, but it felt like we were joined in spirit.

I saw a couple walking together out onto a sand bar exposed at the lower tide, which was under way. I asked, "Have you ever read about the riptides or 'sneaker waves' on the Oregon coast?"

She said she had heard that they can be bad but didn't recall any specifics.

As I watched the couple walking to the end of the sand bar jutting out into the surf, I told Erika a story I read about a honeymoon couple. The honeymooners were standing, embracing on a rocky outcrop, and were hit by a sneaker wave. They were both knocked down, and when the tide receded, the woman was gone, washed out to sea, and the man could not find her.

"Oh, my God," Erika said, "that is totally sad."

"I am always struck by the seemingly randomness of life. Sometimes, your only mistake is being in the wrong place at the wrong time. You can be doing nothing wrong and suddenly your life is changed or it is gone," I said. "Then there are people who are reckless and careless and they seem to get away with it. When I hear of a major car accident on the traffic report or see one, I think, there is a person who didn't expect their day to turn out this way."

Erika said, "I have thought of that, and I can see why you might think about that from time to time, after what you have experienced."

Then she added, "It always seems that when there is an accident, it totally makes people feel better if someone was negligent or doing something they are not supposed to do."

I told Erika about a fifty-three-year-old man who suddenly dropped dead in our office one day. It was very tragic. Then I added, "You know what disturbed me about this? I started hearing comments about the poor guy who had the heart attack. People said, 'Well, he always was kind of overweight.' So they were explaining it away because it was too terrifying to think that any of us could suddenly drop dead also."

I added, "There needs to be some circumstances to blame, then we feel better. That is because randomness freaks us out really badly. I can't control randomness. You are right, if someone was breaking the rules and then was killed, then it feels like they deserved it somehow."

She said, "The poor honeymoon couple was probably doing something several people do each day, but for some reason they paid the price for it."

"Exactly," I said. "When I go to work each day, there are probably three or four ways that I can get to downtown Portland. Sometimes I switch routes because I hear a traffic report. Then occasionally, I just turn instead of going straight, for some reason I do not know. I just decided to go a different way that day. Maybe it is boredom from always doing things the same way. I sometimes wonder when I do that if I am potentially avoiding an accident on my usual route. Is it fate? Is it intuition? Is everything just a toss of the coin? Who knows?"

"It is funny that you are mentioning this because I have thought about this as well. I didn't know anyone else thought this way," Erika said. "If I couldn't find my keys and dropped my papers, I could be running five minutes late and either avoid or be involved in an accident. What if Liz had been five minutes or even two minutes late that day?"

As I thought about her words, Erika quickly added, "I am sorry, I shouldn't have said that."

"No, you are absolutely right. I spent most of the last two years wondering the same thing," I said. "There is no offense taken. Liz wasn't running two minutes late that day, and now my life is on a different path than it would have been otherwise."

"It makes you think, we should spend more time enjoying the moments we do have and not worrying so much about all of the 'what-ifs,'" Erika said.

"I agree, and I think knowing you has helped me to do that," I said.

"Knowing me? How has that helped you?"

"Erika, I realize I have spent too much of my life being fearful of what comes next. But you, you have such a sense of freedom and fun. You are liberating me."

"I am amazed to hear you say that. I don't feel like I have my act together at all," she said. "That is what I find interesting about you: how much you have overcome and accomplished in your life."

"I am trying to let go of my fears and start enjoying all that life offers again," I said.

"Do you know what I think is remarkable about you?"

I said, "No, but anytime things like that pop into your mind, please pass them on."

She gently slugged my arm and said, "I enjoy talking with you more than any person I have ever known."

I gave no response and just smiled at her.

"Isn't it beautiful now?" Erika said, pointing to the beach. "This is a moment when I feel all of the outside pressures are gone and it is just two people who enjoy being together."

"Speaking of random moments," I said, "just think if you had not spilled your purse in the rain at the precise moment I walked by. I might still be just checking you out each morning at the coffee shop. I might have never had the courage to talk to you, and I certainly wouldn't be walking on the beach with you now. There were several unusual things occurring the morning we met. I went the dentist and parked where I usually did not park. You were late because you were picking up your materials that morning, and you parked where you usually do not park. Things could have easily happened a different way, and we would have never met."

"Good, my klutziness has made this moment possible," Erika said. "Were you really checking me out each morning in the coffee shop?"

"I am not so old that I don't notice women like you walking into a room," I said. She just laughed.

We said nothing more, just drank in the beauty and tranquility, as we turned and headed back down the beach towards the house.

"Tonight," she announced as we approached the beach house, "it is my pleasure to cook you my special treat to show appreciation for giving me this wonderful weekend."

"You cook?" I said. "I have never pictured you anywhere but a restaurant."

"Keep it up," she said, "and you will be in a restaurant tonight."

"Sorry, what can I do?"

"I brought most things I need in my bag. Just go get some good French bread and pick out a good bottle of wine, and I will take care of the rest. It should be done just in time to take in the sunset while we eat."

I got to my car and headed to the nearby grocery store. My mind was reeling as I left the beach house. I was in the midst of one of the great weekends of my life. The weather had turned out perfectly, or good enough for the Oregon coast. My early apprehension about going "away" with Erika was disappearing, and we were totally relaxed in one another's presence, just like we were in our life in the city.

I have never felt so natural with another human being. It made me feel guilty to even think that, because I loved Liz for most of my life and still did. However, it was nevertheless true. I don't think I had ever felt this way. It was late afternoon on Saturday. We still had Saturday night and all of Sunday before heading back to the city.

What else might happen this weekend? More importantly, what did I want to happen? What did Erika want to happen? Another question was, why do I always have to ask so many questions? She was probably in the beach house being extremely happy, preparing a meal for her friend and enjoying the moment. I was missing the moment by being angst-ridden about what will happen next. All of this seemed to totally obscure my "Theresa problem." But in the back of my mind, I knew it still existed.

As I returned from the store, it gave me great pleasure to think that Erika was waiting for me in my beach house. I would try to relax and enjoy the wonderful ride I was having.

She was all smiles when I returned and approved of my wine selection. Everything smelled good, and she had scrounged up the things she needed to set a nice table just outside the door, where we could eat and watch the sunset.

We touched our glasses in a toast "to a wonderful weekend at the beach."

"Thank you so much for this," I said. "It has brought me true joy to share this with you."

"My pleasure," Erika said. "It just keeps getting better." I agreed, then I sought some reassurance and perhaps overreached.

"Erika," I said, "what is 'it' to you?" She seemed puzzled by the question.

I said, "I mean, you said it keeps getting better, I just wondered how you define what we are experiencing."

She said, "Why does it have to be defined? Why do we need to label it?

Just as we have talked about, age is just a number someone assigns to us. Some people think those numbers put us in boxes, and sometimes there shouldn't be interaction between the boxes. Those numbers have nothing to do with who we are. The labels on the nature of our relationship have no meaning unless we give them meaning," she said. "Why can't we just enjoy what we have, and what it becomes, it becomes?"

I just let it go and nodded my head.

"Is something on your mind? It seems like you have been troubled by something. Have I done something wrong?" she asked.

"No, I am not unhappy; in fact, I can truly say I have never been happier," I said.

"Then relax and enjoy what we have," Erika said with a smile.

I smiled and tried to change the subject. We sat alone and talked about a variety of things, stopping to comment on the perpetually changing and gorgeous sight of the waves and setting sun.

Finally, I said, "You know, they can't make us go home. If you sold your condo and I sold my house, we could live here a really long time on that money." She just laughed and hugged me.

"I hate to see this day end," she said.

"Me too," I said.

Later, as we departed for bed, she hugged me and thanked me for being so kind to her and then closed her door. I went to my bedroom and got in bed and began reading a book to take my mind off of her. After I turned out the light, I replayed the day in my mind and the flood of feelings I had for her during this marvelous, peaceful day.

I also must admit that I pictured scenes from movies I had seen. The man and woman started out in separate bedrooms, and in the middle of the night, she crawled into his bed because she was cold. Or the woman became frightened and wondered if she could sleep with the man. Or the woman could no longer fight the feelings of overwhelming lust and decided to join the man in bed in the middle of the night. Then I wondered what I would do if one of those scenes were acted out in real life tonight. These were my thoughts as I drifted off to sleep. Her door remained closed all night.

In the morning, I awoke and wandered out into the house to find Erika. Her door was open but she was not in the house. I walked out of the door and saw her standing alone by the surf. I walked out to meet her. As I walked, I reminded myself that I had to get a grip on myself and just be her friend today or I would mess up this weekend, the perfect weekend in the making.

She turned and smiled and said good morning. I said that she looked happy. Erika said, "Now this is the way to begin a day, walk out the door to the beach, right out of bed."

I said I could not agree more.

"Hope the clouds part a little and we have another great day," I said. "You know, this is going to be a great day regardless."

"Totally," Erika said. "No Blackberrys today, no contact with the outside world, just us, okay?"

"Agreed."

It was another day of incredible peace and tranquility. Long walks on the beach and long talks. As we left, the sun was starting to lower on the horizon again. I said, "This doesn't have to be our last weekend ever at this house. We can come anytime you want." Erika said she could easily be persuaded to come back.

The tranquility of the weekend continued as we drove through the forest of beautiful fir trees, headed back to Portland. The quiet music and quiet talk were shattered as we passed the Indian-owned casino and Erika said, "Pull over; we have to stop here before we go home."

I pulled over but was thinking that this was the last thing I wanted to do.

"You want to gamble now?" I said.

She said, "I can't drive by this place without stopping to throw down some money."

"Your clients at the investment firm would love to hear their broker talking like this," I said.

Erika said, "I keep telling you, I am not a broker." I was trying to be spontaneous and to not seem like an old guy who was worried about beating the traffic home, but I did not want to do this.

I got a small stack of chips and decided to go to the roulette table. It was more interesting than standing by, mindlessly dropping money into a slot machine. I did this to kill some time while Erika flitted around, doing whatever it was she had to do before we went home. I was hoping this would be a short stop.

It took me a moment to get reoriented to roulette and what was going on at the table. I was trying to remember about splitting the bets and other nuances of the game as if I was actually going to win anything. Maybe if I lost quickly, Erika would let me go home.

Suddenly behind me, she bounded into me and said, "Put all of these on Red 13."

"Are you crazy?" I said.

"Come on, hurry and do it."

I put all of our chips on Red 13. The dealer called, "Red 13." Erika let out a blood-curdling scream and jumped into my arms.

"That is the most incredible thing I have ever seen," I said.

"I always bet Red 13 and always win," she said. I was stunned.

"We can go now," she said, still laughing hysterically at her luck and my facial expression.

As we walked out, she spotted the karaoke machine in the bar. "Karaoke!" she shouted and started tugging on my arm.

"Oh, no, Erika, I will do anything in the world for you except this," I said. "I can't begin to tell you how much I loathe karaoke."

"Come on, I will help you, it will be fun," she said.

"Erika, I can't even sing in the shower, and singing in public is my worst nightmare. I have never begged you for anything but I am begging you now."

"We are not leaving until you sing with me," she retorted. I walked onto the platform with two chairs and microphones. Fortunately, there was virtually no one in the bar.

"Just watch the screen and get ready," she said. The first song was "Love Shack" by the B-52s. She laughed as I fell about three lines behind and stopped.

"I hate this song, and it is too fast for me to sing," I said. Erika said she would pick another one that would work for me.

It was "Friends in Low Places" by Garth Brooks, which was slower and had a lot of bass. I was equally horrible and finally dropped the microphone. Erika laughed hysterically.

"You are the worst person I have ever seen doing karaoke. It is amazing for someone who likes music like you do," she said as she continued to laugh. "You were amazingly bad," she cackled.

"Thanks, give it to me straight, I can take it, don't feel like you need to hold back."

Erika was laughing uncontrollably and telling me how funny I was.

"Didn't I beg and plead with you?" I said.

"Let me show you how this is to be done, sir," she said.

I sat in the chair and she grabbed the mike. The song "I Am So Into You" by the Atlanta Rhythm Section began. I always recalled it being kind of a dopey song from the seventies. My feelings about that song were about to change.

Erika switched into another gear. She stood in front of my chair and started swaying to the opening bars of the music. She locked her eyes intently on mine. She never lost eye contact with me, and she never blinked.

She began dancing gracefully as she began to sing. I was getting the full treatment, Erika hitting on all cylinders and dancing seductively. She never stopped staring into my eyes, and her long dark hair hung to each side of her beautiful face. It seemed her eyes were high-beam headlights shining on my face and into my eyes. Her long thin body was incredibly graceful, and she was a great dancer.

She continued singing, "Gonna love you all over. Over and over..." This was the non-platonic Erika on full display. It was the sexiest thing I had ever seen. I was actually beginning to perspire, and my heart was racing. This woman was smokin'. I had never been on the receiving end of anything like this. Even last Friday.

Erika moved close to my face, with her eyes fixed on mine, leaning over, stroking my face with her hands, and finishing the lyrics. Her voice trailed off, and she laughed as the music concluded. "Now that's how you do karaoke."

All I could say for a few moments was, "That was incredible!"

"Thank you, I hope you enjoyed it," Erika said as she took a little bow in front of my chair.

"You have changed my opinion of karaoke and the Atlanta Rhythm Section forever," I said. "I suppose you are going to tell me that you think that was better than my Garth Brooks?"

She laughed and said, "You are so cute and a good sport."

Erika grabbed my arm and we began to walk out of the casino. She was teasing me and just having fun. However, I would never forget the way she looked at me and how it made me feel. I don't know if she felt something or not, but I felt like I had a laser beam shot through my body into the core of my soul. Just being her friend was going to be more difficult.

It was like I had been given a little pinch of a love drug that produced incredible hallucinations, and it was quickly gone and I couldn't have any more. Now we were supposed to go back to being "buddies."

I had many things to work out when we returned to the city. I didn't know what would happen or how it would play out. At this moment, my tendency was that I was about to put all of my chips on Erika. I had never seen Erika like this. Could it be the car?

Chapter 14

A FORK IN THE ROAD

As a new week started, I was still basking in the afterglow of my weekend at the beach house with Erika. It was beyond my expectations. Now there was the Theresa problem to deal with. I don't know if I viewed it as a problem or more like a dilemma.

I decided to not stir the pot anymore and just let things and emotions "simmer" a little. That can be an attractive strategy when you are trying to avoid conflict. I have found it often turns out to be just wishful thinking, hoping that somehow the dilemma before you will dissipate. This week would add more evidence to support that theory.

My week progressed on schedule. On Wednesday, Erika and I met for lunch together as usual. I am not sure what she did the rest of the week. I think Erika often grabbed some food and returned to her desk to eat her lunch and keep working. My routine was to go running. I would then grab something at the cafeteria, as I returned, and take it to my desk to eat a belated lunch as I resumed work.

On Thursday morning, my desk phone rang, and I noticed on the digital panel that it was Theresa. The temptation to let it go through to voice mail was significant, but on the final ring, I picked it up and said hello.

"How was your weekend?" Theresa asked.

"Very nice, how about yours?" I said.

"It was beautiful weather but I was a little lonely I guess," she said.

Here we go, I thought.

"Can we meet for lunch today and chat?" Theresa inquired.

My mind raced for a plausible excuse and then, after an uncomfortable silence, I responded, "Sure."

"You were hesitating; are you sure?" Theresa pressed.

I was starting to get slightly annoyed at being pressed. "I wasn't hesitating, Theresa, I was just mentally going through my schedule. No problem."

"Good," she said. "Want to just meet around the corner at that sandwich place at Fifth and Salmon?"

I agreed and then she said, "I will get a table for us."

About 11:45, I walked to the sandwich shop. It is a large open room with lots of tables. It does land-rush business on work days at lunchtime. Fast, good sandwiches and lots of tables. Theresa is always easy to spot with her mane of bright red hair. For the record, I love her hair.

"It is good to see you," she said, rising from the chair to give me a hug.

"Nice to see you too," I said. "Have you ordered yet?"

"No, of course, I was waiting for you," she said. "We should probably get our order in to beat the crowd."

"If you want to hold the table, I will do our order, okay?"

"Perfect," she said. "Just get me the turkey on wheat with no mayo and a Diet Coke."

"You got it," I said, trying to be light and cheery. Meanwhile, I was wracking my brain for a strategy about what I would say to her.

Just as I was getting out of my chair, to my absolute horror, Erika and her friend Jenna came in the door. Apparently, Erika and Jen were meeting for lunch today. Our eyes met and I am sure my face registered my shock and horror at the sudden crisis. As Erika and Jen made their way to a table, Erika said, "Tom, what a surprise," as her eyes moved to Theresa at the nearby table. "What's up?" she asked.

"I need to explain all of this. I am kind of in a weird spot right now. This woman is putting some pressure on me and I was trying to resolve some problems ...," I said as I fumbled for the right words. As I turned to shoot a glance towards Theresa, I noticed there was no one sitting at my table. Theresa had left.

"Where did she go?" Erika said.

"I have no idea," I said, now completely at sea as to my next move. The delicate matter I was trying to handle discreetly may have just erupted into a bloody, full-blown conflict.

"Want to join us for lunch, Tom?" Jen said.

"Uh, I guess my ... I don't know ... no, I don't want to intrude on your girls lunch," I stammered for some response.

"You are never an intrusion, we love you, Tom," Jen said.

"Yeah, come on," Erika said. "You alright?"

"I don't know," I said. "This woman I work with was upset, and I was meeting her for lunch to try to resolve things. Apparently, when I started talking to you, she got upset and split, I guess."

"Wow, psycho chick!" Jen said.

"Yeah," I said.

Erika said, "Join us. Jen and I will go get you lunch while you relax, okay?"

"Yeah, thanks. I will take whatever you are having, Erika."

"Isn't he awesome?" Erika said to Jen.

"Well, apparently not everyone would agree," I said.

"Yeah, like psycho chicks," Jen repeated.

Jen and Erika returned with the sandwiches and began to chatter. Meanwhile, my mind was going 100 miles per hour. I started picturing jilted girlfriends with large knives and a "psycho chick" keying my Porsche. I realized this was a major overreaction and a result of brain damage from seeing too many movies. However, I was really puzzled by what seemed to be an extreme reaction by Theresa.

As my mind was racing, trying to think what would happen next, Erika put her hand on my knee and flashed her blue eyes at me. "Are you okay?" she asked.

I realized I had not said anything since Erika and Jen returned with the sandwiches. "Sorry, ladies, I am just trying to figure out what went wrong here."

"You are too nice and sweet, and if someone doesn't like you, they must be a total witch," Jen said.

"You have always been my favorite among Erika's friends, Jen," I said in an attempt at humor.

Both of them laughed and Erika added, "Jen is right. What's up with her?"

"I will explain later. I am sure there will be more to the story by the end of the day," I said.

Erika looked concerned but moved on.

As our lunch broke up, Jen hugged me and said, "Good luck, sweet man. Don't let the crazy lady get you."

Erika gave me a concerned look.

"Will you meet me after work so I can fill you in?" I offered.

"I will walk down and meet you in front of your building. You can give me a ride home, and we can talk," Erika offered. "Good luck this afternoon."

As I walked back to the office, my distress was turning to anger. What kind of stunt was that? It told me a lot. What, were we in junior high or something? This kind of craziness negates any thoughts of attraction and affection.

When I got back to my office, I had a pretty good head of steam. I immediately called Theresa. She didn't answer. I left a simple and clear message: "What the hell was that all about? Why did you do that? I want to talk to you as soon as possible."

About 2 PM, I went to the bathroom and subsequently missed her call. There was a message when I returned. It was Theresa. "I am sorry, Tom. I handled that badly. I overreacted. I don't know why I did that. Please meet me in the enclave on the seventh floor. It is just after 2, I will be waiting for you."

Geez, this woman has a flair for the dramatic. What if I had a two-hour meeting starting at 2, would she sit there waiting? Our office building has a series of enclaves, or small conference rooms, ringing the inside of the building's core. Each enclave could accommodate about four to six people and is generally used for small meetings and private conversations. Dealing with jilted lovers was not part of the original intent, but it sufficed for that purpose as well. Each enclave is all frosted-glass from floor to ceiling. It allows for privacy but also lets in natural light from the outside windows.

Because of the frosted glass, it is impossible to tell who is in an enclave unless the door is open. If the lights are on, it is assumed to be occupied. I told our receptionist that I had a meeting on the seventh floor and headed for the elevator. Once on the seventh floor, I began walking around the floor, searching for the enclave where Theresa was supposedly waiting. This was the floor where Theresa worked, so she must be nearby.

Finally, I found her sitting alone with the door of an enclave open. I entered and closed the door. "Well?" I said.

"Are you upset with me, Tom?"

"What do you think?"

"I shouldn't have done that, and I am sorry. I was meeting you over lunch to talk about us. When I saw you with Erika, I assumed that was my answer. It was obvious that you felt very uncomfortable being with me when she entered. You seemed very afraid she would see us together. As you talked with her, I thought, I guess I have my answer, so why stay and discuss it?"

"What I am uncomfortable with is you pulling an immature stunt like that and running out on me. This didn't exactly endear you to me."

"Tom, I am so, so sorry. I lost my head and did something stupid."

"Well, since you presumed we had nothing to talk about—what do we have to talk about now, besides how pissed off I am at you?"

Theresa said, "I told you I am sorry. I wish I could take it back. Could we calm down and have a talk now?"

I just looked at her and said nothing.

"Tom, you said you had been thinking about me when I talked to you. Is there any way I can have a chance with you? Are you going to give me a chance to prove how good we could be together?"

It was now easier to have this conversation and be tough with her. "Theresa, I am in a relationship with Erika now. We are just beginning and she means a great deal to me. I am sorry."

"So my timing is off again."

"If that is how you want to put it, I guess it is. Theresa, I do care about you. After we spent that afternoon together, I really was tempted to come back to your house, believe me. I have more respect and affection for you than to take advantage of you in that way. I didn't want to be your lover if I didn't intend to begin a serious relationship with you."

"I appreciate that, Tom. I know Erika is pretty and young, but I think I am a better fit for you. Do you really have a future with her?"

"Theresa, I love Erika. She has changed my life. I am willing to let our relationship develop. There are no guarantees in life. But we fall in love with who we fall in love with. I didn't think it would happen, but it did. Logic has nothing to do with it. This isn't a business deal. I love her."

"I don't need any instruction on falling in love with the wrong person," Theresa countered. "I have fallen in love with a man I can't seem to get to notice me. But I love him anyway. I have tried to wait and hoped you noticed me. Believe me; I know what it is like to have your heart broken by the person you love."

"I am sorry, Theresa," I said. "I never wanted to hurt you. Quite the opposite. You are a beautiful, desirable woman. It is … like you said, I guess … bad timing."

I got up to leave and moved towards the door.

"Wait," she said as she moved towards me.

I saw red flags being raised everywhere. "Theresa!" I warned. "We need to be very careful in here." Being found on top of a fellow employee in a company conference room is a career-ending mistake. For that matter, being found on top of a non-employee in a company conference room is a career-ending mistake as well.

"Lean against the door so no one can come in," Theresa said.

"Theresa ...," I warned, getting very concerned about her next move.

"I will be careful, Tom." She put her arms around me and gave me a passionate kiss. "I love you, Tom. I am not a crazy lady. I am just getting frustrated. I know I can't make you love me," Theresa said as she pushed her body against mine, pinning me against the door. I put my hands on the back of her head and stroked her hair.

"I *am* sorry," I concluded.

"I am still yours if you want me sometime. I can't wait forever, but I will wait ...," she said as she backed off and started to straighten her clothes.

"Good-bye, Theresa," I said and hurried out the door. I couldn't wait to get this afternoon over with and talk to Erika.

I stood in front of my building and watched down Sixth Avenue for a sign of Erika walking my way. Please God, I thought, please let her get here before I run into Theresa. Then I saw Erika coming. I began walking towards the corner to meet her. She greeted me with a hug and said, "How are you?"

"I am always so glad to see you, but never more so than right now. Let's get out of here."

We made our way towards the parking garage. We climbed into the Porsche, without saying much, and then headed out towards Erika's condo.

"So what was that all about?" Erika said.

"I want to give you some background," I began. I told her about Theresa and of her attempt to supplant Liz a few years ago. Then I told her about the day of the baseball game. I told her about going to Theresa's house, somewhat against my better judgment. I told her about how Theresa sat on my lap and started kissing me and told me to "come and get" her and "finish the job" I began that day.

Erika listened patiently as I told her about the weekend phone call and the pressure she was putting on me. We were now in front of

Erika's condo. I pulled to the curb, shut off the engine, and continued my story.

I told her about Theresa's phone call today and the plan to meet over lunch. "I was struggling with a way to tell her I didn't want to be with her. I even told Theresa that I was in a relationship with a woman that I care about very much."

With that, Erika gave me a warm smile and put her arm around my neck. "Let's go upstairs," she said, "then we can continue this for as long as you need to."

Once inside and seated on the couch together, I continued, "I admit that I freaked when I saw you walk in. I didn't want you to see me having lunch with another woman and get the wrong idea. I clearly panicked and made the situation worse. I guess most men would think I am stupid. They would think I should be with both of you. I didn't want to harm anything with you, and I didn't want to have a thing with Theresa on the side."

"You reacted the way you did, not because you are stupid," Erika began. "You did this because you are honorable and good. I am touched by your loyalty to me. However, know this Tom; you don't ever need to work around me. We can always be honest with one another. Always talk to me."

"I am sorry. I didn't mean to deceive you by any means … I wanted to deal with this and not involve you. I didn't handle it well, I guess," I said.

"You are the best person I have ever met, Tom." With that, Erika put her arms around me and kissed me, on the lips, for the first time. It sent electricity through my body. I suddenly knew the difference between love and lust. A kiss from Theresa aroused my lust. A kiss from Erika touched my soul in a way I could not verbalize.

"Erika, I may regret what I am about to say." This got her undivided attention. "Do you tell people who ask that you are in a relationship … a relationship with me?"

"Of course I do," she said, seemingly taken by surprise. "I tell people I have met a wonderful man and that we are in a relationship that is just beginning."

"Thank you, I just needed a little reassurance I guess," I said.

"Do I frustrate you, Tom?" she asked.

At this point in our discussion about being totally honest, I decided to lie and say, "No, you don't frustrate me."

"I know you have to be patient. I am sorry. Never let my carefulness in our relationship be mistaken for not caring deeply about you," she said. "It is by no means you. It is me. I have been coming out of my own dark time, and I am slowly emerging and trying to remake myself. Fortunately, I have the most patient, sweet man in the world as my partner who lets things develop at the speed I am comfortable with. But never misinterpret this as my lack of caring about you."

"I told Theresa that you are a very important part of my life. You are," I said, and we hugged and kissed again.

"Something you need to know, Erika," I said, which caused her to stop and look very seriously at me. I continued, "You need to know I won't ever lie to you. It is not because I am so honest but I am a terrible liar. I could never lie to Liz because she saw through my attempts immediately. You probably can too."

Erika smiled and said, "I think it is an ideal night for a mellow dinner with my favorite person. How about a quiet atmosphere with some nice wine?"

"What? Didn't you think lunch was fun?" I said.

"You poor guy," Erika said. "Let me go freshen up."

Our evening was as envisioned by Erika. Things would not be the same after tonight. We seemed to break through more barriers. I loved being kissed by Erika.

The week went on without further incident and with no contact from Theresa. Then a great opportunity dropped into my lap, and I couldn't wait to tell Erika. Our company had a luxury box at the Rose Garden. Access to the box was controlled at the vice presidential level in the company. Generally, the box was used for schmoozing customers and courting new clients. However, it was also used to reward employees. I had been on the receiving end of that several times for Trailblazers basketball games and concerts.

I got an e-mail on Friday offering me two luxury box tickets for an upcoming concert at the Rose Garden the following week. The communication came from my vice president, and the tickets were available at his assistant's desk. I immediately jumped on that opportunity. I was going to save them to surprise Erika during our Friday night outing.

When I went to pick her up at her condo, I sprang the surprise. "Have you ever been to the corporate luxury boxes in the Rose Garden?" I asked.

"I am just a humble little financial analyst. I am not a corporate high-flier like you," Erika said.

"Well, your luck just changed. I got two tickets for U2 and Kanye West next weekend."

"Shut up! No way. For real?" she asked, as her large blue eyes got even bigger.

"Oh, yeah," I said.

She hugged me and said, "That is so awesome."

"So you will go with me?"

"Aaah, yeah, unless you had someone else in mind as your companion," she said.

I smiled and she said, "Sorry bad joke. That is so exciting. It will be a great concert."

"Wait until you see these boxes," I said. "Free food and drinks, catered goodies, and sitting in plush seats looking out on the arena. When you go the bathroom at a basketball game, you can see the game whether you are sitting on or standing at the toilet. There are two TVs in the bathroom."

"Wow, that fulfills a longtime fantasy I have had," Erika teased. "Obviously, that is some kind of guy fantasy—urinating, watching a ballgame, and still having both hands free to eat Buffalo wings."

"And your point is ...," I teased back.

She just laughed and said, "I can't wait."

"To eat Buffalo wings on the toilet, you mean?" I asked. She just shook her head.

"We don't have to go to Kanye ...," I began to suggest.

"What? We are going to a Kanye West concert, but we don't have to see him?" Erika asked.

"I wasn't sure how much you were into hip-hop, but you like U2, right?" I said.

"Of course, who doesn't like U2?" she said.

"You have passed another important test to show that you are a woman of intelligence and refined tastes," I said.

"Why, because I agree with you?"

"Yeah, that is my standard," I said.

"What is your issue with Kanye West?" Erika asked. "I am not a big hip-hopper, but he is awesome. That will be an incredible show."

"Okay, I am with you. You know hip-hop is not intended to really speak to fifty-year-old white guys?"

"I will burn you a Kanye West CD this week and get you up to speed on him."

A week later, Erika loved the corporate box and all of the trappings.

Kanye West took the stage to a thundering welcome and thundering bass, which literally rocked the house. We stood for most of the concert. Erika sang along, danced and kept giving me seductive looks. Then U2 took the stage. It was a true treat for the senses—Bono and "the Edge" running through their hits, and Erika dancing and flirting with me using her gorgeous eyes and lithe body.

As we exited the boxes at the conclusion of the concert, we began the walk around the big circular arena to get to the parking garage. Suddenly,walking towards us were Jerry and Shelly and Brian and Christine. Liz and my four best friends had gone to the concert together. They had never formally met Erika.

"Well, well, well," Brian said, "look who is here."

We exchanged hugs. It was good to see them again.

All eyes turned to Erika. "Well everyone, this is my friend, Erika Stevens." Then pointing, I identified them, "This is Jerry and Shelly, my neighbors, and Brian and Christine, who thank God are not my neighbors."

Everyone laughed. "Nice talk, Tom," Brian said.

"Ah, we have missed that nasty sarcasm," Jerry said.

"I wasn't being sarcastic ...," I quipped.

Ignoring the banter, the women both greeted Erika. "It is so nice to finally meet you, Erika."

"Nice to meet you as well," Erika said. "Tom has told me a lot about the four of you and your friendship with Liz."

"How nice of you to say so," Christine said. "It is so nice to see Tom being more like his old self. We haven't seen that for a while."

Shelly hugged me and said, "We have missed you, guy."

"I know, I am sorry, I haven't been a great friend lately."

It was Brian and Jerry's turn to focus on Erika. Brian said, "Erika, what is a dazzling young woman like you doing with the likes of Tom?"

"Having a great time," she said. I broke into a big smile.

"Hang on to this one, Tom," Jerry said. "You will never find a woman as delusional about you as Erika."

"Be nice to Erika," I said.

Erika laughed. "So you guys are friends, right?"

"Not that you would know it the way these three carry on," Christine said.

"How did you guys like the concert?" Shelly said.

"It was incredible," Erika said.

"U2 just keeps getting better," I said. "I love the new CD."

"Yeah, we sat out Kanye," Jerry said. "We saved him for the youngsters and sat outside having a drink. Geez, the bass about knocked our beers off the table. How could you stand it inside the arena?"

I looked at Erika and said, "Old white guys never get Kanye West."

She laughed at our inside joke, and Christine cut off incoming retaliatory remarks by saying, "Where did you two sit?"

Erika said, "We were in the corporate luxury box. Tom got a couple of tickets."

"Very nice," Brian said. "You didn't have to sit with the unwashed masses like us."

"So, Erika and Tom," Shelly began, "we are going to have a barbecue at our house next Saturday; why don't you both come? It would be just the six of us. It would be right next door, so pretty convenient."

"That assumes Tom is ever home anymore," Jerry said.

"Hush," Shelly said. "What about it, Erika?"

"Well, we will have to check …," I began, trying to offer Erika an escape ramp if she wanted.

"No, it would be fun," Erika said. "What do you want me to bring?"

"Just Tom," Shelly said. "We haven't seen much of him for a while. It will be fun to get to know you better, Erika."

"Alright then," I said. "We will be there."

I marveled at the prospect of being back with the four of them, with Erika as my new partner.

Chapter 15

IF TOM FELL

A FTER ALL of the rainy days, which can carry over into June during the Rose Festival celebration, finally it was summer in Portland. We have a limited amount of sunny days, but the good news in mid-June is that they are all lined up and waiting for you—one after another, like sailboats on the Columbia River.

The following weekend, Erika and I made plans for the Saturday cookout at Jerry and Shelly's house with Mayers. I was not able to see Erika on Friday night because I had an out-of-town meeting in Seattle and did not get back until late in the evening. I had caught a commuter flight early in the morning Friday and then flew back in the evening. I was anxious to see her Saturday.

I had been thinking about the weekend and decided to propose extending our time together. I called her on Saturday morning to propose that she come prepared to spend the night at my house Saturday after the cookout next door. I suggested we could sleep in on Sunday and have a quiet day together, reading the Sunday paper and just relaxing together.

Erika loved the idea but added one caution:

"Do you want me to park my car in your driveway all weekend? We can be a little more anonymous downtown in my condo. You seem to have a lot of people watching your comings and goings."

"True," I said. "Maybe you could just pull into the empty space in the garage, and then no one would know the difference. Does that sound like fun to you? I have two empty bedrooms in this house."

"Perfect," she said. "Do you have the ingredients so I could make you omelets Sunday morning?"

"Uhh ...," I hesitated.

"Never mind, of course you don't. I have seen your refrigerator," Erika said. "I will stop and get some stuff at the store and bring it with me."

With that, the plan for our weekend was solidified, and I couldn't wait.

My doorbell rang and I was greeted by the sight of Erika in tight denim jeans, a white sleeveless top, and open-toed heels. She had her hair piled on top of her head and was wearing large loop earrings.

"Wow," I said as I opened the door.

"What?" she said. "Is this okay?

"Yeah, it is okay, Erika. You look beautiful. You know I always say 'wow' when I first see you, I just don't say it aloud sometimes."

"That is my sweet-talking man," Erika said as she hugged me and kissed me. I loved that this had become our routine greeting ever since the incidents with Theresa. When we gathered at Jerry and Shelly's, everyone warmly greet Erika.

The party started very slowly. I thought everyone was talking about nothing but grandchildren and retirement. Does everyone my age talk like this? I had told Erika what colorful friends I had, and suddenly an AARP convention broke out. In an effort to jump-start the party and engage Erika in the conversation, I said, "Erika works at an investment firm, so she is pretty tuned in to the market."

Erika shot me a glance that told me she would have preferred I didn't say that. However, all four of them turned their attention to her as she gave her brief spiel about the stock market and the expectations about where it was going. At that moment, she became a fantasy girl for my middle-aged male friends—a hot woman who could manage their portfolio.

That seemed to break the ice, and things moved on from there. Jerry asked if we had seen the summer concerts coming up at the nearby winery. It was an awesome summer venue that offered top acts like Bonnie Raitt and Jack Johnson, while you sat on the lawn, drank wine, or had a picnic. We talked about some possibilities for attending a concert there. Then Erika said, "I hear all of you like Jimmy Buffett concerts. I saw the picture with the five of you and Liz partying."

"Oh, those were great times," Christine said.

"Then there were the Deadhead years, which are chock-full of entertaining stories about the Mayers," Jerry said.

"I don't remember everything about those years," Brian added, "there are chunks of '69 and '70 which I am not sure about."

Everyone started laughing. Christine said, "Don't listen to them, Erika, that is not true."

Jerry said, "This is one of the entertaining aspects about it, Erika. Brian says, 'Yeah, I followed the Grateful Dead around, stoned out of my mind.' Chris now denies any of that happened and has assumed a new identity as a worthwhile member of society."

This followed the usual story line, and everyone was jumping into the fray. Erika laughed at the banter and the well-rehearsed script of old friends telling stories on each other, which get better with each telling, over the years.

Everyone then pitched in to help on the meal. Erika joined Christine and Shelly in the kitchen and helped them while I manned the grill with Jerry and Brian. It pleased me that they were including Erika, and she was being her usual sweet, charming self.

As the meal began, Shelly asked us, "So, how did you two meet?"

I tried to hang back so I wouldn't dominate the conversation, but I wanted Erika to take the lead. I was interested in how she would tell the story.

"Should I do it?" Erika said, looking at me.

"Please," I said. "You will have much more credibility."

"Well, Tom and I had seen one another in the mornings at the Starbucks downtown, but we had never talked. Then one morning, I was trying to unload a box from my car in a pouring rain. I dropped my purse, spilling everything, and my presentation materials were getting wet. Then, all of sudden, Tom appeared from nowhere, put an umbrella over my head, and said he would help me."

"Very nice," Shelly said. "That's our boy."

"Then we just started talking each morning," Erika continued. "Then we started spending more and more time together, and here we are. He has made me really happy, and I love to be with him. We have had some real adventures together."

"Really?" Jerry said. "Adventures with Tom—isn't that an oxymoron?"

"Don't listen to him, Erika; that is a really sweet story. We are so glad you two found one another," Shelly said.

I just enjoyed watching Erika tell our story. They were getting a sam-

ple of her charms—her animated way of speaking and the big, beautiful, expressive eyes.

"Me too," Erika said. "I spent a couple of really hard, lonely years
after my divorce. Tom, as you know, had a very bad couple of years
mourning Liz. He has helped me start having fun again, and I think I
have done the same for him."

"Aaaah," Christine said, "that is so sweet. It is so nice to see Tom
happy again. He even looks different now, thanks to you, Erika."

Jerry couldn't resist a jab: "But he is so old and you are young and
beautiful ...," he teased.

Erika smiled and said, "Tom doesn't seem old to me. There is a big
difference in age but it doesn't change what is on the inside. Tom is
wonderful on the 'inside.'"

Wow, I liked the way Erika told the story.

"This is wonderful," Christine said. "You are apparently just what
Tom needed to bring him back to life."

"It sounds like he has gone through so much sadness, first with his
father and then Liz. He deserves to be happy, because he is such a sweet
person. I bet you all miss Liz," Erika said.

"We do miss her. She was such a great, positive person," Shelly said.
"It hasn't been the same without her, and we kind of lost Tom when we
lost Liz."

"Erika has changed my life," I said simply. "I agree with everything
she said, including the parts about how wonderful I am."

Erika smiled as Brian said, "It is amazing. This one is a keeper, Tom.
I have no idea what she sees in you, but you really lucked out. Be nice
to her."

Before I could respond, Erika said, "Tom is always nice to me."

Jerry said, "I assume that Tom has told you about some of his past—
some of the legal trouble, the restraining orders, and I guess you know
authorities told him to stay away from young girls in coffee shops for
a while ..."

"Shush," Shelly said. "Don't listen to these guys. They are so full of
crap you cannot believe anything you hear from them." Erika laughed
at the outrageous behavior.

I was proud of Erika in front of my friends. She was so gracious talking about Liz and was her genuinely sweet self.

The subject abruptly changed when Erika asked THE question: "I
hear you guys are into Harleys ...." Jerry and Brian immediately came
to life, as if Erika had dropped a handful of quarters into their slots.

They started regaling Erika with Harley stories on one side of the table. It was just a matter of minutes before Erika arose with the two guys and said, "We are going to the garage to look at the Harleys."

"Alright," I said. "Boys, let's be on our best behavior around Erika," producing chuckles from the group. Shelly seconded that, saying, "Jerry ... be very nice to Erika."

Jerry and Brian looked stricken, as if they had no idea what we were talking about. When Erika entered the garage from the patio, Chris and Shelly moved closer to me for further discussion.

"Wow, that is an impressive woman, Tom," Christine said.

"She is so pretty and such a sweet person," Shelly added.

"I am so glad you guys got to meet her. She is incredible, no doubt about it," I said.

"How old is she, Tom?" Shelly asked.

"Thirty," I said.

"She does seem older, but wow, that is pretty young," Christine added.

"I know—but it wasn't about age. It was just as she said. There was an immediate connection between us. I have struggled with our age difference. I hoped it wasn't a problem for her and that she didn't look at me as an old guy," I said.

"Apparently she doesn't," Christine said.

I looked at Liz's two best friends and said, "I couldn't find a way to move on without Liz. Then this incredible woman came into my life. She helped me out of the darkness. I didn't want to move on without Liz. I feel guilty about ... about ... leaving her behind. But I have to."

Both women teared up and hugged me. "It is so good to have you back and to see the old Tom re-emerging. Liz would be happy that you have found Erika," Shelly said.

"We know it has been hard, and we are so sorry. We miss Liz every day ...," Christine said, but her words were interrupted by the firing up of a Harley engine in the garage and the sound of the garage door being raised. While I was having an episode of "Oprah" on the patio, there was some kind of program from Spike TV going on in the garage with a hot girl and motorcycles.

I stood up and said, "Oh, no, no, no ...," and I rushed towards the garage with the two women trailing me. As I entered the garage, I was greeted by the sight of Erika sitting on a Harley, with Brian and Jerry pointing out various gauges, buttons, and switches. "Oh, no, no, no ... this is not happening," I said.

"Chill, Tom," Jerry said. "Erika is a consenting adult."

"Erika is too nice to tell you guys to kiss off," I said.

"Don't listen to him, Erika," Brian said. "He has a thing about motorcycles. We tried to get him to get a Harley and then he found out they didn't come with training wheels ..."

"All right ... enough," Shelly said.

"No, it is okay," Erika said. "This is awesome."

Ignoring all of the chatter, Jerry said, "Want to take a ride, Erika?"

"Yeah, that would be so, so cool," she said.

Jerry went to get helmets.

"Jerry ...," I warned.

Jerry turned to Erika and said, "Do you want to go?"

Erika came over and kissed me on the cheek and said, "Don't worry; this will be a blast."

I looked skeptical as Jerry and Erika put on their helmets and mounted the Harley.

"Just a short ride," I said, "be very careful. There is a very valuable person on that thing."

"Hey, thanks, brother," Jerry said as he pumped his fist over his heart. "Back at you, Tom, I love you too."

"Not you, Jerry ... be very careful," I said. "A short ride, don't end up in Sturgis or something."

"Don't worry, Dad," Jerry said. "I will have her back early." With that, they roared out of the driveway.

"Don't worry, guys," Brian said. "Like Jerry is going to show off or something with a beautiful young woman on the back of his Harley."

"Funny, real funny ...," I said.

About ten minutes later, Jerry and Erika returned, safe and sound. We were all standing in the driveway waiting. Erika dismounted and took off her helmet. "That was awesome," she said. "Thanks so much, Jerry."

"See, I was nice, huh, Erika?" Jerry offered.

"You were a perfect gentleman and took very good care of me," Erika said.

"Thank you, my dear," Jerry said. "You can ride with me any time."

"Oh, brother," Shelly said, rolling her eyes and looking at Christine. Erika noticed that whatever hairdo she had before the motorcycle ride was now trashed by the helmet, among other things. "Yuck," she said. "I guess I look pretty disgusting." With that, she shook her long black hair and tried to straighten it by running her fingers through it repeatedly. I noticed Jerry and Brian were transfixed.

"I guess I look gross now," Erika said.

"Come on, Erika, come with us and we can get away from 'men behaving badly,'" Shelly said as the three women left for the patio.

As soon as they had departed, Jerry said, "Nice, very nice."

"Yeah," Brian said as they looked at me and smiled.

The rest of the evening could not have made me happier. It was a chance to spend one of the golden moments of the summer with my four best friends. It was so good to be back with them. My pleasure was doubled by Erika being there, as my partner, and mixing well with my dearest friends. It was nice to hear them reinforce what I had felt about Erika for so long.

We talked until well after dark. Erika and I departed and went into my house. I was so glad it was not ending there.

"They were so much fun," Erika said. "I really had a great time tonight."

"Thanks so much for being you and charming my friends. I was so proud of you tonight," I said, "in front of my four best friends."

Erika put her arms around my neck and kissed me. "You were such a cutie tonight. I was touched by your worrying so much about me on the Harley."

"It was sincere; believe me," I said.

"I know it was," Erika said. "That's what makes it so charming and sweet."

"Well," I said, "a great man, maybe it was Groucho, once said, 'The secret of success is sincerity. Once you can fake that, you have got it made.'"

Erika laughed loudly. "There is nothing fake about you."

As I helped Erika get settled in an upstairs bedroom, I asked, "What are you in the mood to do tomorrow?"

"Well, you may think I am the most boring person in the world," she began, "but what if we sleep in, lay around in our jammies, and I will make you my special omelets. Then we can just read the Sunday paper together, go lounge on the patio, and watch a movie or whatever. We could just totally chill and be worthless tomorrow."

"Oh, my gosh," I said. "You really are my dream girl. That sounds like the all-time perfect Sunday."

Erika hugged me and kissed me good night and said, "Sleep as long as you want."

With that, a great day with Erika ended. The next day followed Erika's plan perfectly. Our bond continued to grow. It was a perfect summer weekend—basking in the sunshine of having Erika in my life. As evening shadows started to creep into our golden day together, it was time for Erika to leave. I helped load her car, which was hiding in my garage. I waved from the edge of the garage as she departed. Then I noticed, as she pulled out, Jerry popped out of his garage—being the ever-snoopy neighbor. He walked towards Erika's car, signaling her to roll down the window.

"So, Erika," Jerry began, leaning on her driver's side door. "How inconvenient for you?"

"What?" she said.

"I mean, you were here until late last night, and then today you had to drive all the way out here again to see Tom," he said with a wry smile.

I wondered what she would say. Erika gave him a flirtatious smile and said, "Gee, Jerry, I am kind of tired today, but not because I drove out here. Last night, I spent the night with Tom, and we made love like a couple of wild animals most of the night. See you later." She rolled up the window and backed out with a big smile on her face. I nearly collapsed onto the pavement laughing. Erika left Jerry standing in the driveway in a rare state for him—speechless.

Erika and I continued our routine of spending time together on weekends. I was heartened by the increasing affection she was showing me. We kissed when we met and kissed as we parted. She held my hand as we walked together. It felt like perhaps things were starting to turn. I was careful to not fall into a discussion about where we were going in our relationship. I continued to try to be very patient and let her give the signals that she wanted to go to the next level. Even though my hunger for her grew, it was so wonderful that summer to finally have an outlet for my affection and love for her.

I was finally starting to feel more secure about my relationship with her. I was starting to feel more at ease with her. I was letting her come to me at whatever pace she wanted. Meanwhile, I was savoring every moment of loving Erika on these wonderful summer days.

One night, in late June, Erika and I were going to a restaurant on the Park Blocks, which had outside dining. We wanted to spend the fantastic evening enjoying the great weather we were having. As we entered, we ran almost head on into Theresa and a male companion who were leaving the restaurant.

"Tom, nice to see you," Theresa said as she came forward and hugged me. I shot a glance at Erika as I was embracing Theresa. The usual warm, congenial smile that Erika routinely used as her greeting to most of the human race was missing. She looked very stern and serious. Her beautiful blue eyes reflected no warmth.

"How are you, Theresa?"

"I am doing very well; I never see you anymore," Theresa added.

"Theresa, this is Erika."

Erika simply said, "Hello," and nodded her head.

"This is my friend, Doug," Theresa offered.

I was in a hurry to move past this awkward moment. I said, "You have fun and enjoy your evening," as I put my arm around Erika's waist to guide her forward.

"Nice to meet you, Erika," Theresa said. Erika gave a tense smile and nodded as we moved forward into the restaurant.

After we were out of earshot, Erika said, "Well, she appears to have landed on her feet ... so to speak."

I smiled at the manifestation of this feisty Erika and mockingly said, "Well, it was certainly good to see her again, huh?"

"Okay, where were we?" Erika said as we tried to wash the moment from our memory banks.

Then we had a very memorable Fourth of July.

The Goddesses planned a party, and Tamara was going to host it at her new digs in Camas. Erika and I drove over in the Porsche. This was the first time I had seen Erika's friends and their significant others since I had the new car. Erika seemed to be basking in the attention it generated. All of the guys were cranked up in the testosterone zone at the sight of the car. It was fun to talk with them about it. I was also happy to see Tricia was there. There were a few other people I had not met yet. The Goddesses seemed to include Tricia in many of their activities, which I thought was commendable and spoke well of her.

The plan was to have a big traditional Fourth of July cookout in their newly sodded backyard with new patio furniture. After dark, all of the neighbors, including everyone at our party, would join together in the cul-de-sac to share fireworks for a major blowout together.

I had been mulling over several things in my mind, and I was hoping to get an opportunity for a one-on-one discussion with Tricia. I didn't know if it could happen today, but I was going to watch for an opening and then pounce on it.

When I saw Jenna, she greeted me and then said, "Tom, I haven't seen you since the day you were dealing with that psycho chick."

That was the last topic I wanted to talk about, and then Kristen picked up on it. Kristen said, "What? You had a psycho chick after you?" Erika looked like she wanted to end this line of conversation quickly but had not acted yet. Jen's boyfriend was a very hunky, handsome young guy named Ben. Ben looked like some kind of GQ model. I tried to end the "psycho chick" discussion by joking my way out of it.

"It is a common problem that hunky guys like Ben and I have. When you are this good looking, you attract all kinds of attention. Women really see you as a piece of meat. It can be very degrading."

This brought a chorus of laughs. Erika smiled and looked relieved that I diffused the situation. Jen retorted, "So that is how you met Erika, Tom?"

"Nice talk," Erika said, jabbing at Jen.

"No," I said. "Erika is the kind that you spend your life looking for."

This brought a chorus of aws and ooohs from the ladies.

Erika looked pleased and said, "Observe, girlfriends. I do have one friend who is loyal."

Everyone busied themselves helping with the preparations for the party. The guys were about to have their first round of beers on the deck when Tamara's husband noticed that there was no wine for the barbecue. I volunteered to take care of the problem for him and said I would run to the store.

I went inside the house, announced that I was going to get some wine, and said, "Tricia, could you come with me? I need your help."

"Sure, Tom," Tricia said.

This brought a frown and an intense flash of blue eyes from Erika.

I said, "Don't worry, we will be right back, okay?" as I kissed Erika on the cheek.

Jen said, "I don't know, Erika. Do you trust those two taking off in Tom's car?"

"No, not really. I have to kind of watch these two every time they are together," Erika said, in what I think was a tone of levity. "Hurry back," Erika said, looking intently at me with her large eyes, which were conveying volumes of nonverbal communication now—if I was on the correct frequency.

This was my chance. I immediately told Tricia that I wanted a chance to talk with her, which was apparently fine with her.

Upon our return to Tamara's house, we presented the wine we had
selected and rejoined the party. The final preparations for the meal
were under way, and the guys were cooking meat in the backyard.

"What was that about?" Erika whispered to me.

"Your mom wanted to ride in my new car, and it gave us a chance to
chat," I said light-heartedly.

"You initiated it, and Mom has already had a ride in your car," Erika
responded.

I thought, well, that line of defense died a quick death.

"Erika, Erika, why do you always do this?" I said. "What's the big
deal? I was just being friendly with your mother."

"I know. I just thought you were acting strange and up to something," she said.

"I promise I will give you a blow-by-blow account later, okay, sweet
lady?" I offered. "What would I be up to? Your mother and I are probably the two people who love you the most in the entire world. Chill,
okay?"

"I am sorry, I didn't mean to act weird about it," she said.

The partying was beginning on the back deck, which brought an
end to the conversation ... fortunately.

I had gotten some insight into Erika's psyche in my discussion with
her mother. Erika had been more damaged from the divorce than I
imagined. She had actually gone through an experience similar to
mine after Liz's death. I was in mourning and shattered by the death
of my wife. Erika had her self-confidence shattered. She blamed herself
for what happened.

Erika had always been the golden girl. She was smart and pretty,
and everyone liked her. She relished the role as the golden girl. When
she was rejected by Todd and their marriage failed, Erika took it very
hard. I don't think Erika has a dark side. I don't think she has skeletons
in her closet. I do think she has extremely high expectations for herself.
She was damaged—much as I had been, but for different reasons. Erika
may view my trial as no fault of my own, so I deserved sympathy. Erika
may view her trial as her fault for something she did wrong.

The party was great. Portland summer days, with temperatures in
the 80s, are the best. There is little humidity and few bugs, and there
is a wonderful cool moistness to the air. It makes you realize why you
live here and tolerate all of the rainy days. This was one of those pay-
off days. As darkness approached, explosions and whistling fireworks

could be heard over the entire neighborhood, as many of Tamara's neighbors began jumping the gun.

The neighborhood gathering was taking place in the front of each house. Lawn chairs and blankets were set up on front lawns and driveways, facing the circular pavement of the cul-de-sac, in anticipation of the private fireworks show. Neighbors began gathering with bags and boxes of fireworks. All that was needed was for the sun to go a little lower. I planned to help the guys at our party fire off what we had to offer to the celebration in the form of fireworks.

It was cooling off. Meanwhile, the ladies from our party began gathering in the lawn chairs on Tamara's front lawn. A blanket was spread on the lawn in front of the chairs. Erika, who had looked sensational all day in her shorts and sleeveless top, had pulled on a sweater. She perched on the blanket in front of the lawn chairs.

I said, "How are you doing?"

"I am freezing," she said.

"Let me fix that," I said, sitting behind her on the blanket and putting my arms around her.

"You are so warm," Erika said. "It feels so good."

Before I could respond, the other guys in our group approached and said, "Erika, let Tom come and do the fireworks with us."

"Tom can go with you if he wants to; I am not stopping him," Erika said.

She looked at me and I said, "Go ahead and start without me."

The women laughed and Kristen said, "Erika, you are sooo manipulative."

"Shut up," Erika responded. "I didn't say Tom couldn't go."

"Tom," Tamara said, "you passed the test. You have chosen wisely to stay with Erika."

The fireworks began in the street just a few feet away from where Erika and I sat cuddling on the blanket. The other women were perched on the lawn chairs just behind our blanket.

Erika was wearing her hair in a ponytail. Now her ear was exposed and near my mouth. We began to communicate by whispering into one another's ear.

"Is everything okay, Tom?"

"Yes, it is fine."

"Did you have a good talk with Mom?"

"I was going to talk to you about it later, but with you, resistance is futile."

"I am sorry; are you angry with me? Talk about what?"

"I told your mother I had a problem and that I needed her advice."

"A problem?"

"Yeah."

"What kind of problem do you have that would make you seek my mother's help?"

"Erika, can't we talk later—when we don't have fireworks going off in our face?"

"Well, now you tell me you have some kind of problem, but you don't want to talk?"

I was quiet for a moment as we stopped whispering.

"Is it something with me, Tom?"

"Something with you, but it is not your fault. It is my problem."

"Please tell me; you are freaking me out," she said, as we continued to whisper softly into one another's ear.

"Okay." Then I drew closer so my mouth was in contact with her ear. "I said to your mother ... what would happen ... what would happen if I fell in love with your daughter? What would happen if I couldn't just be her friend anymore? What would happen if I told her that I loved her?"

Erika turned her head so it was now lying on my shoulder and she could look into my eyes. The fireworks were casting vibrant colors, which were reflected on Erika's face and in her large eyes as she looked at me intensely.

I said, "I told your mother I was afraid that I could not help myself. I told her that I have fallen quite hard for you. I hoped it wouldn't cause a problem. But then I told your mother I would just have to deal with the consequences ... whatever ..."

With that, Erika kissed me hard with her soft, full lips as she stared into my eyes. She turned slightly towards me and kissed me passionately again. I noticed her eyes, which caught the bright colors of the fireworks, were now moist.

Jen gently pushed my back with her bare foot. "Hey, you two, the fireworks are out there." We didn't respond.

Tamara said, "I think there are a lot of fireworks on that blanket right now."

We ignored them all.

"I am sorry. I didn't want to do it," I whispered. "I really tried not to. I wanted to have the kind of relationship you wanted. I don't want to pressure you. I will still be patient. You can do whatever you want. But I can't help myself. I did fall in love with you. Now I am afraid."

The sky had turned black, and the only faces we could see were those that caught reflections of the serious firepower that was being laid down in the street in front of us.

"Don't be afraid, Tom, and don't be sorry," she whispered, "because I love you too." Then she kissed me again. I hugged her tightly.

"What did my mother say?"

I whispered, "She told me to pack up and leave. She said to stay away from her family."

"Stop it. Really?"

"She said I shouldn't be afraid to talk to you about my feelings. Tricia said she knows you like me too. Your mom suggested I not hide my feelings from you. So now you know."

Erika responded, "I have never been loved like it feels to be loved by you. You have nothing to fear. We will work it out. We *will* work it out. I need just a little more time to work things out, okay? I am sorry."

"I know. I expected that. I would be happy to continue as we have been," I whispered. "But I will wait, wait and see what happens. I just want you to know that I want more, and I want you to know that I love you without reservations or conditions."

We were silent now. I held her from behind as we watched the fireworks in front of us. Then I gently kissed the back of her bare neck, which was inches from my lips. Erika was so soft, and I loved the smell and feel of her skin. She squeezed my hand and kissed it.

I felt some relief. It was now said. That part of the game—that part of the lover's dance—was over. I knew that Erika would need more time to adjust. I don't think she was ready for an intense relationship. Perhaps my openness would cause a problem at some point but I was bursting. That is why I wanted to have some time with Tricia. There was no one else to talk to about this problem.

Erika had been damaged in the past. The hurt was so great that she was afraid to commit and become vulnerable again. Now I was totally exposed. I didn't know where this adventure would go. It was a high-stakes game for me. I had been damaged too. Now I was apparently strong enough to risk it all for the love of Erika.

As I held her tightly in front of her friends and mother on the Fourth of July, I didn't know what was ahead for me. I couldn't wait to find out. The exhilaration of being in love with Erika made me willing to risk everything.

Chapter 16

AUTUMN OF OUR LOVE

M Y SUMMER with Erika continued after that memorable night on the Fourth of July. She made little reference to our discussion on the blanket, somewhat to my disappointment. I had declared my love for her, and she said she loved me too.

The only change in our relationship was the chance I had to kiss her and hold her. Erika permitted more outlets for my affection, and she was more affectionate with me. I decided to be happy with that amount of progress and let her set the pace she was comfortable with. For now, we enjoyed these incredible summer days and evenings together. She knew I loved her, and I didn't need to hide it any longer. We still spent almost every available slot of time together—so what's not to like? I would let things continue to progress.

The events of August seemed to truncate my summer with Erika. I lost most of the first two or three weeks with her due to some encroaching events. I did take a business trip to Denver. I extended my trip and even took some time off so I could do some catching up with Michelle, Rob, and my granddaughters. I had some fence-mending to do in our relationship. The wedges that seemed to be straining my relationship with Michelle were less formidable when I was with her in person.

It was just a couple of days after I returned from Denver that Erika left town. She and her mother had been planning a summer trip to Sacramento to see Erika's brother. Yikes, Sacramento in August. I am sure they would not need coats, as the thermometer hit the high 90s or 100 each day. That is a pretty serious shock for forest-dwellers from Portland. I was glad I got to go to Denver instead.

All of this meant I had not been with Erika for over two weeks, and I was made acutely aware of the void her absence created in my life. I met her for dinner after work on the Friday following her return from Sacramento. We decided to just do dinner and no movie, since we had a lot of catching up to do. I got a warm hug and kiss when she greeted me at the door of number 912. It was so good to see her. Erika looked like she had gotten more sun, since her tan had deepened in the two weeks.

We both marveled at how we felt the loss from being apart that long. We both reviewed our trips and I showed her some pictures I had taken in Denver. We spent a leisurely dinner, which lasted for a couple of hours. After dinner, I suggested we take a walk around the Pearl District and enjoy the wonderful summer evening. We finally landed on a bench outside Erika's building near the fountain. I sat listening to her with my arm around her on the bench. At times, Erika would lay her head on my shoulder. It was wonderful to be back together and touching Erika.

We wanted to spend most of Saturday together. When I arrived at her condo, around 11 AM the next day, she looked somewhat alarmed.

"We have a problem. I am sorry; I didn't know this was going to happen. Todd is coming over in a few minutes to have me sign some papers. He just called this morning," Erika said. "It shouldn't take long, but would you mind giving us a few minutes here to do this?"

"Sure," I said. "Uh … I will just go hang out in the plaza until you have transacted your business. Then come out and get me, okay?"

"Perfect, it shouldn't take long. I am sorry."

With that, I left and went out to the Jameson Square Plaza fountain, across the street from Erika's building. I found a bench. The plaza was already full of people, on what was going to be a gorgeous summer Saturday.

There were several young parents at the tide-pool fountain with their toddlers and preschoolers, who were pitter-pattering around on their tiny feet. There were also several older children and adults wading. The water in the tide pool retreated, and finally the basin of the fountain was empty. The children would wait with anticipation for the next cycle. Moments later, the water would suddenly start cascading over the rocks, and the water in the fountain basin would start to rise again. This brought excited squeals from the children, who either ran from the water or ran into it.

Young mothers in summer clothes spread out blankets and towels as their little ones ran around. The mothers were preparing for an extended siege of the plaza. The lucky ones, who came early, were claiming for their own what small patches of grass existed on the plaza. In anticipation that all of these people were going to get hungry soon, vendors who sell hot dogs, drinks, and ice cream were setting up on the perimeter of the buff-colored stone plaza.

I was distracted by the scene unfolding on the plaza, so I had not realized how much time had elapsed. Suddenly, I realized I had been there for about forty-five minutes. I had selected a bench facing Erika's building. I am not sure why, or what I expected to see. Maybe it was so I could see Erika coming to meet me after Todd left.

It was then that my mind started to focus on Todd. It seemed like a routine matter. Divorced people have to occasionally meet to do some paperwork or whatever. I saw no reason for alarm. Their split had appeared to be amicable, with virtually no contact between Todd and Erika. Forty-five minutes soon became an hour. Then when we were nearing an hour and a half, I began to be concerned.

I saw a young man leaving Erika's building with a manila folder that looked like it contained several papers. I wondered if that was Todd. I kind of hoped not, because he was a very good-looking man. He was tall and muscular with thick black hair, which he combed straight back. He climbed into a maroon Subaru Outback and drove away.

A few minutes later, I saw Erika exiting the front door of her building. She was walking slowly towards the plaza. She pulled some sunglasses out of her pocket and put them on. As she came nearer, she didn't appear to be very happy. I waved as she got closer. Upon spotting me, she headed towards my bench. She sat down without saying a word.

"What's wrong?" I asked.

Without addressing the question, she said, "That took longer than I thought. I am sorry you had to hang out here for so long."

"There are way worse places to spend your time on a day like today," I said cheerily. Then I tried again: "Is everything alright?"

"The paperwork was no big deal. It was just a waiver form or something that ex-wives have to sign when you make an election on your retirement and 401k and that kind of stuff," Erika said. "But there was more than that on his mind."

"What?"

"He told me that he wants to get back together. He wants to try again. Most of the time, he was telling me that he has really changed and that he still loves me. Todd asked me to consider giving him another chance," Erika recounted, and she appeared to be very rattled.

It was impossible, on this beautiful summer day, to detect that in our lives storm clouds were beginning to gather on the distant horizon. The storm would not hit now, but the clouds would continue to thicken, signaling trouble ahead. These storm clouds went unnoticed by Erika and me, as we had many other things on our minds at this point.

"What did you tell him?" I cautiously asked.

"I told him that I didn't like that he suddenly popped back into my life from nowhere and hit me with a bunch of stuff like that. This stirs up things I was trying to forget. I had put all of this behind me and moved on," Erika said. "Now all of a sudden, the issues from the past come flooding back into my life." The more she talked, the more unstrung Erika appeared.

I reached for her hand and held it. "I am so sorry, Erika," I offered. "Was he nice about it? You didn't feel threatened or anything, did you?"

"No, no, he is always nice. He is a pretty laid-back guy, but he told me that he realizes he still loves me. Todd said he has tried to go different directions in his life over the past couple of years, but now he realizes that he made a big mistake. He said he still loves me and that he has really changed and blah, blah, blah ...." The frustration seemed to pour out of Erika now. "He said he has really changed and wants a chance to prove it to me."

My concern was building. This can't be good news.

Fumbling for words, I asked, "What did you say?"

"I told him I was in a relationship and that I couldn't think about this now," Erika said. "He asked if he could call later next week after I have had some time to think about it. Todd said he didn't expect an answer right away, but wanted me to know how he felt and wanted to give me a chance to think about the things he said."

I was temporarily at a loss as to what to say and said simply, "Oh."

It was as if Erika had detected, for the first time, that this development was starting to hit home with me. "Don't worry, Tom," she reassured me. "I will take care of this. It is not anything that you need to be concerned about. I will deal with it. It has just kind of thrown me and upset me this morning."

"Okay, I understand," I said, "but please, let me help if I can. Talk to me about it."

"Don't worry, it will be okay. Todd is a very gentle person. Don't get the idea that he is stalking me or being aggressive or anything," she offered.

"If you don't mind me asking, what happened with you and Todd? If it is none of my business, just say so."

"No, I have never talked with you about that," Erika replied. "We were young and met in college. It was a pretty whirlwind relationship, and we decided to move in together during our last year at college in Eugene."

"So Erika's a Duck," I said in an ill-advised attempt to lighten the mood, referring to her being a student at the University of Oregon. "I never realized that until now."

"Is that a problem?"

"No," I said. "I went to Portland State, or at least finished there, during my checkered academic pursuits, but some of my best friends are Ducks."

"Nice to hear," she said.

"You were telling me about you and Todd when I interrupted."

Erika continued, "We lived together during our senior year and then moved to Portland together to start our careers. I was in finance and Todd in the high-tech IT world. After a couple of years, he asked me to marry him and I did."

I didn't sense a great deal of passion as she told me the story. Erika seems very passionate and romantic to me, but I wasn't getting that vibe from her at all as she told me about how they began as a couple. Of course, they are divorced and I am in love with Erika—so that could be coloring my perception of the story.

"Did you two love one another? Was it special at one time?" I blurted out.

"We did, but it was never very romantic in that sense. Todd just wasn't that way. Don't get me wrong, I shouldn't bag on him. We had a lot of fun together, and he seemed right for me. We were very young, however, and as we matured and grew in our careers outside of college life, we seemed to go different directions. He still liked to hang out with his college buddies and seemed, after awhile, to not be very interested in the things I was interested in."

"What made you finally decide that you didn't want to be married anymore?" I said as I intruded further into her personal life.

"For starters, during our first year of marriage, he forgot my birthday and our anniversary."

"Yikes, that is the quick route to becoming an ex-husband."

Erika said, "It is not that my birthday or anniversary is so important, but it became part of a pattern. I was just there in his life, but I wasn't an important part of it. We really did grow apart, and I decided one day that I could do better. Things had changed, and we didn't seem to belong together any more. I didn't want to divorce, especially after what I saw my mother experience, but I didn't want to spend my life in this situation when I could make a change."

"I think that is pretty brave and commendable to make those kinds of midcourse corrections to be a successful person," I offered.

"I didn't feel successful though," Erika said. "I had failed to have a successful marriage, and I didn't understand why Todd didn't seem to love me anymore. What had I done?"

"You are asking the wrong person. I cannot comprehend how someone could become apathetic about being with you," I said. "I don't think you did anything wrong, Erika. I really don't. You are so easy to love. On that subject, I am an expert."

She buried her face in my shoulder, and I put my arms around her.

"I am so sorry, my dear Erika," I said. "I am so, so sorry. This should have never happened to you."

Erika said nothing but just continued to lean on my shoulder. A thousand questions were racing through my mind, but this was probably not the time to press her. Was she seriously considering Todd's proposal? Or was she just temporarily knocked off-kilter by this sudden development?

When she raised her head, I could tell there were tears behind her sunglasses. She reached beneath them to wipe away her tears.

"Does it ever get easier, Tom?" Erika pleaded. "Does life get any easier as you get older?"

"Well, to some extent, I don't know if it gets easier or just different. Of course, I thought life was pretty good until my wife was suddenly murdered," I said. "But I know what you are asking."

"How do you get through all of this? I look at you, that you found the person you loved and had a successful marriage. You raised two good children. You got established in your career and are successful. You have overcome a terrible event in your life and have landed on your feet," she said, "but how did you get through all of that? I seem to be stuck on the first steps and can't get by them."

"I appreciate the complimentary summation of my life, but there were a lot of bumps and pains involved to get all of that done. I am hardly going to be the one to come out with a series of self-help books on how to overcome life's challenges," I countered. "Until you came into my life, my defense mechanism was to crawl into a dark hole, curl up in a ball, and hope life went away."

"But you did find a way to have a successful marriage," Erika said. "How did you find a way to get along that well and stay married for, what was it …?"

"About twenty-nine years," I said.

"Wow, that is a long time to get along with one person," Erika said.

"Yeah, Liz would undoubtedly agree," I offered, "it wasn't twenty-nine years of bliss and no conflict. It is hard work. It is a hundred compromises. It is giving up part of yourself so you fit with the other person. I have heard people say marriage is a 50-50 relationship. I don't think it is. If you are willing to only give your 50 percent, you won't make it. You are going to have to give more than that. If your partner does the same—gives more—then you can be successful."

"I feel like Todd quit giving to me," Erika said sadly.

"I know, baby, I am so sorry. I don't understand that because when you love someone, I think you are willing to pretty well give everything," I said.

"That is what is so wonderful about you—your willingness to give," Erika said.

"It is because I really care about your happiness," I said. "I think that is one of the keys to having a good relationship, or marriage."

"Then there is that," she said, pointing to the children playing in the fountain. "It terrifies me to think about being someone's mother. How could I ever do that?"

"Erika, you would be an incredible mother. You are very loving, intelligent, and sweet. You have all of the tools. Someday, there are going to be some very lucky children who get Erika as their mother," I said.

"I wish I had as much confidence in myself as you have in me," Erika said.

"It makes me really sad to hear you talk like that," I said. "I wish you knew how incredible you are. You shouldn't be afraid, Erika. You have so much to give those you love. Your confidence really got rattled, I can tell. Don't give in to fear, Erika."

"Give in to fear?" Erika asked.

"You can't go through life holding back or never trying because you might fail," I said. "Believe me, as the voice of experience, I have made a lot of mistakes and still do. I certainly made mistakes in my marriage.

I certainly made mistakes raising my children. I still mess up my relationship with them, and they get mad at me."

We stopped talking for a moment and watched the children playing in the fountain.

"Look at those children, Erika; there is a lot of happiness out there. A lot of happiness is out there waiting for you. Don't be afraid. Step out there and go get it," I pleaded. "Someday, a little boy or a little girl will come into your life, and your life will be changed forever. But you won't mind because it will be the most wonderful thing that ever happens to you."

"Oh, Tom," Erika said sadly, "I was trying to get the courage to move on with my life. I was almost there, and then Todd has to show up and throw me into a muddle. It brings back all of the things I didn't want to come back."

"There was something people kept saying to me when Liz died. At the time, it really pissed me off," I said. "They would say, 'Well, life must go on.' Sure, what the hell, my wife died, but just quit whining and move on. Just get another wife and you will be fine. Is that what they were suggesting?"

Erika looked at me very intently.

"I know people were just trying to comfort me, but that one phrase really annoyed me. I would think, 'Oh yeah, says who? Why does life have to go on?'" I said, with my frustration making its way into my voice. "But you know what—it is true. I don't like it, but it is true. Life DOES go on. You are going to make mistakes. You are going to get your heart broken. You are going to have moments of incredible exhilaration and moments of terrible despair. You have to find a way to meet the challenges and ultimately triumph."

"Oh, Tom, you are so patient with me," Erika said. "You are so good for me."

"I am so sad when I see you sad," I said. "What can I do to put a smile back on that beautiful face?"

She just buried her face into my shoulder again. I held her closely as I asked the question that had been hanging in the air for a while: "What are you going to do, Erika? About Todd, I mean?"

"I don't know," she said. "He was being very sincere, but I said I am in a relationship and now was not a good time. He asked me if I would think about it and talk to him again. I finally said I would."

I just nodded.

"I told you," Erika said, "please don't worry. I will work this out. I just told him that, because I didn't want to spend all day in my apartment debating it. I needed to get away for a while and think," she said. "I just needed to talk, like we just did. Thank you."

"Erika, I am hardly an objective bystander. I obviously don't want Todd to have his request honored," I said. "I *do* understand someone saying they have never stopped loving you and they want you back. If I got that chance, I would never let you go."

Erika smiled for the first time since she entered the plaza.

"What do you want to do today, beautiful lady?" I asked.

"I want to be with you," Erika said. "Let's take a walk. I am kind of a mess." She removed her sunglasses and wiped her tears. Her blue eyes were red and sad. We walked across the plaza, which now resembled an anthill, with lots of Portlanders swarming everywhere, worshipping the sun and enjoying the plaza fountain.

Our walk took us down the sun-drenched streets of the Pearl District. We passed all of the quaint, funky shops and restaurants we had enjoyed on all of those rainy days. They now took on a different ambiance in the bright sunlight. We continued to walk down the street from the plaza, and somehow we ended up at Powell's City of Books. It is no trivial undertaking to go browsing for books at Powell's, which is one of the largest bookstores in the world.

There are over 1 million books in this store, which is multileveled and takes up a whole city block. There are 3,500 sections and 68,000 square feet of space jammed with books, both new and used. When my kids were young, Liz and I would give them each a $10 bill and let them go roam through Powell's, finding used books. It was a great rainy Saturday activity. I asked Erika if she wanted to go in.

"Sure," she said.

It seemed to be a good diversion. It provided a nice way to push the reset button on our day. We both left with a bag of books and stopped to get an ice cream at a nearby shop as we headed back towards Erika's building. I was trying to be very tender with her. I had never seen Erika this upset before. My strategy appeared to be working.

After grabbing some lunch, I asked what she wanted to do that would make her happy. She seemed stumped, which is unusual for Erika.

I needed to pull something out of the hat quickly.

Then suddenly, I said, "I've got it. Do you trust me?"

Her smile returned and she said, "Uh-oh ... I get nervous when you get that gleam in your eye."

"Do you trust me?"

"I think it is a little late to say no to that question," Erika said.

"It is a beautiful day, let's put the top down. I have a surprise for you," I said.

"Okay, what do you have planned?" she said.

"It is a surprise," I said.

She took my hand and said, "Lead the way." Her beautiful, warm smile returned.

I drove east out of Portland a few miles, down the beautiful Columbia Gorge, which is a national scenic area. There is a series of cliffs overlooking the Columbia River. The gorge is full of incredible nature trails, and there are seventy-seven waterfalls on the Oregon side of the river. I felt like I knew just the place to take Erika.

It was incredible to drive the Porsche with the top down on a day like this. It seemed to help Erika unwind as she totally surrendered to the experience. She just let her long hair blow in the wind. She was relaxing and enjoying the ride.

I turned off of the interstate highway and took the old highway, which is a holdover from early in the twentieth century. I have seen historic photographs from the 1920s with pictures of Model As driving up the old highway, back when it was the new highway. It was quaint and gorgeous. It puts you in touch with the beauty all around you, whereas on the new interstate highway, you just blow past the scenery as quickly as possible. I turned off the old highway at Horseshoe Falls. This waterfall takes an incredible 176-foot drop from the top of the cliff to the river below. It was spectacular.

"Wow, this is so amazing," Erika said.

"Have you been here before?" I asked.

"I don't think so," Erika said. "I would have remembered this."

"Come on," I said, reaching out for her hand to lead her down the trail towards the falls.

"Where are we going?"

"It is a surprise," I said as Erika started to smile and follow me down the trail. The winding trail went through incredibly lush foliage and steep ridges covered with ferns, which loved the atmosphere of being constantly misted by the thundering waterfall.

I led Erika down the trail to a chamber that was carved into the rock and allowed us to walk behind the falls.

"Oh, Tom," she said, "this is awesome."

"Do you know, this is supposed to be one of the best places to kiss in the entire Columbia Gorge?" I asked.

"You drove all this way, so you could kiss me behind a waterfall?" Erika asked, with a smile on her face.

"Yeah, do you have a problem with that?" I said.

She put her arms around my neck and gave me a long kiss. We were getting wet. I reached out and touched the water thundering off of the cliff. It splashed on Erika, who squealed and splashed water on me. We kissed again. Then we sat on a rock and just watched the water rushing past us, crashing into the river. We were temporarily lost in our thoughts.

"How do you know this is one of the best places to kiss in the gorge?" Erika asked. "Do you bring all of your girlfriends out here to the waterfall?"

"I try, but you are the only one to go for it so far," I said.

She laughed. It was working.

"I actually have a book that lists the most romantic kissing spots throughout the gorge. It gives them a number rating—from least romantic to the most romantic."

Erika began to laugh louder now. "You have a book? You have been studying this? I thought this was just spontaneous ..."

"It was well-planned spontaneity," I said. "It appears I am just this smooth, suave guy who does these incredible things, but this is not easy, you know ... it takes hard work to be this good."

Erika continued to laugh. Her hair was mostly wet now and hung limply at the sides of her face. She never looked more beautiful as the sparkle returned to her blue eyes. We continued to sit on the rock and watch the hypnotic sight of the cascading water.

"Is this the best place ever to spend a warm day?" Erika finally said.

"It was the best one I could think of," I offered.

"You never disappoint, Tom," she said.

"I hope I never do, Erika," I said. "Do you want to go?"

"No," she said. We continued to sit there silently until she started to actually get cold.

We walked down the trail into the warm sun and back to the car. Our day ended back in "our restaurant"—the Asian one on the ground floor of Erika's building. She insisted that she freshen up after being doused in the waterfall and sitting on the rock ledge.

As we parted, she kissed me good-bye and said, "What would I do without you, Tom?"

"I hope you never find out," I said. The statement seemed to take on a more serious meaning that day.

A few weeks later, I saw Josh in the lobby waiting for an elevator.

"Hey, Josh, how was your summer?" I asked.

"Awesome. How about yours? Didn't I tell you that driving that Porsche around with the top down on a summer's day was better than sex?" Josh said.

I said under my breath, and somewhat to myself, "It is better than the sex I am getting."

"What?" Josh asked.

"Never mind. You were absolutely right, Josh. I had a dream summer, thanks to your car. It *is* incredible. How is the Beemer treating you?"

"I love that car, man. The ultimate driving machine, bro, right? Cheryl loves it too."

"How is Cheryl doing?" I asked, wondering how the pregnancy was progressing.

"She is great, her stomach is starting to pop out there, and we can feel the baby kicking," he said.

"Good for you, Josh, you are in for a great experience. Take care, buddy," I said.

Josh then departed for his floor and left me with my thoughts. As September had progressed, Erika seemed more troubled and preoccupied. I actually wondered if she and Todd had started seeing one another again." I had stopped seeing her regularly each morning, as had been our routine for so long. She now sporadically came in to the coffee shop some mornings. When I did see her, she said she was running late or had not slept very well.

When we were together, it seemed like she was somewhere else. Her blue eyes, which were always riveted on me when we were together in the past months, now sometimes looked disconnected from our conversation. I wondered if maybe the end was near.

As far as I knew, the only time she had seen Todd was when they met in her condo. Other than that, she had told me that Todd had called a few times and sent some e-mails. She assured me that he was being very kind about it—in fact; he was trying to woo her back to him through his communications.

My despair was starting to build. It felt like we were starting to just go through the motions, instead of the "magic" and easy compatibility we had enjoyed up to this point.

I even started wondering if I had made a mistake back in May when I rejected Theresa. Maybe I should have heeded Dave's early warnings about giving myself over to Erika. How would things be now if I had decided to go with Theresa? After all, Theresa was just asking me to "try" her and to give her a chance.

My concerns continued to mount as the month wound down. The great run of Indian summer days was just about gone. The fall rains would start any day now. It seemed symbolic. Those golden moments of the last summer were now being dulled by cloud cover, which turned the sunny days back into gray days. It was time to talk.

Before I could bring it up, Erika had some news.

"Tom," she said, "I am trying to get this all resolved with Todd. I need to ask your indulgence."

"I want to talk to you about that topic also," I said.

"You do?" she asked. "Let me tell you what has happened, and then we can discuss it. I can't meet you Friday night because I am going to meet Todd for dinner and give him my answer."

"Which is?" I asked.

"What do you mean? You know what my answer will be," Erika said. "I am not getting back together with him. You know I have had trouble figuring out how to handle this. Todd and I don't talk that often and rarely see each other. I wanted to talk to him face-to-face and not just send him an e-mail or something."

"Have you and Todd been seeing each other regularly since he approached you?" I asked.

"No, I just told you that we haven't seen each other," she said. "Don't you believe me? Why do you think we have?"

"I guess ... I just assumed ... part of it, is just the way you have been acting. When you are with me, I feel like you are somewhere else. I have wondered if you need some time away from me. Some space to work out whatever you want to do, and then, if you still want to be with me ... I would be happy to come back," I said.

"Do you want to go away from me?"

"Of course not. But something feels broken. Do you want to take a break from me? Am I putting too much pressure on you by hanging around all of the time?" I asked. "You haven't been talking to me about this. I have wondered where Erika went. How come Erika has that far-away look in her eyes now when I talk to her? Where did you go?"

"Tom, please don't go away," Erika said. "I have been so mixed up, and I have been fighting my way back to you. I hope this Friday night puts it all to rest. I really do. I am so, so sorry."

"The last month has confirmed all of my most paranoid fears about our future," I said. "This is what I feared when I told you that I loved you and that I was afraid. I was afraid that because I fell in love with you, it would change our relationship, and you wouldn't like what it changed to."

"I know, you sweet man," Erika said. "I am afraid I have really trampled on your feelings lately because I have been so into myself. Do you wish you had made other choices? Do you wish you had gone with Theresa instead of putting up with me and my problems?"

"Let's talk about Theresa for a minute," I said, as she looked a little surprised that I pounced on that topic. "When Theresa approached me, much as Todd approached you, I had a choice to make and I made it. I didn't take a month or more to figure it out. I didn't want to do that to you ... I didn't want to do that to us."

"Theresa was someone you knew at work; Todd was my husband," Erika said.

"Point taken, but it doesn't invalidate the choice I had to make," I retorted.

"She would undoubtedly take you back, so if you have regrets ..."

"Don't do that, Erika; that is not what I meant. How much clearer could I make my choice? I want you, you are all that I have ever wanted," I said. "Come back to me. Can it be like it was? Can it even be better than it was? I just want you back from wherever you have been. I don't want to fight with you, just come back."

She picked my hand up off of the table and kissed it. "Friday night is it. I am resolving it. Just trust me to handle this the way I feel I must. I promise I will come back to you. That has never been a question in my mind. Please hang in there just a little longer."

I just nodded and smiled at her.

"I am looking so forward to celebrating your birthday at the beach with you," Erika said. "You and I need time away from all of this."

Chapter 17

SHELTER FROM THE STORM

Erika had been pressing me about the date of my birthday. She threatened to call Christine or Shelly or even my mother. I finally told her that it was October 20. Then she started pressing for what I wanted for my birthday. I could think of something, but I wasn't sure she was ready to give that particular present. If she witnessed me blowing out my birthday candles and making a wish, it wouldn't have taken much imagination on her part to know what I wished for—I felt I had made it clear.

Before I told her when my birthday was, I taunted her, telling her that I knew her birthday was January 14. She wanted to know how I found out, but I wouldn't tell her.

Erika asked, "So what do you really want for your birthday?"

"That is a pretty loaded question," I said. "Surprise me."

"Stop it!" Erika said. "You have to tell me something you really, really want."

"The only thing that fits that description is you," I said. "That is what I really, really want."

"You have that," she said, smiling and teasing me. Surely she realized my meaning was deeper than she was admitting.

"Okay," I said, "I would like to have you spend the weekend at the beach house with me. I would like for you to take a Friday off, if possible, so we could be there longer. I don't know if that is possible, but the monetary value of a day off would be your gift to me, in addition to the gifts I always get by being with you. You asked, and now I have told you. If you can't do the Friday thing, that is okay, I would take a regular weekend."

She had a big smile on her face and said, "You got it! You could have anything, and you want to spend time with me?"

"Yes," I said, "there is nothing I want more."

She smiled, kissed me on the cheek, and said, "A weekend at the beach is a pretty good gift for me too."

"If you enjoy my gift, then that is so much the better."

The plan was now in place for another beach house getaway with Erika. This would undoubtedly be a different experience than the one last summer. The Oregon coast, in the late fall or winter, can be a hostile place. The coast usually gets Portland's rain times four.

If we could leave Portland on Thursday night after work, this could maximize our time at the beach. Erika said she thought that sounded perfect. A major storm was brewing off the coast and was supposed to move inland overnight.

It was probably going to be a good weekend for reading a book while the storm raged outside. A good foul-weather pastime at the Oregon coast is "storm watching" on just such a weekend as the one that approached us. If you were lucky enough to have a vantage point out of the weather, like a beach house, it was a thrilling experience to watch the waves being whipped up in the storm. It was truly spectacular to have a front row seat for a display of the ocean at full fury as huge waves crashed onto the beach. Erika had never experienced that and was excited at the possibilities.

As we left Portland for the eighty-eight-mile drive to Lincoln City, it appeared we were going to get our money's worth this weekend. The wind was picking up in Portland, and the closer we got to the beach, the stronger the winds became. There was going to be a lot of rain following these winds onto the coast, and I hoped to be in the beach house by the time that happened. We stopped for a quick dinner on the way to the coast, anticipating that when we got to the beach house, we would just hunker down for the night as the storm's fury came on shore.

The drive to the beach from Portland can be pretty treacherous on a stormy night. The road passes through large, beautiful forests of seventy-five- to one-hundred-foot-tall Douglas fir trees, which can potentially come crashing down in high winds, blocking the road or, worse, crushing your car and you. The rain was starting in earnest as we pulled into Lincoln City. It had been getting pretty dicey to safely drive through the forest.

As we pulled into the driveway of the beach house, the rain was pounding us. Small branches were coming off of the trees and pelting my car and the driveway. I was a little concerned about leaving the Porsche in the driveway to weather the storm. We ran for it and got inside.

"This is going to be an exciting night," I said. "I am so glad to be here now, but this will be different than our idyllic summer weekend at the beach house."

"Definitely," Erika said, "but this is going to be exciting. It is very nice to be back in your beach house with you."

"I am hoping this will be a good experience for you and I hope you will not be disappointed," I said.

Erika said, "I am a big girl. I can handle it, and you do not need to take responsibility for the storm or my fun this weekend. I am pretty sure I will have lots of fun, being marooned in a beach house with you while a storm rages outside. Sounds awesome to me, and it will be another adventure for us."

I said that I was hoping for a stormy weekend but I didn't want to be interviewed by a reporter on the weekend news as I surveyed my demolished beach house. Such storms were fresh on everyone's mind in the fall of 2004, since the Atlantic Coast had just suffered through the deadliest and costliest storm season on record. Fortunately, we were on the Pacific Coast.

"Go ahead and settle in, and get the lights and heat on," I said. "I will go outside and get a few logs to start a fire for us."

"You are going outside?" Erika asked. "It is scary out there, be very careful."

We settled in for the night as the storm continued to rage. The lights flickered a few times, as can often happen on stormy nights like this. But I had a fire going, and I had Erika with me. That was enough for a great night.

I looked into her beautiful eyes twinkling in the firelight and said, "Erika, thank you for making this a memorable birthday weekend for me. I am so lucky to have you in my life and to do these kinds of things with you."

"Have you ever been told how incredibly romantic you are?" she asked.

"Actually, no, I don't remember anyone saying that to me. I risked your life dragging you through the forest in a horrible storm ..."

"You are, you know; very romantic. What is incredible to me is that you don't seem to realize it, but that is just how you are wired," Erika said sweetly.

"I just want to be with you, and you make me very happy, Erika."

"Happy birthday, Tom," she said, smiling at me. "Is it fifty-four?"

"I thought you said that was just a label, right? You know, it is strange," I replied. "I have actually stopped thinking about birthdays since I started hanging out with you. In fact, I think I am getting younger."

She laughed off my comment and said, "I feel myself decompressing already. This is awesome here."

"Oh yeah," I replied. "This week has been a killer, and I was ready for this. Knowing I had a weekend at the beach with you may have actually made the rest of the week harder. I wanted to bolt for the door all week long."

"The storm can rage on outside now because I am safely inside with my great protector," Erika said.

"Is that how you view me? I have never considered myself in those terms."

"You know," Erika said, "my father was not around much, and I never really felt safe and secure with anyone, even my ex-husband, like I have with you."

I replied, "There is no accounting for taste, Erika. I find it impossible to imagine someone not loving or cherishing you."

"That is because you know how to make a woman feel special. You are the first man who has ever opened car doors for me, brought me flowers, or been tender with me in so many other ways," Erika said.

"I guess I am just old-school or something," I said. "Erika, I hope I don't come off like your father or, worse yet, grandfather. I try really hard to not be that way. I want to be your friend, but I don't want to be an old guy to you. I guess it is inescapable, I am an old guy."

"A little birthday blues going on here?"

"The forties were okay, but heading into the fifties sucks. I am starting to feel like I am changing, and not for the better," I said.

"Look at you," Erika said. "You are a successful man who has raised his family and now is spending his birthday with this 'incredible, amazing young woman' in your very own beach house. You have a Porsche now. You could do worse."

"Since you put it that way, I am feeling better. I wish we could somehow make our age difference go away," I said.

Erika said, "I have told you several times that your perception of yourself, and how you look through my eyes, is apparently very different. You are not 'an old guy,' you are a very charming man and my dear friend, who I obviously trust implicitly. Isn't that good enough?"

I thought to myself, truthfully, no, but I would settle for it for now, like I always have. I said, "I guess I wonder, as Paul McCartney once sang, will you still want me when I'm sixty-four?"

"Oh yeah, I remember hearing something about that group," Erika taunted me. "It was like before I was born, but what were their names ... there were four of them, right?"

"So ends the birthday pep talk by Erika," I said.

"By the way," she said, "what the heck is going on outside? Listen to that." We heard a series of crashes and bangs as the storm roared on. We looked out the window, but could really not see anything as torrential rains hit the windows facing the beach.

"Let's turn out the lights and sit here to watch the storm, okay?" I said.

"Spoken like my true, romantic, and young-at-heart friend," Erika said. With all of the lights out in the beach house, it occurred to me that this blackness could become nonoptional as the night's storm continued.

"I am going to locate the candles before we go to bed, just in case," I said to Erika.

"Wow, were you like a Boy Scout or something when you were younger?" Erika teased.

"No, I spent most of my time scouting girls."

Erika laughed as I started going through drawers, trying to locate candles and matches.

"How long is the power usually out here when there is a problem?" Erika asked as I continued to rummage through drawers and cabinets.

"An hour or a week, or anywhere in between. There is probably only a 50-50 chance we will have coffee in the morning."

"Spoken like a true Portlander," Erika said. "A tree may fall on me ... that's okay; the power may be out for a week ... we can handle it; we can't make coffee ... oh, no, we are all going to die."

As the fire died down, we headed to our separate rooms for what would likely be an interesting night's sleep. Erika hugged and kissed me and said good night.

I lay in bed thinking about the discussions we have had about her marriage and Todd's attempts to win her back. It seemed to conjure up Erika's demons. I now thought that maybe it was not so much demons as it was an almost irresistible opportunity for Erika to correct what she viewed as her major failure. I could not understand how someone could be married to Erika and become indifferent to her. If she were mine, there would never be a doubt about how much I loved and cherished her.

But now I sympathized with Todd's efforts, even though I did not want him to succeed. He made a serious effort to win back the heart of the woman he loved. Todd also wanted to make up for his mistakes. One of the mysteries of the human heart is that we love who we love. We do not know why, particularly. We can list outward signs as to why we are attracted to that person, but we do not know what makes us fall *in* or *out* of love.

I do not know why Erika has so gotten to me. In some ways, I wish I didn't love her so much and so completely. This could, and likely will, end badly for me. She is probably just too young for me and not looking for a romantic relationship with me. I wasn't looking for this to happen and never imagined falling in love with a thirty-year-old woman. The odds could be long that she would someday love me like I loved her, but I couldn't resist.

After our romantic encounter on the blanket on the Fourth of July, she had given me little acknowledgment of what was said that night. She had not referred to it directly. I told her I had a problem, and I confessed my love for her. Didn't it register with her? She told me she loved me too. What does that mean? How long do I have to be patient? I had probably overcommitted too early. I tipped my hand. That is always the risk with being the first one to say, "I love you." The other person now has the strategic advantage.

But I just couldn't deal with this as a tactical game. It is Erika who has brought me back into life. I think about her all of the time. I don't want to be without her. Just as it seemed things might be moving my way, the upheaval came with Todd re-entering the scene. I was suddenly feeling somewhat discouraged at my prospects with her. Perhaps, my long-suffering patience with our relationship was wearing thin. Perhaps, it was having another birthday. My frustrations were boiling over a little tonight for some reason.

This was my state of mind as I dozed off amid the raging storm outside and as I pictured Erika lying alone in her bed during the storm. What restful sleep there was that night was short-lived.

The intensity of the storm increased. I had been at the beach house on many stormy nights, but this one was creeping up the all-time list of nasty storms. The rain gutters were clanking as the howling wind shook them. The walls of the house were actually vibrating as wind gusts hit the house broadside. The beach side of the house was taking a real pounding. I was awake, and there wasn't much chance of going back to sleep.

Then suddenly, it was like a vision appearing in the doorway. My bedroom door slowly swung open, and Erika appeared in light-colored pajamas, carrying a candle. "Tom, are you awake?" she said quietly.

"Very much awake," I said.

"I think the power is out, and there is no heat," Erika said.

I reached for the nightstand lamp and flipped the light switch, to no avail.

"Do you want to put on some more layers and come in here with me?" I offered.

"Yes," she said.

I lit both candles and pulled on a sweatshirt over my t-shirt. Erika reappeared with a hooded sweatshirt and socks, carrying her candle. She climbed into bed and put her candle on the nightstand.

"I wanted a stormy night but, I am sorry, this is not exactly what I had in mind," I said. "Are you all right with trying to survive the storm together in here?" I asked.

"I am freezing," she said.

"Let's get warm, or try." I extended my arms, and she backed into me to cuddle. I put my arms around her from behind and grabbed her hands, which were clutched in front of her.

"Your hands are really cold," I said.

"Ya think?" Erika replied. "How come your hands are so warm?"

"I will take it as a personal challenge to keep you warm," I said.

We lay there cuddling, and I rubbed her hands with mine. I felt her body next to mine as she backed into the arch of my body.

"That is nice," she said. "I forgot how much I loved to be cuddled. Todd never liked to cuddle; he said it annoyed him when he was trying to fall asleep."

"You are really trying to make me like Todd, aren't you?"

"No, I ..."

Before she could complete her answer, I said, "You are in the clutches of one of the great cuddlers, and I assure you, I am not annoyed."

"It is starting to feel good, thank you," she said.

We remained in a tight ball, with my arms around her and my face buried in her thick black hair. We were listening to all the sounds of the storm and not talking. I was starting to be distracted by the feel of her body next to mine and the wonderful smell of Erika I was experiencing by having my face buried in her hair.

She broke the silence by saying, "When you have fantasized about sleeping with me, is this how you pictured it?"

"Oddly enough, it is. I pictured you wearing three layers of clothing and us freezing to death."

She laughed. "So, you have fantasized about sleeping with me?"

"Wait a minute, is this one of those questions women ask where you get in trouble regardless of the answer, like 'Does this dress make my butt look big?"

"Well, is it?"

"What?"

"Is my butt too big?"

"Erika, seriously, tell me, do you think you have a big butt?"

"No, it is okay."

I said, "I knew if I lived long enough, this moment could one day happen. I have found the one woman in America who doesn't think her butt is too big."

"Now we can tell all of the gossipy people who seem so interested in us that we have, in fact, slept together," she said.

I laughed and said, "This reminds me of a Valentine's Day a few years ago. I planned a Valentine's getaway with Liz to the beach house. I even went to Victoria's Secret to pick out a nice nightie for her."

"For her or you?" Erika asked.

"Whatever. We came here, and it was a stormy, windy night, and the power went out. I am sure all of the restaurants, which were packed with Valentine's couples, were thrilled with the power company when things went black. The beach house was without power, and all my plans were ruined."

"You didn't get any action, huh?" Erika asked.

"Liz was one of those women who would want a sweater in equatorial Africa. So I didn't even get to hold her like I am cuddling you. She put on every stitch of clothes she had and piled blankets on her.

The nightgown never made it out of the box. Happy Valentine's Day to me."

Erika laughed. "Sweet plans, though, you get points for that. Isn't it funny how plans don't quite come together sometimes? Like tonight."

"True, but I could do way worse than holding you by candlelight."

We continued to talk quietly, and I launched into a story about something else that happened at the beach house long ago. Then I noticed that she was not responding and had dozed off. I listened closely and could hear her rhythmic breathing, indicating she was again warm and asleep. I was having another moment to remember with Erika. In her past, she had wondered if Todd loved her and she had wished he would hold her. I did both, intensely.

When I first became aware that the night was over, there was dim light coming through the blinds into the bedroom. The other sensation was that there was no feeling in my right arm. Erika apparently had not have moved since we went to sleep. I tried to adjust my arm to restore blood flow without waking Erika. I flexed my hand to try to get rid of the tingly feeling. I was enjoying holding Erika so much I did not want it to end. If amputation of my arm was necessary later, because there had been no blood flow for four hours or something, I was willing to pay that price.

I didn't hear the wind pounding outside any longer, but it was still cold in the house and the bedside lamp was not on. So I assumed the power was still out. I also had no idea what time it was. Erika started to stir. My arms were still around her as she put her hand on my hand. I started to pull out my tingly arm and looked at her.

"How are you doing?" I said.

"Great; I slept so well after you cuddled me and made me warm," she said.

"Were you comfortable? I didn't crush you or anything, right?" I said.

"I acted like I was pretty comfortable, since I didn't move all night, wouldn't you say?"

"I hope I didn't snore in your ear or molest you during the night. You know I can't be responsible for what I might have done in the middle of the night while I was holding you and sleeping."

Erika said, "Oh, nice disclaimer. So last night you were free to grope all you wanted, huh?"

"No, I ..."

Erika giggled and said, "You couldn't have found me anyway, in all of these clothes. You were a perfect gentleman as usual. There was some deep breathing going on in my ear, for a while, but no snoring. The deep breathing was kind of exciting ..."

"Really? I wish you had awakened me, if that were the case."

She laughed and rolled over to face me. Her face was just a few inches from my face as we lay side-by-side. Her hair was in disarray. However, her blue eyes were locked on mine, and she smiled. It had an incredible impact on me, and I couldn't take my eyes off of her. We said nothing for a few moments but just continued to smile at one another.

"Another adventure added to our list," Erika said.

As we continued to stare at one another, I said, "I know I am definitely getting the best of this situation."

"What?"

I said, "I know what I look like in the morning and now I know what you look like in the morning. You are way better."

She laughed. "You are not so bad to look at."

"But using any measuring stick, you are better."

"By the way, happy birthday, Tom," she said and kissed me.

"Thank you for doing this crazy thing with me."

"I wouldn't have missed it. It is awesome."

"I wonder what it is like outside," I said. "What if it was like one of those science-fiction movies, where we walk out on the beach and discover all of civilization was destroyed while we were asleep, and you are the last woman and I am the last man?"

"You wish! I think you watch too many movies."

"You are probably right. At least we would have you in the gene pool as earth began again."

She laughed. "Yeah, all of the world would be tall, skinny girls."

"Answer a question for me. Do pretty women know they are pretty?"

"What?"

"Tell me, despite all of your silliness and disclaimers, you know you are a very attractive woman, don't you? Haven't you been treated differently all of your life because you are pretty?"

"I guess I am okay. I have told you the things I don't like about myself, but I don't feel like I have been treated differently."

"Okay, let's take a test ..."

Erika started laughing and said, "I love your hypotheticals and your theories," and she continued to laugh.

I pressed forward. "How many traffic tickets have you received in the last five years, Erika?"

We continued to lay face-to-face. I loved to watch the expressions on her face change from this close-up perspective. I loved watching her eyes twinkle and flash, and she responded to me.

"What are you talking about?" Erika said. "What does this have to do with anything?"

"Answer the question, how many?"

Erika said, "I don't know. None, I think. I have had a few warnings."

"A few warnings! Damn cops. I knew it."

"Where is this going? How many tickets have you had?"

I said, "Probably, five tickets, so like one a year."

"Well, then, you should be more careful," Erika said.

"Or I should have beautiful black hair and big blue eyes," I said.

"So you are saying that I don't get traffic tickets because I am pretty?"

"Gee, do you think?"

"You are so full of crap. That is so not true."

"Yeah, whatever. You know the odds of me getting a warning and the cop saying, 'Hey, it could happen to anyone, so you be more careful in the future, cutie pie.'"

With that, she poked me in the ribs and said, "That is so not true. Hey, did I just detect that you are kind of ticklish?"

"No, not at all."

She smiled.

"There is another side to being perceived as pretty."

"Hey," I said, "I am well aware of the burden of people liking me just because I am incredibly good looking."

"No, seriously, some people think a woman can't be smart and attractive. If you get a promotion or something at work, is it because you are smart and qualified and earned it? Or is it because you are pretty? One time, I applied for a job in my company, and I was competing against a middle-aged woman. I actually had more experience in the skills needed and had an advanced degree that she didn't. I got the job, and I know she thought it was because I was young and attractive. She really hated me after that."

"Well, I guess smart and pretty beats smart and ugly ..."

"Okay, that's it. If I went to your office, would the staff that you have hired all look like Charlie's Angels with push-up bras?"

"No, no, I was just kidding. I don't really feel that way," I said.

"I know, you just enjoy being a bad boy and messing with me."

We stopped talking and just looked at one another and smiled.

"Thanks for keeping me warm and being my wonderful friend," she said.

"It was my pleasure, and I am sorry it was such a weird night."

"Not as far as I am concerned," Erika said.

"What time do you think it is?" I asked.

Erika got up on one elbow and picked up my cell phone from the nightstand. "Whoa, it is almost noon!"

"Are you up for a walk on the beach to take a look at the aftermath?"

We got out of bed and walked to the front door. When we opened it, we saw the beach littered with debris and massive piles of seaweed, all of which came on shore in the storm. Oregon beaches also can get huge logs washed onto the beach during a storm, and last night was no exception. The wind was still blowing but nothing like the night before.

"What do you think?" I said, wondering if she wanted to venture out.

"There is no power, so why not take a walk?" Erika said. Just then, her cell phone rang in the back bedroom.

"Oh, hi, Mom.... No, we are fine.... We have no power but we are doing okay.... Yeah, Tom has candles and extra blankets, and he has got us all safe and warm.... You are right, he is...."

Erika leaned away from the phone and said, "She said to tell you hi, and that you are awesome."

I just smiled and nodded.

"Don't worry," Erika said into the phone, "we are okay.... Yeah, we head back tomorrow.... How's Portland?"

Erika listened for the response and then said, "Okay, see you when I get back, love you."

Then turning to me with a smile, she said, "Mom says she knows I am always okay when I am with you, but she was just checking."

"I really *do* like your mother. Of course, I am used to being showered with constant positive feedback from my mother...."

Erika laughed. "Mom said it rained tons in Portland last night, but everything is fine now."

"It figures," I said, "the coast got pounded big time. Now all we need is some electricity."

We bundled up and headed down the beach.

"Erika," I said as we walked, holding hands. "I need to talk to you. I am fighting for survival here. I am confused. Could you help me?"

"What? What is wrong?" she said.

"This has been a bit of a tumultuous time at the end of the summer, and I have tried to let things run their course. I am trying to keep up with where we are. What is it you want of me? Do you want anything of me?" I asked.

"What do I want of you?" she asked in a puzzled tone. "Where is this coming from, what is troubling you?"

"I don't know where I am with you. What did our discussion on the blanket on the Fourth of July ... I mean ... what did the things we said that night mean to you? I am not just imagining that night—it *did* happen, right?" I asked in a frustrated tone.

"Of course it did, Tom. Why are you saying that?" Erika asked, with a very concerned look on her face.

"It seems like you have ignored what I told you that night. I confessed to you that I was concerned. I told you that I had a problem. I even took my problem to your mother for advice. I told you I was afraid. I told you I love you.... I am still afraid and I still love you," I said as my voice was beginning to get out of control and reflect my exasperation.

"I am so sorry, Tom. I have not treated you well. Since that night, so much has happened. We were apart for a while, in August, and then this thing with Todd really messed with my mind. I was trying to get my head around all of my feelings, and I was really struggling," she offered. "I took advantage of you."

"I know you have had a tough time. I offered, and still offer, that if you need some space, I will go away for a while.... I understand ...," I said.

"I don't want you to go away, Tom. It is me, not you. I am so screwed up. I don't know if I am ready or capable of getting back into a serious relationship ... that is what I meant when I said I will need some more time," Erika said.

"But those are the words of someone who is being analytical—not someone who is in love and can't help themselves. I didn't want to fall in love with you. I didn't want to jeopardize our relationship. I am afraid of rejection too," I said. "I am taking a real chance. One of my friends warned me, when I first started seeing you, that I should not get too attached to you. He said I should be careful because, he warned, sooner or later, you would leave me because our age difference is too great."

"Why would someone say that?" Erika asked.

"Because my friend is afraid for me. That is one of the things I am referring to when I say I am afraid," I countered. "Help me, Erika. I am trying to understand. That night on the blanket, you told me that you loved me too.... I am confused.... Have I misinterpreted everything?"

We suddenly stopped walking. She looked at me and started to cry. She put her arms around me and said, "Tom, I am so, so sorry. I do love you.... I really do love you. I have never met anyone like you. *Never.*"

"Are you afraid to have a serious relationship with me, Erika? Just tell me ... just tell me now. I will try to understand if you don't want me in that way. Please just tell me—what I said in the beginning—what do you want from me?"

"I want you to be my friend; I want you to be with me every minute. I am never as happy as when I am with you. And yes, I do love you. Things are beginning to change for me too, Tom."

"What do you mean, change?"

"We started out as good friends, but just recently things started to change for me. I have begun to fall in love with you also. I really have. I realized it for the first time on the blanket that night," Erika said, wiping tears from her eyes. "I was afraid that this relationship you and I have had would change. I didn't want to lose that. I was afraid too, Tom. I was afraid to go to the next step and lose what I had with you."

"Are you afraid to expose yourself to love again because you were so hurt in your divorce?" I finally asked.

"Yes, Tom. I had my heart broken. I blamed myself. I never wanted to open myself up for that kind of pain again. I know it is wrong and irrational, but I can't seem to shake my fear," Erika confessed.

I grabbed her tightly and said, "My beautiful, beautiful Erika. I am so sorry you experienced that. I love you. Trust me, I will never hurt you. Just take my hand and venture out there with me.... I will keep you safe, just like I did last night. You asked me before we came here ... what do I really, really want? Last night, I finally came up with the answer while I was holding you as the storm raged outside."

She raised her head and looked into my eyes. Tears ran down her cheeks in the cold, moist air. I continued, "What I really, really want is to hold Erika amid life's storms that will undoubtedly rage around us. But we will both be safe together."

"My dear, sweet Tom," she said, "don't ever doubt again that I do love you ... please. I am catching up; I ask your patience a little longer. I am trying. I am really trying. Just hold me, be my friend, and love me."

Finally, there was a break in the tension. "If there is one thing I can't stop doing, it is loving you." I took her face in my hands and said, "You make me crazy, but the pain is so exquisite," trying to inject some levity into the serious talk.

She smiled and brushed away her tears.

Suddenly, I said, "By the way, where in the hell are we? We got a little carried away talking ... is that Tillamook Head up there?"

Erika laughed. Tillamook Head is a famous landmark on the coast near Seaside, Oregon, which is about ninety-three miles up the coast from Lincoln City.

It wasn't Tillamook Head, but we did turn around and walk back towards the beach house.

"Are we okay, Tom?" she asked.

"We are okay, Erika. Thank you for your assurances, and thank you for loving me."

We walked with our arms around one another's waist. It was a cold, gray day after the storm. The moisture in the air chilled our bones. The entire landscape—both land and sea—were made up of shades of gray. I had a hooded sweatshirt on under my coat. I removed my coat and put it around Erika's shoulders. We said little on our return trip. We just held one another closely.

By the time we returned, the bedside lamp was on, indicating the power had been restored. I heard the heater going. After taking warm showers, we spent the day relaxing, reading, and talking. I really felt I had cleared the air. I was now at peace with Erika and felt we were back in synch.

Erika planned a birthday dinner at a local restaurant. Of course, she slipped away to talk to the waiter so they could provide the most humiliating display possible for my birthday, with singing and a cupcake with a candle.

When we returned to the beach house, I lit a fire and we got cozy. I could tell Erika was still a little sleep deprived. She tried to hang in there but her eyes were closing as she felt the warmth of the fire.

"Sorry I am being such a dud, but this is so wonderful in front of the fire. It makes me sleepy and so relaxed."

"Sleepy and relaxed are two of the reasons to have a beach house," I said.

I laid some pillows in front of the fire and asked Erika to join me. She laid her head on the pillow on the floor. I sat by her.

"I want to tell you a story."

"A bedtime story! It has been a while. I seriously hope I stay awake through the story."

I said, "I hope I make it interesting enough to hold your attention."

"I saw this in a movie once ...," I began. "One of my all-time favorite movies."

Erika interrupted and said, "A movie ... you like movies ...? I had no idea."

"Be nice or we will skip the bedtime story," I said mockingly.

She laughed and said, "Sorry, I will be good." I began to run my fingers through her long black hair as I told her the story.

"A soldier met a beautiful princess at a ball given by the king ..."

"Cool, a princess story," she said.

"Quiet, please," I said. "The soldier thought she was the most beautiful thing he had ever seen. He immediately fell in love with her. The princess was impressed by the soldier's strong feelings. She told the soldier that if he would wait under her balcony for a hundred days and a hundred nights, she would come to him. The soldier waited patiently through rain, snow, and wind. Birds pooped on him, insects bit him, but still he waited. The princess watched the soldier faithfully waiting each night to earn her love. He stayed at his post for ninety-nine days."

"So what happened?" Erika said, suddenly sensing the seriousness of the parable.

"In the parable, the soldier's strength gave out and he could not come back for the hundredth day. One more day and he would have earned her love. When the character in the movie is told this parable, he reenacts the test and tries it on the woman he loves. The woman in the movie peeks out of her window each night and sees the man standing, patiently waiting. She comes to him on the hundredth day and they fall in love."

She looked deeply at me and said, "I like the movie ending better. I promise I will not let you waste away waiting."

"I want you to know that I will gladly wait, in snow, in rain ..."

"I know you will," Erika said.

"In the parable, the soldier was sustained by the hope he had for ninety-nine days that he could actually have the princess for his own. But in the end, he was disappointed. His hope was in vain," I concluded.

With that, we kissed deeply and stared into one another's eyes in the glow of the fire.

"I will try not to disappoint you," Erika said softly.

"Thank you for a wonderful day and a wonderful birthday," I said. "I loved my gift."

"My pleasure."

I continued to run my fingers through her hair and lightly rub her face. She closed her eyes and enjoyed my caressing. Soon, she was asleep.

I continued to enjoy looking at her sleep by the fire and lightly touching the woman I loved. We had come a long way since the night when she was sick. I could now be open in my love for her. I hungered for more. But after the turmoil of the end of the summer, this weekend I felt like I finally had Erika back.

I helped her up and we headed towards the back bedroom.

I said, "If you get cold tonight …"

"Thanks, I will keep that in mind, but I think my heater works now."

"I am not so sure," I said. "I think that one is kind of unreliable. The one in my bedroom is really good, so … if there is a problem, or if you would just like to be held by someone who loves you … I am behind that door over there."

She shook her head and sleepily said, "Thanks for the offer, and I will keep you in mind if I require your services."

"Please do," I said. She hugged me and went off to bed.

Chapter 18

MASKING FEELINGS

THE SUMMER had passed quickly and I had seen little of Dave. We would occasionally run into one another and talk. We had not had lunch together since that day when Erika broke down on the freeway. A lot had happened this past summer.

I called him and arranged to meet him for lunch at the Blue Note one day in October. I had asked to meet him for a talk before Erika and I had gone to the beach for the stormy weekend. Some of my concerns that I wanted to discuss with Dave had seemed to dissipate after my talk with Erika at the beach house.

Still, I felt very anxious about her holding back. I found myself being jealous of Todd. I still felt uneasy about how my declaration of love in July had seemed to have so little impact on Erika. Even though she was affectionate and sweet to me, I was wondering if I was becoming more of a father figure to her, or her "best friend."

Dave and I met at the underground hamburger place.

"Sorry we haven't gotten together for a while, the summer seemed to go so fast," I said.

"You know, I wouldn't blame you if you didn't want to have lunch with me," Dave said. "I owe you an apology for last time. I felt I said some things I shouldn't have said about you and Erika. It really is not my business."

"Actually, that is not my take on it at all," I countered. "It turned out that you were right on about many things. Let me tell you what happened."

This really got Dave's attention.

"One day, early in September, I went over to Erika's condo. She informed me that her ex-husband was coming by to have her sign some papers. It was supposed to be kind of a quick thing. An hour and a half later, I was still cooling my heels in the park, and then Erika finally came out to meet me."

"Whoa, what happened?" Dave inquired.

"Well, she said that her ex-husband was trying to talk her into coming back to him," I continued. "She says she won't do it because she is in a relationship with me. But she agonized for the next month about the things he said to her."

"A month?" Dave said incredulously. "Damn. If she had made her decision, why did it take a month?"

My answer was delayed, as our burgers came.

"Erika said that she was trying to figure out the best way to handle it, but that I shouldn't worry."

"Was she seeing her ex during this month?" Dave asked.

"Actually, I accused her of that, and she got really upset and said she had not seen him. They just talked. He was trying to woo her back. Her ex-husband said he still loved her and realized that he had made a big mistake."

"Wow, so where did all of this leave you?" Dave asked. "You know, you can always pull the plug, leave her before she leaves you, if it appears things are going south."

"It left me hanging out there for sure, but I feel better after this last weekend," I suggested.

"What happened over the weekend?" Dave said.

"We spent a long weekend at my beach house and got caught in the wild storm that hit the coast. We ended up sleeping together and having long talks about our relationship," I said.

"Well, congratulations; it finally happened," Dave said.

I started to explain that we slept together as in slumber, not as in sex, but I decided to let it lie. I actually thought I didn't need to be constantly explaining my relationship with Erika to others … even Dave.

"So I do feel better about things right now," I said. "I feel like Erika and I are back on the same page. I think things with her ex are now behind us. She still values me more as a friend than a lover, but I can wait. It is moving that way."

"Well, good; that does sound better," Dave said.

"However, your points were very valid, and I thought about them much of the summer, especially when Todd, her ex-husband, reappeared on the scene," I said. "You were right on, and I want to thank you for giving me a heads-up about some of the potential hazards. Really, Dave, thanks for your concern. No apology is necessary."

"I sincerely hope things work out with Erika," Dave offered. "Erika is so charming and beautiful, and there is such a difference in you. I hope I never see you in the state you were in after Liz died. That was painful to watch for those of us who care about you."

"Thank you," I said. "You know, I had some good talks with her mother about this also."

"Really? That is interesting. Her mother?"

"Erika's mother is a very cool lady. A real hottie. I love to talk to her."

"Wow, is she like our age?"

"Yeah," I said, "but she is very supportive of my relationship with Erika. She also told me that Erika was pretty damaged by her divorce. It was something akin to what I went through after losing Liz. Erika is just re-emerging also."

"Interesting," Dave said, as he appeared deep in thought.

"And … it makes me nervous when I see you with that look," I pressed.

"No, no, nothing is wrong," Dave said. "What do I know? I wonder if Erika is ready for a serious relationship yet."

"She is getting there, I think," I said. "That is what she tells me. But you know, I have decided that I need to step back and take a deep breath. You know I can be wrapped a little too tight sometimes."

"No way, you?" Dave said mockingly. "What do you mean, take a deep breath?"

"Do you know how wonderful my life is right now, compared to the last couple of years?" I exclaimed. "I can't begin to tell you … well, you know as much as anyone … but my relationship with Erika has resuscitated me. She pulled me out of the darkness. I love her so much. This wonderful, beautiful, exciting woman wants to be with me. If it ends someday, then I still have so much to be happy about. I didn't think I could ever come back after losing Liz. And look at what has happened."

"You are right, my friend," Dave said, "and I am so happy for you. It is just … no … I am not going to start again …"

"Don't do that to me, now you have to spill it," I said.

"I guess I am just always worried about you because you are my friend. I want you to stay just like you are now, because it is so good to have you back," Dave offered.

"But ... there was going to be a 'but,' wasn't there?" I asked.

"But ... just be careful. I have found this to be true with myself ... and maybe you are wiser than I am ... beautiful women can be dangerous," Dave said.

"Yeah, I have noticed," I said, attempting to shrug it off.

"I mean that sometimes, we are so distracted by the beautiful package that we do not look carefully enough at the contents, you know?" Dave reasoned. "Just be careful."

"I will try, I will really try," I said, "but I seem powerless to resist the spell she casts over me."

"My final word of advice to you is this," Dave said, as I leaned forward to glean the wisdom he was about to dispense, "you should enjoy the ride with your beautiful Erika and continue to be as happy as you are now. You should stop accepting advice from well-meaning friends who don't know what the hell they are talking about."

"Like who?" I asked.

Dave just smiled and said, "It is so good to be with you again. Let's not be strangers. You and I haven't taken a long run together for a while. Let's do it soon."

"You got it," I said. "I would really like that. These fall days are so fantastic for running or anything else."

As the end of October neared, Erika told me that she and her friends were planning a Halloween party. The Goddesses were excited; they had not had a Halloween party for several years. Erika was hosting it at her condo.

Erika excitedly told me about the big plan. She and Jen had found a costume rental place that they thought was reasonably priced and had awesome costumes. The ladies were really revved up about the pending party and selecting costumes.

I listened patiently and then informed Erika, "I just don't do Halloween. I have issues with Halloween."

"What?" she said. "I am not having a Halloween party without you, and I am having a Halloween party. Come on."

"Erika, I have issues with Halloween. I have always hated it."

"Issues?" Erika asked. "Like religious issues, or what?"

"No, I just had some bad experiences as a kid and have never liked it," I said.

"Didn't you like to dress up and get candy?" she pressed.

"Well, initially, but I told you I had some traumatic experiences, and it has left me with issues about Halloween."

Erika looked serious all of a sudden. I think she was wondering if I had been molested or suffered some other serious trauma. "What happened to you?" she asked.

"Well ... I got beat up on Halloween once by the school bully, and it ruined my costume ... and ever since then, I haven't liked Halloween," I said.

"What?" Erika said. "The school bully beat you up? Tell me about it."

"Well, this guy, Russell Johnson, was the meanest kid in our elementary school. We all came in costumes one day for Halloween. Russell was dressed like Dorothy from *The Wizard of Oz* ..."

Erika interrupted, "Your school bully was dressed like Dorothy from *The Wizard of Oz*? You had a really sexually conflicted bully, didn't you?"

"He wore the blue gingham dress and the red shoes and everything. He had a wig on with ribbons and pigtails ..."

Erika started rolling on the couch, laughing hysterically. "Tom, are you telling me that you don't like Halloween because Dorothy kicked your ass one Halloween?"

"Well, yeah ..."

She was now cackling loudly and added, "And Toto, too?" Erika then fell over on the couch laughing. "That is the funniest thing I have ever heard."

"I am revealing a moment of childhood trauma, and you are laughing hysterically," I countered.

"I am sorry, this one tops all of the Tom stories ...," she said, as she continued to laugh.

After she stopped laughing, she said, "So that was like in the fourth grade or something, and you have written off Halloween forever?"

"Yeah," I said, "and I am not too crazy about *The Wizard of Oz* either."

She began laughing again, held out her arms, and said, "Come here. You poor guy." She hugged me but continued to snicker. "I will help you with the costume and get you back into Halloween, okay?"

"No, I don't like Halloween ..."

"I know, sweetie, but trust me ... I will be gentle with you. Let me help you confront your fears."

"Are you making fun of me?" I asked.

"No, I am not," Erika said, trying to keep a straight face. "I will walk you through this, and it will be fun. I will pick out a costume for you at the rental place."

"Minimalism, okay, Erika?" I said. "Like just a hat and now I am a cowboy ... or something like that."

"Minimalism?"

"Yeah, I don't want to be a clown or a bear or lion or something weird like that," I said.

"Trust me, okay? I will be sensitive to your needs," Erika said, trying to suppress a giggle. "No lions or tigers or bears—right?"

"Funny ... nor tin men either."

"I got it."

"What are you going to be, Erika?"

"I am still struggling with that."

"Hey, remember in the third *Star Wars* movie when Princess Leia was a slave girl?"

"Yeah, right," Erika said. "You would love that."

"I would love that. It would help me feel better about Halloween," I said. "Or what about a mermaid?"

Erika asked, "How come all of the costumes you suggest for me require that I remove my clothes?"

I shrugged my shoulders, and she just rolled her eyes and smiled.

Erika and Jen were picking up the costumes. I was supposed to come to Erika's apartment on Saturday afternoon before the party, and they were going to help me get ready.

When I entered apartment 912 that day, I was greeted by Erika, dressed as a witch. She had on a fairly short black dress with black tights. Her thick black hair was streaked with purple, and she wore black nail polish and black lipstick. Jen, who is an adorable, petite woman with long blonde hair, was wearing a Cat Woman suit. Jen is barely over five feet tall and is an interesting companion for Erika. I am sure it adds to Erika's phobia about being a "giant woman."

"What do you think?" Erika said.

"You guys look awesome," I said. "Erika, you look amazing. You look like Erika's evil twin sister. It is pretty erotic, actually."

"Well, don't get your hopes up too high," Erika said.

"Jen, you look hot," I said.

"Thank you so much. Do you think Ben will like it?"

"Oh yeah," I said. As I went to kiss Erika, she warned me to be careful so I didn't get black lipstick on me.

"Okay, I can't take the suspense any more. What have you two done to me?" They led me back into the bedroom and showed me an old-fashioned-looking suit jacket with tails and weird striped pants. I looked puzzled.

"Groucho," Erika said, "your hero. You can be Groucho Marx. Jen and I will draw the mustache and eyebrows on you."

I hesitated and saw their anxious faces awaiting my verdict. Finally, I nodded and said, "Okay."

Erika and Jen squealed and clapped their hands. "So we did good, huh?"

"You did good, Erika ... and Jen," I said, smiling. Erika and Jen laughed and hugged one another. They exchanged high-fives. They were obviously trying really hard.

"Go change and sit in this chair, then Jen and I will do the rest," Erika said.

I put on the Groucho suit and returned to the kitchen chair. Erika and Jen readied their makeup kit and bent over in front of me to begin working on my face. Suddenly, I was distracted. As Erika bent over in her witch's costume, I could see all the way to her navel, inside the V-necked dress. Erika never showed much cleavage, but now here she was, all barely contained in a small pink bra. I, of course, enjoyed the view immensely.

Then after a few moments, I said, "Erika, I have a question. Do you think a pink push-up bra is a good choice with a witch's dress? Don't you have a black one?"

Her blue eyes went wide. She stood up and put her hand over the front of her dress. Erika gasped and said, "I guess this is pretty low cut ... I didn't realize ..."

"I am not complaining, mind you," I added.

"Maybe you could wear a cami or something under it," Jen suggested.

"And it is not a push-up bra, either," Erika responded.

"Really?" I said. "Impressive."

Jen started laughing and said, "Down, boy."

"I will fix that in a minute, but we have to finish your face now," Erika said. Then Erika bent over me again and warned, "Thomas, I want some eye contact with you."

"Erika, my favorite thing has always been to look into your beautiful eyes ... until now," I said.

"All right, knock it off, you two," Jen said, taking charge. "We have to get this done. Tom, be quiet and just stare at Erika's ta-tas. Erika, finish the eyebrows. I will do the mustache." Then Jen added, "We should have gotten Tom the Harpo costume. Harpo doesn't talk."

I smiled.

Jen said, "Erika, I didn't know Tom was such a naughty boy."

"Oh, he isn't really," Erika said, "he just has this little mischievous side, and he acts naughty."

"Isn't doing naughty things how you become defined as naughty?" Jen asked.

"Hey, I am still here; you two are talking about me like I am not here," I said, "and Jen, the Harpo remark was impressive. You know the Marx Brothers. My esteem for you is rising."

"Thank you so much," she said. Then with a smile, Jen asked, "While we are talking about Erika's body, have you seen her tattoo, Tom?"

"Erika has a tattoo?" I said, completely surprised.

"Shut up, Jen," Erika warned. "You are so evil."

"Oh, yes, Erika has a tattoo," Jen said mischievously. "I am surprised you haven't seen that part of her yet."

"Jen!" Erika said. "Don't do it!"

"Erika, where is your tattoo, and what is it?" I asked.

"Well, that is a little secret, but one you will have to look forward to discovering," Erika said. "A lady must maintain some aura of mystery."

"You know, tattoos seem to be a generational thing, and my generation kind of doesn't get why your generation loves tattoos," I said. "But doesn't a 'lady' [as I made air quotes with my fingers] lose her 'aura of mystery' [I made another air quote] when she pulls down her pants and bends over a table in a tattoo parlor while some greasy guy draws a butterfly on her tush?"

Jen now started laughing loudly.

Erika looked perturbed and said, "That is not what I did."

"Not quite," Jen said.

"Jen, you are so going to pay for this," Erika warned.

"When did this happen, Erika?" I asked.

"Well, one weekend when the Goddesses were having a 'girls weekend,' we got a little carried away and things got out of control. All four of us got them," Erika said. "Shut up, Jen, no more."

"Hey," I said, "I enjoy a good cat fight as much as the next guy, Erika, but you shouldn't start a cat fight with Jen today," referring to her Cat Woman costume.

Jen purred, made a clawing motion, and said, "Yeah, Erika, I have the tools."

"I could whip your scrawny little butt ...," Erika teased. "I am so going to get even with you for this." Erika then said, "You are done, Tom, check it out."

"I have to admit, that is pretty cool," I said. "This could be my best Halloween ..."

Jen interrupted and said, "Since Dorothy kicked your butt?" She and Erika erupted into laughter again.

Chapter 19

REMEMBERING THAT WHICH
WAS LOST

THE STRANGEST thing happened on the Wednesday before Thanksgiving. I was sitting in the house, waiting for Michelle and her family to arrive from Denver. I just happened to be looking out of the front window in my living room when for a minute ... for just a minute ... I thought I saw Liz walking around the corner of the garage and up the front walk towards the door.

It sent an electric jolt through my body, and my first thought was ... it was Liz coming home from somewhere. It would have been a routine sight two or more years ago. Liz had been running errands or out with a client and was coming home. Then I realized it was Michelle.

Michelle had changed her hairstyle since I last saw her in the fall. She had cut her long blonde hair and changed it to a shorter style. The new hairstyle was almost exactly how Liz wore her hair at the time of her death. The odd moment of confusion had a strange effect on me.

All of that day, I thought more about Liz than I had for most of the year. Despite the joy of having Erika in my life, I found myself missing Liz. If only that could have been Liz walking up to my house ... how different things would be.

Maybe it was the gathering of the family that made me nostalgic or melancholy for Liz. It was another moment like I had suffered through during the first two years. This holiday was going to be another time when I was reminded that Liz was missing. Now Erika would be my partner at the family dinner.

The family would all be together for Thanksgiving. This Thanksgiving would be the first time we had all been together since Liz's funeral. Michelle and Rob and the girls had flown in from Denver. Alan was flying in from San Francisco. My mom would be here, and so would Erika.

Michelle and Mom were going to work on the dinner preparation on Wednesday and Thursday morning. Erika would join us midday and be here for Thanksgiving dinner. This would be the first time Erika and my kids had met.

Erika was basically alone for the holiday weekend. She informed me the week before that her mother had started working for a friend's travel agency and loved it. Tricia was going to spend the Thanksgiving weekend with her travel agency buddies in Vegas. It was under the guise of "orientation."

I said it was the first time I had ever heard of someone going to Las Vegas to "get oriented." It usually has the opposite effect. I was impressed with Tricia's plans. I said, "Have I told you how awesome I think your mom is?"

Erika replied, "Yeah, every time I mention her name."

I was starting to wonder if Erika didn't like the lavish praise I was always heaping on her mother.

After my brief moment of hallucination when I saw Michelle, I warmly greeted her when she knocked on the door. She had come to the door alone, since one of the little girls had fallen asleep on their way from the airport. Michelle wanted to pull the van they had rented into the garage and let her sleep a while longer as they unpacked. I pushed the button to raise the garage door so Rob could pull in next to the Porsche. He started smiling when he first spotted it.

Michelle, Rob, and I had decided that renting a van was the way to go, especially since my purchase of the Porsche, or "that funny little car," as my mother described it. I was splitting the cost of the van with them. This would also facilitate our planned trip to the beach house. While Michelle was in Portland, she wanted to spend some time at the beach house after Thanksgiving, before they returned to Denver on Sunday. Alan would accompany us to the beach house also. He would return to San Francisco on Sunday. I was looking forward to spending time with my children and grandchildren at the coast.

Erika would join us for Thanksgiving and then hit the stores with the girls on "Black Friday" the next day. The after-Thanksgiving sales were the equivalent of Super Bowl Sunday to the Goddesses. After everyone flew out Sunday afternoon, I was going to Erika's condo to do some catching up following the long weekend.

Rob was a huge sports fan and was way into the Denver sports scene. It so happened that the Denver Nuggets were in town Wednesday night to play the Trailblazers. I got tickets so Rob and I could go together. Rob thought it was the ultimate stroke of luck to catch a Nuggets game in Portland with me. He was even more excited to be driving in the Porsche to the Rose Garden.

Meanwhile, Michelle was going to begin the meal preparation for Thanksgiving as a proxy for her mother. Michelle would stay home with the girls. She also wanted some time in the house alone to go through some of her mother's things.

Thursday morning, I picked up Alan at the airport and wanted to make sure I got home before Erika arrived. I didn't want Erika to arrive and be alone with my mom, Michelle, Rob, and the girls. About fifteen minutes after Alan and I arrived, Erika pulled into the driveway. I greeted her at the door and introduced her around.

She and Alan hugged and Michelle and Rob greeted her more formally but warmly. My mother said, "It is good to see you again, Erika. You look very pretty." I was grateful for that. Erika was dressed in a blue sweater with a white blouse underneath and gray wool pants. It was simple but elegant, a classic Erika look. Any time Erika wore bright blue, it turned her wattage up a few notches so she looked great.

Erika immediately asked Michelle and Mom what she could do to help them. Erika went to work helping set the table. I went into the kitchen and offered to help also and to watch Erika's back, in case there was an outbreak of undesirable behavior from my daughter or mother. Michelle was very congenial to Erika—so far, so good.

The table seating alignment was me at the head of the table, Erika was on my left seated next to Alan. Rob was on my right. Michelle was at the opposite end of the table between my granddaughters and my mother. I love Rob but I was kind of hoping Michelle would sit by me. I wanted Michelle and Mom to engage in the conversation and not sit grumbling under their breath at the end of the table like some grouchy Pharisees.

As dinner began, Rob and I immediately fell into a conversation about the Blazers and Nuggets and the prospects for the Broncos as the football season headed into the home stretch. Rob was a lot of fun and a total ESPN fanatic. He was a walking encyclopedia of the Denver sports scene. I cocked an ear in Erika's direction and heard her and

Alan talking about environmental law and San Francisco. Mom and Michelle were occupied with getting things passed and food distributed to Brooke and Emily.

Rob directed a shot in Alan's direction.

"Too bad you were not there last night, Alan. You could have seen your Blazers struggling against a young, rebuilding Nuggets team."

"Yeah, yeah," Alan fired back, "rebuilding seems to be a word that gets used in Denver a lot. Portland is just retooling. We will be back."

"I am sure you are still traumatized after collapsing in Game 7 in LA against the Lakers in the 2000 playoffs ...," Rob said, knowingly pushing a hot button with Alan.

"Dad," Alan said, "didn't you inform this guy when he wanted to marry Michelle that there were certain things we didn't speak of in this house?"

Before I could answer, Rob pressed on: "Up by 13 over Shaq, Kobe, and the Lakers ... in LA ... fourth quarter ... and the Blazers take the biggest swan-dive in NBA playoff history and end up watching the finals on TV."

Alan said, "Michelle, control your husband ..."

I said to Rob in mock sternness, "Rob, there are two things we never speak of in this house: Game 7 against the Lakers in 2000 and the draft where the Blazers took Sam Bowie instead of Michael Jordan."

With that, Rob started cackling and slapping the table.

"Rob," I said, "that is like showing a Red Sox fan the tape of the Bill Buckner error in the World Series."

The jabbing and laughing continued, and then Michelle said, "All right, you guys, knock it off." Then she added, "Erika, these guys are so bad. When they get going like this, my mother used to be ready to throw them out of the house. One is as bad as the other."

Erika laughed and said, "So I see," as she reached below the table and patted my leg. I put my hand under the table and squeezed her hand.

Alan said, "Michelle, did you know that Erika is a Duck?"

"No, Alan, I didn't."

Here came the banter about the rivalry between the University of Oregon (the Ducks) and Oregon State (the Beavers).

"Erika," Alan said, "notice how the table just kind of naturally divided into Ducks on one side and Beavers on the other. It's kind of a sixth-sense thing ..."

"I hate to burst your bubble, Alan, but I think Dad asked Erika to sit by him," Michelle said. "It wasn't some mystical Duck karma that you emit."

Erika asked Michelle, "So I presume that you didn't go to school in Eugene?"

"Oh, no, no, no," Rob said, joining the fray. "Michelle and I both went to Oregon State, and we met there."

"Oh, nice," Erika said. "Why did you end up going to school in Corvallis?"

"That is the question …," Alan said. "I ask all of my friends from Oregon State that question; it is baffling."

"That isn't what I meant," Erika said, smiling at Alan.

"I know it isn't what you meant, Erika," Michelle said. "Just ignore him. A lot of my high school friends were going to Oregon State, so I did also."

I interrupted Michelle and said to Erika, "Wasn't I telling you the other day how wonderful it is to have children?"

Erika laughed and then asked Michelle, "So how did you and Rob meet?"

"We actually were both working summer jobs at the same place, and that is how we got together," Michelle said.

"Yeah, there was this cute blonde girl who kept throwing herself at me so I decided to give her a try …," Rob offered.

Michelle rolled her eyes and said, "Whatever. I think you were the smitten one, Rob, and you kept bugging me."

"Isn't love wonderful?" I said sarcastically. Just then Emily, the three-year-old, came over to sit on my lap as the meal was winding down. She whispered in my ear, and I got up from the table and went to help her in the family room. I could hear the conversation continuing, with the good-natured jabbing and laughing.

When I returned, my older granddaughter was perched on Erika's lap, and all eyes were on their exchanges. Michelle asked me where Emily went.

"I started her video for her again," I said.

"Oh, geez, the flying ponies for the twentieth time?" Michelle asked, and I nodded in the affirmative. "Why didn't you make her watch something else, Dad?" Michelle pushed.

I just shrugged my shoulders.

My mother joined the conversation and said to Michelle, "That is always the way he was with you kids, he would let you do anything you wanted. It was always your mother who had to discipline you kids."

I rolled my eyes and said, "Wait, can we confine our criticisms to the twenty-first-century mistakes I have made? There are plenty of those. You can no longer criticize me for the twentieth-century mistakes ... what is it, Alan? You are a lawyer ..."

"Yeah, it is the statute of limitations. The statute of limitations has expired on all of the things Dad did to screw up our lives last century."

"Yeah, statute of limitations," I said. "By the way, thanks so much for that, Alan," I added sarcastically.

Meanwhile, Brooke was inspecting Erika's necklace and large earrings.

"Those are so pretty," Brooke said.

"Thank you," Erika responded.

"I like your long black hair too," Brooke said.

"Well, I think the blonde hair like you and your mommy have is very pretty, so you are very lucky," Erika responded.

Then Brooke abruptly switched topics and said to Erika, "You know, I had a grandma, but she died in a car crash."

"I know," Erika said. "That is very sad, but you have a nice grandpa."

Brooke looked at me and smiled and said, "We are going to the beach tomorrow."

"Oh," Erika said, "are you going to the beach house? That is such a pretty place. That will be fun."

At the mention of the beach house, Michelle shot me a look that lowered the temperature in the room. Michelle then said, "Brooke, quit pestering Erika."

Brooke climbed down and said, "You are pretty."

Erika responded saying, "So are you, Brooke." Erika gave her a hug before Brooke departed into the family room to watch the flying ponies.

I smiled at Erika, and she put her hand on my knee under the table.

Then Mom asked, "So how is everyone getting to the beach with that car your dad bought?"

Alan jumped to my defense: "Grandma, that car Dad bought is one of the finest cars in the world, and it is awesome."

Rob chimed in, "Yeah, Grandma, that car goes 0 to 60 miles per hour in less than five seconds, and it will top out at 200 miles per hour. It is an incredible car."

My mother looked at Rob like he was speaking Mandarin Chinese. Then Alan took a crack at it. "It is a great car, Grandma."

"I just thought it was impractical, and why do you have to go that fast, Rob, when the speed limit is 55?" Mom said.

"Of course it is impractical, Grandma," Alan said. "But Dad is just trying to have some fun."

Mom just shook her head and looked at Michelle for solace. I looked at Erika, and she gave me a smile and was barely stifling a laugh.

As evening shadows began to come across the dining room, our Thanksgiving dinner concluded. We all helped clean up, and then it was time for Erika to go home. She had been so gracious and had really attempted to connect with the family. I appreciated it so much.

As she said her good-byes, I announced I would walk her out. I put my arm around her shoulder as I accompanied her to her car.

"Thanks so much, you sweet lady," I said. "You were a hit, as usual."

"It was fun," Erika responded. "I will miss you. Have fun at the beach and call when you are free."

"I wish you were going to be there with me," I said.

"You need time with them," Erika suggested. "Good luck."

I kissed her and wished her well on her shopping adventure the next day.

As I re-entered the house, before I could speak, my mother, who had been stationed near the living room window, said, "That was quite a good-bye kiss."

"Were you watching me out the window?" I asked. "Were you spying on me?"

"I wasn't spying on you," Mom said. "I was just looking out the living room window; is there a law against that?"

"I expected you to flicker the porch light at me, Mom," I said, referring to her favorite tactic from long ago. When I was a teenager and Mom thought I had been parked in the car with a girl for too long, she would flash the porch light. My kids were enjoying the exchange, seeing my mother chiding me about kissing my girlfriend in the driveway.

"She is great, Dad," Alan offered. "You look very happy when you are with her."

"I am," I simply said.

Michelle said, "She seems very nice. I liked her, Dad. I am glad you are having fun again." I was grateful for the seemingly positive review. It could have been more enthusiastic, but I would take it, I guess.

Friday, after we arrived at the beach house, I kept trying to get close to Michelle, but there seemed to be a barrier. We walked and played with the little girls on the beach around midday. It was very foggy at the beach. From the house, we could not see the water. If you were at the edge of the surf, you could not see my house or the other houses spread out along the strip of beach. It had a very confusing effect. As you walked along the edge of the surf, you could not really tell where you were, since no landmarks were visible because of the fog.

When we returned to the beach house, we had a round of Thanksgiving leftovers that we had transported to Lincoln City. Rob had turned on an NBA game between the Lakers and Dallas Mavericks. Then both of my granddaughters went down for afternoon naps.

After lunch, I suggested, "Hey, let's go take a walk on the beach together, just us."

Michelle said, "We can't, the girls just went down for naps."

Rob interjected, "Hey, go ahead. I will hold down the fort here."

"Yeah, you just want to watch the game," Michelle countered.

"Hey, Rob is just helping out," Alan said. "I am sure he would volunteer to watch the girls even if it wasn't a tie game as the fourth quarter was beginning." Alan and Rob both snickered.

Michelle finally agreed.

So, Alan, Michelle, and I headed out on the beach, just the three of us. I really couldn't remember the last time just the three of us were together. Not even during the post-funeral times were the three of us alone together.

"This fog is weird," Alan said as we left the deck and started walking on the sand.

"Yeah, I don't ever remember seeing it exactly like this," I said. "The fog seems to surround you. It is very disorienting. You lose your bearings quickly as you walk down the beach."

We proceeded to walk down the beach into the thick fog.

"You know," Alan began, "being at the house yesterday and being here today makes me really miss Mom."

"Me too," I said. "It is what I have been struggling with for almost three years. She is missing. There is a big hole in my life. In all of the places that I love to go, like here, she should be with me but she is gone. It is very, very hard."

Michelle was quietly listening and then said, "Apparently Erika has been to the beach house ..."

"Yeah, she has, Michelle," I said, "twice. She is my good friend and companion. It is very comforting to have her with me." I bit my tongue to keep from saying, "It is my house and my friend, so what is the problem?"

"I really think she has been great for you," Alan said. "You act really different now, more like your old self."

"So is she the same age as Alan and me?" Michelle pressed.

"Basically," I said. "I have been troubled by the age difference, and I wanted you two to like her. I didn't want you to be disturbed by her age. But you know, it hasn't been about age. Our relationship has been about two lonely people who needed one another."

Michelle didn't respond to my explanation, but changed topics. "So what's going on with the guy who hit and killed Mom? Where did all of that end up in the courts? Is he is prison now?"

I said, "I don't know."

"You don't know," Michelle said briskly. "Don't you care?"

That comment ignited the dynamite that had been placed on the logjam of my relationship with my daughter.

Alan sensed Michelle had crossed the line and added, "Geez, Michelle."

I could no longer hold back. "Don't I care?! Don't I care?! You know, Michelle, I only get one life. I don't get another. My life was ruined when your mother was killed. It is not going to get better! It was ruined! You have no idea what I have gone through. I can't become this bitter person who walks around all day, shaking my fist at God because I got ripped off. I can't go sit in a courtroom and listen to the life story of the guy who murdered your mother and the details about how he did it! I just can't do it, Michelle. I need to find a way to survive this and salvage something of what is left of my life."

Michelle looked startled. I had never spoken to her like that.

"Michelle, why are you so mad at me? The three of us have suffered an incalculable loss. It is not my fault, Michelle. It is not Erika's fault. Why won't you cut me any slack? Why don't you like me anymore?"

Michelle stopped walking and faced Alan and me. Her fists were clenched and tears of rage were tumbling out of her eyes and down her cheeks.

"I will tell you why! I am so damn mad because that stupid bastard hit my mother, and my life got ruined too! I am twenty-nine years old, and now my mother is gone. I can't call her! I can't do things with her! I can't ever be with her again! It is not fair. But that isn't even what makes me the angriest. My little girls don't have a grandmother. They will never remember her! My mother should have had thirty more years with my girls. My girls will never know how wonderful she was. My mother will just be a photograph on a bookshelf to my girls, and it makes me so damn mad. I will never get over this!" she screamed. "Never!" She stamped her feet on the sand.

I rushed to Michelle and embraced her as she wept uncontrollably. These were the bitter tears of a truly broken heart. I began sobbing audibly also. Alan put his arms around both of us. The three of us sank to our knees on the sand and continued to cry and embrace.

I finally pulled away and began to speak. I told Michelle about the experience I had earlier in the weekend when she walked up the driveway.

"When I saw you," I said to Michelle, "I would have given anything … anything … if it had really been your mother coming home." This caused Michelle to cry out, an almost primal scream of pain, and she embraced Alan and me tighter.

I pressed on. "I want you to both know the feelings of my heart," I said through my tears. "I so wish it had been me who was taken in the accident. Why did it have to be her? I would gladly switch places, and I wish it had been me."

We continued to embrace and audibly sob while kneeling on the sand on this steel-gray, cold day. The moisture in the fog and from our tears caused our breath to show each time we spoke or exhaled.

Michelle held me tighter and kept repeating, "Daddy, I am so, so sorry."

It was as if a poisonous infection had been purged from our systems. The infection had almost been fatal to us, but now it was out. In time, we would be healed. The rest of the weekend, it felt like I had my kids, particularly my beautiful Michelle, back with me.

Wherever Liz is, I hope she could look down on that cold, foggy day on the beach and witness Michelle, Alan, and me shedding bitter tears for what was lost.

Chapter 20

LETTING GO

A FTER I told my family members good-bye at the airport, I immediately dialed Erika on my cell phone.

"Hey you, would you like some company?" I said.

"Absolutely, I have several things to show you, and we can catch up on things," she said.

"I can't wait," I said. "See you in a few minutes."

I can actually say it is a few minutes from the airport to Erika's condo downtown. The Portland Airport is actually in Portland and is a short hop to connect to the Banfield. Conversely, the Denver Airport, where Michelle and her family were headed, even though it is state-of-the-art and an incredible facility, only gives you the illusion that you are really in Denver. It is a pretty long drive to Denver from that airport. It feels like you are in Kansas.

When Erika opened her door, she was wearing denim jeans and a lime-green, V-necked sweater, which showed much more cleavage than she usually did. She also had bare feet.

"Hello," I said as I kissed her. "Don't you look great! I like your sweater, is that new?" I still had not gotten over the thrill of walking up to Erika and kissing her when I saw her. It still seemed wonderful that I could do that.

"It is a new top," Erika responded. "I thought you would like this one."

"Very much," I said. "It is a different look for you; very nice, very sexy."

"You don't think it is too much, do you ... too low cut?" Erika asked.

"Oh, no, I think it is gorgeous," I said.

"Why am I asking you?" Erika responded. "How far would my boobs have to be hanging out before you would object?"

"Pretty far ... actually, on second thought, I still don't think I would object," I said.

"I just remembered who I was talking to and how ridiculous it is to ask you a question like that," she said. "You have been obsessing about my breasts since Halloween."

"That is not true," I said defensively. "I started obsessing about them way before that."

She smiled and hugged me. "You are so bad. But you think this sweater is okay?"

"Yes," I said. "Seriously—being objective about your cleavage—I think it looks great."

"Never mind," Erika said. "I do have other new things to show you. We had quite an outing. I spent way too much money. Are you up for a little fashion show?"

"Most definitely," I said. "Watching you modeling different clothes for me will definitely brighten my Thanksgiving weekend. What kind of clothes will these be?"

"Don't get too fired up ... no new underwear or lingerie. Dresses, tops, pants, you know ..."

"I wasn't even thinking such a thing; are you implying that I am some kind of ..."

"Not implying," Erika said coyly. "I will show you my new clothes but you have to behave."

She proceeded to go into her bedroom and change clothes and then return to the living room to show me her purchases. She was so cute and delightful. It was a feast for the eyes. I had permission to stare at Erika as she modeled her new clothes for me.

The knock-out punch came in the form of a tight-fitting little black dress, which was hemmed just above her knee. It didn't show much skin, it would be business attire, but it really was very flattering to Erika's sleek, long body.

"Alright, that is amazing," I said as she entered the room, wearing her new black dress with bare legs and feet. "Erika, you look gorgeous, that is so flattering to your body. Very impressive."

"So you like that one?" she said.

"It is spectacular," I said. I reached for her hand and said, "Come here."

I guided her over to sit on my lap.

"What do you have in mind, Mr. Walker?" she said as she smiled and flashed her eyes at me.

"I don't know, this dress just made me want to grab you."

"So I guess that means you like it?"

"I guess it means I like you," I said, and she put her arms around my neck and we kissed. I released her and she smiled at me again. Our eyes met and we just stared at one another for a few moments.

Finally, she said, "Did I tell you that my feet are so destroyed? I definitely wore the wrong shoes. I wore some new heels to go shopping, and my feet are killing me. That is why I am not wearing any shoes, even though my feet are kind of cold."

I helped her off of my lap and said, "You lay down on the pillows on the couch. Put your feet on my lap. I will see what I can do about your sore feet, and you tell me about your shopping adventures."

"Oh, yeah," Erika said as she maneuvered into position.

She laid her freshly pedicured feet on my lap and reclined into the pile of pillows on the opposite end of the couch. When I started to massage her feet, she closed her eyes and fell deeper into the pillows in an almost orgasmic spasm and said, "Aaaaw, don't stop."

"I love it when a woman says that," I said.

Erika ignored my comment and continued to writhe in ecstasy on the pillows with her eyes still closed.

"Many women have said 'Don't' and 'Stop,' but you are the first one to ever use them together in a sentence when referring to me," I added.

She smiled, continued to close her eyes, and said, "This is the best."

As she continued to revel in my foot massaging, she began to tell me about her weekend. The girls did party and shop pretty hard. She started to tell me about the new shoes she bought.

"You got more shoes?" I said. "How many shoes do you have now?"

That popped her blues eyes open, and she asked, "How many DVDs and CDs do you have?"

"Okay, I withdraw the question."

Erika then continued to tell me all of the details of her outing to Bridgeport Village, a very chic, new shopping area of upscale stores.

It had been the Goddesses' first serious excursion to Bridgeport, and it sounded like a marriage made in heaven.

Erika continued her monologue about the Bridgeport assault. As I concluded the foot massage, I lifted her foot and kissed it. This stopped her mid-sentence.

"You kissed my foot," Erika said softly.

"Sorry, I guess I got carried away in the moment," I said.

"I am soooo touched by your tenderness," Erika said softly, "I have never experienced things like this before."

"Neither have I, Erika," I said. "I am sorry if I can't keep my hands off of you tonight."

"I am sorry if I frustrate you," Erika said.

"Erika, do you remember the story I told you at the beach about the soldier and the princess?"

"Of course I do."

"I am happy to wait. Erika, we are just beginning, we have all of the time in the world. There is no hurry. I will not pressure you, and I want to assure you that you have nothing to fear by taking my hand and stepping into whatever our future will be."

Erika was quiet for a moment and looked deep into my eyes. "Tom, I always feel safe and secure with you. You are the best friend I have ever had. I am not ready to let go of my friend's hand."

"You don't have to be afraid, Erika. We are in no hurry. I want to savor what we have and look forward to our future."

Erika smiled and hugged me and held on for a long time. Then she let go and looked at me and asked, "Are you hungry?"

"For anything but turkey," I said.

"You know, I have kind of been lonely this weekend," Erika said. "I had fun with my friends on Friday, but on Saturday and Sunday, it seemed everyone was gone. I don't like being alone."

"I used to like it more than I do now," I said, "but you ruined it. I don't like to be alone anymore either."

She gave me a quick kiss and then stood up, turned around, and lifted her hair. "Could you unzip me?"

"For future reference, my answer to that question will always be yes."

She snickered, and then, as I unzipped her new little black dress, revealing only a bright blue bra and her smooth, tan back, I slipped my hands inside her dress to embrace her around her bare stomach. I then kissed her neck and shoulders and said, "Oh, Erika, how did I get so lucky to have you come into my life?"

Erika said nothing, but stood with her arms over her breasts to prevent her dress from falling to the floor. I held her bare midriff a little longer, then kissed her neck again and released her. She turned and smiled at me and said, "So does this mean I should keep this dress and not take it back to the store?"

"Yeah, I would say I enthusiastically approve of that dress," I said, "and I think in the future, every time you buy clothes, this is how we should evaluate your shopping trip."

She smiled and said, "I will be right back," and headed into her bedroom to change.

I had done a lot of thinking over the last week or so. I no longer wanted to have these angst-ridden talks about where our relationship was going and wondering what the next steps would be. I wanted to savor each moment with Erika. I wanted to enjoy the ride, and I thought there was no reason to hurry. We had lots of time ahead of us; there was no reason to rush. I had never been happier in my life at the end of the triumphant Thanksgiving weekend.

I felt I was finally back from my long, lonely journey in the darkness since I lost Liz. I was now reconciled with my children. I loved Erika more than I ever had. Each day with her was something I longed for but would never have dared imagined possible. It appeared on this rainy November holiday weekend that I had all of the time in the world to be with Erika. There didn't appear to be anything that could stop us now.

But the clock was ticking. The storm clouds threatening our relationship, which were barely visible in the distance in September, were now growing more ominous. But I was caught looking the other way. I still hadn't noticed the approaching storm on the horizon.

Erika and I walked to a South American restaurant in the Pearl District on the Sunday after Thanksgiving. We snuggled under an umbrella as a persistent mist fell on the city. The evening lights, which were just coming on, gave the city a magical appearance. The soft colors and mist falling from the dark sky made it appear that Erika and I were walking through a watercolor painting.

We shared an appetizer and both had large salads. It was a wonderful antidote to the heavy food of Thanksgiving. I told Erika that I wanted to tell her what happened at the beach.

Erika said, "I really enjoyed being with your kids."

"You were certainly popular with my granddaughters."

"I had a great talk with Alan, and I tried to make some progress with Michelle," Erika said.

"Well, we had something extraordinary happen at the beach," I said.

Erika's eyes widened and she anxiously awaited the news.

I told her about the moment on Friday when Rob stayed with the little girls while Alan, Michelle, and I took a long walk together on the beach.

"Michelle got right to it," I said. "She asked me if I knew what was happening in the courts with the guy who killed Liz. When I said no, I wasn't following the legal proceedings, she asked if I didn't care."

Erika gasped when I told her that and continued to intently listen for my next words.

"I kind of lost it, and everything came pouring out of me. I told her and Alan that they had no idea of the pain I had gone through. I told them that I could not bear to go sit in a courtroom and listen to the details of this guy's life or the specifics of how he killed Liz."

"Oh, Tom ...," Erika said, with a concerned look on her face.

"I told them that I can't be some bitter person going around and demanding justice because my life got ruined," I said. "In order to survive Liz's death, there are certain things I can't do."

Erika continued to listen intently.

"I can't live in the past and I can't put myself in the position where I am constantly reminded that Liz is missing. I have to make a new life."

I continued, "Alan had mentioned that he really missed his mother when he came to the beach house. I said that is what I have been contending with for almost three years. Liz was missing everywhere I looked. Everything made me sad when that was the mode I was in. My coping strategy, however flawed, was to avoid being reminded that there was a big hole in my life. Then I told them that I had to find a new life and make new dreams, not just dwell on the old ones, which were now gone."

Erika was riding on my every word and hardly moving. I said, "It was then that Michelle asked if that was what my relationship with you was about. I said it was, among other things. Then things exploded between Michelle and me. I simply said, 'Michelle, I don't know why you are so mad at me. We have suffered an incalculable loss, but it is not my fault and it is not Erika's."

"Wow," Erika said. "How did she react to that?"

"That is when all of the poison started pouring out. Michelle basically started screaming and shaking her fists. She said she was frustrated and mad because she was robbed. She was robbed of being with her mother. She was robbed of seeing Liz be with her daughters, and most of all, she was angry because Brooke and Emily would never really know Liz. Liz would just be a photograph from their distant past...." I suddenly started becoming overcome with emotion and teared up.

Erika tenderly put her hand on mine. She then picked up my hand and kissed it and continued to hold it.

"Sorry ...," I said. "Then it happened. We all started crying and hugging one another. It was very foggy, and the three of us just stood in the fog, embracing and crying. We were finally mourning Liz together. We were finally back together. We were still angry about what happened, but not at one another. Michelle kept repeating, 'I am so, so sorry, Daddy.'"

I had to stop now and wipe my eyes with my napkin. Erika had tears rolling down her cheeks.

"I am sorry, Erika," I said. "I was anxious to tell you this but I thought I could control my emotions better."

"You keep making me cry in restaurants," Erika said, wiping her eyes. "Everyone looks at us like you are breaking up with me."

"Then they are probably thinking, 'There is the stupidest man on earth,'" I said.

Erika smiled as she wiped her eyes.

"I am sorry, I didn't mean to do that to you in the restaurant," I said as I looked into Erika's face, which was illuminated by the golden candlelight.

"I am not blaming you," Erika said. "You just keep saying things that touch my soul. What happened after that?"

"I felt united with my children. I felt I had Michelle back. It was one of the best moments of my life," I said as I lowered my head, trying to keep my emotions in check. "I told them I was so sorry that I cut them out of my life, and I promised I would be a better father and grandfather."

"You dear, sweet man," Erika said, "they are so lucky to have you."

"Then I told Alan and Michelle what I had privately, in my darkest hours, thought for so long about the accident," I said. "I so wish it had been me instead of Liz. Why couldn't it have been me, if it had to be someone? If I could change things, I would gladly take Liz's place, and she would still be with them. Liz would have many wonderful years with her granddaughters ... I so wish it had been me."

I buried my face in my hands and was now quiet.

When I raised my head, Erika looked thoughtful and alarmed. "Tom, don't ever say that again. I know you are so giving ... I know you would give your life for Liz and your children ... but the world would be a darker place without you. I can't imagine what my world would be like without you."

"Seriously," I said, "my children would be okay with Liz. They would have mourned me, but Liz would have handled it so much better than I did. The three of them would have moved on in time and been fine. You would be fine without me. There are so many possibilities for you."

"How can you say such things?" Erika protested.

"What would you be doing if we had never met? You probably would be back with Todd, right?"

"Not necessarily, and I don't want to have this discussion," Erika said. "My point is that I am so sad to hear someone who is so special to me say there would be no impact if you never came into my life. My friendship with you has so enriched my life. I understand what you were saying to your children, and it is so extraordinarily kind and giving, but please don't ever say that again, Tom."

"I am sorry, I just felt that way," I said.

"Tom," Erika said, with her large eyes boring into my own eyes, "your love, your tenderness has healed me. I was damaged and broken, and you have made me whole." She touched my hand and continued to lean forward as she said, "I have intimately known you for this past year, and I have seen your kindness make the world a better place for so many people. Promise me you will never say that again."

"I promise," I said simply.

"What else happened at the beach?" Erika asked.

"You know what I think really happened this weekend?" I offered. "I think all three of us finally said good-bye to Liz. We are sad to leave her. We got screwed. We got robbed. It shouldn't have happened. But it did. We have to go on from here."

"That is so wonderful," Erika said. "I am so glad there has been some degree of peace and reconciliation."

"It feels so good to have my sweet Michelle back. You know, she was actually asking me about you and our relationship. But after our walk on the beach, it was like she was really interested. Not the snapping, angry kind of reactions she had before," I said. "I told her how important you are to me and how you helped me find my way out of the dark times."

Erika just smiled, and I think she wanted to say something, but decided to let me talk it out.

I continued, "You know, Michelle was the sweetest little girl. She was a great teenager. Michelle was always pretty, she was smart, and she was always on task and organized. Michelle was always the best daughter you could ever hope for. I have missed that Michelle."

"That is such great news, Tom," Erika said.

"You know, my description of my daughter sounds like your mother telling me about Erika," I said.

Erika just looked down and said nothing.

"Your mother tells me that she is glad to have Erika back too," I said.

Erika continued to be silent and just looked at me and squeezed my hand.

"You know, Erika, I have told you some of the things people said to me after Liz's death, but there was one I have never told you. A woman, who apparently knew Liz, but I had never met, came to me at the cemetery and said, 'Your wife was an angel ... I guess God needed more angels.'"

Erika looked surprised and said, "What?"

"That was my reaction also. That wasn't comforting, I thought it was just odd," I said. "I thought I don't know what the work load is like for God's angels, but we could sure use some more down here."

Erika smiled and shook her head.

"I guess God owed me one. It took a while, but sure enough, another angel showed up to rescue me, just in the nick of time," I said.

She smiled at me and continued to hold my hand. Rain was now pounding on the window, and we viewed the street through the rivulets of water running down the windowpane. We stared at the nighttime scene outside amid the downpour. We said nothing. It was a moment of great peace and melancholy as we pondered all that had cumulatively occurred in our joined lives.

Erika finally broke the silence, saying, "I am so happy that things worked out this weekend and that you had the time. You must be exhausted."

"You know, now that you mention it, I am," I said.

"All of this outpouring of emotion can be very draining also," Erika said.

"It is. But you know, I feel that a tremendous burden was lifted this weekend," I said. "I feel like maybe I am all the way back from wherever I had gone. But I am not the old person. I am a new revised version of myself."

Erika started to respond, and I suddenly interrupted: "Oh, and there was another development," I blurted out. Erika's eyes widened and she waited for the news.

I continued, "After the smoke cleared from our talk on the beach, Alan announced that he has met someone. He is spending Christmas with her and her parents in the Bay Area."

"Wow, so this is serious?" Erika asked.

"Apparently," I said.

"So Alan is in love, huh?"

"Very much so, I guess."

"That is great news."

Then I said, "Let's see if love can conquer all."

Erika gave me a puzzled look.

I pointed outside and said, "Remember how we thought an hour or so ago that it would be romantic to take a walk in the rain to the restaurant?"

Erika groaned as she saw the rain pounding hard against our window. She had apparently forgotten the car was not parked nearby.

"If it is raining twice as hard," I asked, "does that make it twice as romantic?"

"I will call a cab," she said.

Chapter 21

CHRISTMAS WISHES

IT WAS now the first weekend in December, and it was time to go take in the holiday festivities downtown and maybe do some Christmas shopping. Knowing that I would be experiencing all the things the city had to offer with Erika really was thrilling. Despite her making fun of my holiday enthusiasm, I really do love the weeks prior to Christmas. Sharing it with the person you love the most is a major enhancement to the holidays.

As I drove to her condo, my mind went back to a year ago when I had wandered the downtown streets alone. That Christmas just didn't work for me.

Last Christmas, Alan stayed in the Bay Area because he couldn't get enough time off to make it worth flying to Portland. Michelle and her family went to Rob's parents' house since it was their turn to host the family Christmas.

I kept the fact that I was alone a secret, because the last thing I wanted was some well-meaning family inviting me over for Christmas morning. People meant no harm and were just being kind. However, I was getting annoyed at how everyone I met in the month of December kept asking me if I was going to be okay. I wasn't sure if I was going to be okay, but I wanted to work that out myself. I most definitely didn't want to talk about it.

I felt like a character in one of those sappy Christmas movies. I was the poor, pathetic widower who lived alone, who had no one to share Christmas with. So as a project, some nice family takes him in and gives him a bowl of soup.

I wonder if all single people feel that way during the holidays. You are the brown shoe in a world full of tuxedos. All of that was gone as I contemplated the holidays with the bright light that had come into my life—Erika.

As she opened her door to me, I thought she looked unusually pretty. Of course, I think I always thought that. She was wearing blue jeans with knee-high boots, a bright red sweater, and a scarf. There is a reason that I distinctly remember what she wore that day.

"Very nice," I said as I saw her.

"Why, thank you. You don't look so bad yourself," she said.

"Are you ready to have some fun? I am way ready to have some fun with you, after the 'joy' of the family gathering at Thanksgiving."

She chuckled and said, "It actually turned out well."

"It did, but it wasn't exactly light-hearted. I am ready to spend a little uninterrupted time with you."

With that, we were out the door.

"So tell me, my director of fun, what is today's itinerary?" Erika said.

"You probably went to Santa Land at Meier & Frank department store when you were a kid, didn't you?"

"You mean go see Santa?"

"No," I said, "you know the monorail that takes the children through the magical land and flies over Santa's house and stuff."

She started laughing. "No, I don't know what you are talking about."

"What? You never went to the big ten-story Meier & Frank's with Santa Land on the top floor?"

"I guess not," she said. "My family never wanted to come downtown at Christmas because of all the traffic."

"You poor abused child, no wonder you are the way you are. That will be our first stop," I said.

"Riding the monorail?"

"No, you're a little too big for that," I said.

"Thanks. I know I ate a lot at Thanksgiving."

"No, silly, you are about a foot and a half too tall to get on the monorail, but we can go watch. I haven't been there for years."

Erika said, "I suppose you came downtown every year with your kids?"

"Of course."

"How did I guess that?" she said. "You must have been a real hoot as a father during the holidays."

"I thought I was just normal," I said.

"Darlin', I don't know how to break it to you, but I doubt you were normal. You are abnormally fun. Have you always loved Christmas so much?"

"Yeah, I guess so. I used to wake up my kids on Christmas morning if they slept too long."

Erika started giggling and said, "Is this why they moved away?"

I took Erika to Santa Land, and her eyes sparkled like a small child's as she looked around and watched the little kids get on the monorail that ran along the ceiling of the tenth floor. "This is incredible," she said.

We then walked out into Pioneer Square and looked up at the big city Christmas tree.

"Since you work down here, have you seen them chop down the Christmas tree after the holiday?"

"No," she said. "It is just always magically gone when I come by the square after Christmas."

"It is a major logging operation. They trim off all of the branches, and guys climb up there and take it down in sections with chain saws. Amazing. Want to go do a little shopping?"

"You are asking me a question like that?" Erika queried.

"What does Erika want for Christmas?"

"Just being with you; I have been too naughty this year for a gift."

"No doubt you have been naughty," I said. "You know, it is not too late to pull it out of the fire. Santa is still watching you to see if you are naughty or nice. In fact, I just saw some other guys watching you, and I think they were wondering if you were naughty or nice."

Erika rolled her eyes and shook her head.

"But what do you want anyway?" I persisted in asking.

"Don't do anything crazy, okay?"

"Like I would ...," I responded.

Then she was distracted when we entered the mall and we over-looked the big chair where children were having their picture taken with Santa.

"They always have an awesome Santa here," I said, "no fake whiskers; this guy always looks great and has a real beard, and he is the real deal."

Mockingly, Erika said, "So are you telling me the other guys are fakes, but the one here is the real one?"

"Yes, that is what I am telling you."

She started laughing and said, "Well, we better take a closer look."

As we approached the throne of Santa Claus, Erika was charmed and distracted by two adorable Asian children sitting on Santa's lap.

I took out my wallet and said to the attending elf, "My daughter would like to have her picture taken with Santa," as I handed him a $20 bill.

"That is so not funny," Erika said.

I told the elf, "She was a very difficult child who I could never get to sit on Santa's lap, but I thought I would try again this year."

"Shut up," Erika said. "This is not happening."

I said to the elf, "See? She is still a really obnoxious child."

I turned to Erika and said, "Come on, it is already paid for."

The elf gave encouragement, and Santa's lap was now free.

"Come on," I said, "I am sure it would be the highlight of Santa's day to have you sit on his lap." With that, the elf started laughing.

Santa observed the standoff and gave some encouragement: "Come on, little girl, don't be afraid of Santa."

"There you go," I said to Erika.

She lowered her head, started towards Santa, and said to me, "Seriously, you are so gonna pay for this."

It was a silly moment, but one that would become frozen in time. There was Erika sitting on Santa's lap with her arm around his neck, looking embarrassed but smiling her dazzling smile and cocking her head against Santa's in the perfect pose. She was looking at me when the picture was taken. I was standing next to a person dressed like an elf with striped stockings. I was beaming at the woman I loved as I teased her on our happy day together. Ironically, it was the only picture taken during our time together.

As Erika got off of Santa's lap, she looked at me and started walking towards me, shaking her head. The elf asked me how many pictures I wanted, and I replied, "Two copies."

"You are in so much trouble. I am going to get even," Erika said.

"It is a cute picture," I said, showing it to Erika. "Santa looks happy too. Who can blame him? I think I heard Santa telling the elf he wanted a set of those pictures also."

"You are so hilarious," Erika said sarcastically, with a big smile on her face. "Let's get something to eat."

Over lunch, we talked about how difficult it is to know what to get various family members for Christmas. Then I said, "You never answered my question; what do you want for Christmas?"

"I told you," Erika protested, "I have been too naughty. Do you know how much I spent on Black Friday? I just want to be with you for Christmas."

"I am sure that this afternoon, Santa moved you from his 'good' list to his 'very good' list," I said.

"Just keep being my friend and keep making me smile," she said softly.

"So you are not going to help me?" I asked. "But I *am* going to get you something for Christmas. This is your official notification. Would you help me figure out something for my kids and my mother?"

"Sure," she said. "What about you? What do you want? You are such a brat because you seem to buy yourself anything you want."

"Like you don't," I said. "I notice some of these women's shops have your picture on the wall. They probably make their revenue projections by finding out when you are coming to the mall next."

"Funny boy," Erika said. "So you are dodging the question."

"And your answer about what you want for Christmas is ..."

"I gave you my answer," Erika said.

"What?"

"I said I want to be with you."

"You have that, my love, but that is not an answer. You can't wish for world peace and stuff like that ...," I said. "Okay, let me try this, what dollar limit should we set?"

"I am not answering that question," Erika said.

"Oh, so I am going to show up with a Burger King gift certificate, and you are going to give me a trip to the Bahamas."

"That is part of the fun," Erika said. "Just follow your feelings."

"I have a really bad feeling about this; it feels like a trap. Is this a test? This is going to be some kind of cat-and-mouse game between us, right?"

Erika shook her head and said, "It is nice to see that you have the true spirit of Christmas. So do I get to be the cat or the mouse?"

Later in the month, I asked Erika if she had ever been to the Living Room Theatres.

"I don't know what that is, but I am sure I am about to find out, and I am probably going there," Erika responded with a sly smile.

"No, no, I never force you to do anything," I said. "I only present options."

Erika laughed and said, "Okay, give me the briefing."

"These theatres are basically across the street from Powell's City of Books. We could walk there from your house," I suggested. "You can watch a movie, but in big comfy chairs, and order food that is delivered to you while you watch the movie."

"No way," Erika said, suddenly seeming intrigued. "You have undoubtedly been there."

"Yeah, I have."

"Lucky guess on my part," Erika said.

"But it is like restaurant food: salads, salmon, halibut, sandwiches ... they even have a wine bar," I continued.

"I can drink wine in a comfy chair and watch the movie?" Erika asked.

"Yep."

"Now do you possibly have a suggestion for a movie we might see at such an establishment?" Erika asked, mocking me.

"You know I do."

She began to laugh.

"We never saw *Lost in Translation*. It came out before we were 'partners,' but I have always wanted to see it with you. Remember it was an Oscar nominee, great movie. Bill Murray, Scarlett Johansson ..."

"Okay, I get it now. Two hours of looking at Scarlett."

"No, no ...," I protested. "Well, I do like to look at Scarlett."

"You have a thing for these young hot women, don't you?"

"Why would you think that?"

Erika smiled and gave me the look, which consisted of partly closing her big eyes and intently staring at me with the bright blue slits. She always did this when she was not buying what I was telling her.

"I am nondiscriminatory, though," I responded. "I like older hotties too. Helen Mirren, Diane Keaton, Patricia Clarkson ... have you seen Julie Christie lately ... whoa!"

"Okay, calm down, I get it. Back to *Lost in Translation*."

"Well, it is the story of a middle-aged man who meets a young, attractive woman while they are both traveling in Japan. There is a real connection between them as they spend more and more time together."

A smile crept across Erika's face. "Oh, yeah, like that could happen. So why would you want me to see a movie like this?"

"No, don't go there. It is not an autobiographical thing."

"Are you going to make me dye my hair blonde after seeing this movie? Are you going to go all *Vertigo* on me?"

I smiled, "No, but nice *Vertigo* reference. Our viewing of classic movies is paying off." I pressed on. "This movie is about relationships and connections between people. They are both married but are somewhat lovelorn. They are both jet-lagged and trying to get their bearings in the strange culture of Japan. I love this movie. Sean Penn won the Oscar for best actor last year. Sean was incredible in *Mystic River* but I thought Bill Murray should have won the Oscar for this movie. I am anxious to get your reaction to it, and I wanted to watch it with the person I am most connected with."

"Since you put it that way, let's go," she said.

Erika and I walked over to the theatre, which was about six or seven blocks from her condo. The city was decked out in its holiday decorations. We walked holding hands in the cold December air. Erika loved the experience at the theatre. We both took a glass of wine into the theatre and picked out some chairs to sit in as we waited for the delivery of our entrees. Erika was looking at a pamphlet about the theatre.

"We are so having your birthday party here next year," she said.

"What?"

"Did you know you can rent these rooms, have a private screening and food? Invite family and friends. How cool would that be? Have you ever done that?"

"No, this place has opened in the last two years or so. I haven't thrown any parties for myself in the last couple of years."

Erika just smiled and squeezed my hand as she continued to read the pamphlet.

In my fragile, neurotic, and insecure state, it gave me enormous satisfaction to hear that Erika still planned to be around next October.

When the lights went down and the previews were over, the movie began. The opening scene of *Lost in Translation* shows a tight shot of a woman's hips as she lies on her side on a bed, wearing pink panties. The opening credits roll over this image.

Erika leaned over and asked, "Is this why you love this movie?"

"No," I whispered, "but you have to admit, this is the best opening credits sequence *ever* in a movie."

Erika was really touched by the film. She reacted the same way I did when I saw it almost a year earlier. We had a talk about relationships and connections between people as we walked home in the frosty night air.

At the end of the movie, Bill Murray's character realizes he will never see Scarlett's character again. Their relationship has been largely platonic to this point. Bill Murray has his cab stop and he runs down the street to catch Scarlett and tell her good-bye. He embraces her and kisses her. Then he whispers something in her ear, which causes Scarlett to cry. We cannot hear what he tells her. He then leaves, in all likelihood forever.

"What do you think he whispered to her?" Erika asked.

"I don't know, I have always wondered about that," I responded. "I think they discover that they are truly soulmates. Regardless of what happens in the rest of their lives, they will always cherish the moments they had together."

"I think so too," Erika said softly.

"I don't know what it is about that movie," I said. "It is creeping up my list of all-time favorites."

"Did you like it before you met me?" Erika asked.

"Yes, but I like it more now. But then again, I like everything more since I met you."

We walked mostly in silence, just contemplating the movie and our discussion.

"I can see why you like it so much. It is so you," Erika said.

"Do you like it?"

"I love it."

As Christmas neared, Erika and I continued to tease one another about our potential presents. It appeared that Erika was going to spend Christmas with her mother. I didn't want to impose. I didn't tell Erika that my mother was actually flying to Cleveland to spend the holidays with my brother, something she had not done for many years. The way the dice were falling this year, I would be alone.

Alan would be with his new love in San Francisco, Michelle and her family would be staying in Denver after their Thanksgiving trip, and Mom was headed to Cleveland. I thought if I could spend Christmas Eve with Erika, I would be okay alone on Christmas Day. We could exchange our gifts on Christmas Eve.

I floated this plan to Erika and was hazy about my Christmas Day plans, because I didn't want to interfere with the plans she and Tricia had. I knew Erika would never let me be alone if she found out.

Late in the afternoon on Christmas Eve, I went to Erika's condo with my gift. I had really racked my brain and stressed about what to get her. It was unusually cold for Portland on that day. It was freezing outside. Erika greeted me at her door. She put her arms around my neck and kissed me with a little extra passion.

"Merry Christmas, Tom."

"Merry Christmas, beautiful lady."

Her eyes immediately focused on a small gift bag I was carrying.

"Don't let the small size fool you," I said. "It is actually the keys to a matching Porsche so we will both have one. It is parked outside with a big bow on the top."

She smiled and slugged me playfully in the arm. This bantering about gifts had been going on for days and had been our main source of entertainment through the buildup to Christmas.

"Where's yours?" I asked.

"My gift for you is in the bedroom," she said.

"Mine is in the bedroom? So you *did* guess what I wanted," I said.

"Funny boy, you can't be naughty or you will get a lump of coal."

"So who goes first?" I said.

We both looked at each other and smiled. "This is starting to feel like an exchange of prisoners ... all right, ladies first." I produced a small velvet box from my bag, which obviously came from a jewelry store.

Erika's face registered genuine surprise.

"It's not the little jewelry store box you think, but I hope you will like it."

Erika opened the box. Inside was a necklace with a heart-shaped pendant, with small diamonds surrounding the heart.

"Tom!" she gasped. "You shouldn't ..." then she just stopped and hugged and kissed me.

"Is it okay?" I said.

She got tears in her eyes and said, "I should have known you would get the perfect thing for me."

"I will take that as a yes."

She took off the necklace she was wearing and immediately put the new necklace around her neck. Erika gave me her sweetest smile and then hugged me for a few moments. As she pulled away, she kissed me again.

"I love you, Erika," I said.

"I love you, Tom, I really do," she said.

After she wiped some tears from her eyes, she said, "You know I can't follow that."

"I bet you can."

She produced a small gift bag. "Now I am afraid about this."

"Anything from you is special, Erika."

I opened the package and found she had purchased a full spa day for me, with a massage and the whole bit.

"Do you like it?"

"I love it, Erika, I have never done that."

"It isn't too girly, is it?"

"No, sweetheart; thank you."

"Here was my logic. Tom spends so much time taking care of everyone else. He spends so much time making sure I am happy. It is time someone pampered Tom and took care of him."

"It is wonderful, Erika. That you had those thoughts about me makes it an incredible gift. You are my beautiful gift this year."

We embraced for a long time, savoring our moment together at the end of this wonderful year. I never imagined my life could turn around like this.

"You are going to stay for a while, right?" Erika asked. "Can you hang with me and share some goodies and Christmas Eve with me?"

"You couldn't drive me out," I said.

She lightly touched the heart on her necklace and said, "I love it, Tom."

I just smiled and cherished watching Erika being truly touched by my gift.

Erika had several snack items and hors d'oeuvres prepared.

"Is this okay?" she said, gesturing towards her plates.

"You are beautiful and intelligent, and you can cook too? Wow!"

We sat at her kitchen bar and talked as we munched holiday goodies. After a while, Erika looked over my shoulder and said, "Is it snowing?"

"It was really cold when I came over here," I said as we both walked to her small balcony.

Erika opened the sliding door and said, excitedly, "It is!"

A white Christmas is very rare in Portland, and Portlanders do not handle snow well.

"It *is* snowing!" I exclaimed.

"It is so beautiful; look how big the flakes are," Erika said.

We stepped out on the narrow balcony so we could take in the beautiful scene unfolding before us. I put my arms around Erika to keep her warm.

"It is magical. The city looks so beautiful," I said as the large flakes continued to fall faster.

Then Erika, being a true Portlander, said, "I wonder if the roads are going to get bad."

"I don't know."

"By the way," Erika asked, "what are your plans for tomorrow, are you with your mother?"

"Uh, actually, she went to Cleveland to be with my brother."

"So you are alone tomorrow?"

"Well, it kind of turned out that way, but I will be okay if I just have Christmas Eve with you."

"Tom!" Erika said incredulously. "You were planning to be by yourself tomorrow?"

"Well, I knew you had plans with your mom, and I didn't want to push myself into everything."

"Tom, I am mad at you for keeping that from me. There is no way you are alone tomorrow. You can join Mom and me. It will be awesome."

"I don't want to impose ..."

"Tom!"

"Okay ...," I said, and before I could say more, Erika looked at the snow falling and said, "Why don't you just stay with me tonight?" She turned and faced me as we stood on the balcony in the snow. The large flakes were sticking to Erika's long black hair. "Stay with me," she continued, "watch Christmas movies with me. I'll pop some popcorn and we can cuddle on the couch and watch movies. Don't go."

"It is impossible for me to resist you saying 'Don't go,' but sweetie, I don't have any stuff with me."

"We can work it out," she said, turning on her charm and staring at me with those magnificent eyes.

"I am utterly incapable of countering that," I said.

"Good, let's go inside and get warm."

One of Erika's sofas folded down into a futon-like bed. She put on *The Bishop's Wife*, the wonderful old Christmas movie with Cary Grant and Loretta Young. We cuddled under an afghan and watched the Christmas movie. I was starting to feel exhausted but there was no way I wanted to miss a minute of this. After that movie, Erika got up to do the popcorn. We then settled in for the second part of our double feature. We put on the old version of *Miracle on 34th Street*.

What a way to spend Christmas Eve. I held her in my arms as we started our second movie. I felt myself dozing off. I felt Erika relaxing and going limp in my arms. She was now asleep. The only lights in the room were from Erika's Christmas tree and the television. I gently leaned forward to look upon that beautiful face in the dim light. How I love this woman!

I gently removed the remote from her limp hand and turned off the television. Sleep in heavenly peace. I just relaxed in the glow of the Christmas tree lights. It was a wonderful moment.

Amazingly, when I suddenly awoke, it was morning. Erika was still sleeping in my arms. We had slept all night together on the couch. I knew we had both been burning it at both ends recently. Now, in the wonderful security of one another's arms, we collapsed in deep slumber.

In a little while, Erika stirred. She looked confused and then said, "Oh, my God, did we sleep here all night?"

"Apparently."

"Wow," she said. "I guess you and I were pretty exhausted."

"Happy too," I added.

She turned and smiled at me.

"You know what?" I asked. "I really believe in Santa again."

"Why?" she said, looking at me warily.

"When I talked to Santa at Pioneer Square a couple of weeks ago, I told him what I wanted for Christmas. When I awoke on Christmas morning, there it was—the thing I most wanted for Christmas, in my arms."

She smiled and said, "Merry Christmas." We kissed each other good morning. We emerged from the couch and both felt like we looked horrible.

Erika washed my shirt while I took a shower. She showered and looked her usual dazzling self when she emerged from her bedroom. Erika gave me an extra toothbrush that had never been used, and we were starting to feel decent again.

The plan was to meet Tricia for a holiday buffet at the Heathman Hotel, one of the great and grand old hotels downtown.

"Are you sure your mother will not mind?" I asked.

"Are you kidding? She will be excited to see you. My mother totally loves you."

As we entered the Heathman lobby, we saw Tricia. She and Erika hugged and then Tricia hugged me and kissed me on the cheek.

"I am so sorry to be intruding, Tricia, but your daughter has great powers over me and she insisted."

"Don't be silly, it is great to have you here. I am so happy to see you," Tricia said.

"I understand you have been a busy lady, traveling around, getting involved in your new business," I said.

"Oh, yes, I have a lot to tell you. What a nice surprise to get you here with Erika."

"Mom, Tom was planning to be alone today rather than intrude on our mother-daughter thing," Erika said. "How sweet is that?"

"Tom, Erika and I do not want you to be alone on Christmas. You should have never even thought such a thing."

As we were seated at the elegantly decorated table, Erika held out her necklace and said, "Look, Mom."

"I presume from Tom," Tricia said.

"Of course," Erika said.

"Very nice, that is so pretty," Tricia said. "So what have you two been doing?"

I looked at Erika and she said, "Go ahead."

Tricia's eyes turned to me.

"Well, I came to see Erika late yesterday afternoon so we could exchange our presents, then it started snowing, and Erika thought it was too dangerous for me to leave."

Tricia looked at Erika and smiled.

"Obviously it wasn't, but she was very convincing. She always is, anytime she talks to me."

Erika smiled.

"We lay down together on the couch and started watching Christmas movies. We watched one and then somewhere during the second movie, we both went to sleep. The next thing we knew, it was Christmas morning. We slept together on the couch last night," I concluded.

"What is it with you two? You are always falling asleep or getting stranded or some funny thing," Tricia said. "You two are hilarious together."

"You know, Tricia," I said, "when I first started hanging around with Erika, I had heard that she sleeps around, but I had no idea what they meant."

Tricia started laughing, and Erika rolled her eyes at me.

"The truth is that I didn't want to be alone on Christmas Eve, and Tom was such a sweetheart, he stayed with me," Erika said.

"You have a found a gem, Erika," Tricia said. "No doubt about it."

I turned serious for a moment. I said, "I want you both to know how horrible the last couple of Christmases have been in my life. I want you to know that I will never be able to tell you both how much joy you have brought me this year."

Both women got tears in their eyes. I raised my glass and said, "To my return from the long dark tunnel. To the best year of my life, thanks to Erika and Tricia. Merry Christmas." We touched our glasses in the toast. Now I had four beautiful blue eyes looking at me through the mist of their tears.

Chapter 22

NEW YEAR'S EVE

ERIKA WAS planning a big New Year's Eve party at her condo with the Goddesses and their significant others. What a year 2004 had been.

One year ago, there was no Erika, and I stayed home alone on New Year's Eve and just watched some movies and tried not to think about the state of my life. I now felt like a completely different person. I looked forward to almost every day and especially those days when I would be with her.

It was just a week or two after New Year's Eve last year that I first noticed Erika coming in for her morning coffee.

Now I was trying to pick out the right clothes for that night's party, which would make me appear hip and cool enough to accompany the lovely Erika into the New Year.

As I was making my plans my phone rang. It was Erika and she had a proposal. "Why don't you bring your overnight bag with you and stay in the guest room tonight? It will be really, really late when the party subsides, and I so don't want you out dodging drunks driving home," she said.

"I am there; that is very nice," I said. "You know, it might be good to suggest to the others that they arrange for cab rides so they are not dodging drunk drivers either, or becoming drunk drivers. I guess I am a little sensitized to that issue."

The city cab companies were offering rides to those who had been drinking in an effort to keep them off of the road and safe.

"That is a great point. I should have been a little more sensitive about that as well," Erika said. "I will call the ladies and suggest that."

"What can I do to help you get ready for the party tonight?" I said.

"Come early; I am sure there will be things, as scattered as I feel today. Plus it is always nice to have you hanging out with me. But it is totally up to you, come as soon as you can," she said.

"I will try to get there by mid-afternoon or so, but call me if you need anything," I said.

"Okay, it will be awesome."

"Erika," I said, "thanks for everything."

"See you soon," she said, as her phone clicked off.

I loved the thought of another "sleepover." It put me in a special class that meant I was something special to Erika. Ever since our trip to the beach together, I felt like my relationship with Erika was back on track. The Todd upheaval appeared to be behind us. Erika seemed not as distracted and troubled. Erika had been very loving and affectionate. Our talk at Thanksgiving had also eased my mind considerably. I sensed that tonight might be something special. Erika and I were going to celebrate our year together.

Even though I always wanted more, there was so much to be happy about. It had been one of the best years of my life.

In my suit, dark shirt, and dark tie, I wanted to look cool and not like someone's accountant. I hoped I was pulling it off. I hit the buzzer by Erika's unit number and said, "It is me."

"Come on up," she said and the door clicked open. She greeted me in her robe, but this was a silky one, not the usual terry cloth one I had seen before. It was very nice.

"Did I overdress?" I said.

"Always with the witty reply," Erika said, as she hugged and kissed me.

She smelled sensational, and I could tell she had taken her makeup and hair to the next level and looked very, very nice. I wondered how many levels she had.

"No, silly," she said. "I don't want to be stirring bean dip or something in my party dress. You haven't seen my new dress yet, huh?" I raised my eyebrows in interest and then shook my head no.

"All of the ladies got new party dresses during the Goddesses' post-holiday shopping extravaganza, and tonight is the 'reveal' night. Hope you like it."

"I didn't see this at the Thanksgiving fashion show you gave me?"

"No, I deliberately didn't show you this one. I was saving it for tonight."

"If it is better than the little black dress, I can't be held responsible for what might happen."

"Well, it is way better than the little black dress."

"Really? I better consult with my cardiologist. Now I am enthused about tonight. It is nice to see you finally taking an interest in your personal appearance," I said.

"Come and help me," she said. She gave me a hip check and let me know my sarcasm had registered with her.

"Here, this is for you," she said, as she slipped an apron over my head and tied it behind me.

"What is up with this?"

"I don't want you to mess up your clothes, and besides, you look very cute and domestic."

We spent the afternoon scurrying around the apartment, doing whatever Erika needed done. It was hard not to be distracted by the silky robe, which made her appear much more curvy and bouncy than the terry cloth one did.

"Be calm," I kept telling myself. Erika seemed to keep raising the level of her sexuality and flirting with me. She seemed different tonight.

Finally, the transformation of the condo to the party mode pleased Erika. I thought it looked great about an hour or so ago. But an experienced man like me has learned to keep my opinions to myself and follow my lady's lead in such matters. It was getting dark and nearing party time. "Would you be a sweetie and light the candles for me while I finish getting ready?"

"Sure," I said, as she hugged me and said, "You are totally cute in your apron."

I removed the apron and proceeded to hunt down the candles she had scattered everywhere. The candles gave the condo a golden glow, and it looked really great.

She suddenly emerged, and I felt the air being sucked from my lungs. Erika was wearing a bright blue, sequined dress with spaghetti straps. It was a few inches above her knee, which made her long legs look even longer.

"What do you think?" she said.

I really could not speak except to say, "Oh, Erika …"

"I think he likes it," she said.

"Wow, you really outdid yourself this time. You look incredible. I am truly speechless."

Her blue eyes were even more electric blue with that dress, and she was wearing the necklace I gave her for Christmas.

"Do you think it fits okay? It isn't too much, is it? I ate so much junk during the holidays that I worried about getting into it."

"Well, Erika, I can safely say you got into it. You are stunningly beautiful. You have truly blown me away. As to the question, 'Is it too much?'—If I kept attacking you in the little black dress, you could be in big trouble tonight. Or I am." I took her hand and kissed it. I said, "My beautiful, beautiful Erika, you take my breath away."

She laughed. "You are so sweet. I hoped you would like it."

"Can I touch?" I asked as a came closer to her.

She flashed her eyes at me and said, "It depends on where."

I gently took both of her hands and leaned forward and kissed her. I said, "I don't look like I belong with you tonight."

"Says who?" she said, as she turned on the lights in her magnificent eyes and pointed them at me. Erika then turned to make some last-minute adjustments in the party preparations.

I am in so much trouble tonight, I thought. My "friend" looks incredible. This could be the night I get hauled away by the cops. Witnesses will tell Channel 2 News that "this man seemed to be gentle and had no history of violence. Then he suddenly started attacking the young woman who was hosting the party for no apparent reason." Is it too late for a cold shower? The buzzer sounded, signaling the party was officially on.

New Year's Eve is always an interesting moment when you are marking the passage of time. For me, it has always been a time of reflection to ponder what has gone before and think about what was ahead. I am always fascinated by the adventure ride that is our life.

On New Year's Eve 2001, I could have not foreseen that a few weeks later, my wife would be killed; I would descend into a dark, solitary time where I would re-evaluate everything. I would be put on a path that would lead me to this night—a place I never imagined I could or would be.

Then there was New Year's Eve 2003, which I spent alone in my empty house, which had become a crypt to me. I was trying to figure out where to go and how to get there. I wanted to make the blues go away and be happy, but I wasn't sure how. I could not have foreseen that I would meet a woman named Erika who would chase all of the clouds away. A new, unimaginable bright light had shined on me, and suddenly life became a wonderful sunny day. Nothing would ever be the same after we met in the most mundane of ways—grabbing our morning coffee.

Now there was this joyous event. A celebration, really, for Erika and me—a year of being happy and finally leaving behind the darkness we had both experienced in our lives. Little did I know that things were about to profoundly change again.

As midnight neared, the party revved into high gear. We turned on the television to watch the countdown on Times Square. The champagne glasses were being set up and filled in anticipation of the big moment, which was less than ten minutes away now. I was talking to a couple of the guys when Erika leaned over the back of the couch. She whispered into my ear, "Come with me for a minute." I excused myself and wondered what was going to happen next. She took my hand and led me into her bedroom.

"I just wanted a private moment to tell you how I love you, Tom, and how wonderful this year has been with you," Erika said.

"Thanks for the best year of my life," I said. "I love you so much, Erika."

Erika put her arms around my neck and gave me a full, passionate kiss and said, "Thank you." I grabbed her and began kissing her beautiful long neck. I worked my way down her neck to her breasts. She began to caress me and push herself against me. She grabbed my face and kissed me passionately again. The passion and desire for Erika, which I had tried to hold in check for all of these months, was now pouring out of me. I burned with an intense desire for this woman, who had become the love of my life. Our hearts were pounding, and we were both breathing hard.

She pushed me gently away. I looked at her and smiled. Erika leaned forward and put her forehead against mine. She then turned her blue eyes on my eyes. It always had an overwhelming effect on me.

"We better get out there or we are going to miss midnight," she said.

"I will catch the replay," I said breathlessly.

"Wait," Erika said, and she took her finger and removed lipstick from my lips and face. She quickly grabbed her lipstick and touched up her smudged, attacked lips as she led me by the hand out of her bedroom.

"It won't last," I said, and she gave me a sly smile.

Tamara, Kristen, and Jen were at the counter doing the final preparation of the champagne for the midnight toast. As we emerged, they all smiled and Kristen said, "Wow, you two look kind of out of breath. Time for a quickie before midnight? What have you two been doing?"

"I am not that quick," I said.

They all laughed, and Erika gave them "the look" and said, "Shut up."

Midnight came and Erika and I kissed again. I hoped there would be much more happiness ahead for us in 2005. Maybe tonight was going to be a landmark in our relationship. This might be the night that things begin to turn in another direction. There were certainly hopeful signs.

"Happy New Year, baby," I said to her as we kissed at midnight. I was hoping that this was not all a dream and that because I had kissed the princess at midnight, I wouldn't turn back into a frog. Everyone was in a great mood, and it was one of the most joyous New Year's Eves I had ever experienced. I felt true and unfettered happiness at that moment.

The party seemed to get a second wind after that, and there was lots of laughing and fun. Before we knew it, the clock said 3 AM. As the last couple left, they said, "You kids behave tonight."

"Now that was a serious party," I said, as we closed the door.

"I am so totally wiped out. I think the last time I sat down was two days ago," Erika said, as she kicked off her shoes.

"Let's go sit down on the couch," I suggested. She moaned as she sat down and fell over with her head on the sofa pillow. After the heat that had been generated between us all night, I wondered what would happen when we were alone. The problem was that we were both completely spent physically.

I said, "Lay down, maybe I can help. Roll over on your tummy."

She complied without saying anything. I began to rub the soles of her feet with my hands.

"You are so awesome," she said.

I continued to rub her feet and then gently returned them to the couch. I pushed away her long hair to expose her back. I began to rub her bare shoulders. She was incredibly soft, and her flawless skin looked luminescent in the soft light. Her face was covered by her thick mane of hair.

Her voice was barely audible.

She said, "Leave it to you to chill me out when I am so exhausted."

"Yeah, I seem to have a talent for making you sleepy," I said.

I couldn't resist. I unzipped the back of her dress and unhooked her bra to facilitate a more complete back rub. She never flinched. Her long legs were exposed almost completely.

She lay with her beautiful, tan back and shoulders completely bare and her mane of thick black hair spilling over her shoulders and covering her face.

There she was in front of me, the object of my total affection and desire. The unattainable golden goddess that was always just out of my reach. It was very late; I was exhausted, and we had both had too much to drink. I am sure this was the moment when I could have become Erika's lover. But I did not want to do it this way. I didn't want our first time to be when we were both exhausted and had too much to drink. I wanted her so badly, but not this way. I wanted Erika to give herself to me when she decided that she wanted to be my lover.

My impaired brain was fuzzy. I felt I could be on the verge of threatening a nearly perfect year and a perfect evening with my beautiful Erika. Maybe it would be the beginning of a new phase. Now was not the time for either Erika or me to make this decision about taking our relationship to the next step.

"Why did you stop?" she said.

"I think we need to go to bed, my love."

"I drank too much," she groaned. I zipped her dress up.

"Happy New Year," she mumbled through a mass of hair and bleary eyes. She sat up on the couch. I hugged her and held her for a moment, stroking the back of her head.

"You are right, as usual," she said. I kissed her soft, beautiful lips again.

"I love you, Erika. You were so beautiful tonight. I will never forget this New Year's Eve."

Erika just kissed me passionately again and said, "Good night, my dear friend. I love you."

It was the perfect ending to the most wonderful year in my life. I could not get over the dramatic turnaround my life had taken. Erika had brought about a miraculous transformation. As bad as I felt my luck had been when I lost Liz, now I was having extremely good fortune to have Erika.

We staggered into our beds. I could have not foreseen the events that were shortly to overtake me. I felt I had just completed a dream night with Erika. I went to bed so excited and so hopeful. I had never felt closer to her. We seemed in perfect synch. It seemed that she finally felt about me the way I had felt about her for so long.

When we re-emerged, the first morning of 2005 had already come and gone. Unfortunately (or maybe fortunately), the terry cloth bathrobe had reappeared.

"Are you alive? I feel so horrible," I said.

"I can't tell yet," she said.

After we cleared our heads and nibbled on a light first meal, Erika said, "I never got a chance to tell you about the latest with that task force thing at work."

"Oh yeah, did they make any decisions?"

"Yes, I am on the team, and it is actually going to start on the fast track right away," she said.

"That is great, Erika, congratulations. Remind me again what the scope of the project is."

"It is a business change initiative where people from various offices are going to pull together and try to streamline procedures and brainstorm more efficient ways of doing business. I think it will be pretty exciting. We will be reporting our recommendations to the top executives, and it will be a high-profile assignment."

I said, "Are you glad about it?"

"Oh, yes, I think this could be the opening I have been waiting for. Since I got my MBA, I have been positioned to move up but haven't had any real chance yet. This could be it. I am the representative of the Portland office, which is one of the biggest ones," she said.

"Way to go. That is a nice way to start a new year."

"Thanks; the only bad thing will be the project is going to be headquartered in Seattle, so I will be there during the week but back in Portland on the weekends," she explained.

"How long will that last?" I said.

"I think six weeks, but we will get more details this week."

"I am proud of you, Erika; you will do great in that kind of environment. I will miss you during the week, but at least I will get to see you some on the weekend, right?"

"Of course," she said. "I will keep you posted."

"That is cause for celebration," I said. "How about some champagne?"

"That is not even funny," she said. "Look at this place, it is totally destroyed. It would be easier to just move. I am not sure it can be saved," she said, surveying her condo.

"As soon as I am able to stand, I will help you clean up. That was one great New Year's Eve party and one great hostess last night," I said after a long silence.

"You liked it? Do you think everyone had a great time?"

"You knocked that one out of the park, my love. I don't know how they could not have had a good time. Great job," I said, as I leaned over and kissed her. "It is appropriate to have the best party ever after the best year ever," I offered.

"Thanks for being so cool with my friends last night."

"I genuinely had a good time with them. They are great," I said.

"Everyone loved you and thinks you are so much fun and funny," Erika said. "How could anyone not love you?"

"A surprising amount of people seem to find a way," I said. She just laughed.

"The problem with partying hard on New Year's Eve and waking up after noon on New Year's Day is the short turnaround to going to work tomorrow," Erika said.

"That is a really revolting thought," I said. "We better get busy cleaning up so we can regroup before morning."

After a couple of hours of cleanup, I gathered my things and prepared to leave.

"It was totally fun," Erika said. "Thanks for all of your help to pull it off." She again kissed me and stared into my eyes for a moment and smiled. I just smiled back at her and basked in the loving gaze of those wonderful eyes.

"I don't know what this week is going to be like yet," Erika said. "I will just have to call you when I get more information."

Chapter 23

LETTING HER GO

THE SECOND day of the New Year was very busy. After the hiatus of the holidays, things really kicked into high gear at work. It was very hectic. Erika called me about mid-afternoon and said she had talked with the task force people; she needed to fly to Seattle the next day.

Erika asked if I could take her to the airport on the morning of the third. She was to spend the remainder of the week going through orientation sessions in Seattle. I would then pick her up on Friday night when she returned to Portland. We hurried to the airport; she only had enough clothes to get her through a couple of days. I walked Erika to the security checkpoint at the airport. She put her arms around me and kissed me and said with a smile, "See you Friday."

There was about to be a major snafu that would threaten our plans. Generally, Portland has very mild winters compared to the rest of the nation. There are mild temperatures in the 30s and 40s and lots of rain. January is one of the rainiest months for Portland.

However, sometimes an arctic blast can come down the Columbia Gorge, hitting Portland head-on. When this arctic air from the gorge meets the moist, rain-laden air coming off of the Pacific, it can disrupt life for several days. The rain combined with cold air can cause an ice storm that coats everything—roads, trees, cars, sidewalks, everything—with a layer of ice. There is really no way to combat this, and it tends to paralyze the city for several days. In the worst-case scenario, it can also coat power lines and add power outages and no heat to the plagues it can visit on the city.

Thursday, an ice storm hit Portland. It can take a while for warmer air from the Pacific to scour out the Portland area. This allows the ice pellets or freezing rain to transition into regular rain as the temperatures warm above freezing.

Erika called me on Thursday and said it appeared everything was encased in ice between Seattle and Portland, so she couldn't get home. That was really disappointing and also caused Erika some significant problems. She now would have to go for another week before coming home to get her clothes packed for a longer stay.

The ice continued through most of the weekend. I didn't go to work on Friday, nor did most people in the Metro area, as the ice storm continued its grip on the city. It made for a lonely weekend. I was stranded in my house. Most importantly, there was no Erika. I already missed her and wished we had some time to follow up on our romantic New Year's Eve.

Finally, after a ruined weekend, regular rain began to fall from the Portland skies Sunday night. The ice began to melt just in time for everyone to return to work on Monday morning. Erika called me on my cell phone Monday while I was in the office.

Apparently, the project team had met and discussed the dilemma. It was decided to get an executive hotel room for each team member so they could stay in Seattle. The room would be an "apartment" for the individual team members for the duration of the project. This action was taken because, given the time of the year and the unpredictability of January weather, team members could just spend the remainder of the month in Seattle.

Erika was to return home on Wednesday to pack for the extended stay in Seattle. She would then fly to Seattle and not return until the project had ended.

It made perfect sense from a business point of view. It is a decision I would have probably made had I been in charge of the team. However, on a personal basis, this was a crushing blow. After Wednesday I wouldn't see Erika until sometime in February. She would be gone for her birthday and probably for Valentine's Day, two events I was really looking forward to spending with her this year.

I picked up Erika at the airport on Wednesday morning. She needed to pack up quickly and catch the 5 PM shuttle flight back to Seattle. She was understandably stressed out when she arrived. I warmly greeted her and offered to help her any way I could.

We went back to her condo, and I helped as she packed whatever she would need until she returned to Portland in February. Suddenly,

February seemed like a long time away. I was trying to keep a positive spin on the events that had been thrust on us. However, as we left for the airport, I had a bad feeling in the pit of my stomach.

Erika and I exchanged concerns about how much we would miss one another. We promised to stay in touch. I said I would e-mail her. We could use our Blackberrys, as we always had. I told her I would love to talk to her whenever I could, but I felt reluctant to call because I didn't know what I might be interrupting. Erika promised to make every effort let me know how things were going.

I somehow couldn't avoid the sinking feeling that fate was again dealing us some cards. It could be some cards we didn't want. As I walked Erika to the security barrier, we hugged and kissed. I held onto her for as long as I could and then finally had to let her go.

Erika made her way through the security maze, and before she left to go down the concourse, she turned, smiled, and blew me a kiss. I watched her until she disappeared from my view. I had a terrible feeling of foreboding as I turned and walked alone to the parking garage.

I hated January. I always had. There is absolutely nothing to recommend January. There is nothing to look forward to, and the weather is awful. That is how I felt even before Liz was killed in January. Now Erika was leaving me to suffer through January in solitude. Of course, on the other side of the coin, I had found Erika a year ago in January. Still, it was very hard to feel any optimism.

I trudged on alone in January, working towards the end of the time she would be away. As the month continued, it became harder to have any contact. When I did contact her, she seemed different … distracted … not wanting to talk. I attributed it to the grind of such a project. I had been on a few special projects myself, and one of the casualties is your personal time and privacy. I am sure, because they were all housed in the hotel together, that there were many late-night work sessions and meetings. Project members can become like captives in these situations. They can be in a conference room for extended periods of time. Food is brought into them, so they don't leave. These types of projects tend to grow, filling the time available, as pressure builds to meet project goals.

Most of our exchanges consisted of e-mails on our Blackberrys, where we exchanged a couple of sentences of information, told each other how much we missed being together, and then usually signed off with "See you soon."

Finally, it looked like Erika's freedom was near. She said they were beginning to dismantle the project headquarters and pack up their apartments. I thought she might be home on February 16, but she sent an e-mail saying her return to Portland would be delayed a couple more days.

After the delays, I got a phone call from Erika about midday on Monday, saying she was back in Portland.

"Come over to my condo as soon as you can get away. I have some things I need to tell you, and we can catch up on what has happened," she said.

It sounded innocent enough, and I was looking forward to seeing her and hearing how her project went. I was very excited to begin to reclaim my time with her. I was hoping we could pick up where we left off.

Where we left off was the New Year's Eve party, when I felt things may be changing with her. She was very affectionate and treated me more like her boyfriend. We nearly became lovers on that night, and there had been serious sparks exchanged between us. I had really missed her, and it had seemed that she was gone much longer than six weeks.

The project schedule did not go as we had expected. But hopefully, we could put that behind us and get back to our life together. I left work early and did not plan to return. Instead, I was excited to spend the remainder of the day with Erika.

As I parked and approached her building, I felt my excitement growing. It had been a long time since my last visit. As I looked upwards and spotted her windows, it was comforting to know she was really there. I buzzed her unit number, and there was no reply, just a buzz to admit me into the building. I expected a big greeting when she opened her door, but instead something seemed wrong. She hugged me and thanked me for coming over. It suddenly felt like we were starting a business meeting.

I began gushing and telling her how much I had missed her and how good it felt to have her back in town. She smiled and said, "Let's sit down. I want to tell you what is going on." This seemed to have a very serious tone.

"This project turned out to be a much bigger deal than I ever imagined." I nodded my head in agreement as she continued, "That is both good and bad. I have been offered a position in Seattle to head the team to implement the business change results of the project. I am going to take it. I think this is the chance I have been waiting for, and I don't see how I could turn it down. It will mean a chance to get into management and more money, and they are offering me a relocation package."

I was stunned. I was fumbling for words and the appropriate reaction. I never saw this one coming. All I could manage to say was, "You are moving to Seattle?"

"Yes," Erika said with a tortured expression on her face. "I need to do that as soon as possible really."

"I am a little shocked, and of course, I have mixed feelings from a selfish point of view ... but congratulations, Erika, that is really great news." The horrible news was slowly sinking in.

Without acknowledging my meager response, she said, "There is another development also."

I was still reeling from the first punch, and a bigger one was right behind it.

"Todd and I are going to try again. We are getting back together."

"What, you mean here or ...?"

"No, in Seattle."

"Todd is moving there with you?"

Erika said, "No, Todd already lives there. He has for quite a while. Todd is the technology troubleshooter for his company, and he has been living around the whole Microsoft world up there in Renton and Bellevue."

I had always assumed Todd was still somewhere in Portland.

"Excuse me," I said grabbing my forehead. "I am still trying to catch up with you. How and when did this happen? I am more stunned about Todd than about your job. This is devastating. This last fall, did Todd live here or in Seattle?"

"He lived in Seattle; I should have told you that. When he came down this fall and had me sign those papers, he was living in Seattle. I somehow thought you knew that, and that is why I didn't understand when you thought we were seeing one another regularly. I am so sorry to hit you with this," Erika said. "I have been rehearsing ways I would tell you how all of this has happened in the last several weeks. There was no good or easy way. This is the hardest decision I have ever made."

"So this fall, I was wrong, you weren't seeing one another regularly. But now, while you have been in Seattle, you have been seeing each other regularly?" I said, trying to comprehend what I was being told. "Did I get that right?"

"Yes," she said, as she buried her face in her hands.

"At what point were you planning to let me in on the secret? I run over here today, thinking everything is good and we can resume our life and our relationship. Then I find out I am about four weeks behind the curve!"

"Let me try to explain," Erika pleaded.

"I ... I can't get my mind around you and Todd getting back together. Why?" I said. "I thought things got resolved last fall. I thought this was a done deal. Didn't you decide that you and I were in a relationship, and you told Todd you weren't getting back together, right? You make me think I must have imagined some events.... Why are you doing this? What has changed?"

"He has really changed. He is a different person now. We have both done a lot of growing up, and I am certain things will be different this time. I didn't know things would turn out this way. Events overtook me, Tom. It all seemed so right when I was in Seattle. Now I come back here, and it is horrible to have this conversation with you. It is horrible to think of leaving you!"

Still reeling, I blurted out, "So basically, you and I are never going to see each other again?"

"I hope that is not true, but things are definitely changing," Erika said.

"What happened to 'I am in a relationship with Tom'?" I buried my face in my hands and tried to form rational thoughts, but I was feeling like my brain was in shock after a traumatic accident. All I could manage was, "I am confused, when did this happen? I thought you were busy 24/7 with the project."

"We contacted one another, or I contacted him to tell him I was in Seattle on the project." Erika continued, "One thing led to another and we started spending a lot of time together, having long talks. It laid the foundation for our reconciliation, as it turns out."

Finally, I was able to construct a few sentences. "I guess my reaction or approval is not really important here. A good friend to you would be happy to hear the news that you have a new job and you are patching up your marriage with your husband. Can you understand how much trouble I am having seeing your point of view right now? But I love you, Erika! I have given myself totally to you. I have waited patiently for you. We have talked about this for weeks ... months ... but now all that talk was meaningless and for naught. You assured me that I wouldn't be disappointed and that you loved me too. You never did, did you?"

"Please don't say that," Erika replied. "I do love you, but I discovered that I still love Todd too. I was forced to choose, and it is so painful."

"Erika, I tried to play the role and be patient, hoping you would notice me. I hoped at some point you could love me too. I know I can't make you love me if you don't."

"I do love you," Erika said, as tears began to well up in her eyes.

"Not in the way I love you, Erika," I said. "I need you like I need air and water, not like you were just a fun person to hang out with. I guess I am embarrassing myself now, because I really never had a chance, did I? This was all drawn out, but the ultimate outcome was probably never in doubt. I am sure you thought I was too old for you and there really wasn't a chance, maybe ever, of a romance between us." With that, I lowered my head and buried my face in my hands, which rested upon her kitchen table.

"I am so sorry," Erika said. "As all of these developments have hit me since I went to Seattle, it made me really think about leaving Portland and leaving you. I have loved you deeply, Tom. I still do. There has never been anyone like you in my life."

"Great," I said. "I am so confused. You tell me how much you love me and how important I am to you. Now you are going to live with Todd in Seattle. Can you understand my confusion and how these things don't seem to fit? Now we will never see each other again. You don't know how you could live without me, but starting tomorrow, you are going to find out."

"I hope this doesn't mean we won't ever see each other again," Erika said.

"Erika, that is exactly what it means. I can't come and hang out with you and Todd. I can't come to your house and sit back, watching Todd enjoy what I desperately wanted but can't have. In what universe do you think this means we are not saying good-bye?"

"Please don't be mad at me or hate me," Erika sobbed. "Oh, Tom, I will never forgive myself for hurting you."

"Erika, it is impossible for me to hate you. That is my problem. You and I have never had any fights or cross words between us, but don't you realize that you have broken my heart? You have really broken my heart," I repeated. "I am sorry to not be happy for you.... Please tell me that you see this from my point of view. There has never been anyone like you in my life. How will I ...?" My voice trailed off as I realized it was really over. I had no more options but to leave Erika.

Erika continued to cry uncontrollably.

"Did you love me, Erika? In the way I loved you? In our final moments, it would just make me feel a little better to finally know. Did you ever contemplate spending the rest of your life with me? Did you ever want me?"

"When I met you," she began, "I was not looking for a permanent relationship but I wanted to have some companionship and some fun. You were perfect. I tried to keep it that way, and you seemed to be okay with it."

"But did you ever love me, Erika?" I interrupted and pushed the issue. "It apparently no longer matters, but I would like to know that before I go."

"I have loved you since that night on the blanket. I was trying to work through things but I told you repeatedly to never doubt how much I loved you. Our last few weeks before I left for Seattle were really something extraordinary to me. I loved you and wanted you. I wanted you so badly on New Year's Eve. You need to know that. We ran out of time. I couldn't make it work with these new opportunities. Events seemed to overtake us, and I must now do these things. I really never thought this day would happen. I never thought I would leave you."

I could no longer speak. I was afraid I was about to be really frustrated and angry. "It doesn't have to be this way. Please, please, don't leave me," I whispered, as I looked at the floor and shook my head.

Then I looked intently at her face. Her beautiful blue eyes were now red and sad. The sparkle I loved so much was gone.

"Erika, I have never loved anyone the way I have loved you. And I mean no one! Probably not even Liz."

"I am so, so sorry, Tom, I never wanted to hurt you. You have done so much to help me, and there will be a void in my life without you."

I had to fire off one more shot: "You will have Todd to fill your void, who will I have?" With that, I got up from the kitchen chair and started for the door.

"I don't want it to end like this," Erika said.

"Neither do I, believe me. What did you think would happen today, Erika? I really hope it all works out for you. I sincerely do. I hope you are happy in your new life." I grabbed the doorknob and was on my way out the door.

"Are you going to be okay?" Erika asked.

I just looked at her and said, "No, I really doubt it. Erika, I will always love you. I don't think this will happen again for me."

"Will you come and tell me good-bye before I leave town?"

I nodded and left her standing at the door. She stood in her doorway, watching me go to the elevator and then disappear as the doors closed. I tried to not look directly at her, as it was much too painful.

I never went back. I never told her good-bye. She didn't call me, and I didn't call her.

As I left her building, I felt I was almost staggering. I had no inkling that any of this was coming, especially today, when I was so excited that she was back. The wind had picked up and rain had begun to fall. I climbed in behind the steering wheel of my car. I sat stunned, almost not able to move. I buried my face in my hands on the steering wheel and fought back the tears, which were starting to flow.

I had been angry a few minutes earlier and was really going at Erika. Now I was not angry, I was devastated. I wasn't sure I could drive home. Then I thought the last thing I wanted to do was drive back to my empty, lonely house. A flood of conflicting feelings was starting to wash over me. I felt horrible that I had treated Erika as I had and made her cry. But she ripped my heart out and stomped on it, and she deserved some backlash.

I wonder what had gone through Erika's mind over the last week or so. How did she think it would go when she told me? Did she really think I would be happy and congratulatory about her new job, her move to Seattle, and the patched-up marriage? My mind was reeling from one extreme view to another, and I couldn't form a rational thought.

I sat in my car for the longest time, like I was suddenly paralyzed, both mentally and physically. I was incapable of making a decision about what to do next or where to go. I didn't want to be seen in public. I was suddenly terrified that after all of the joy of this past year, this moment was reminiscent of the day Liz died and its aftermath. I can't sink back into the abyss ... I can't.

I started my car and drove aimlessly around the Pearl District and downtown. Finally, I saw a drive-through java place and got a cup of coffee and pulled into a parking spot to sit and drink it. My hands were actually shaking, and I felt I was completely falling apart.

I didn't want to eat anything; in fact, I felt like I might be sick. I did have one rational thought. Today was Monday. I so wished it was Friday and I didn't have to go to work tomorrow. I pulled out my Blackberry and wrote a note to my boss and my staff, informing them that I was ill and would not come to work on Tuesday. Upon completion of that e-mail, I held my Blackberry in my hand and stared at it, wondering if I should write to Erika. What would I say? I didn't want to leave things this way but there was no reprieve coming, they would have to be left this way.

I finally took the freeway on-ramp and headed for home. I was replaying the final conversation over and over in my mind, thinking of different things I should have said and how badly I handled myself. How it pained me to treat Erika in this way, even though her news had completely devastated me. How would I ever begin to put my life back together again after another crushing blow? Dave's worst fears for me had now become a reality.

My mind went back to the mystery of the randomness of life. I had discussed this numerous times with Erika. If Liz had been five minutes or even two minutes later or earlier, she would still be alive and there would have been no two years in mourning and no one year with Erika. My life took a completely different course, all because a drunk driver entered the intersection at the exact moment as Liz's car. What are the odds it would happen?

And now this. Why did this project have to happen so quickly after New Year's Eve? On New Year's Eve, Erika was passionate and fiery. She kissed me multiple times that evening. We were on the verge of becoming lovers. She even admitted it that day. She felt it too. What if we could have had four weeks or three weeks or even two weeks after that before she had to go to Seattle? Maybe, if we had become lovers, she never would have wanted to leave me. What would have happened in those weeks in January if she had been in Portland? I would so love to have had the chance to find out.

I have had a good life compared to many, many people. I can't say I have had a bad life. But why couldn't I have caught a break here? It was so close to working out. Why in the world was she choosing to go back to Todd?

I flopped on my couch without removing any clothes when I came in the door of my house. I held onto one last straw and obsessively checked my cell phone and Blackberry for a message. Maybe Erika would call or text and tell me that a terrible mistake had been made and she was sorry.

After all of the years of listening to music ... all of the songs about people who have had their hearts broken or are feeling the blues ... I now understood this on a whole new level. I did not want to know how it felt to have a broken heart. I now did, in spades.

I lay with my eyes closed and not moving. My mind was still racing with all of these random thoughts, and somehow it just all shut down. I awoke to a dark, silent house. I don't know how long I had been asleep. To my disappointment, I wasn't having a bad dream. I was still living in my nightmare.

I stayed awake until 2 or 3 AM, mindlessly channel surfing on my television. I would occasionally stop and watch something, hoping if I could get involved in some show or movie that it would take my mind off of my own situation, at least for a little while. Maybe it could apply a little Novocain to the throbbing pain I felt where I used to have a heart.

I staggered off to bed finally and fell dead asleep. When I awoke, it was reminiscent of the first morning after Liz's death. I had a horrible nightmare. I was hoping to wake up and find Liz sleeping next to me. She wasn't, and as I returned to consciousness, it made me realize that Liz was indeed gone. All of those things apparently really happened.

Now as I returned to consciousness, I wondered how all of the events of Monday could have occurred. Did they really happen? Unfortunately, they did occur. Now there was no more Erika.

When I returned to work on Wednesday, I felt I was still in a daze. I needed to get reinvolved in something, however, and not be alone with myself any longer.

The award for the worst timing ever would have to go to my friend and co-worker Megan, who regularly dropped by to chat. Shortly before lunch on Wednesday, Megan slid into the chair by my desk and said, "We haven't had a chance to talk for a while. Let's catch up. How are you and your hottie little girlfriend doing these days?"

Megan didn't realize it but this was akin to asking Mrs. Lincoln how she enjoyed the play. "We are doing okay," I said, trying to just pass it off and not answer her question.

Megan said, "Yeah, well, she is a beautiful woman, and I have spied you two out on the town together over the holidays. I have seen how you look at each other. There are some serious sparks there."

Just stick the dagger in and start twisting, I thought. "Actually, she is moving away and taking a job in Seattle," I said. I didn't want to discuss that either, but I could not take any more talk about the sparks between me and my hottie girlfriend.

"What?!" Megan said. "How can she leave you? Is that it?"

I wished I could take the paperweight on my desk and beat Megan into sudden unconsciousness to make this conversation end. "I think that is it, Meg. I think it is over."

"You poor, sweet man, how are you coping with this?"

"I was just leaving for lunch to survey the bridges over the Willamette River to see which one is high enough to kill me if I jumped off," I said.

"Oh, I hope you are kidding," Megan said.

"I am, but truthfully, I am not doing very damn well. This isn't a subject I am ready to have a lot of conversation about yet, okay?"

"I am so sorry, and when you are ready to talk, you just call me, all right?"

Yeah, right, I thought; don't sit by the phone waiting. But I replied, "Thanks, Meg, I will."

There were other conversations to be endured over the next few weeks. Notably, there were mostly unpleasant conversations with my mother and my children. I had to listen to my mother telling me, "Erika seemed like a nice girl but it is probably best since she was a little young for you." Mom had an enormous talent for stating the painfully obvious.

Michelle was much more charitable and said she was sorry it all turned out that way for me. She asked, "So is it over?" I said it was.

"Dad, I am so sorry. I know she really meant so much to you," Michelle said. "I am sorry you have to be sad again. What are you going to do now?"

I told her I had no idea.

The best conversation was with Alan. When I told him Erika was going back to her husband and moving away, he said, "Dad, I am so sorry. Erika was awesome. I feel so bad for you. It was so much fun to see you at the holidays because you were so happy. I don't know if I have ever seen you that happy. You looked really different to me—so excited. You didn't really deserve this one, Dad, after all you went through with Mom's death." Finally—someone had seen my problem from my perspective, not just my problem from their own perspective.

"Thanks, Alan, I really appreciate your understanding. I really haven't had anyone to talk this over with. I really so hoped it would work out. I thought it was going to. Alan, I want you to know that I really, really loved Erika. I miss her so much. I don't know if it can ever happen again."

Alan said, "I can understand how you could grow to love her so much. She is incredible. You two seemed like a great match when I saw you together."

"Really, did you think so, Alan? I didn't know what everyone thought. She is about the same age as you and Michelle, and I wondered if everyone thought I was some weird old guy chasing a young woman."

"No, Dad, there was something special there between the two of you. I felt it and was happy that you had found someone so well-suited to you. The age thing was weird at first, but when I saw you two together, it made me happy and I forgot about the age difference."

"Thanks, pal; your words are a comfort to me."

"Hang in there, Dad. I am sorrier than I can say."

"I love you, Alan."

"I love you too, Dad. I will call you later. Good-bye."

Alan had found a woman in San Francisco who would change his life. He would know what I had felt for Erika. They would marry and she would become a great addition to our family.

Eventually, the word was out and there was no more conversation about me and Erika. There was a new problem, however. Ghosts.

The ghost of Erika was everywhere. In all the places that would give me enjoyment or comfort—she was there. I remembered where we had sat in my favorite restaurants. I couldn't run through the Pearl District now on my noontime jogs without looking up at her building, or passing the bench where we sat by the fountain or recalling the night she was sick and I held her. Then, of course, there were the wonderful memories of New Year's Eve.

Erika's ghost inhabited my movie theatres, the walkways along the waterfront, and of course, my morning coffee shop. It even made me melancholy when I went to my beach house one weekend alone. I thought of holding her on the stormy night. I remembered the sunset colors reflected on her face and in her beautiful eyes when I sat on the deck with her on an idyllic summer weekend together. I couldn't even drive by the stupid casino without recalling our epic karaoke session.

The only picture I had of Erika from our time together was the one with her sitting on Santa's lap. That moment from our day of enjoying the city at Christmas had been preserved.

I wish I could have preserved the whole day in some kind of time capsule. If I could preserve it, I would occasionally reopen it and re-experience my day with Erika. Of all the things Erika and I did together, this was remarkably the only photograph I had of her. There were no photographs taken of us together. It wasn't planned that way, it just turned out that way. I don't know why we never took a camera with us on our outings. I guess we thought we were just beginning and had a lot more time.

Over the months ahead, I wished I had just one good picture of Erika's face; a nice head shot that captured her essence. I would have liked to have that on my desk at home. But then again, maybe it was just as well because it might have made me sad every day.

Instead, I would occasionally take the "Santa picture" out of my desk drawer and look at it longingly. It would remind me that the thing I had wanted so deeply and passionately was the one thing I couldn't have.

But it also brought great joy. It helped me recall the one wonderful Christmas when I loved Erika, a time of hope and true happiness, when I had her with me and anything seemed possible. It seemed like many more wonderful times were stretched out before us.

During the past year, I had been growing increasingly restless about living in the suburbs in my too-big-for-me house. Now, it was intolerable. Before 2005 would end, I sold my house and moved into a small condo in the Park Blocks downtown. It was two blocks from my office building and right in the middle of everything I cared about in Portland. It was a block from the art museum and performing arts center and a block off of Broadway and all it had to offer. I sold off many of the things in my house, much to the chagrin of my family, especially Michelle.

They didn't really want any of the things I sold but I had the feeling I was supposed to maintain a monument or memorial to their childhood or their mother or something. I needed a life that fit who I was and was becoming. It was one of the many things from Erika that enriched my life. She helped me make this decision and change, even if it were in absentia.

One night, Erika and I saw a loopy movie about memories and failed relationships. The premise of the movie was that a technique had been developed where you could hire this company to erase painful memories. In the movie, the company would come to your house and hook electrodes to your head. After they turned on the fictional machine, it would erase any memory of painful love affairs so you never had to recall them again. The philosophical point of the issue raised by the movie was this: If such a machine existed, would you hire them to erase the pain of a failed love affair and remove the pain you felt from a broken heart?

I am broken-hearted and lonely for Erika. However, if such a machine existed, I would not want to erase a single memory. I cherished every moment I spent with her. She made me glad to be alive. I looked forward to every day when I had Erika in my life, especially those days when I would be with her. I wouldn't want to miss anything, even the sadness and melancholy I felt now.

My life had gone from sunny and happy back to gray and overcast for now. I doubt there will ever be another Erika. But I will anxiously await another sunbreak.

Chapter 24

SOME TIME LATER ...

IT HAPPENED while I was with a group of friends at the Portland Art Museum. I had finally rounded up some companions to go see a Monet exhibit I was really interested in. I vowed to go by myself if I couldn't get everyone's schedule together to get it done.

One of Liz's good friends recently had divorced, and I had asked her to be my companion for the night. I had always liked her, and I didn't want to go as the single one in a group of couples. I had a few dates since my relationship with Erika ended. They were all first dates and no seconds. I was having trouble getting re-enthused. Perhaps Erika had set the bar pretty high for those who might follow. I was still comparing any woman I associated with to Erika.

The plan was that we would do the Monet exhibit and then go out to dinner. It sounded like a good evening. I hadn't seen some of this group of friends for a while. I was looking forward to this and my mood was pretty upbeat. I was ready to have some fun after a tough week, and I had been trying to see this art exhibit since it opened a month earlier.

Then I saw her. As I rounded a corner, I saw Erika and her friends from her Portland days standing nearby, admiring a painting. "Oh, Tom!" Jen shouted as she spotted me. The Goddesses greeted me briefly and then told Erika to take her time. She could catch up with them in the next gallery. My friends were surprised and seemed to instinctively drop back and disappear. Ryan said, "We will catch up later and give you a moment." I said to my date, "Sorry, I will need a minute."

After they had all disappeared, those big beautiful blue eyes met mine. Her face lit up and she moved towards me. We hugged tightly, and as I went to pull away, she held onto me and didn't let go. She gently rubbed the back on my head in a tender, affectionate way. I was deeply touched to get a reception like that from her. How I had longed for her touch.

Old feelings were suddenly resurfacing. We didn't speak for what seemed like a long time as Erika held me. Then she pulled back and smiled that beautiful smile. Her eyes twinkled and she said, "How have you been? You look so good."

I said, "I guess I am doing reasonably well, but I can't begin to tell you how happy it makes me to see you." She smiled and hugged me again.

I said, "You look fabulous, as usual. You look happy."

She slightly diverted the subject by saying, "I am, but it is so, so good to see you again."

"What are you doing here?"

Erika said, "We are having a girls weekend out—a meeting of the Goddesses. So I came down from Seattle and we wanted to do Monet." Then she added, "I get a big bonus by seeing you, one of my favorite parts of Portland."

"Lots of good memories, I hope," I said.

"Of course they are. I am so sorry how things worked out. I never wanted to make you unhappy, and I have missed having you in my life."

Before I could reply, she said, "What's going on with you?" We had been getting too close to an uncomfortable topic, so things seemed, to my disappointment, to turn more superficial.

I gave the superficial reply, "Oh, I am alright I guess. I have been really busy at work. Alan is getting married in a few months. Remember, he met someone in San Francisco? So that will add some excitement to the next few months."

"Oh, good for Alan, he is such a good guy. Tell him I send my congratulations," Erika said in her usual charming, animated way. Her voice was starting to turn to her more formal voice and not the warm, intimate tones I loved.

I said, "I hope things are good for you in Seattle."

"Thanks," she said. "Todd and I are working things out and we are doing well. The new job is stressful, but it was the right move."

"Good," I said. "I hope you are happy." I made no reference to Todd.

Her smile faded and she said, "You will always be a very special part of my life. You will find someone else, and that woman will be the luckiest woman in the world to be loved by you. You have so much to give."

I was thinking, I don't want the luckiest woman in the world—I want Erika.

I was stunned by her words and was fighting back tears, which I felt beginning to form in my eyes. I did not want to do that in front of her, and I was surprised at this upwelling of emotion. I thought I was over her. Apparently, I wasn't even close. I could no longer talk. She seemed to sense that. I just tried to make a mental snapshot of her beautiful face.

She hugged me quickly and said, "So good to see you; I guess I better catch up with my friends."

She turned and walked away as I quietly said, "Good-bye, Erika." I don't think she heard me say that. I watched her walk across the gallery and tried to memorize the moment. My mind went to all of the times I had dreamed of running into her in some public place. I don't know why I fantasized about doing that. When I was in big crowds or visiting Seattle, I always wondered if somehow I would see her again.

One time in a restaurant, there was a woman sitting with her back to me. She had a tall, slender body and long black hair. I knew it wasn't Erika but I couldn't take my eyes off of the woman because she made me think of Erika.

I watched Erika until she disappeared out of the large, long room. About halfway across the room, she turned and briefly flashed those magnificent blue eyes at me and smiled. She then continued walking. I watched her hair bounce, her familiar walking gait, and her hips sway. These were all nuances of Erika that I had become so familiar with.

She was gone again. Why had I hoped to run into her again sometime in a public place? Now I had that familiar empty feeling again. There was a large void in my heart for the woman who brought me back from a dark place and into the warm sunshine of her love. I loved her, I could never help loving her, and loving her intensely, even though it largely went unfulfilled. I couldn't make the moment last. I couldn't hold onto her. I couldn't keep her.

About six months later, there was another unusual turn of events. I received a wedding invitation from Jenna. She and Ben were getting married. The invitation included a handwritten note from Jen, which said simply, "I would love to have you come. I hope you can."

I had always really liked Jen, and we had some good times together. I was very moved that she would hunt me down and invite me to her wedding. My only hesitation was seeing everyone else again ... especially Erika and Todd, who would undoubtedly be there. I had longed to see Erika again ever since our relationship ended. Now I was wondering if I could possibly stand to go to the wedding, or would it just be too uncomfortable.

Finally, I decided I would go and at least make a brief appearance out of respect and affection for Jen. It was an overcast but mild day for a backyard wedding. I was hoping the sun would break through the clouds before the wedding was over. The brief ceremony was already over. I went late intentionally. I made my way into the backyard and saw a lot of familiar faces. I suddenly felt like I didn't belong there and almost bolted for the car. I would say a quick hello to Jen and Ben and then get out of there.

There was a loosely formed reception line around Jen and Ben, including Kristen, Tamara, and of course, Erika. There were also a few guys in tuxes milling around. They were apparently Ben's entourage. It was going to be impossible to see only Jen. I would have to see everyone. I took a deep breath and forged ahead.

Erika had her back turned to me while talking to some other people. I moved in close to Jen and said, "Congratulations, beautiful." Jen turned and saw me. She gave me a big hug and thanked me for coming.

There was a stir, and I was greeted by several others in the party. When I looked back towards Erika, she had noticed my entrance and was smiling and watching as I greeted the wedding party. It was really difficult to see her again in this social setting but yet it was wonderful. Seconds later, my discomfort took a huge leap when I noticed that Erika apparently was pregnant.

I moved towards her.

"Tom, you are so kind and sweet to come to Jen's wedding," Erika said, "but then, that is what I would expect from you."

Before I could answer, I guess I was caught staring at her stomach. "And yes, I am expecting, about the first of November."

"Congratulations, Erika," I said. "I told you some day there was going to be a lucky little child who would have you as a mother." She smiled and hugged me. Erika suddenly pulled away and said, "Todd, come here...." I was now face-to-face with Todd.

Todd rushed forward and said, "Is this Tom?"

"Yes," Erika said.

"I have always wanted to meet you, Tom," Todd said warmly. "Erika has told me so much about you. You are a very special person in Erika's life, and it is so nice to finally meet you."

I was definitely overwhelmed and surprised. I seemed to stand frozen for a moment and could not speak. Finally, the words came: "Todd, it is good to meet you as well. Congratulations to you and Erika. This little child is going to be very lucky to have the two of you for parents."

"That is very nice of you to say so," Todd said. "We are trying to get ready. Come and see us sometime. I would like to get to know you better."

I smiled and said, "I should probably be going."

"Don't rush off, Tom," Erika said, "everyone is so glad to see you. You should say hello to my mom, at least, before you leave." With that, Erika gestured towards a table where I saw Tricia sitting and talking with some other people.

"Okay," I said softly to Erika. "You take care of yourself. You look radiant today, as always." I hugged her and headed towards Tricia's table. This was both wonderful and extremely painful, I thought. I had to get out of there. This was not good to stay and hang around. If anyone else felt even a fraction of the discomfort I was feeling, I was a real distraction at the happy wedding.

As Tricia saw me approaching the table, she greeted me with a warm smile. Tricia looked even prettier to me than I had remembered. Her hair had a more golden tone to it, and she appeared to have been getting more sun. She looked tan and striking. This made her vivid blue eyes even more dramatic.

"Tom, what a wonderful surprise," Tricia said. "It is so great to see you again."

I hugged her and kissed her on the cheek and said, "I am very glad to get the chance to see you again."

"You know, I have actually thought of calling you in the last year," Tricia said. "I wanted to talk with you and see if you were ... doing all right, I guess."

"I actually had the urge to call you too, Tricia," I said, "I really did, but then I thought it was best if I just stayed away and let it go. I have missed seeing you, though."

Tricia got a kind of sad look on her face and just nodded.

"It is a funny thing, I have missed all of the people I became fond of, like you, while Erika and I were together," I offered.

"I guess I haven't seen you since we had that Christmas dinner together," Tricia said.

"That is right. What a nice day that was," I said. The music started and several couples started dancing, including the bride and groom. My mind wandered for a minute and went back to the wonderful day in downtown Portland, when I had Christmas dinner at the Heathman with Erika and Tricia. That happy day now seemed like a long time ago.

"How have you been, Tom?" Tricia asked tenderly.

I shook my head and wasn't sure how to respond. "Okay, I guess. Frankly, I am not sure I have recovered yet from Erika. I have tried. But nothing is ..." Words failed me and I just shook my head slowly.

Tricia broke the uncomfortable silence by telling me that she recently started working full-time for a friend's travel agency. It was going to give her a lot of opportunities to travel, and she was really excited. I told her I thought she was perfect for that job.

"Was that the same travel agency you were with when I saw you last?"

"Yes, that's right," Tricia said, "you remembered."

"This is like a new exciting adventure for you then, isn't it?"

"It really is, I have been traveling a lot, and I have done so many things I never thought I would ever get a chance to do," Tricia said.

"That is just the best news," I said. "When I heard you were going that direction with your life, I thought it was the perfect fit."

"It seems so," Tricia said. "I am having a great time. And I am getting paid for it besides."

I smiled and told her I was actually starting to count down the days when I could retire from my company. I was ready to do something else besides working for the insurance company.

"I can't believe I am talking about retirement," I said to Tricia.

"It sure goes fast, doesn't it?" Tricia said, looking somewhat melancholy.

"It sure does," I responded. "And now you are going to be a grandmother I hear ... or see."

"Yeah, how about that?"

"Well, you will love that experience, and your grandchild is a lucky little kid."

"Thanks, Tom; you have two, right?"

"I do. They are great. How did you and I get to be grandparents, Tricia?" I asked. "Funny how, in your mind, you haven't changed since you were young, but then you look in the mirror ..."

Tricia laughed and completed my sentence, "Then you look in the mirror and say, 'Yeah, I guess I do look like someone's grandmother.'"

"Well, when I look at you, Tricia, I just think, 'They don't make grandmas like they used to.'"

Tricia laughed and said, "Aren't you nice? You know, Tom, I think being in your fifties is not a bad place to be. You have a lot of hard things behind you. It is time to have some fun, don't you think?"

"I definitely do."

Tricia reached over and put her hand on mine. "Tom, I am really sorry that things ended the way they did. It made me very sad for a long time."

"Thanks for saying so. I, of course, did not want it to end that way either. You know, Erika really brought me back to life after my wife died. I wanted to change and move on but I didn't know how. Erika was the catalyst. I will be forever grateful to her for that."

"Oh, Tom, I am so glad. It is hard to imagine how hard this has all been for you."

"Now look at her," I said, pointing to Erika. "She looks very happy."

"She owes much of that happiness to your impact on her life; she and Todd realize that," Tricia said.

I looked out at the couples dancing, including Erika and Todd. I noticed the pregnant Erika looking at Todd the way she used to look at me. Now it really was time to get out of there, I thought. My threshold of pain had just been exceeded.

As these thoughts rushed through my mind, my legs began to move so I could rise from the table. I think Tricia sensed my uneasiness. Before I could rise, Tricia asked tenderly, "You haven't found anyone else yet? Someone is sure missing the boat not hooking up with you."

Ignoring the first question, I turned and looked into Tricia's eyes and responded, "Funny you should use those words, because I used those very words to Erika one time when I was talking about you. I said, 'How is it your mother is still single? Someone is sure missing the boat.'"

"Really?" Tricia said.

Suddenly, the sun broke through the overcast and began to bathe the wedding party in golden light. We were both silent for a minute.

I stopped watching the dancing and looked at Tricia. She smiled and broke the silence, saying, "I don't know how comfortable you would be doing this, but would you be willing to meet me at the dock sometime to test our boating skills?"

It took me a moment for her metaphor to sink in.

Slowly, a smile crept across my face and I said, "Would you like to dance?"

Author's Note

THIS BOOK is something of a love letter to the City of Portland. I love it much as Tom loves Erika. I worked in downtown Portland, Oregon, for over twenty years. I have wandered its streets, alone and with those I love. Nearly all of the venues depicted in the book are real and at least as wonderful and charming as depicted in the book.

The only exception is Blue Note Hamburgers, which is a fictional business. It is a compliation of two lunch spots I know in downtown Portland.

All of the characters exist only in my imagination, and any resemblance to friends or associates is only coincidental. The only possible exception is Josh. There really is someone as crazy about cars as Josh—my son Scott, who helped me make sure the car data was accurate in that chapter.

Sadly, I have yet to find anyone who will trade me their Porsche for my car.

I really did work in the Public Service Building downtown for many years but the companies that occupy it in the story are fictional. I have attempted to state some of the historical information about Portland as accurately as possible based on reliable sources.

I really did see a man in a suit of armor riding a white horse to propose to a woman on Valentine's Day in downtown Portland. I really did kiss my wife behind a waterfall in the Columbia Gorge. Such are the charms of the Portland area.